SHADOW KISSED

MAGIC SIDE: WOLF BOUND, BOOK 4

VERONICA DOUGLAS

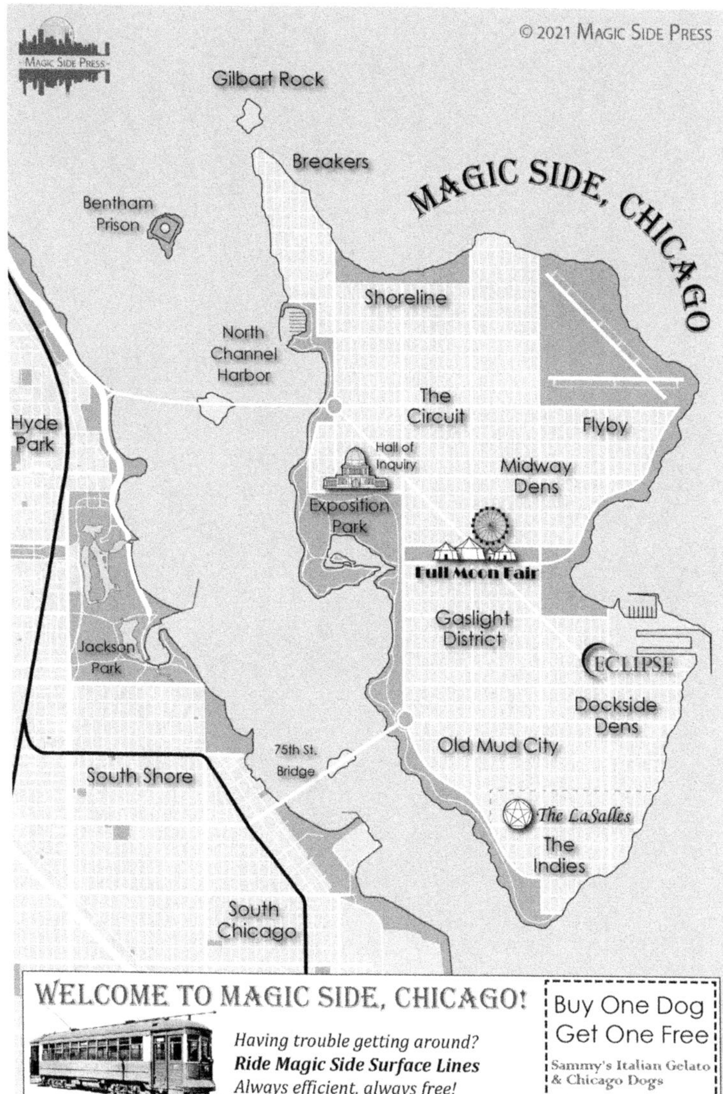
© 2021 Magic Side Press
Magic Side Press
Gilbart Rock
Breakers
Magic Side, Chicago
Bentham Prison
Shoreline
North Channel Harbor
The Circuit
Hyde Park
Flyby
Hall of Inquiry
Midway Dens
Exposition Park
Full Moon Fair
Gaslight District
Eclipse
Jackson Park
Dockside Dens
75th St. Bridge
Old Mud City
South Shore
The LaSalles
The Indies
South Chicago
Welcome to Magic Side, Chicago!
Having trouble getting around?
Ride Magic Side Surface Lines
Always efficient, always free!
Buy One Dog
Get One Free
Sammy's Italian Gelato
& Chicago Dogs
(limit one per customer)

OUR STORY SO FAR...

In *Untamed Fate* (book 2), our heroine Savannah Caine finally defeated Ulan Kahanov, the blood sorcerer who'd drained her blood in book 1 and had been haunting her dreams. She discovered that Kahanov had actually been possessed by the ghost of Victor Dragan—a powerful twin-soul who Savy's aunt had defeated years ago.

Savannah's victory came at a cost. Kahanov cut her with the Soul Knife, creating a wound that wouldn't heal, despite her werewolf blood and Jaxson's magic.

At the beginning of *Dark Lies* (book 3) Savy found herself struggling to come to terms with being a werewolf as well as the revelation that Jaxson was her fated mate—a fact that he'd hidden from her. Despite her mistrust and resentment, she was about to have much bigger problems on her hands.

Ghosts began appearing with warnings and threats, and on a highway outside of Magic Side, she was attacked by a gang werewolf bikers. She learned that the bikers were hooked on a super-drug that Kahanov had manufactured by refining the blood that he'd stolen from her in book 1, *Wolf Marked*. The bikers' supply had run out, and they were hunting her down to make more.

The bikers brazenly attacked her outside of Eclipse, forcing Savy and Jax to take the offensive. They tracked the bikers to a bar and, after a rumble, interrogated them. To their shock, they learned that the ghost of Victor Dragan had returned and taken possession of the leader of the motorcycle club, turning it into a cult. His goal was to bring back the Dark Wolf God, a sinister and dangerous deity from werewolf lore intent on wiping humanity off the map. Savy also learned of a werewolf prophecy that claimed that a twin-soul (like Dragan and Savannah) would bring back the Dark God, and steal the souls of the pack.

Savy went to her aunt for help, but discovered that Laurel and her parents were responsible for originally binding her wolf when she was a child. Driven by rage and betrayal, Savy lost control of her magic and attacked her aunt. In horror at what she'd just done, she fled.

With the clock ticking on the Dark God's return, Savy and Jax recruited a team of Order agents and converged on Pere Cheney cemetery to disrupt the cultist's ritual. They succeeded, stopping Dragan from bringing back the Dark God. Needing a new host, Dragan attempted to possess Savy, but she fought him off. Unfortunately, he escaped by possessing someone else.

That left Savy and Jax with the question: how do you trap a ghost? Savy made a bargain with the ghost-witch that haunted Pere Cheney to find out, and learned they needed Dragan's bones to trap him and destroy him for good. Unfortunately, the only bone remaining was in the possession of a notorious vampire who'd cut off Dragan's finger.

With the help of Damian Malek and Neve Cross, they visited the vampire's mansion in San Miguel de Allende. Negotiations broke down when he got a whiff of Savy's blood and attacked. They killed him, and escaped with the finger by the skin of their teeth.

While our heroine and hero were in Mexico, Dragan

possessed a new host and infiltrated Bentham prison, one of the most secure locations in the magical world. He took it over during a riot and locked the place down so that no one could get in and disrupt his ritual.

Savy and Jax convinced the Order's archmages to sneak them in through a secret access tunnel beneath Lake Michigan. They found the prison overrun by possessed cultists and Dragan on the verge of completing the ritual to summon the Dark God. The only step remaining was the bloody sacrifice of a twin-soul: Savannah.

They battled Dragan on the roof of the prison and came within an inch of losing their lives, but at the last second, Savy trapped him using a talisman that they'd made from his bones. Having saved the prison and everyone inside from certain death, Savy used her Aunt's Orb of Destruction to annihilate Dragan once and for all.

Upon leaving her aunt's house, the Dark God spoke in her head: *Your sacrifice is accepted, little wolf. Together, we will bring darkness upon the world.*

Overcome with horror, Savy realized that she was the twin-soul prophesied to free the Dark God, not Dragan. If the rest of the prophecy came true, she was destined to steal the souls of the pack.

She fled Magic Side to protect the pack, and set her mind to finding a way to fight the Dark God, the prophecy, and her fate...

And that is where our story begins.

1

Jaxson

I pulled my truck onto the shoulder and killed the engine, leaving the road in darkness.

Savannah was close. Every fiber in my body rose to her call—a deep, resonating ache that pulled me toward her like a moth to flame. The power of our mate bond.

It had been over twenty-four hours since she'd fled Magic Side, and it was all that I could take. I needed her. I couldn't purge my mind of her. The softness of her body, the taste of her lips, the heady scent of her desire. The memory of the night we'd rutted like animals.

Fuck.

I slid out of the cab and slammed the door. Faint light filtered through the trees that covered the Indiana Sand Dunes, and a cool onshore breeze brought with it the sweet, earthy scent of oak and hickory. And something else: citrus and sunshine. Maybe a mile away, but with werewolf senses, it was like pressing my face against her bare skin.

Heat spread through my veins, and my wolf surged in my chest.

Soon, my friend.

I strode down the asphalt road before slipping into the trees. The state park was closed for the evening, and apart from the scent of the small animals that inhabited the dunes, there was only one other creature here tonight—my mate. A twin-soul. The person prophesized to unleash the Dark Wolf God's wrath on the world and to steal the souls of our pack.

The first part of that prophecy was coming true, but I refused to believe the second. Savannah wouldn't betray our pack. Somehow, we had to stop the impending catastrophe before everything unraveled.

The fucking fates had a diabolical sense of humor.

My boots dug into the loamy sand as I tracked Savannah's scent through the thin woods that had sprouted from the ancient dunes. I could see why she was fond of running in this place. It was quiet and desolate, compared to the parks of Magic Side. No exhaust or sound of horns or people—just lake, sand, and trees.

The resonant ache of our mate bond intensified as I reached the crest of a dune.

Wisps of sand drifted along the beach, carried by the steady breeze that churned the dark waters. And there, at the edge of Lake Michigan, stood Savannah, a beautiful siren luring me to my doom.

Her hair whipped around her shoulders as she gazed over the turbulent water, lost in thought. As if suddenly sensing someone watching, she scanned the empty beach, then finally turned to face the dunes. Her eyes drifted across my position, then flicked back and locked onto me.

In a swift movement, she shifted and fled.

I felt like she'd kicked me in the gut. My mate didn't trust me.

Yes, she wanted to be alone. She was still wrestling with the fact that defeating Victor Dragan had inadvertently released the Dark Wolf God. But while that discovery had shaken Savannah to her core, it was learning of her role in the prophecy that had driven her out of my arms.

Perhaps she thought that by running, she was protecting me and the pack. But I could see the truth. Deep down, my mate didn't trust me to help her carry this.

I swiftly stripped and kicked off my boots, preparing to shift even as the thought spread like poison in my veins: was she going feral?

I'd seen it before. Wolves who had been hurt and betrayed learned to trust no one, and every reaction was to run or fight. And since coming to Magic Side, Savannah had been betrayed and battered and hunted without end. Was it any wonder she no longer trusted me? Fury tightened around my heart, anger not at Savannah, but at myself.

I'd failed.

Stop, my wolf said. *It's time to leave human thought behind.*

Human thought, with all its recrimination and confusion and self-deception.

I let my animal spirit take over, and my muscles knotted as fur erupted across my skin. Within seconds, I was on all fours and running, my paws tearing through the sand as the clarity of wolf thought focused my mind.

Bring her home.

Savannah was fast and had a long lead, but I was faster still. I raced along the ridge, and when she broke off toward a path into the forest, I bounded down the sandy embankment after her.

The thrill of the hunt sank into my bones.

I leapt over a downed tree, and Savannah must have scented me because she beelined in the opposite direction. I wound through the trees after her, and then suddenly, she was gone.

Pausing, I scanned the forest. I couldn't see her, but I heard the faintest of footfalls slipping over the loose sand. Soft creeping. Pride swelled within me.

My little wolf is cunning. Was she planning on doubling back?

On instinct, I whipped right, out of the woods and down the face of a dune. I erupted onto the beach right in front of her, pinning her against the edge of the lake.

Savannah skidded to a stop, with her head lowered and fangs bared. *Don't come any closer.*

Apart from the sea breeze that ruffled her auburn-tinged fur, neither of us moved. I knew that if I pressed, she'd resist. If I backed down, she'd run. So I made neither an advance nor a retreat, just locked her there with my gaze.

She stared back at me with unwavering golden eyes. It was like gripping a knife by the blade.

Hell, that was *every* moment with Savannah Caine. But I would never wish to dull her edge. That edge was what made her fierce and beautiful and perfect.

Finally, Savy shook her head and began to shift.

Her arms and legs lengthened, and the fur faded away. She twisted gracefully until all that was left was a beautiful woman, naked and unmarred, with her crimson hair whipping around her. Her bare chest rose and fell with heavy breaths, and desire threatened to tear all other thoughts from my mind.

"Fine," she snarled in frustration. "You caught me, Jaxson. But I'm going for a swim."

With that, she spun and slipped into the lake. She *knew* my wolf would hate that.

With a warning growl, I shifted, too. As my body transformed, the clarity of wolf thought drained away, replaced by the swirling miasma of human thinking.

Frustration. Anger. Desire.

I was furious with her as much as I was with myself, but

there was nothing to be done about that. I strode out into the gentle waves and dove in after her.

Cold, dark water rushed around me and cleared my mind.

Bring her home.

That was what mattered. Lone wolves didn't thrive, and she wouldn't last long on her own with the Dark Wolf God coming for her.

For a second, I spotted her kicking through the darkness, and then I lost her as the murky waters closed in around her. When I surfaced, Savannah was already waiting in the shallows. Beads of starlit water descended one by one across her bare skin. Transfixed, I followed each rivulet as it wound its way around her body. Then, like the witchy woman she was, she slowly formed a black dress of shadows around herself.

I didn't feel the need to hide behind magic. I was *alpha*. Rising from the water, I growled, "You made me hunt you down."

Savannah looked away. "I had to get out of town. It's safer for everyone."

I took a hesitant step through the shallows toward her. "You need to stop running, Savy."

"I'm not running." Her head snapped back to me. "I'm staying away because I'm trying to protect you and the pack. The prophecy—which *you* repeated to me—says I'm supposed to take the wolves from every werewolf who resists the damned Dark God. So not only did I release him, but I'm the werewolf antichrist as well."

Her voice burned with pain and resentment, but all I could hear were the echoes of my own words, foolishly recounting the prophecy of the Dark Wolf God before I realized it was about *her*.

A twin-soul will come to power. They will be the harbinger of destruction.

I shook my head as I approached her. "We can't be sure of what the prophecy means."

She stretched out her hand, and dark tendrils of smoke swirled around her fingers and coalesced into the form of a wicked bronze blade.

The Soul Knife.

She raised it and pointed it at me. "It's pretty clear what it means. If the Dark God gets his way, he's going to take control of me, and I'm going to cut out the souls of everyone in the pack with this—just like Dragan tried to do to me."

My eyes flicked to the wound he'd given her with the blade. It still hadn't healed.

Cara, one of our pack members, hadn't been even that lucky. We'd watched him ram the blade into her helpless form and sever her soul in the Dreamlands. She'd lived, but he'd left her a woman without a wolf—a truth that only Regina, Sam, and I knew. No one else, not even Savannah. The guilt of that failure was mine to bear.

But what if that was our whole pack's fate, all of us without their wolves? Was this the end the prophecy warned of?

It took all my strength to keep my signature and expression steady. "You're not Dragan. We'll find a way to stop this."

"I killed Dragan trying to prevent the Dark God from returning, but I just gave the Dark God exactly what he wanted. I refuse to be a puppet again." With a snarl of frustration, Savannah hurled the knife into the sand, then dismissed it into tendrils of smoke with an angry flick of her wrist.

I couldn't help but breathe a sigh of relief when the cursed thing disappeared.

My mate left the water and headed toward the beach, her shadow dress fluttering behind. "Until we figure out what's going on, it's safer if I stay away."

In a step, I closed the distance and grabbed her wrist, spinning her around. “No,” I snarled, with a ferocity that made her eyes shoot open wide. “You’re coming back to Magic Side. With me.”

She tugged against my grip. “Jaxson—”

“Please,” I said, “we can figure this out together. Please, Savy. Trust me.”

2

Savannah

Jaxson's hand locked around my wrist, but it was his eyes that pinned me in place, burning like golden stars against the night sky.

The signature of his magic vibrated the air, a cascading waterfall of sensation. It woke every nerve in my body, as if I'd been sleepwalking through the last decade of life. The rich forest scent and snowy taste of his magic made me feel like I'd stepped straight from the lake onto the porch of a warm cabin in the silent winter woods of Wisconsin, hundreds of miles from Magic Side and all my problems.

It pulled me toward him, and it took everything I had not to submit. It would've been so easy to give in and go with him, to pretend that the Dockside alpha was strong enough to make the coming storm disappear.

But I knew he couldn't. That was up to me.

"Let me go," I said, my voice low and about as steady as I could hold it.

For a moment, he held on in silence, and then his grasp softened as he reached up and brushed my hair. "I want to give you the space you need, but we've only got six days—"

I stepped away as my mouth turned sour. "Six days until the Dark Wolf God returns? Until he enslaves our people and turns Magic Side into a mound of rubble and ash? Do you think I don't realize that? I spend every waking minute dreading it."

"We need to make a plan."

"I have a plan," I snapped as a moment of frustration pierced me like a knife. Did he think I hadn't considered what I was going to do?

I turned my back on him and began trudging up the dune toward the tree where I'd hidden my clothes. Jaxson followed.

"If the Dark God wants me to cut out the souls of the pack for him, then I'd better make sure I can't, and no one else can, either. I'm meeting Neve tomorrow, and I'm going to hand the Soul Knife over to the Order. They have a magic vault that's supposedly impregnable. If the blade is locked in there, I won't be able to use it against anyone."

Jaxson nodded as he climbed the dune beside me. "That's a good start."

His voice was low and approving, reflecting back none of the frustration I'd felt. He was patient, and I needed that right now.

I stopped in my tracks and dug my nails into my palm. He wasn't going to like the next part. I sure didn't. "I'm going to ask —if and only if things go really bad—whether they can lock me away in there. To keep the pack safe. Obviously, with what happened with Dragan, Bentham isn't secure enough, and if the Dark God starts to take cont—"

"No."

Jaxson spoke so quietly, it was almost inaudible. But the power behind that single word shook me to my bones, like an earthquake erupting inside of me. Every muscle froze, and I couldn't step forward or protest or even breathe.

His command was absolute. Undeniable. Irresistible.

Jaxson stepped up behind me and whispered in my ear. "I'm your alpha, and I forbid it. Imprisonment is death to a wolf."

He was so close, I could practically feel his heart beating. Struggling for every ounce of control I could muster, I parted my parched lips and rasped, "I will do what I have to, to protect—"

"No. You're letting this prophecy control you. Don't. We don't yet know what it means."

Frustration burned my neck, but I surrendered just a little. He was right. I was allowing my fear of the prophecy to control me.

Jaxson circled around and lifted my chin, so I had no choice but to look up into those intense, impossibly golden eyes. "I suspect the Dark Wolf God would like nothing more than for you to lock yourself away. He's been trying to control you or kill you since you stepped foot in Magic Side. Somehow, you're a threat to his plans. We just have to find out why."

The glow in Jaxson's eyes dimmed, and his power over me faded, but I didn't move away.

The trace of a warm smile softened his stern expression. "You're powerful, Savannah, and you're the one the Dark God is afraid of. But you don't have to fight him on your own. You're part of a pack."

How I wanted to believe him.

I was so tired of the running and the unending fear. Tired of having to be strong and earn every breath I took. I wanted to be able to release just a little of it. To lean on someone else.

We were so close to each other that half a step would do it. We'd be skin to skin, my robe of shadows meaningless between us. I could just melt into him and let the world fade away, even if only for a moment.

Instead, I nodded and stepped back. Maybe one day, we'd have that chance.

I stepped behind the tree where I'd stashed my clothes, plucked my undies from the crumpled pile, and pulled them on beneath a billowing cloak of shadows. "I get it, Jaxson, I really do. I don't have to do everything on my own—not that I was planning to."

From the approving way the alpha watched me, I began to get the sense he didn't have to be able to see me to appreciate the dressing process.

His eyes never wavered. "No more running off. I'm with you, whether you like it or not."

I pulled my wet hair back. "I guess that means you're coming to Pere Cheney with me, then?"

Surprise cut across Jaxson's face. "Pere Cheney? Why? To see the ghost?"

"I swore an oath to bring her a headstone," I said as I fastened my bra. "I don't like being beholden to anyone—not you, and certainly not to a half-crazed long-dead witch who swore she'd *torture my soul and fill every waking moment of my life with cold and pain* if I didn't follow through with my end of the deal."

"I shouldn't have let you speak to her alone," Jaxson grunted, his voice tinged with frustration and protectiveness.

I shimmied into my shirt, wincing as I pulled it over the damn wound in my shoulder. "The ghost gave us a hint on how to defeat Dragan. I'm hoping that if I follow through with my side of the bargain, she'll give us a clue on how to defeat the Dark God. Maybe she knows a weakness of his or something."

Jaxson nodded. "Your plan is good. Getting rid of the knife and meeting the witch. Regardless of whether she helps us, we don't need to make another enemy at the moment."

I smiled slightly while I pulled my tight shorts over my ass, a little regretful that the cloud of shadow blocked the view. I mean, he'd seen me naked. We fucked, for heaven's sake. Why was I wrapped in shadows?

You're afraid of letting him through that rusty armor of yours, Wolfie murmured in my mind.

What are you calling rusty? I teased back with mock anger.

At least I had my wolf.

My phone buzzed. "I bet that's Casey, wondering where the hell I am. We need to roll."

"Casey," Jaxson said flatly. It wasn't a question, but rather a statement of all that was wrong with the world.

"He's got the headstone in his car. I didn't know anyone else shady or skilled enough to find an unbreakable tombstone at a moment's notice."

Jaxson's jaw clenched. "Fine. But we're taking my truck. Your Fury won't make it up the back roads, and Casey's ride is a piece of shit. I trust it less than I trust him."

I dismissed the shadows and grabbed my phone to text my cousin. "Where's your truck parked?"

"On a pull-off on Highway Twelve, near the boundary road. He'll know it when he sees it."

I texted Casey. His response was quick: *Jaxson? WTF.*

"Yeah, my cousin might not be keen on the idea, either." I pocketed my phone.

"Follow me," Jaxson said, and took off running through the woods.

I had my Swiftley boots, so it was easy for me to keep up with him without breaking a sweat. My feet pounded into the sand as my soul breathed a sigh of relief. It was good to run together.

I didn't know why I'd run from him before. Instinct, I supposed. A dread of what was coming tightening around my throat. The fear that I would be the one to hurt him, to hurt the pack.

I couldn't face that.

Hush, Wolfie said. *Stop worrying. Just focus on his buns.*

She was incorrigible, but my eyes darted down involuntarily. The sight was enough to drive the dread away for a moment. Feeling a little flush rising, I wondered if I might work up a sweat after all.

When we neared the road, Jaxson slowed and stopped by the bushes where he'd stashed his clothes.

"Give me a few minutes to talk to Casey," I said, tearing my eyes from the hard angles of his body. "We haven't cleared the air."

Jaxson nodded and started dressing. I lingered for just a moment, then made my way to the road through the cluster of oak and hickory as my stomach tightened.

Last time I'd seen or spoken to my cousin was at Aunt Laurel's. She'd tried to stop me from leaving, and I'd lashed out with my magic. I'd bolted out of the house, leaving Casey cradling her with a look of abject horror on his face.

Since then, he'd learned that I was a werewolf and Jaxson's mate. And now, I had to tell him I was the werewolf antichrist. Shit.

We'd become so close, yet I'd kept so much from him. And I hadn't returned any of his calls.

How the hell did I expect him to forgive me?

I stopped dead in my tracks, the guilt of everything weighing on my shoulders like massive iron chains. It had taken all the courage I had just to text him to ask for help with the gravestone. How was I going to face him now?

My leg kicked forward as Wolfie took control, and I yelped in surprise.

Stop that. I'm going! I snapped at my wolf.

Didn't seem like it.

"Savannah?" Casey's voice echoed through the trees.

I sighed and trudged out of the forest into a whirling morass of doubt, guilt, and fear.

Jaxson's big black truck was pulled off to the side of the road, lit up by the headlights of Casey's RAV4 parked haphazardly behind. My cousin was leaning against the hood with his arms crossed.

I didn't need werewolf senses to read his mood: *pissed.*

3

Savannah

"Just because I've agreed to help you does *not* mean I forgive you," Casey said as he popped open the back of the RAV4.

Heat crept along my neck. Why couldn't he just say, *Hi Savy, I'm sorry everything has gone to shit. I'm here to help.*

I clenched my fists, and it was all I could do to stop my fangs from popping out. "Forgive me for what? For being a filthy werewolf? Or for attacking Aunt Laurel?"

He held up his hands. "Geez, Shaggy, no need to go to Defcon Two. Mom feels terrible about everything that's happened. All of it, I swear."

I hugged my arms around myself and dug my nails into my skin.

Aunt Laurel.

I wanted to hate her for helping my parents cast the spell that bound my wolf, and even worse, for hiding the truth of what I was. But after everything she'd done for me, all I felt was shame. I'd lost control and attacked her, and even if it was an accident, I'd hurt the woman who'd taught me magic and opened my eyes to the unlimited possibilities of this world.

I bit my lip and looked away.

Casey gently touched my arm. "I know she's forgiven you, Savy. Hell, I think she feels like she deserved what happened."

Nausea wound around my gut. That just made it worse. She didn't deserve any bit of what I'd done.

I shrugged off his touch. "What about you? I saw the way you looked at me."

My words were sharper than I expected—twisted and bitter, pushing him away. But the truth was, I was desperate for his forgiveness, even more so than hers.

Casey lowered his hands and hooked his thumbs through his belt loops. "Look, when I was a kid, Mom had beautiful straight hair. One time, she grounded me for stealing, and I got so mad, I lost control of my magic and burned off all her hair. It's been curly ever since. I remember that every single time I look at her."

I tried to imagine Aunt Laurel bald. It didn't work.

"Magic is hard to control when it's new. That's the reality of our world. You were rightfully angry, and your magic went haywire. That's happened to me and to every other kid in Magic Side."

I looked away as shame flushed my face. "I'm not a kid."

"Duh. Most kids have way more experience. You've been doing spells for what, almost a month? Cut yourself some slack. If my mom can forgive you, then you can forgive yourself."

Shame flushed my neck. "Yeah, that's not something I'm ready for."

I moved toward the gravestone in the back of his ride, but he blocked my way. "Not so fast. Part of the bargain is that you get over your shit and tell me everything. Like *everything*, because I've got a feeling I don't know half the crap that's going on around here."

He was right about that, but *everything* was going to be a long conversation.

I walked over and lowered the tailgate of Jaxson's truck. "Fine. But first, help me move the damn tombstone over, okay?"

Casey rolled his eyes. "Why *is* Jaxson coming along? This was supposed to be cousin time."

"Because he is," I growled as I headed back to the RAV4. "He literally hunted me down. I don't think he's going away."

Pinching the bridge of his nose in frustration, Casey sighed. "Great. Fine. But let Jaxson put the tombstone in his own damn truck, then. It took a couple of huge dudes to load it up."

I frowned at him. "I'm a werewolf. Just help steady it."

I slipped my fingers under one end of the granite slab and gave Casey a steady glare. He shrugged and grabbed the other side. "Okay, but if I slip a disc, you're paying the medical bills."

We heaved the damn thing upward and staggered back from the car. "Oh, gods, this is heavy!" Casey grunted.

My arms strained, but we shuffled in tandem toward the bed of Jaxson's truck.

Casey's end got progressively lower until he was practically crab-walking. "We need to put it down, Savy! It's got to be four hundred pounds!"

With an exasperated snarl, I scooped my body forward and heaved the gravestone up and out of his hands. "It's two hundred, tops. Just help me lower the thing without scratching up the truck. It's new."

He jumped into the bed and helped me set the stone down gently. "Damn. I knew werewolves were strong, but this She-Hulk business is going to take some getting used to."

"Yeah, well, frankly, I can't believe that you're remotely okay with me being a werewolf," I muttered as I shut the bed.

Casey shoved his hands in his pockets but didn't climb down. "Screw that. That's on page two of the list of things I'm pissed about. Number one is the fact you didn't tell me about it. I'm hurt, Savy. I don't know that I'll ever be able to trust anyone ever again."

Yup. He was going to milk this for all it was worth.

I rolled my eyes. "Can you *honestly* blame me? After all the werewolf hate you throw around?"

He shrugged. "Well, if I'd known my cousin was a werewolf, maybe I wouldn't have said some of those things."

I blinked, dumbfounded by his logic. "You realize that makes *absolutely* no sense, right? You need to start thinking about shit differently now. I'm a werewolf, and I'm part of the pack. If I'm going to trust you, I need you to let go of whatever hate you've got left."

Casey sighed audibly. "I know. I get it. I'm here for you, fur and all."

4

Jaxson

I pressed my cell phone to my ear and headed toward the highway. "What do you mean, you've made no progress?"

"Exactly what I said," Sam muttered back across the line. "I've interrogated half of the cultists the Order has locked up in Bentham. Seems like Dragan didn't tell them shit about what will happen when the Dark God returns. Most won't say much, and the really crazy ones just keep repeating gibberish about how the Dark God is liberating our kind from the tyranny of men—and I don't think they mean gender inequality. I'm pretty sure none of them have any idea what they signed up for."

I ground my teeth. "Dragan must have told at least one of them what was going to happen when the Dark God returned—what they'd need to do to prepare. A location, signs, somewhere to meet, anything."

"I'm trying everything I can," she said sharply. "But feel free to get your ass back here and ask them yourself."

A long silence stretched between us, and finally, Sam sighed. "Sorry, Jax. I was out of line. I'll keep trying."

"Good," I growled softly. "I'm heading up to Pere Cheney

with Savannah to tie up some loose ends, so it's on you. If there's anything to learn, I know you'll find it."

After another pause, Sam asked, "Is Savannah willing to meet with the council? We need to get ahead of this before the pack finds out about her."

I already knew that proposal wasn't going to go over well.

"I'm working on it," I said, pushing some low brush out of the way. "The prophecy has her spooked. The first step is getting her back to pack lands and around others of our kind. She needs support. Then we can bring up the council."

With that, I hung up and followed Savannah's intoxicating scent to the highway.

Frustration clawed at me.

I'd called pack loremasters all around the Great Lakes, and so far, all I'd discovered were hazy warnings and ancient legends. Whispers about how the Dark God would return and reduce the world of man to ash and stone. How he would purge the earth of its human plague and restore it to the way it should have been—wild, with werewolves on top, of course.

Just threats and myths. No specifics. No clues how to stop it from happening.

Sam was the only one I'd told so far about Savannah's connection to the prophecy. I hadn't even mentioned it to Regina, but that would have to change. We needed help.

I stepped to the edge of the tree line and admired the woman standing beside the bed of my truck.

My mate. Herald of the apocalypse.

The brightness of Casey's headlights made her hair look like flowing fire, and the backlighting, combined with her cocked stance, gave her plain white shirt and cutoff jeans shorts an almost exotic effect. I drank in each curve of her body with my eyes, desiring everything I saw. The one night we'd spent together was burned in my mind, and seeing her naked again on the beach and sensing her desire had need screaming through me. It had been all I could do to stop myself from taking her right there.

Unfortunately, a repeat of that one night wasn't going to be an option. Her idiot cousin was here—and standing, for no gods-damned reason, in the bed of my truck.

I stepped into the beam of his lights. "Get. Off. My. Truck. *Now.*"

Casey went white for a moment, then hopped down, muttering, "Fucking alphas," under his breath.

I let my claws slowly slip out and stepped very, very close.

He inched back and raised his hands. "Whoa there, Wolverine. I was just helping Savy."

She turned and gave me a pleading glare. *Please be civil.*

Sighing, I retracted my claws and fished my keys out of my jacket. "Thanks for your help, LaSalle. We've got it from here."

Casey shook his head. "Oh, hell, no. You're not getting rid of me so easily. I'm coming with. Do you know how much trouble it was to get a freaking tombstone enchanted at the last minute?"

Savannah touched his arm tenderly. "And we really appreciate it, Casey. I mean it."

"You owe me big time," he muttered out of the side of his mouth.

I glanced at the gravestone lying in the bed of my truck. It was red granite with an ornately carved trim, and inscribed, *Here lies the witch of Pere Cheney—remembered forever while her accusers are long forgotten.*

I raised my eyebrows. "No name?"

Savannah bit her lip apprehensively. "Yeah, that's a bit of a problem. She didn't give me one. She just asked for a beautiful, unbreakable gravestone that would last forever."

I looked over at Casey, who seemed lost in thought. "Will it?"

He shrugged. "Hey, forever is a long time. Let's not get into specifics. As far as you folks are concerned, it will."

I narrowed my eyes. "You did the enchantment yourself, didn't you?"

He glared back at me and ran his hands through his hair. "Yeah, I mean, where else was I going to get an enchanted gravestone on the weekend?"

I wasn't sure how much I trusted his prowess as an enchanter, but I unlocked the truck anyway. "Fine. Let's just get this tombstone up to Pere Cheney before it explodes in a ball of flame. It's going to be a long drive."

As it turned out, the four-hour trip was longer than I could've possibly imagined because Casey didn't stop talking.

He'd spent the last decade messing with our business and manufacturing wolfsbane, and now, I couldn't get him out of my car. His incessant questions had my blood pressure soaring, and I had to dig my claws into the steering wheel to keep calm. With the gas pedal pressed to the floor, I uttered a small prayer to the moon mother for patience as each mile marker flew by.

Sitting in the back middle spot, Casey leaned forward between our seats. "So, okay, I'm still wrapping my head around this whole mates thing."

"I don't want to talk about it anymore, Casey," Savannah moaned.

"What would happen," he continued, completely unfazed, "if you got pregnant? Would you have babies or puppies?"

I spun around. "Why, for the sake of the fates, are you here?"

Casey leaned back and tucked his hands behind his head, and I turned to the road. "I'm not letting my favorite cousin face a dead witch without magical backup. What if the old specter goes off the rails? No way I'm letting Savy get possessed."

"Too late." Savannah sighed. "I've already been possessed, just not by her."

"What? Really?"

"It was Dragan," she spat. "He was a fucking asshole."

"Wow. Okay, this is all news. Either way, I'm not letting my cousin get possessed *again*," he grumbled. "What I don't get is why all this is such an emergency. Dragan's dead. You obliterated his soul. Then, according to Mom, you just panicked and ran off."

Savannah bit her lip, and I shook my head subtly.

"You guys aren't telling me something," Casey said in a suspicious sing-song.

"It's nothing," I muttered. "Let's just focus on the—"

"I'm the herald of the apocalypse," Savannah blurted, and darkness crowded in around my vision.

"What?" Casey yelped.

"This is wolf business," I growled. "Stay out of it."

But Savannah turned her fiery eyes on me. "I'm a wolf, he's my cousin, and the rest of my family are going to be dead if we don't stop what's coming. So frankly, wolf business is *everybody's* business right now."

"Holy shit...are you serious?" Casey squeaked.

My claws extended fully into the wheel. "She is *not* the herald of the apocalypse."

"The werewolves have a prophecy," Savannah told Casey. "A twin-soul—*me*—will make a sacrifice that releases the Dark Wolf God. Apparently, obliterating Dragan's soul counted as that sacrifice. I know that because the Dark God literally told me himself. We have a little less than six days until he returns, and when he does, he's going to spread madness among the living and wipe human civilization off the map."

Casey grabbed the seat backs. "Fuck. Prophecy be damned, but if you have a psycho-murderous wolf god speaking to you, we've got to tell Mom and the Order, ASAP!"

I slammed on the brakes and jerked the truck to the side of the road as my fury boiled over at last. Casey screamed, and Savy clung to my arm for dear life.

When the truck finally rumbled to a stop, I turned around and let my presence fill the cab. "You will not speak a word of this to anyone. Prophecies are unreliable. We thought Dragan would be the one to release the Dark God, so we took the bastard out. If the wrong person hears of this and puts two and two together, they might decide to do the same thing to Savy."

Casey sank down into his seat. "Oh, fuck."

Savannah looked out the window. Her raging emotions vibrated through the air—despair, terror, fury. I wanted to comfort her, but I had to lock this down, once and for all.

I let my eyes go brilliant gold as I pressed Casey with my full power. "You'll tell no one until we understand what's going on. Got it, LaSalle?"

He swallowed hard. "Got it. I'll be as silent as the grave. I promise."

"Good," I said, pulling back onto the highway. "You start now. For the rest of the drive."

5

Savannah

We bounced down the old trail, Jaxson's headlights sweeping the darkness ahead of us. Finally, we rolled to a stop at the entrance to the Pere Cheney cemetery. It was little more than a clearing in the woods, with patchy grass and crumbling gravestones.

This place was as forgotten as the people buried here.

Well, all but one.

Hopefully, this works.

I wasn't quite able to shake off the menace in the warning she'd given me: *I will hunt down that missing sliver of your soul and make sure you never sleep again.*

So yeah, not someone to be messed with.

I opened my door and slid out of the truck, and Casey followed.

"This place doesn't look like much," he muttered. "I thought it would be, you know, spookier. Cobwebs and shit, and grotesque statues."

The cemetery wasn't so much sinister as neglected by time. Then again, I could sense the ghosts lurking here, and that made it eerie enough. I shrugged as I dropped the tailgate. "To be fair, last time we were here, this place was teeming with possessed werewolves trying to summon the Dark God."

Jaxson heaved the granite stone from the bed like it was a sack of feathers, and Casey's eyes nearly popped out of his head. "Where do you want the gravestone?" Jaxson asked.

I bit my lip as I scanned the overgrown clearing. There were a few standing markers, but nowhere that felt special. "I don't know. She didn't have an actual grave. Somewhere prominent, so anyone who visits can see."

Walking out across the strange, crunchy, moss-infested grass that grew in the cemetery, I searched for a spot. I put my hands out like my godmother, Alma, used to do, trying to feel the energy of the place, but I sensed nothing other than mild creepiness. That sixth sense of hers wasn't something I'd ever been able to cultivate, though it brought back good memories to try.

Finally, I reached a spot that felt a little more *right* than all the others. "Here, I think. I don't really know."

Jaxson brought the stone over, raised it over his head, and slammed it into the ground like a pile driver.

It sank about four inches into the earth. *Damn.*

He packed the dirt around it with his foot as I tried to ignore the way his shirt stretched over those broad shoulders.

"So, what now?" Casey asked as he approached. "Do we wait for Bloody Mary to show up, or do we do voodoo to summon her?"

"I'm not sure, really," I admitted. "Last time, I just shouted a lot until she came out."

"Cool, cool, cool," Casey said doubtfully.

Giving him a dirty look, I cupped my hands around my mouth. "Ghost of Pere Cheney! We brought your gravestone!"

We waited. Nothing happened.

Jaxson raised his eyebrows, and I motioned the men back. “Be patient, and give me some space.”

Wishing I knew the ghost’s name, I shouted again, “Ghost of Pere Cheney, I’m here to fulfill our bargain! I’ve brought you a headstone that will never break, will never weather, and will last long after these others have turned to dust. You’ll never be forgotten.”

Casey made a guilty, hedging expression, and I rolled my eyes.

For a long time, there was nothing. Then suddenly, my wound began to itch. I held up my finger to my lips in warning as a soft chill deeper than the night air washed over my skin.

We were no longer alone.

Slowly, I scanned the cemetery until at last, a pale, spectral light emerged from the woods. I held my breath as the witch of Pere Cheney slipped from behind the trees and drifted effortlessly across the grass. Her long, ratty hair framed a youthful face, and her threadbare dress trailed in wisps behind her on wind that I couldn’t feel.

Anger tightened my fists. She couldn’t have been more than a teenager when they’d hanged her, probably because she’d gotten pregnant out of wedlock or broken some archaic religious laws.

Humans were monsters.

The ghost approached cautiously, as if somehow, I were a threat. “I remember you, shadowed one. We had a bargain.”

“Here is your gravestone, as promised.”

“Who are you talking to?” Casey whispered, his eyes as wide as I’d seen them. “Is she here? I don’t see—”

I quickly shushed him. “Yes. I told you, I see ghosts. Now be quiet.”

The ghost paid our exchange no heed, floating instead to where the gravestone stood. She put her hands over her mouth in a way that made a lump of sorrow form in my throat. "It's beautiful. Perfect."

"No one will forget your story now," I said softly, stepping over.

She wrapped her hands around the stone, a sob hovering at the edge of her voice. "Those people hanged me in the woods, and they let the wolves and birds fight over my bones. This is all there is to remember me."

"I'm sorry," I whispered.

Like the shadow of the earth passing over the moon, her eyes went dark. "The fools should have let me live. I cursed that town with plague and disease until not one of their offspring was left breathing. Until it was nothing more than a desolated patch of earth, and all of them rotting in the ground alongside me."

My skin crawled at the sudden venom in her voice. She was possibly a little unhinged. I began to back away.

She flicked her infinitely dark eyes on me. "It doesn't have my name. Why doesn't it have my name?"

Aw, shit.

Somehow, it didn't seem like arguing *you didn't tell me your name* was going to be a viable defense.

My mind spun like Robin Arzón, and I swallowed hard. "Of course not. That's, uh, part of the mystique. People who come here and see this stone will want to know who you are, and they'll go crazy hunting through books and archives searching for your story. The harder you make them work for it, the better they'll remember you."

Practically purring, she traced her fingers over the granite slab. "What is in a name, anyway? They will remember who I was. What I did. Let them look."

I licked my lips. "We had a bargain. I brought you your eternal gravestone, but you still owe me another answer."

Her eyes flared with unearthly light, and she disappeared. My stomach dropped. *Shit, shit, shit.*

I spun around, looking for her. "Please, don't go!" I shouted as I ran toward the woods. "You promised you'd help me! The Dark Wolf God is coming back, and I need your help to stop him! We had a bargain!"

As I stepped into the dark shadows of the trees, she was suddenly there, looming over me. "It's dangerous to ask boons of the dead, you know."

All traces of her earlier gratitude had vanished, replaced by the cold menace of her floating, ethereal form. My skin lost its warmth, and I began to recognize the depths of her madness and how dangerous the specter might truly be.

But I stood my ground. "How do I stop the Dark God from returning?"

Her face contorted into an expression somewhere between disgust and pity as she floated backward. "It's too late. You released him. You can't stop him from returning now. He's already got his claws in you. Now, do not call for me again."

Dread seeped into my soul. "What do you mean? Please! Help me."

Like a viper, she lashed out and jabbed her finger into my wound. I gasped as her touch sent ice racing through my veins.

"You're broken, and your defenses are breached," she hissed. "Can't you feel him prying you apart from the inside?"

Every muscle in my body knotted. "The Dark Wolf God?"

"I can feel it. He lives in you now. You are doomed to serve his will."

She slipped away, but I stretched out my hand in pleading. "Wait! I don't understand. How is he inside of me?"

An ethereal wind buffeted the spirit as if to blow her away, but her head turned back, and she locked her hollow eyes on me. "You're a broken ship, and he is the sea. He's spilling through the cracks, and soon, he will consume you. I can sense him here, even now. I've lingered too long."

With that, the ghost vanished into a stream of glowing mist. Terror and despair pulled on me like heavy chains, and I let my outstretched hands drop.

"What's going on?" Jaxson growled. He wouldn't have heard her half of the conversation, but he would have certainly sensed my fear.

I instinctively grabbed his hand and started tugging him toward the truck. "We should probably get out of here."

As we stepped out of the woods, Casey started to blurt something out, but I froze in place, hand raised to silence him and straining to hear. The air was unnaturally quiet, and the only sound I could make out was the drumming of our heartbeats.

As we stood there, a chilly frost began to creep through the wound in my shoulder, and I sucked in a sharp gasp of pain. It was far worse than the ghost's touch, like a blade of ice slowly pushing toward my heart.

Run! Wolfie whispered in my mind.

6

Savannah

The Dark Wolf God was here. His presence was unmistakable—dark, bitter, and angry. It burned into my wound and seeped into my bones like a bitter chill.

My breath fogged the night air as we waited, silently measuring every sound in the forest.

Suddenly, a shadow flickered in the corner of my eye.

"Did you see that?" I whispered.

"See what?" Casey hissed, doubt rattling his voice.

Jaxson sniffed the air and scanned the woods. Like a cobra, he was coiled and ready to strike. His strength practically thrummed around us, and for a moment, the vibrations of his power calmed my pounding heart.

We waited, watching and listening.

Another shadow flicked through the woods.

"There! Between those trees." I pointed. "And another!"

"I still can't see anything," Casey whispered. "Should I light it up with my magic?"

"No." I quietly crept forward. "Just stay alert and stay put. Jaxson and I will handle this. We can see in the dark."

Jaxson stepped up beside me, and his heat made the air seem frigid. "I feel a presence."

"It's *his*, though it's weaker than when the Dark Wolf God first spoke to me."

"It might be his spies. Or agents. We're definitely being watched."

I strained with all my senses, hoping for the crack of a twig or even the rustle of leaves, but I sensed nothing other than the familiar scents of Jaxson and Casey amid the forest. Out of nowhere, the branches of a tree swayed, and a shadow sped away.

I didn't hesitate. My legs erupted into a full sprint as I tore through the brush and foliage. I was a wolf. *I* was the hunter.

"Savannah!" Casey's shout echoed from far behind.

Jaxson was at my side in an instant, flying through the brush and downed trees. "What is it?"

"I don't know," I snarled between heavy breaths as I ducked between two bushes. "But it's straight ahead of us, and I'm not letting it get away!"

The dark shape wove between the trees, using the shadows for cover. Perhaps that could've shielded it from Jaxson's eyes, but the shadows were my playground, and my magic let me see what others couldn't.

My fangs and claws erupted as fury consumed me, and I punished the earth with every step I took. Was there no place that I could be free of the nightmare? My life had become little else but fear and anger and suffering. It was *his* fault. Whatever he'd planned, I wouldn't run, and I sure as hell wouldn't roll over.

The rage pulled me on, driving me past the point of control and reason. I became one with the hunt; nothing else mattered.

As I jumped across a small gully, the black shape broke left.

I tried to pivot as I dug my foot into the earth, but I slipped.

Jaxson vaulted over me to avoid my tumbling form as I crashed to the ground.

Pain cascaded through my side, but I was up again before I even stopped rolling. I gritted my teeth against the agony in my foot and charged, pulled onward by the chase.

Just then, a shadow flashed beside me, and an icy chill rippled over my skin. Was there more than one?

With a sudden snap, my spine contorted, and I shifted mid-stride, faster than I'd ever shifted before. Agony wrenched through my body as my wolfish form shredded through my clothes. Before I'd finished another stride, my paws hit the earth.

A feral rage consumed me. I would hunt. Kill. *Destroy* whatever *he* had sent to haunt me. I delighted in the sudden surge of power that rose inside. I could tear the whole world apart.

Low brush and branches ripped across my face as I tore through the woods after the shadow. I wove around trees and leapt over logs. My feet propelled me with more power and strength than I'd ever had. My wolf and I were in sync, and we moved as smoothly as smoke. Hell, we were almost flying.

The shadow I was pursuing turned right, and before I could react, my wolf angled hard to intercept. She'd taken full control, so I let her steer. The woods were her realm.

Something glinted up ahead, and for a second, I caught the silhouette of a figure moving through the trees.

My wolf surged forward and sprang, jaws wide.

The shadow screamed, and I only felt contempt for my prey's pathetic cry of horror.

Wait a minute. Casey?

The realization struck me in the gut at the same time as the air around me erupted in a billowing sheet of flames. Just before my paws collided with Casey's chest, a heavy force slammed into my side. I hurtled sideways and tumbled head over heels. The dirt and leaves extinguished the patches of flame on my fur.

A massive wolf landed beside me, shaking the earth. *Jaxson.*

Before I could thank him, I was up on all fours, snarling. With a burst of speed and my fangs bared, my wolf charged Casey as he scrambled back.

Horror twisted my gut.

Stop! I screamed at my wolf, but no response came.

I tried to force her aside, but she didn't relinquish control. What the hell was happening?

Suddenly, Jaxson's hulking form was between us, with his lips pulled back in a savage snarl—*Submit!*

I skidded to a halt, then shot left. But Jaxson moved to intercept.

Stop! I commanded my wolf, but she wasn't listening. It was as if she weren't there. I struggled to gain control, but it was like grasping at mist.

Jaxson growled deep and low. His power and presence hit me like a windstorm, vibrating through my body and pushing me to my knees, giving me one command: *Shift.*

Did he realize my wolf was out of control?

I strained to obey, but my limbs wouldn't return to my human form. My jaw clenched as I struggled to force the shift, drawing power from Jaxson's presence and wrapping it with my own will.

Finally, my shoulder popped. Agony jolted down my spine, but I drowned it in anger. *I will have control!*

My body shook as my magic pulsed through me, and I howled in pain as the transformation came. My spine snapped, and my ribs began to realign. Time stopped having any meaning. Jerking and shaking, my human form fought to rip its way free of the wolf until I was left panting and naked on the ground.

I sucked in a lungful of air and moaned in frustration as I rolled over. Jaxson, now human himself, knelt beside me and took my hand. "You okay?"

I could sense his concern and worry.

"I don't know." I blinked, and the dark trees above me blurred into view. A few moldering leaves clung to my sweat-streaked back as I sat up. I quickly called my magic and cloaked myself in shadow. "Where's Casey?"

I looked around frantically, but there was no sign of my cousin.

"He should be about fifty feet to the north and staying put. That is, if he did what he was told," Jaxson growled, though I could hear the doubt in his voice.

Yeah, our family wasn't great at that.

With my head throbbing like it was the morning after an all-night bender, I took Jaxson's hand and rose on unsteady feet. "What the hell happened?"

"You tell me," Jaxson said quietly, without judgement. "You charged off into the woods, chasing something. Then you turned, shifted, and chased down Casey. You seemed like you wanted to take a chunk out of him—not that I blame you, but..."

"Oh, my God." Terror crept up my spine. "There were shadows moving through the trees. Didn't you see them? I mistook Casey for one of them...then my wolf, she wouldn't give me control back."

"You've had that problem before," Jaxson said softly, though his eyes glistened with worry.

"This was different, Jax. *She* was different. She wanted to attack him, I think, or at least, she couldn't tell friend from foe. I could feel it." I whispered the words, not wanting to admit the gravity of what I said even to myself, though my voice had a panicked edge to it.

My wolf—she'd gone rogue.

The ghost's words slipped into my mind: *He's already got his claws in you.*

Was this the Dark God's doing?

Shaking with fear and confusion, and desperate for a rock to cling to, I stepped forward and grabbed Jaxson's arm. Every inch of my body wanted to get closer, to have him hold me, but our nakedness was a barrier I couldn't quite step through.

I needed his warmth.

Jaxson nodded subtly and appraised me with a concerned expression etched across his face. "You got caught up in the hunt. It happens. We'll sort it out. You'll be okay."

Lies.

7

Savannah

Jaxson knew things weren't right with me and my wolf, but now wasn't the time to press him on it. We had to get out of Pere Cheney.

"Is Casey okay?" I asked.

Jax gave a noncommittal grunt. "He'll be fine. He might have nightmares for a few weeks, but they'll fade. As far as he's concerned, we say you were trying to protect him, got it? We don't need any more trouble with your family."

Guilt and shock knotted my stomach. "But that's not what happened, is it?"

He shook his head. "For now, it's the easiest story, and one he needs to believe. As for what's going on with your wolf, we'll sort that out later. We should get your cousin and get out of these woods. There's bad magic here."

I tightened my grip on his arm before he could turn away. "Did you see anything?"

Jaxson's eyes hardened, and his gaze scanned the trees behind me. There was a long pause before he spoke. "No."

My stomach plummeted, and my knees suddenly went weak.

What was happening to me? Had the shadows been my imagination? Was I losing my mind?

Jaxson glanced out into the darkness, searching. "I didn't see it or smell it, but I felt it, whatever it was. Something dark, ice-cold. I don't think you were chasing ghosts—or in this case, maybe you were. You see things I can't."

That was true. Between ghosts and shadows, my eyes were open to a sinister world. I hoped that was it, and not just me going crazy.

A shudder rippled down my spine. "This wasn't ghosts. It was the Dark Wolf God."

Before I could take another breath, Jaxson pulled me tightly against his body. "We'll figure this out. I promise."

I didn't dare breathe. We stood skin to skin in the midst of the dark woods. I could feel his heat and wanted nothing more than to melt into him, to hide in his warmth and take refuge from the world.

My heart began pounding faster than before.

And then, just as quickly, he released me and looked away. The cold night air flooded into the space between us, and my skin mourned the loss of his touch.

Jaxson cleared his throat. "We should go. Let's grab your idiot cousin and get out of here before anything else happens."

Always, there was disaster looming. How I wished I could hit pause, just for a moment, even if I had to march on to my doom after. I was so tired of the sword hanging over my head.

Giving Jaxson a regretful look, I reached out and traced a finger down his chest, channeling my magic to slowly drape him in a cloak of shadow like my own.

He raised an eyebrow, and I gave him a half smile. "If Casey sees you naked like that, he'd probably try to burn his own eyes out."

With a rough laugh that pushed back a little of the chill

around us, Jaxson turned and started making his way through the brush. "Hopefully not. I had to shift into human form to *order* him not to panic. He was freaking out."

"I'm sure seeing you shift in front of him calmed him right down. God, he's going to be traumatized for life," I muttered as I picked my way through the brush beside Jaxson. We headed in the direction of Casey's scent—which was a hell of a lot more than fifty feet away, and definitely not north.

We found him three minutes later. It wasn't hard. He was standing against the largest tree he could find with fireballs blazing in each hand.

"Casey? Are you okay?" I shouted from the darkness as we approached.

"Savannah? What the hell is going on? And *no*, for your information, I am *not* okay. A werewolf just tried to eat me, and I got to see John Holmes here naked. So no, I am never going to sleep again."

"Just don't shoot," I said as I emerged, hands raised.

"Do you have any idea how fucking scary you two look right now?" he snapped, dismissing one—and only one—of his fireballs. "You're like a couple of severed heads floating out of the darkness. Human heart muscle wasn't meant for this kind of *bullshit*, Savannah. I think I'm having palpitations. Start explaining, *now*."

Right. We were cloaked in robes of shadow. I hadn't considered the optical effect at night.

Before I could respond, Jaxson cleared his throat. "There was something in the woods. You were in danger. Savannah, in wolf form, tried to knock you down, but you fireballed her."

My mouth went sour. He'd chosen his words so carefully that it made me sound like a hero and a victim instead of a half-crazed assailant. Every phrase was true, yet together, they were a lie.

"That was you?" Casey asked. "Do you have *any* idea how terrifying you are? Never, *ever*, do that shit to me again. What the hell were you chasing?"

My shoulders drooped at the bitterness in his voice. "I'm really sorry, Case. That's...not how I wanted you to meet my wolf. I was chasing a shadow creature, but I couldn't catch it. I don't know what it was. Probably one of the Dark God's minions."

"And we should get out of the woods before more of his servants arrive," Jaxson said, scanning the darkness.

We picked our way back through the bushes as I tried to think of a way to apologize to my cousin for so many things. I just kept digging myself deeper.

As we neared the truck, Casey finally broke the silence. "Don't be so glum. We both nearly killed each other tonight, so let's consider it a learning opportunity." Casey shouldered me gently and gave a sly glance at Jaxson ahead of us. "For instance, I learned what you see in Jaxson. Wow. I mean, like, *wow* girl."

Scorching heat flooded my neck and face, and I stopped him in his tracks with my finger jabbed against his chest. "We are not discussing *that* part of my life. Got it?"

"Fine. I think I already know everything I need to."

I spun and stalked after Jaxson, flushed all the way to my burning core. Idiot cousin. Jaxson, of course, had heard every single word, and I could smell the scent of his smugness. *God save me.*

Jaxson unlocked the truck, and I slipped into the passenger side while Casey climbed in the back. My cousin wasn't the only one with whom I needed to work things out. I closed my eyes and concentrated on the spirit of my wolf.

Wolfie? Are you there? Can we talk about what happened tonight?

No response.

Wolfie?

A deep dread settled over me.

What was happening with my wolf? Was the Dark God intruding on our connection?

A litany of questions tightened around my heart as we backed out of the cemetery and headed down the dirt road.

Had I really brought the Dark God with me, like the ghost had said? And what had she meant when she'd said that he had his claws in me, that he'd consume me like the sea?

All I knew was that with each passing minute, I felt more and more like a liability to Jaxson and the pack, let alone my own family. I was losing control of my wolf. What if I lost control of myself?

Dragan had taken over my body before—first, to make me walk into the arms of a lurking noctith demon, and then he'd tried again in Pere Cheney. If Dragan could do that, then the Dark God would be powerful enough to make me dance like a puppet and turn me into the monster of werewolf legend.

The twin-soul will steal the wolves from every werewolf who resists them and will leave your people weak before the Dark God.

I had to get rid of the Soul Knife. And if things kept going to shit, *really* to shit, I needed to find a way to lock myself away, despite Jaxson's objections. Maybe then, the pack would have a chance.

8

Savannah

I parked my Fury in the temporary parking outside of the Hall of Inquiry. We'd driven all night back to the dunes, where Jaxson had dropped Casey and me at our rides. We'd all headed to Magic Side as dawn started to creep above the horizon and made good time until we hit the outskirts of Chicago.

Already exhausted from the sleepless night, I was pretty sure the rush hour traffic had sucked the last breath of life from my soul. I texted Neve that I'd arrived, then took a sip of the Zinger I'd picked up on the way. My nerves didn't need the buzz, but my tired body did.

Heaving myself up, I climbed out of my Fury and groaned as the aches and pains of driving crept down my spine and into my legs.

Jaxson pulled up in his truck behind me. I headed over and pounded on his door, and he rolled the window down. "I'm going to ditch the Soul Knife," I said. "It shouldn't take long."

He nodded. "Need me to come in?"

"I'm not sure you're allowed," I replied, recalling our last encounter in the Hall of Inquiry. "Can I crash at your place after? I don't think I'm in any state to deal with Aunt Laurel."

A smile crept up at the corners of his mouth. "Of course. I'll be here when you get back."

I did my best to hide my reaction and walked away. "I need sleep, Jaxson."

Neve waved from the stairs as I made my way across the square out front. The weathered stone of the neoclassical building matched the gray sky.

"Hey, there." She pulled me into an embrace, then held me at arm's length as she eyed me. "You look..."

"Like an exhausted mess?" I prompted. "I've been chasing shadows through the woods and driving all night."

"Pretty much. I thought you'd take some time off after everything that happened at Bentham," she said, laughing. "That place is a shitstorm magnet."

I smiled dully. "Yeah, well, I'm not sure we solved anything at all. We defeated Dragan, but I'm pretty sure we woke a monster in the process."

Neve glanced over as we climbed the steps to the brass doors. "What do you mean?"

My stomach suddenly clenched. How much should I tell her? Jaxson's warning was still fresh in my mind. *We thought Dragan would be the one to release the Dark God, so we took the bastard out. If the wrong person hears of this and puts two and two together, they might decide to do the same thing to Savy.*

I hadn't known Neve long, but I trusted her. As for the rest of the Order, however, I wasn't sure. Even if they were well intentioned, the Hall of Inquiry probably leaked rumors like a rusty sieve. The wrong someone might hear, but I had to tell Neve something, even part of the truth.

I rubbed my tired eyes, hoping the Zinger would kick in. "The wolves have a legend of a Dark Wolf God that will bring devastation to our world. Well, I think killing Dragan woke him, and now everything is messed up."

Neve stopped and put a hand on my shoulder. "First off, I know that tone of voice. Whatever is going on, don't blame yourself for this. You stopped a catastrophe at Bentham. We saw the runes Dragan burned into the roof of the prison. By the looks of the spell, he was going to send the whole place, along with its magic, nuclear."

I recalled Dragan's words, shouted toward the sky: *I have prepared your altar, great one! A sacrifice unlike any before.*

Neve squeezed my shoulder gently. "That explosion would have hit the lakeshore with a tsunami, Savy. So whatever else happened, you stopped a lot of people from dying."

Or had I just deferred their fate?

She released me and gave me a warm smile. "Cheer up. You're not on your own. I'm here to help, and so is the Order. What can we do?"

Taking a deep breath, I said, "First, I need to get rid of the Soul Knife. I think it has a role to play, either in my hands or in someone else's."

"I see why you wanted to unload it so quickly. The good news is that Archmage DeLoren is waiting to take it and lock it in the Vault. But if there's anything else you need, let us know."

Could you lock me in there, too?

I held my tongue on that one.

Neve turned and headed up the last steps into the Hall of Inquiry with me right behind, and we pushed through the front door, avoiding a few officers on their way out.

The front room was bustling with employees arriving to work. Breaking out of the crowd, I followed Neve down a marble corridor to an open elevator.

I shoved my hands in my pockets to keep from fidgeting as I

watched the glowing numbers on the door descending...1, 0, B. "So, what exactly is the Vault?"

Neve flashed me a grin. "It's a magically concealed labyrinth with hundreds of portals that lead to hidden rooms scattered around the world. It's the best place to keep something safe and practically impregnable."

The nerves fluttering in my chest eased a smidge. "Good."

The sooner the cursed thing was locked away, the better.

Bing. The doors opened at level V. We followed the warmly lit corridor around several corners until we reached a heavy brass door.

I eyed the symbols engraved into the metal. Electric energy pulsed around us, and my skin prickled. "It's beautiful."

"And deadly. No touching," a gruff voice sounded right behind us, and I jumped.

"Archmage DeLoren." Neve smiled. "Nice to see you again. This is my friend Savy."

The older man tilted his head slightly as his blue eyes narrowed in on me. "Detective Cross said that you are in possession of a cursed weapon that needs to be locked away?"

With difficulty, I stole my attention from his bushy, caterpillar-like eyebrows. "Uh, yes. The Soul Knife, which belonged to an Italian mage. I've been storing it in the ether for safekeeping, but I need to get rid of it. Someplace safe that no one can access."

"A Soul Knife," he grunted. "I haven't seen one of those for ages. A particularly medieval and fiendish weapon. You can be assured that it will be safe in the Vault. It's impregnable."

Neve glanced at the weathered archmage, and something flashed across her face that caused his gaze to harden with an undercurrent of annoyance. What the hell was that about?

It didn't matter. I held out my hand to call the knife, then hesitated. "Once it's safe in the Vault, I won't be able to summon it back, will I?"

The archmage furrowed his brow. "Once something is inside the Vault, it's impervious to outside magic. No power on this Earth could summon it because it is no longer on this earth."

The tension in my shoulders eased. "That's what I wanted to hear."

I rubbed my palms on my jeans and focused my mind on the Soul Knife to summon it to me, imagining how it felt in my palm.

Nothing.

Pressing my lids shut, I dug deeper, recalling the patinaed bronze blade, the inscribed runes and raised ridge that cut down its center. My magic strained, and I tasted the knife's signature—oaky and rich like wine on my tongue—but I couldn't seem to draw the cursed thing from the ether.

I opened my eyes and growled in frustration.

DeLoren cocked one of his hoary eyebrows. "Is something wrong?"

"I can't summon it," I said in surprise.

"Have you summoned it before?" he asked, the slightest undercurrent of irritation in his voice.

I held out my hand again and gave a snarl of frustration when the knife didn't appear. "I've done it dozens of times. Something's wrong."

"Hmm." The archmage rubbed his beard thoughtfully. "Maybe your mind is unfocused. Let me see if I can help."

Unfocused? I paused and shot him a piercing glare. I was exhausted and stressed. I hadn't slept in a day, and the Dark God was looming over everything I did. So yeah, maybe I was unfocused.

Neve stepped up beside me and squeezed my shoulder.

"Take a breath, Savy. You've been through a lot recently. You've got this."

I inhaled deeply and nodded. "Okay. Let's try again."

DeLoren's magic flared and enveloped me like a warm blanket, but I still couldn't get a sense of it. I cleared my racing thoughts and focused on the Soul Knife. The heaviness of the blade in my hand. The coolness of the metal.

The sound of wheat blowing in the wind hummed in my ears. It was close.

And then, a cold weight tugged against my magic and sent a shiver down my spine as the wound on my shoulder ached. A deep voice rose in my mind: *Why would you want to give up your claws, little wolf? We have so much work to do.*

The Dark Wolf God.

Creeping terror clawed at my heart, and my eyes flew open.

"Shit," I gasped, dragging my hand through my hair. Was he blocking my magic? Trying to control me?

Neve looked between DeLoren and me, worry in her eyes. "What happened?"

Jaxson's warning to Casey burned in my mind: *Tell no one until we understand what's going on.*

I could trust Neve, but the archmage? I didn't know him. If they learned that the Dark God was trying to take control of me...

"I need some fresh air." The walls of the corridor were constricting, and the magic pulsing off the Vault was making me nauseous. My head throbbed, and my heart began to race.

I didn't pause to explain, but just bolted down the hall and punched the call button on the elevator a half dozen times.

You can't run, little wolf. Sooner or later, you will submit to me, the Dark God said.

Terror coursed through my veins, and when the doors

opened, I threw myself inside, jamming the starred button for the lobby. *What am I going to do?*

"Hey, wait up." Neve slipped between the closing doors. "What's going on, Savy? You're freaking me out."

Her signature filled the small space, and after a moment, it felt like I could breathe again. That the dark presence in my soul had lifted.

Her vivid eyes shone with concern, and she pulled the stop button on the elevator. "Talk to me."

I swallowed hard, chest heaving. "He stopped me from releasing the Soul Knife."

"Who?" she asked, eyes bright with concern.

I pressed myself against the back of the elevator. "The Dark Wolf God. I heard his voice. I think he wants to use me."

"We should tell DeLoren."

I grabbed her arm and whispered, "No! There are prophecies about the Dark God...and about me. If people misinterpret them, it could go really, *really* badly for me. I need to figure out what's happening first."

Neve's expression turned grim. She nodded and released the stop button.

The elevator lurched up to the main floor, and the doors opened. She followed me across the foyer and out the front doors. The sky was still overcast, blotting out the fading sun. I slumped onto the stairs and stared out across the green expanse of the Midway. "Please don't tell anyone yet."

Neve sat down beside me and squeezed my hand. "I won't say anything, and you can count on my help, one hundred percent. We'll figure this out, gods and prophecies both. I know things probably feel wildly out of control right now—I've been there—but we're all in charge of our own destinies, even though it may not feel like it at times."

I nodded, but I wasn't sure I believed it.

How did one fight one's own destiny? More to the point, how did one defeat a god?

Kick 'em all in the nuts? Wolfie prompted, and I smiled softly. That had been my motto once, back when my biggest problems were a rundown car and customers skipping out on tabs. Problems that a Belmont girl could reasonably be expected to face.

Might still work, she suggested.

I closed my eyes and responded, *I haven't heard from you in a while*

Things...have been different. Fading in and out. There are longer and longer gaps. I don't know how to explain it, and it's making me nervous.

"You and me both," I muttered.

"What?" asked Neve.

I blushed. "Just talking to myself. Sorry."

She leaned over and bumped my shoulder. "Don't worry, we just have to work through the problem. Stop fretting over the big picture for a moment, or you'll get overwhelmed. Something is clearly up with the weapon you have, so figuring that out is the first step. Perhaps it's a curse. I know a diviner..."

Taking a deep breath, I stood. "You're right, but I think I have to talk to my aunt. She helped me bind the knife in the first place. Maybe she can undo the spell."

Neve smiled and rose as well. "Okay, then that's step one."

I slipped out my phone and pulled up Laurel's number. My finger hovered over the screen, emotions thrashing inside me.

She'd bound my wolf. She hated my mate and my pack. But even though I'd hurt her deeply, she'd always been there to help. And I needed her help now, more than ever. Whatever it took, it was time to reconcile.

9

Savannah

"I'm so glad you called," Laurel said as I stepped into her kitchen. The sweet warm aroma of snickerdoodles hit my senses, and my mouth began watering.

She wore a paisley apron that was dusted with flour. "You look like you saw a ghost, Savannah. Tell me what's wrong."

My aunt looked at me with a troubled expression that twisted my gut. She was such a cluster of contradictions. I knew that in her dealings, she could be hard and ruthless. She was a lethal sorceress, and probably one of the most dangerous people in Magic Side. And yet, here she was baking me cookies from scratch.

I took a seat at the kitchen island and fisted my hands to keep them from shaking. Last time I'd been there, I'd used the Sphere of Devouring to destroy Dragan's soul. There was no easy way to explain all the shit that had unfolded since.

But she needed to know. If anyone could help me sort things out, it was her.

So I spilled my guts and told her everything. The Dark Wolf God. What had happened at Pere Cheney. The Soul Knife.

When I'd finished, a weight had been lifted from my shoulders, but Aunt Laurel looked pale and distraught.

A buzzer went off, and she jumped up and took two baking sheets out of the oven. The rich cinnamon scent wafted off the piping-hot cookies as she set the sheets on the stove to cool.

"I've heard of the legends of the dark one. Just pieces and hearsay, but this..." She paused and turned to me. Worry lines etched her forehead.

"Is bad," I finished, the words catching in my throat. "I don't know what to do."

Laurel nodded and began moving the cookies to the silver cooling racks she'd set on the counter. "You've got a good start. Don't panic, and seek help from people you trust. I learned that the hard way. When I was younger, I thought I had to carry the world on my shoulders until Rhia—an old mentor of mine—knocked some sense into my head."

She broke the edge off of one of the cookies and sneaked it in her mouth. "I know I told you not to go to the Order before, but you were right to try to give up the Soul Knife. I'll help you summon it, and I can remove the spell so you can bring it to the archmages and lock it away in their ridiculous vault."

Hope and relief flared within me. "You could do that?"

She slid two cookies onto a plate and handed it to me. "Of course I can. I cast the spell, didn't I? Together, we should be able to summon the blade. Removing the magic bonds will be easy."

Thank God.

As I heard Casey stir upstairs, I bit into a cookie and moaned at the warm, sugary goodness. Hints of vanilla, butter, and caramel flooded my tastebuds. Being a wolf had its benefits, and heightened senses were top on my list. Everything tasted way better.

Or actually, in some cases, way worse. Burritos from gas station hot shelves, for instance.

Laurel took the stool opposite from me, and I brushed off the crumbs from my hands before placing them in hers.

"Focus on the knife like I taught you," she said, closing her eyes.

Laurel's magic wrapped around me like a familiar hug. I squeezed my eyes shut and went through the process that had always worked, envisioning the signature, the feel, the details of the knife.

But just like earlier, I couldn't call the Soul Knife to me. It was like my tether was severed, or at least restrained.

Worry crept under my skin, but I reached harder, searching for any connection with the cursed blade. My aunt's signature pulsed, and the buzzing of bees and scent of cloves filled the room as she intensified her efforts. The little symbols she'd drawn on my palm appeared, but the knife did not.

After a minute, I released the breath I'd been holding and pulled my hands free of Laurel's. "It's not working."

"I can see that." Her brow was furrowed, and the intensity of her gaze sent chills up my spine. "This is very unusual. I sensed the Soul Knife, but its connection with you is different."

"Different?"

My palms suddenly felt sweaty. Different wasn't necessarily bad. I'd always been different. But the way Aunt Laurel said it sent panic coursing through me.

"Like the spell has been tampered with. Altered," she said. "Another magic has crept into the bond."

Shit. "The Dark Wolf God."

She stood up abruptly and placed her palms on the table. "I'll look in my spell books to see if there's any way to counter the magic that has reworked the original spell. There must be.

But for now, you need to be extremely careful. Who else knows about you and the prophecy?" Laurel asked.

"Just me, Jaxson, and Sam. And Neve at the Order."

My aunt looked at me knowingly. "It might be safer if you move back in with us. If the rest of the pack gets wind of this..."

They'd kill me?

I shook my head, even though doubt crept into my heart. "I'm safe with Jaxson."

"Are you certain? I don't trust those wolves, Savannah."

Heat flushed my neck, and I had to tamp down the defensiveness that surged. "I'm a wolf, and I trust him more than anyone." And that was the truth.

Laurel stiffened and turned to the sink to vigorously clean the dishes. "I know you share a bond. Trusting him that much makes sense, though I don't understand the ins and outs of such things. It's not like you have a choice about it."

Somehow, her tone was frustrated and disapproving and hurt and accepting all at once—but it was her words that sliced deep. "Every choice I make is mine."

Fuck the fates.

I stood to leave, the legs of the stool scratching against the linoleum floor.

"That's not what I meant, dear. The fates push us toward things, but the choices are always ours. I just know how strong the mate bond is, and I know that what you feel for Jaxson is real. I may not like it, but that's not for me to decide." Sadness floated around her, dousing some of the flames of my anger. "You're my niece, and I love you."

I bit my lip. "All of me, or just the LaSalle half?"

Laurel reached out and placed her hand on my arm. "All of you. You may not believe it, but your mother and I...we weren't like sisters, but we had an understanding. A closeness, even. We both loved your father so much, and that gave us common ground." Her hand dropped away. "I'll try to remember that. After your parents died, and I thought I'd lost you, too, I let bitterness get the best of me."

I wanted to leave it there, as if her feud with the pack had been about her brother, but I couldn't. I knew better.

My gut tightened with the fear of what I'd learn. "Your issues with the wolves go deeper than that. You've got dossiers on dozens of North American packs. And you've been keeping them updated."

She flinched, and shock and anger crossed her face. "What were you doing snooping in my office?"

I squared my shoulders, trying to hide the guilt and shame. I'd trespassed and violated Laurel's privacy, but the information she'd collected on the werewolves was dangerous and motivated by bad intentions.

"I was desperate. I was trying to deal with becoming a werewolf. I asked you about my mother over and over, but you were hiding something. I was looking for anything I could find about her, anything to explain what was happening to me. I didn't expect to find...werewolf profiling."

Her signature crackled. "You shouldn't have gone in there. You had no right."

Unwilling to back down, I balled my fists in frustration. "You should have told me the truth about my mother when I asked. You had no right to keep my heritage from me. What I did was wrong, but that doesn't make your lies or stacks of dossiers any more ethical."

Laurel pressed her fingers to the bridge of her nose and slumped back against the wall. "I know."

A long, stiff silence dragged out between us before she finally sighed and looked out the window. "It doesn't make me any less culpable, but your grandfather collected most of that information. Knowledge is power, and I'll admit I've made use of it, even added to it. But only ever to protect our family and our interests. Your grandfather had different intentions, but I swear to you, I'm not him."

My stomach twisted, and bile rose in my throat. He'd died fifteen years before, but I'd met his ghost lurking in her office. He'd called me a dirty little half-breed snoop, claimed that Laurel would skin me alive if she caught me in there. "He hated my kind."

Laurel's jaw stiffened. "Your grandfather...he is part of the reason we have the reputation we do. He was a loyal but hard man. And when it came to the werewolves, he was bitter, vengeful, and filled with hate. If he could have wiped the Laurents out, I think he would have."

I was glad I'd never met the bastard while he was alive. I dug my nails into my palms. "Why? Why do we have this feud?"

She looked at me with broken eyes. "The death of his brother. Before that, the death of a Laurent, and before that, a LaSalle. It goes a long way back."

A cycle of hate repeating over and over. Like the death of Jaxson's sister, Stephanie, and the plans on Billy's wall to kill our whole family.

Laurel stepped up and took my clenched hands. "But I'm not him, Savannah. Your mother changed that. Your birth changed that. I had to change."

"He was why my mom and dad left," I whispered.

She nodded, tears brimming in her eyes. "In part. If he knew that your father had fallen for a wolf, he'd have hunted them both down."

"I know. I found the photo album on the shelf. And the letter from my dad." I fought back my own tears and anger. If it weren't for my bigoted grandfather, life might have been different for them. For me.

She worked her hands into mine. "It was the wolves, too.

Your father was just as afraid of them as he was of your grandfather. Maybe it had something to do with this prophecy. All I know is that this feud took my brother and sister-in-law from me, and I thought it had taken you, too. I hated them all for that."

"If this feud took so much from you, and if you're not like your father, then why do you still have stacks of files on werewolves? Why can't you just let it go?"

Laurel stood and fetched a copper teapot from the cupboard, and began filling it. She set it down hard on the gas stovetop and leaned against the oven. "Insurance. The pack hasn't been kind to us, and the Laurents have been at our throats since our family settled on this island. Jaxson's father, Alistair, is much like mine. Though you may know Jaxson, so do I. And I'm not certain that he's that much different from his father."

Frustration tore at me. I didn't believe that. I'd never met Jaxson's father, but I knew who Jaxson was. Every day we'd spent together, I'd seen more and more of his soul.

"I don't care what you think you know. He's brave, he's loyal, and yes, he can be ruthless. But he'd do anything to protect his pack, even swallow the death of his own sister."

Laurel's shoulders wilted. "That was a horrible accident."

Unable to face that story right now, I shoved it out of my mind and crossed my arms. "Ending this feud would protect our family and theirs. So end it."

Laurel gave me a mournful look. "You've changed so much since you first showed up on our doorstep. If you can do that, if you can adapt to all this madness, then maybe there's some hope for the rest of us."

I opened my mouth, but at that moment, Casey trudged into the kitchen halfway through a giant yawn. He patted me on the head as if I were a favorite family pet. "Hey, Cuz."

Casey made his way around me and pulled a box of Count

Chocula out of the cabinet. He paused midway through setting it on the counter and looked between me and Laurel. "Wait, what are you doing here? Did you two make up?"

Laurel, her sad expression hidden at the first sight of him, gave him a kiss on the cheek as she fetched two mugs and a box of loose-leaf tea. "We did. Or we're getting there, I hope?"

She glanced at me, and my chest loosened.

Laurel accepted what I was and had forgiven me for what I'd done. She loved me, and she was willing to change. We might not agree on everything, but we'd cleared the air, at least. "We're all good, but I'd better get going."

"By the way, did you ever figure out what that key I gave you was for?" Laurel asked as I turned to go.

The key. Damn, I'd forgotten about it. My mother had given it to Laurel, and Laurel to me. I rummaged through the coin pouch of my wallet and pulled the tiny gold-plated key out. It was a peculiar shape, with an ornate G on it. "I haven't had a chance. You have no idea?"

Laurel shook her head. "It was just for safekeeping. She didn't say."

"That thing?" Casey asked through a spoonful of cereal. "That's a key to a safety deposit box."

Laurel and I looked to my cousin, who stood there with mussed hair and a dribble of milk on his chin.

"What?" he asked, suddenly confused.

I held the key up. "You're telling me that this key is to a lockbox?"

He nodded and shoveled another spoonful of sugary cereal into his mouth. "Yeah. That's what I said. That one belongs to Gold Trust Credit on Sixty-Third and Razorback."

Holy crap. My cousin was either a genius or full of shit.

Laurel folded her arms over her chest and lifted a brow at her son. "And how do you know this?"

"Because I have boxes all over town. I use them for...uh, you know. Keeping stuff?"

I wrapped my arms around Casey and gave him a squeeze. "I love you."

His spine straightened, and he looked down at me suspiciously. "Who the hell are you, and what have you done with my cousin?"

10

Savannah

Thirty minutes later, I climbed out of my Fury and glanced up at the golden sign fronting Gold Trust Credit.

My senses were instantly alert. The familiar scent of pine and melted snow sent shivers skating up my spine. *Jaxson.*

Searching the street, I spotted him strolling down the sidewalk toward me holding two takeout cups from Magic Bean. It had only been a few hours since I'd seen him, but suddenly, it felt like days. I tried to ignore the way he made me melt, but the strength of his stride and the way his jacket stretched over those broad shoulders reminded me of the way we moved together. Just his scent sent shivers running somewhere else.

A knowing smile tugged on his lips as he noticed my interest, and I blushed. Yeah, werewolf senses could be a real pain in the ass.

He handed me a cup, and my mouth watered at the rich scent of cardamon and cinnamon. "Thanks." I took a sip of the sugary mocha latte and sighed with relief. I was running on fumes.

When I'd told him about the key, he'd insisted on meeting

me here—something about not wanting to leave me alone, though I suspected that was as much for his benefit as mine. I quickly explained the key situation as we headed up the sidewalk.

"So Laurel has no idea what's inside the lockbox?" Jaxson asked as he opened the glass door for me. A bell dinged as we entered.

"She has no clue."

Bank tellers sat behind glass windows, while at least five tiny, winged creatures flitted about behind them carrying receipts and wads of cash.

"What the…?" I watched as one of them deposited a stack of hundred-dollar bills into the palm of a woman with broad-rimmed glasses. She didn't even look up. She just took the cash like it was no big deal.

Jaxson chuckled beside me. "First time seeing an imp, I take it."

"I think I saw some at the Archives, but these are so tiny." They were no bigger than a foot and cute as all hell. "Can I have one?"

He grunted. "Imps are more like assistants than pets. They're single-minded and ornery and best suited to busywork. You're better off getting a dog."

One of the imps glared at him but went about its task.

We waited in line behind a woman who had a small child next to her. He was holding her hand, and he turned his head and looked up at me. I wasn't good with kids, but this one was cute. I smiled at him. He blinked, and when he opened his eyes, they were no longer blue but a pale green with vertical pupils.

I frowned, and a lizard-like tongue darted out of his mouth. I must have gasped or had a horrible look on my face, because his mother glanced back at me and gave me a death stare.

Jaxson cleared his throat as the woman towed her son up to a teller.

Embarrassment burned my cheeks, but a teller about my age waved us over. Every time I started to get comfortable in Magic Side, it peeled back another layer. It felt like home, but I had a feeling that this pattern of awkward discovery was going to stick with me for a long time.

"Hi. I'm here to collect my belongings from this box," I said, and slid the key to the man. His signature smelled like popcorn, but I couldn't find any indications as to what kind of Magica he was.

"Name?" He examined the key and looked up at me.

"Savannah Caine. Though it might be under LaSalle."

His fingers flew over the keyboard in front of him, and his eyes darted to me when I said LaSalle. "Do you have any identification?"

I pulled out the ID card I'd gotten from the Order when I'd first showed up in Magic Side. He examined it, narrowing his eyes at the photo and then at me.

Seemingly satisfied, he slid the key, ID, and a golden token under the glass partition and said, "Box one-oh-six. Take the hall on your right, first left, five rows down."

"Well, that was easy," I muttered, but stopped short when we came face to face with a giant vault door. An enormous horned demon guarded the way. His signature smelled of ash and blood, and I sucked in a sharp breath.

He extended a clawed hand and spoke in a voice that was like grinding stone. "ID and token please."

I carefully placed it in his palm. He studied both, returned my ID, and slid the coin in a slot on the door.

The handle began to spin, and a burst of steam shot out from small vents in the steel plates. It swung wide, and the demon ushered us in.

Silver lockboxes lined the walls from floor to ceiling, and a narrow set of stairs on wheels was parked at the end. We took the first left, and I counted five rows down, dragging my finger over the black numbers inscribed into the boxes.

My heart pulsed harder, and I swallowed. "Thanks for being with me, Jax. I don't have much of anything that belonged to my parents, and I'm a little nervous to see what it is."

"Of course. I figured I'd better be here in case they denied you access. I wouldn't want you to try robbing the bank."

I narrowed my eyes at him. "That was almost a joke."

Finally, I found it: one hundred six. It was no bigger than a shoebox.

I fitted the key into the brass hole and turned until it clicked. Pulling the small door open, I peered inside.

Excitement thrummed through my veins as I reached in and withdrew two white business envelopes. The thickest one was full of crisp hundred-dollar bills. I sucked in a breath. There had to be at least fifteen grand here, if not more. "Holy shit."

Jaxson whistled low.

I flipped open the other envelope and pulled out several folded sheets of paper. A letter—and written in my mom's handwriting.

Savannah –

If you're reading this, then something has happened to us. I'm so sorry, honey. We always wanted you to have a "normal" life, but sometimes, the fates have other plans. You were the best thing your father and I ever did, and we will always *love you.*

Trust your aunt Laurel. She sacrificed more for us than anyone. She will explain everything. Just know that what we did, we did to protect you. You might be angry, but one day, I hope you'll understand what it was all for.

Don't let anyone push you around. You've always been stronger than you realize, and though the fates may have set the course for things to come, you will always have the power to fashion your own path. You're an artist, after all.

You have family in Silverton, from my side. When you're ready, I know your grandfather and cousins would love to meet you. He was so excited when you were born, and his heart is like yours. Go to him and reconnect with your roots.

Take care, honey. Love you to the moon and back.

Mom

My eyes blurred, and I swallowed hard as I unfolded the other sheet. On it was my grandfather's address in Silverton, Colorado.

Jaxson gently rubbed my back. "I'm so sorry, Savy."

I nodded, and a tear slipped free. "What would have happened if I'd never come to Magic Side? If I'd just kept on driving? I'd never have any of this. Not Laurel. Not this letter. Not my family. Not you."

"I would always have found you." He pulled me to his chest, and like a dam breaking, my tears finally fell. He held me tight and pressed his lips to my forehead. "You're right where you belong, where you're loved. And safe."

His words seemed to crack my chest further open, and by the time I was finished crying, Jaxson's shirt was damp. I wiped my eyes and nose, feeling a rush of embarrassment. "Sorry. There's just so much to deal with, so much of the time."

"You've got nothing to be sorry about. I understand."

I dried the last of my tears with my wrist. "Let's get out of here."

"Where do you want to go?"

"I don't care. Somewhere that's not a wall of boxes. Somewhere quiet, somewhere I can breathe without a demon looking over my shoulder."

He nodded. "I know just the place."

11

Savannah

We loaded up in Jaxson's truck and wound our way through Magic Side as a thousand thoughts swirled through my mind. My parents. My family. My wolf and the Dark God hanging over it all.

Twenty minutes later, we parked in a lot at the edge of the shore. A narrow channel separated us from a small, wooded island.

Jaxson didn't explain, and I didn't press him. I was too exhausted, so I just followed him over an ornate wooden and iron bridge that looked like it belonged in another time.

As I reached the middle of the bridge, I stopped short. Something had changed. The island, with its trees and flowers, was still the same, so what was it?

Then I heard it: stillness. A silence that was like your first breath of air after a dive. I glanced over my shoulder just to make sure the city was there.

It was—but the sound of traffic and screeching breaks and sirens were gone, as well as the eternal rumble of city life to which I'd acclimated since leaving Belmont.

It wasn't that everything was completely silent—quite the contrary. Birds argued in the trees overhead, and the buzz of bugs filtered through the tall grasses. The leaves, which were beginning to turn orange, fluttered in the wind

But that was it. No city. No incessant gray noise.

A surprising spark of anger flickered in me. Why couldn't the world be like this all the time?

"Welcome to the Garden of the Wolves," Jaxson said, a soft smile tugging at the edge of his lips. "There's a magical barrier around the island that keeps the city noise out. It's a good place to reflect—my favorite place in our lands here."

Breathing deeply, I nodded. "I think I needed this."

I followed him along a path lined with wild, flowering weeds that were several feet tall and resplendent in purple, white, and yellow blossoms.

The path led to an old grove of trees. Tucked away, beneath the shade of the canopy, sat an ancient, weather-beaten mausoleum with a peaked roof, stone pillars, and a pair of ornate metal doors. Beneath the arch, the limestone blocks had been engraved with the name LAURENT.

Jaxson sat on a little stone bench. "I come here when I need a quiet place to think or I want to be near my sister. Sometimes, I can almost imagine her listening."

I sat down beside him. "We've never really talked about her, Jax."

"We don't need to," he growled, then his expression softened. "This is just a good place to come to wrestle with the ghosts of our past."

My parents. The promise of family in Colorado.

I sat with him quietly for a long time, savoring the soft sound of the birds and wind rustling the leaves. Savoring a single moment free from the Dark God and the chaos of the world falling apart outside.

I linked my arm through his. We were an island for each other in the midst of it all.

At last, Jaxson bowed his head. "When Stephanie died, my father lost it. He blamed me. And when he couldn't handle the pain anymore and fell apart, I had to pick up the pieces. I never had any time to grieve her death, and eventually, too much time had passed. So I just come here, never certain of what I should say or how I should feel."

I could see his grief, all bottled up. It was in the tension in his back and the coil of his muscles. And I saw it in every action he took—his rage, his anger, the ruthlessness with which he led the pack.

Haunted by guilt and grief and longing.

I placed my head on his shoulder. "I'm sorry, Jax."

We sat like that for a long time until he cleared his throat. "I was never meant to be alpha. It wasn't a path I chose, but one I had to take. That was Stephanie's fate, not mine. She'd been trained for it. I was just her muscle. A thug."

I sat up. "You're not a thug, and you've done well. The pack is thriving."

He gently squeezed my hand. "I know it is. But when I started out, I was in over my head. I only managed it because of Regina and Sam. You need to trust them, like I did. You don't have to carry everything on your own. You're part of a pack. They'll stand by you, no matter what. We need to tell them."

So this was what it was about: come clean, admit the monster that I was. I shook my head. "Regina wanted to string me up when we first met."

He stood. "You won her over, Savy, and she'll be your staunchest defender. You need to trust me in this."

I rubbed my temples.

I was so tired. Tired of running. Tired of hiding the truth, first about my wolf, then about the prophecy.

You might like being the Lone Ranger, Wolfie whispered in my mind, *but something tells me we're going to need a fucking high-powered posse to bring down the Dark God. I'm with Jax, let's tell the pack.*

I'd told Casey and my aunt and Neve, but only because I had to. And because I wasn't prophesized to betray them. The pack was different.

Hey, this way, they can't say you didn't warn them. Anyway, you're going to crack if you hold on to this much longer.

That much was true. I stood and stretched. "Fine. We tell them. If they don't freak, then we go from there."

"Good." Jaxson grinned. "They're already waiting in the parking lot."

"*What*?"

"I figured I'd win you over. Let's go."

Cocky alpha.

You like him that way, my wolf observed.

Shut up, Wolfie.

Trepidation and irritation fought for dominance in my gut as I followed Jaxson back to the bridge, where indeed, Sam, Regina, *and* the loremaster were waiting.

Sam raised a six-pack that was already missing a few bottles. "Jax said to bring beer. What's up?"

Regina pulled one out, popped the top, and handed it over. "Jax said things were fucked and that you needed our help. So here we are."

Stunned, I took the beer and looked at each pack member. At least we were on the silenced side of the bridge and no one else would be able to hear.

Ready for a leap of faith? Wolfie asked.

Nope.

I took a long pull of the beer, and then I told them everything.

12

Savannah

"Fuck Dragan, and fuck the Dark Wolf God," Sam growled.

I'd just finished explaining how I happened to be the horrible monster of werewolf prophecy, that I had accidently released the Dark God, and that I would soon be stealing all their souls.

I dried my eyes with the back of my wrist.

Regina crossed her arms. "Okay. Clearly, the fates are out to screw us, as usual. So we work the problem. We need to take the Dark God out of the picture before he fucks over Savannah and the rest of us. If we can stop him from returning, then the prophecy will be moot." She pivoted toward me. "Any ideas?"

I raised my eyebrows. "Honestly, I thought you guys might just want to get it over with and string me up."

She glared. "Nobody messes with my pack, and you're part of my pack. We take him down."

"Yes, but he's a god," Sam muttered. "How do we take down a fucking god?"

The loremaster cleared her throat. "The Moon did once before, so it's possible."

Sam laughed. “Yeah, she seduced and drugged him. I don’t think that’s going to work again, and I’m sure as *hell* not signing up for *that* job.”

The loremaster glared at Sam. “Don’t be daft. It’s a story. A metaphor with a grain of truth, and a lesson for those who *listen*. But the Moon did *something* to him. We’ll have to ask her how to do it again.”

Ask the Moon? I gaped. “Is that even possible?”

She snorted. “Wolves have called on the Moon in times of trouble since we first set foot on this earth. There are old rituals, magic that has been passed down from grandmother to grandmother.”

“How?” Jaxson asked. “Tell us what you need.”

The loremaster cleared her throat and doodled sheepishly in the hard dirt of the path with the end of her cane. “Well, the problem is, I’ve done moon calling, but I’ve never actually tried to summon the Moon herself. They’re old rituals, and the details are fuzzy.”

Jaxson shrugged. “At this point, we don’t have much to go on, and fuzzy is better than nothing. How do we proceed?”

The loremaster put two palms on the top of her cane and rose. “Well, first, we have to find ourselves a Moon temple—a place of her worship.”

“A Moon temple? Are there any of those still active?” Regina asked.

The loremaster squared her shoulders. “I said it was an *old ritual*. Even an abandoned one will do.”

Jaxson grunted and folded his arms. “Well, if ruins are what you’re looking for, I’m pretty sure I know who can find us one: Neve Cross.”

A couple of hours later, Jaxson and I followed Neve back to her desk in the Archives. Though she had an office with the other detectives, she said she preferred to work in the company of books.

I couldn't help but be awed by the place. Though I wasn't a researcher and I preferred to read thrillers, I could appreciate the wonder of being surrounded by some of the world's most ancient and powerful books. I also couldn't help the envy I felt for Neve, who seemed to have it all—magic she was comfortable with, a job she loved, and a partner who was mad about her.

"The Moon has many temples, but this is the closest one I could find next to a portal, so it'll hafta do." She tore a page from a notepad and handed it me. "These are the coordinates."

"To where?" I asked.

"The island of Delos. It's the birthplace of Apollo and Artemis, and there's a small temple to her there."

"Wait a second, Artemis?"

Neve nodded and paged through a weatherworn book. "Selene, Diana, Artemis, they are all personifications of the Moon." She handed the book to me, which was open to a black-and-white sketch of the goddess Artemis. She wore a flowing gown, and a crescent moon crown adorned her braided hair. I traced my index finger over the image, my eyes drawn to the bow in her hand and the majestic wolf beside her.

"Is that the Dark Wolf God?" I asked.

Neve shrugged. "The Moon attracts creatures who are drawn to the lunar phases. Wolves, in particular, are closely associated with her. It's no wonder the Dark God was smitten with her."

Neve handed Jaxson a folded sheet of paper. "These are the coordinates. Myrto will greet you and show you to the Temple of Artemis. She's an archaeologist who works on the island, and she was the one who agreed to let you use the portal."

I frowned. "But I thought all portals were open to Magica."

"Correct," Jaxson said. "But not all portals have free access."

"That's right. The one that you'll be traveling through is a minor portal, and its use is controlled. Delos is a sacred island full of history. The Ephorate of Antiquities of Cyclades doesn't want Magica tramping around the archaeological site, performing unsupervised magic and rituals. I doubt the gods and goddesses would like that, either."

Right. That's exactly what we were going to do. Nerves fluttered in my gut. *God, I hope the Moon comes when we summon her.*

Jaxson's phone buzzed, and mine vibrated a second after. A text from Sam: *We're outside.*

Neve led us out. "Good luck, and tell me how it is. I've always wanted to visit Delos. So much history...but alas, so much to do here. The chaos never stops."

A glint of envy shone in her eyes, and I could sense her pining to tag along, but she'd told us yesterday that she was on an important case and shouldn't skip town.

I gave Neve a hug, wishing that she was joining us. "Thanks again. We owe you big time."

Neve waved her hand through the air. "Psshh. It's what friends do for each other."

Despite the unease that was gnawing at it, my heart swelled at Neve's words. My life was epically fucked up, but I'd managed to find my tribe. That was something I'd cherish, no matter what happened.

An officious and impatient clerk escorted us out of the Archives, and we found Sam and the loremaster waiting for us on a bench across the front plaza.

"How'd it go?" Sam asked.

"Well, we've got the location of a temple," I muttered. "So let's find out how to take down the Dark Wolf God."

13

Savannah

Unfortunately, getting to Delos required using a portal, a mode of transport with which I was still getting comfortable. I had no idea how some people used them for daily commutes—it felt like having your body disassembled and dumped into a washing machine, then put back together again.

Jaxson's driver dropped us off downtown at the edge of Rain Bridge Plaza. It was like O'Hare Airport, except the lines were shorter, and you were less likely to lose your luggage.

The wide plaza was ringed with dozens of wrought iron archways. Long lines of people had formed in front of each of the gateways, traveling to and from destinations in the magical and non-magical worlds. One by one, they stepped through and disappeared, while every so often, a different person would step out the back of the doorway.

The real mind-bending feature of the place—aside from all the vanishing Magica, which I'd now come to take for granted—was the floating river that wound overhead, the Rain Bridge. It was a living sculpture that gently misted all the people who passed through.

I followed Jaxson as he headed to the front of one of the lines and glared. The people in line dutifully shuffled back to let us cut. In the past, an alpha stunt like that might have embarrassed me, but at this point, we were on our way to save the world. The foodie on his way to get fresh biscotti in Milan could wait a bit.

"I haven't left Magic Side for a decade," the loremaster said as she shuffled forward with her cane. "I'm ready for an adventure."

I glanced back and arched my brows at Sam, who was standing beside the old woman, probably worried that she might stumble and break a hip. As if reading my thoughts, Sam's lips tightened, and she shook her head.

I wasn't sure how to properly act around the loremaster. She was old and wise and definitely to be respected, but she had a fierceness about her, and I didn't want to coddle her.

I stepped to the side to let her go ahead.

She raised her eyebrows. "What? Age before beauty? Are you kidding me, child? You and the alpha are going first in case there are any beasts lurking on the other side."

I flushed red, but the loremaster looked over at Sam and winked.

Jaxson entered the coordinates that Neve had given us using a dial on the side of the portal. The translucent veil covering the ringed doorway began shimmering in the afternoon sun. Jaxson's lips pulled up slightly into a smile, and he offered me his hand. "Ready?"

His question was simple, but the way he looked at me implied so much more. Would I step with him into the unknown?

With a gaze that intense and smoldering, how could I not follow a man like him anywhere? I swallowed and took his hand. He continued to watch me, though his eyes betrayed a hint of delight.

Yeah, he knew how my body reacted to his attention.

He gave my hand a light squeeze that made my stomach summersault, and then we stepped through together.

With a rush of magic, the ether sucked us into the void of space. My stomach flipped for real as my body was pulled in countless directions. Just as I thought I couldn't take it anymore, I stumbled out onto a set of narrow stairs beneath a night sky.

Nausea swam in my gut, and I doubled forward. My balance was shit, though, and my foot slipped, and I fell.

With a single fluid motion, Jaxson slipped his arm around my waist. "Steady, there."

His heat pressed into me, and his eyes dropped to my lips. Hell, I was in trouble here.

My neck flushed, and I awkwardly peeled myself out of his grasp. "Thanks. That was a rough ride."

"Minor portals like these don't get a lot of use. The magic degrades if it's not maintained," he said, giving me an amused smile.

Clearly, he'd enjoyed catching my fall. I wasn't sure if that annoyed me or made me wish we'd been somewhere private when it happened.

My gaze drifted to the stars and faint clouds above.

Right. Greece was hours ahead of Chicago.

I took a moment to inspect our surroundings as best I could in the dim light. Since I'd first shifted, my night vision was getting better and better.

We stood in an ancient well or cistern of some sort. Low walls of stacked granite slabs enclosed the water feature, their surfaces etched by dark watermarks.

I wasn't sure how deep the green pool behind us was, but it looked stagnant. At least the portal hadn't dropped us in the water. The only thing worse than wet boots were slimy wet boots.

Ascending after Jaxson, I emerged into a windswept landscape filled with standing columns and the crumbling ruins of countless ancient structures off in the darkness. My pulse quickened as the wonder and magic of the place buffeted the air around us.

I was broken from the spell by the loremaster's grunt from behind.

"My fates! That portal had the jitters. Who do I complain to around here?" The huge grin on her face told me that she'd been absolutely unfazed by her trip through the ether. Sam laughed beside her, and I felt the heat on my neck spread. Why was I the only one who got portal-sick?

Footsteps approaching over the rocky ground pulled my attention, and I glanced over my shoulder. A bobbing light approached, and Jaxson stiffened as I put my hand up to shield my eyes from the glare.

The beam of light swept down to the ground, and after a second my vision adjusted, revealing a petite woman with a pixie haircut.

"You must be the people Neve sent. Welcome to Delos." She had a faint accent and wore cargo pants and a white T-shirt that accentuated her sun-kissed skin and green eyes. "Sorry to keep you waiting. This place has been shut down for hours, and it took longer than I planned to get past the night guardsmen—even though they know exactly who I am."

She flashed us a warm smile and extended her hand to me. Her signature smelled of earth and rosemary and felt cool and calm. I was immediately drawn to her, and I was sure it had everything to do with her magic, whatever she was.

"I'm Savy. This is Jaxson, Sam, and our loremaster. Thanks for meeting us so late at night," I said, shaking her hand.

"Night is better," Myrto shrugged. "Better than having you folks pop out in the midst of a tour group."

"Neve told us that you'd be able to show us to the Temple of Artemis?" Jaxson asked.

"Yep. Right this way," she said cheerfully, heading down the path in the opposite direction than the one she'd come. "I'd give you a tour of the place if the moon was up, but it's a bit dark, and I imagine you're pressed for time."

"Thank you so much, but the clocking is ticking," I said regretfully. "The portal we came through, was that a well?"

"That's the Minoan Fountain. It was one of the island's public fountains, but long before that, it was a sacred spring that belonged to the nymphs." She gave me a wink.

Was she a nymph? Her signature was unfamiliar and tasted like raw honey. She definitely wasn't a sorceress or werewolf, or hell, a demon or vampire, for that matter.

Myrto led us down the weatherworn dirt path, her flashlight sweeping the way ahead. Like ghosts of the past, the ruins were pale and barely visible in the faint starlight. I couldn't help but feel a pang of regret for not being able to see the place in its former glory, or even the light of day.

Suddenly, the hair on my neck stood on end, and I got the uncanny feeling of lightning about to strike, or of being watched.

I slowed my steps and scanned our surroundings. My attention settled on the outlines of a large building to our left. Broken columns and other pieces of architecture littered the interior, and a rectangular slab with a bull head was set on three supports.

Nothing moved in the ruins, but something wasn't right.

Myrto must have noticed my gaze because she paused to flick her light toward the structure. "That's a stoa. It doesn't look like much now, but it was once a covered walkway with statues. Right beyond it is the Sanctuary of Apollo, where we're headed."

I glanced back at Jaxson and met his eyes. He gave me a subtle nod.

Something was up, and he knew it.

The air was almost heavy, and something about the old magic of the place started to shimmer and shift almost imperceptibly. Myrto drifted into conversation with the loremaster, but Jaxson and Sam both had their eyes fixed on the darkness.

One moment, all three of us stood there listening and searching for scents. Then a crunching and grating sound echoed from the distance, almost like stones being moved.

I stepped up beside Sam and Jaxson. "What *is* that?"

Jaxson's nostrils flared, and then his body tensed. "Loremaster, Myrto, quiet—something's headed our way."

"What?" Myrto asked, glancing over her shoulders.

I felt a rising swell of dark energy rush over me.

The Dark God.

"I think we're in trouble," I whispered.

Before Jaxson could respond, two starlit shadows appeared at the junction in the path about a hundred yards ahead. My blood iced.

About the size and shape of lions, the feline creatures began to prowl toward us. Something was off about them. Their bodies were too sleek, and they moved with an unnatural gait.

Whatever they were, I had no doubt who'd sent them—the Dark Wolf God, to stop us from calling the Moon. But how had he known?

For a second, one paused, searching. The instant its soulless black eyes locked onto us, it bolted in our direction, and its partner was right on its heels.

I shouted a warning as adrenaline surged through my veins, and I instinctively shot forward with Jaxson and Sam to protect Myrto and the loremaster, who were about twenty paces ahead.

"Fates! What's going on?" Myrto exclaimed.

The two beasts closed the distance in a flash.

Jaxson launched forward, colliding with the first in a crash of flesh and stone. As they skidded across the ground, the beast roared and kicked out with its hind leg, sending Jaxson flying back.

He landed on his feet with one hand on the ground as Sam hurtled into the second feline.

Her shoulder hit first, and she ricocheted with a horrifying crunch of bone and a pained grunt, as if she'd run into a brick wall. She practically had. The felines were made of stone, animated statues from a lost age. With a swift pounce and swipe, the stone lion rammed her into the low wall of the stoa.

Rage filled me, and I let the thrill of the hunt take over as I bounded over the crumbled wall.

The creature reared up to finish Sam.

With my adrenaline burning, I leapt forward and grasped its raised foreleg, using my momentum to pull it off balance.

I landed in the dirt, but it crashed into a broken column. Unfortunately, before I could even get up, it had righted itself. The thing prowled forward, its dark eyes focused entirely on me.

Then its head jerked unnaturally to the side, and it turned on Sam.

What the hell? Why wasn't it coming after me?

"Hey!" I jumped to my feet and released a quick blast of shadows. It jerked its head back at me before turning its attention to Sam, who was now backed up against a low wall.

Realization dawned. The Dark God was controlling it like a marionette. He was going to kill my friends and leave me alive because he was planning to use me the same way—as his puppet.

Fucking bastard.

My magic swelled, like rivers of ice water spreading through my veins. Charged near to exploding, I released my magic in a torrent. "Stay back!"

Dark tendrils streamed from my palms, and as if obeying my command, they wound around the creature, ensnaring it in a cage of shadows. The stone monster leapt but slammed into the cage as if was made of iron. The creature roared from within, but my shadows muffled its bellows.

I'd never used my magic this way before, but desperate for any form of control, I imagined the shadows closing in like a vise. My pulse quickened and delight sang through me as I felt the beast being crushed beneath the force of my shadows.

When at last I released them, there was nothing left of the creature but a mountain of rock chips. For a second, I thought I heard the voice of the Dark God: *Good. You see there is strength in shadow.*

"Fuck you, and fuck your magic beasts!" I shouted, my chest heaving with anger and exhilaration.

Grunting, Sam pushed herself up from the rubble. "Thanks for stepping in."

Her shoulder drooped strangely, and blood seeped from a gash on her thigh. She was wounded but okay.

I spun to find Jaxson as dread flashed through me.

I started running as soon as I spotted him on the path about a hundred feet away.

Somehow, he'd managed to pin the first stone lion. While its jaws snapped inches from his face, Jaxson seized its head and mandible and twisted.

He couldn't be serious.

His eyes flashed gold, and his muscles corded as he strained against the stone beast. Suddenly, a crack of rock split the air, and then, with the grating of stone and a primal snarl, Jaxson shattered its neck. In seconds, the whole thing disintegrated into dust in his hands.

My jaw dropped as I stumbled to a halt. He'd just snapped the head off a stone lion.

I knew he was strong, but *holy shit.*

I sucked in a breath of relief, but it was instantly extinguished by a warning shout from Sam. Three more shapes bounded through the ruins on our right, straight for Myrto and the loremaster.

Jaxson was already moving to cut them off, but the cats were fast, and he wouldn't intercept them in time. I could.

As I darted forward and leapt over the low wall, I threw up a billowing barrier of shadows between my friends and the beasts. "Run!"

Myrto grabbed the loremaster's shoulder and ushered her down the path. Although they were hidden from view, if the beasts had decent senses, the veil wouldn't do my friends any good.

It was up to me.

"Savy, get out of there!" Jaxson roared.

Anger coursed under my skin, dispelling my fear. I had to protect the loremaster. She was part of the pack and our key to summoning the Moon.

I moved without fear or hesitation. The Dark God had made it clear he wanted me alive and planned on making me watch him kill my friends and allies.

Screw that.

The beast at the front bounded over a series of ruins opposite the path, heading for the shadow veil. My heart thudded in my ears as I flung my hands forward and released the last of my pent-up magic. A ball of crackling wild energy pummeled into the airborne monster. The thing snarled as the force knocked it onto the path. Chips of stone scattered in the air, but the shot hadn't been enough to kill it.

The remaining two beasts broke off after Sam and Jaxson,

and protectiveness surged through me. But the creature I'd blasted was up on its feet again, and its attention was now solely on me.

Minor miscalculation. The Dark God needed me alive, but not unharmed.

The lion growled as it circled around me, its lips curled back, revealing a set of unnaturally long marble fangs.

Stone crashed behind me, and it was all I could do not to be blinded by the urge to go to Jaxson.

Protect the others, I thought I heard him say in my mind.

My muscles throbbed. It was taking everything I had to keep the veil of shadows up—and it was weakening. I'd spent too much of my magic. Fear crawled over my skin.

Wolfie, I could use some strength.

But she didn't answer. I was on my own.

The feline took a step forward, but then, as if an invisible leash pulled it back, it tensed and stopped. It released a ferocious growl and tried to move, but again, it couldn't. Something was wrong. The thing looked confused or conflicted.

It wanted to kill me, but the Dark God had put it on a leash.

This was my chance. I just needed to hulk out and rip its head off like Jaxson had done.

Fat chance without a boost from my wolf—or even with it. But I had to do something.

I spotted a column chunk five feet away. It would be heavy, but I could probably lift it and bash its head in, as long as the lion stayed on its tether.

Still wary of the beast, I extended my claws and slowly crept forward. The beast thundered and struggled against its invisible bonds.

Then suddenly, it was free.

In a flash, its front paws rammed me, sending me flying backward. I hit the dirt hard, and the air left my lungs in a gasp of pain. I struggled, and horror rocked me as the creature stepped over me and pressed down on my chest with its paw. Its breath was hot and pungent as it curled its marble lips and growled.

Was this how I would die? Death by a mythological lion beast?

Fucking fates.

I called my magic, but my veil of shadows had already dropped, and my stores were spent. I dug my claws into its stone leg and tried to heave, but I couldn't budge it an inch.

The lion spread its jaws wide and reared back to strike. But just before its teeth grazed my skin, a detonation of rock shards burst above me.

Choking on dust, and with pain screaming from a thousand places on my body, I rolled to my side and flopped onto my back, totally spent. *What the hell just happened?*

14

Jaxson

The lion clamped its jaw around my forearm, and bones cracked. His immense weight pinned me the ground, but my rage and pain and fear for Savy sent new strength surging through me.

With a roar, I braced my free hand against its snout and pulled down with my trapped arm, slowly levering its jaws apart. Its teeth sank into my flesh, hitting bone, but my boiling adrenaline dulled the pain. With a gasp and a swift movement, I ripped my arm free, and its jaws snapped shut on thin air. Rolling out of the way of its savage claws, I jumped to my feet and stumbled over to a large block of stone.

Time to end this.

A stabbing pain shot through my forearm as I grabbed the stone block and pulled it from the dirt, but I fought through and heaved the block into the air.

The creature lunged, but I was ready. At the last second, I shifted right and brought the slab down on its head. Chips of rock sprayed, and the feline bellowed as a thin crack appeared along its neck.

It stumbled, and I took my shot again, bringing the stone down onto its skull. Gasping for breath, I struck over and over until its neck finally snapped, and the possessed thing crumbled.

I spun, searching for Savannah.

The last lion had her pinned beneath it and was about to sink its fangs into her throat.

Terror seized me, and I raced toward her, even though I knew it would be too late.

"Use your magic!" I roared.

The beast lunged for her neck, then exploded into a cloud of shrapnel. I shielded my face as rock fragments tore into my chest and arms, but I didn't stop running.

I dropped to my knees beside my mate, who was staring up at the starlit sky and trying to roll over. Her body was tattered and torn with fresh cuts from the shrapnel, but the wounds were already beginning to heal.

"Sam and the loremaster..." she wheezed.

I stood and shouted for them.

Sam clambered over a pile of rubble. "Alive, mostly. Also pissed."

Myrto appeared from behind a broken wall and helped the loremaster to her feet. "We're over here and unharmed, thanks to Savannah."

I turned back to my mate and slipped my hand beneath her to help her sit up. "Where are you hurt? You look like you got hit by a bomb blast."

"Pretty much, but I think I'm okay," she grumbled. "That was a little close for comfort."

I brushed a loose strand of her hair behind her ear, unable to help myself. "Too close. Next time, blow up the monster before it gets on top of you."

She grasped my shirt as I helped her up and met my eyes. "It wasn't me, Jaxson. It must have been the Dark God."

"That blew the lion up? I don't understand—I thought those were his creatures."

She bent her head close to mine. "He's obviously trying to stop us from calling the Moon, but I think he's trying keep me alive at the same time. Because of the prophecy, and what I'm supposed to do on his behalf."

Bile burned my throat. He wanted her for himself.

"Are you guys okay?" Myrto asked, her face wrought with confusion and panic.

"A little worse for wear, but alive," Savannah said as she stepped back quickly. Then her face went pale at the sight of my wounded forearm. I could sense her discomfort and the instant desire to heal me as her eyes flicked up to mine. "That looks bad."

It was a wicked sight, with bloody fang marks. The bone was cracked, but it would mend.

I shook my head. "I think we need to get to the temple."

Sam limped over. We'd tag-teamed the second cat, but it had shattered her collarbone and left a deep gash in her thigh. I gave her an appreciative nod. "You saved my ass back there. Thanks."

The loremaster dug her walking stick into the dirt and hobbled over. "It seems the Dark God is trying to dissuade us from calling the Moon."

Savy nodded. "You're all targets when you're with me. Are you sure you want to carry on?"

"You're stuck with us." Sam dusted the dirt from her jeans. "But that Dark God is really starting to piss me off."

Savy grunted. "*Starting*?"

Myrto had gone white as a sheet. "I don't know who you're talking about, but I'd like to get you off this island as soon as possible, for your sake and mine."

"You do not need to worry, child. The moon mother watches over us," the loremaster said, and pointed with her cane. "Lead the way to the temple. We've got work to do."

Mytro swallowed and, after a moment of hesitation, led us on. We followed her past the time-worn vestiges of buildings that no doubt had been dedicated to many different gods. Ancient magic thrummed off the stones and columns that littered the ground, attesting to the sacredness of the place.

We were all on high alert. With Savy drained and Sam and me busted up, we were in no shape to weather another ambush.

Finally, we stopped in front of a raised rectangular structure. About the only things still standing were three columns in various states of collapse. "This is it," Myrto said. "The Temple of Artemis."

The ground around us was strewn with architectural pieces organized in rows. In the dim light, I could just make out a honeycomb decoration carved into the faces of the stone blocks nearby.

It was entirely unimpressive.

"This is it?" Savannah asked, bewildered.

The loremaster shot her a piercing glare. "Hush now, child, lest the moon mother hears you."

Sam smirked as Savy pursed her lips.

"Actually, the sanctuary is dedicated to Apollo, Artemis's twin, so her temple is a minor feature," Myrto said.

"So typical. The man gets the sanctuary, and his sister gets a shrine," Savy whispered.

She wasn't wrong.

"If you're okay, I will leave you to it," Myrto said, fretting with a tiny tuft of her shirt. "Can you find your way back to the portal?"

Unease pulsed off her, and I sensed her urgency to get the

hell away from us. "We'll manage," I said. "Thanks for your assistance."

"Hey," Sam said, "Are you going to be okay going back alone?"

"Thanks, but I know this place like the back of my hand. And I can move fast when I want to. Anyway, I'm pretty certain that if more of those things show up, they'll be looking for you, not me."

Myrto forced a smile before turning and hurrying off.

The loremaster climbed the two front steps, and Sam darted forward to help her. I stepped up beside Savy, inhaling her citrus sunshine scent. Reaching out, I picked a fleck of stone that was embedded in her neck.

She flinched, and her eyes dropped to my lips. "Let's hope the Moon shows up."

Sam took up a spot as a lookout on the stairs, while the rest of us headed toward the back of the temple. The inside of the sanctuary was, frankly, more disappointing than the outside, just a patch of crumbled stone that was probably smaller than the living room in my penthouse.

The loremaster shooed us out of her way as she lit a bundle of sage and sweetgrass and wove it through the air. "I've never tried to call the Moon like this—a full apparition. So prepare yourselves, because I have no idea what's going to happen."

Savannah gave me a nervous glance.

The loremaster raised her arms to the sky and spoke in an unfamiliar language. "Matrem lunarem invocamus ut se ostendat."

She pounded her walking stick on the stone once, twice, and on the third time, the air around began to vibrate like a swarm of bees—a low drone that reverberated unnaturally around the space. Then she began to pace in a circle, moving her staff and chanting, her voice in harmony with the atonal drone.

For a moment, there was no change, but then a strange and unfamiliar power began to swell beneath our feet—the magic of the temple.

As it intensified, I took a step closer to Savy, and I caught the sign of subtle movement—not within the temple, but in the sky overhead. It began to spin. We looked up in amazement as stars began to spiral above us, a whirlpool of light. Then the stars faded into pure darkness as a white light crept overhead, bathing us in a silverly glow—the Moon.

Energy pulsed, and a blast of wind rushed past us. I grabbed Savy's arm to hold her upright. My eyes adjusted to the new light just in time to see a woman in a flowing gown materialize before us. Her magic was dense and rich, like an exotic bloom on a hot summer night, and tasted of vanilla.

"Where the hell am I?" Her silvery blonde hair cascaded over her shoulders as she took in her surroundings—namely us —and she frowned. "Oh."

Shock rolled over me. We'd actually summoned the Moon.

"Moon mother." The loremaster, practically panting with exhaustion, bowed her crooked frame. "Thank you for blessing us with your presence. We called upon you to ask of your assistance."

The Moon looked at us with an expression that betrayed a strong sense of doubt. She twisted her hair.

"I'm flattered that you thought to call on me, but I'm afraid I don't do blessings for just anyone. Who are you?" The goddess's pale eyes flicked to the floor, searching. "And where are my offerings? Are there no sacrifices?"

The loremaster balked but moved in stride. "Of course, my goddess. Offerings. Each of us has brought you a favored possession." Casting me a sharp glance, she hobbled forward and set a stone on the pavement. "This is my lucky stone."

I arched my brow. *Fuck.* Apparently, some details of the

pagan ritual hadn't made it all the way down through werewolf lore.

I had nothing important on my person, and the two things I cherished most were here with me now. Savy glanced up at me, and something inside my chest tugged.

Sam stepped forward and placed a bead bracelet on the floor. The loremaster scrutinized it, but Sam just shrugged. "It's very special."

I hoped the goddess couldn't smell lies.

I pawed around in my pockets and withdrew a crumpled hundred-dollar bill. The loremaster nodded with mild approval and looked to Savy, who looked flustered.

With a sigh, Savy kicked off her Swiftleys, shooting me a look that said, *I can't believe I'm doing this.* She placed the boots beside the other offerings. "These are my second most sacred possessions."

The loremaster grunted. "Precisely what is required."

Savy glared at Sam and me, muttering under her breath, "You're buying me another pair as soon as we get home."

I couldn't help the smile that formed on my lips. I didn't let anyone make demands from me, but Savy could ask anything, and I'd give it to her.

15

Savannah

My mind reeled. I was staring at a goddess. Like, an actual goddess.

She was breathtakingly stunning and bathed in an ethereal soft light that seemed to emanate from within her. With extraordinarily long silver-blonde hair, she was so beautiful that I suddenly felt very, very small.

The Dark God had spoken to me and appeared in the clouds, but this was real. She was right *here*.

That raised the fairly key question—what the hell was a god or goddess, anyway? An immortal supernatural being?

I shook the thoughts from my mind. There were a lot of questions I'd have to ask later.

The Moon casually strolled up to the meagre offerings before her. Her movements were graceful, like a dancer, but I supposed that's how one moved when one was a goddess.

I swallowed and found my mouth watering from her signature. For whatever reason, it reminded me of Alma's cookies.

She frowned at the odd array of offerings but knelt to inspect each of them.

I glanced away for a second, and my jaw slowly dropped as I realized the temple had changed. I'd been so taken by the goddess before us that I missed the fact that we were now standing in a roofed space with walls.

I looked back over my shoulder. The night sky had returned to normal, and stars peeked through the six columns that fronted the temple. Complete columns. I looked up, and a roof rose above our head. The temple had reformed.

"My God," I whispered, tugging Jaxson's arm and motioning him to look around us. Directly across from us was another building—the ruins that had littered the ground earlier were gone, and the sanctuary had risen in their place. Jaxson's hand squeezed mine, and he gestured at the Moon mother behind me.

Right. Steady on, Savy. Remember why we're here.

The goddess scooped up Sam's bracelet and tossed it aside before picking up one of my boots. Her lips pursed in what I assumed was disgust, and she dropped it. "Your offerings displease me."

She stuffed the hundred-dollar bill into a fold in her dress. It had pockets?

The stone that the loremaster brought glinted in the goddess's light. She picked it up and examined it, and seemingly satisfied, she stuffed it in her dress as well.

The goddess put her hands on her hips. "Clearly, people in your age have forgotten how to properly petition the gods. Whatever happened to sacrifices and grand processions? Or naked dances, even, if that was your thing."

I bit my lip as my doubts mounted but spoke up anyway. "I'm sorry, great goddess, but we desperately need your help, and there was no time to prepare."

She looked around and clucked her tongue. "In one of Apollo's temples, too, of all places. This one is barely a closet. I had extraordinary temples once. Wonders, even." She sighed and turned back to us. "Well, I'm here. Tell me what you need from me, and I'll consider your request."

"The Dark Wolf God is about to break loose. We need your help to stop him," I blurted.

For a second, she made no movement. Then her fists tightened, and her expression hardened. "Are you certain? How did this happen?"

The magic in the room began to swell, like the moon slowly rising over the horizon. It was cold and warm, soft and harsh.

Utterly intimidating.

I couldn't help but take a step back, but I knew I had to put it all on the line. "He's breaking free. He's spoken to me."

"To *you*?" It was more a statement of disbelief than a question.

Terror of her majesty overwhelmed me. I'd just confessed to a god, and not in the slightly removed Catholic way. She was right here.

The Moon waited for my answer.

I swallowed as the horrid words formed in my mouth. "I believe I set him free. I'm a twin-soul. And I killed another twin-soul that was trying to release him. Apparently, that was the sacrifice he required."

Rage burned in her eyes, and the temple shook around us. Jaxson clasped my arm, and I dug my nails into his hand.

But then her rage faded to embers, and the quaking stones calmed. When she spoke, it was all softness and deep sorrow. "You didn't release him, child. He stacked the cards of fate against you. He's always been a puppeteer."

I hung my head, and Jaxson softly touched my back.

It wasn't my fault.

That was a good thing, right? But why did I suddenly feel worse? I'd desperately wanted to be acquitted, but somehow, her words made me feel small. Like a pawn. Something foolish, something to be toyed with.

The stone lions flashed in my mind, pulled and jerked about like marionettes. They were puppets.

But I was not.

My heart hardened. I'd played a role in all of this, and I had a role still to play.

I looked up and met her soft and consoling eyes. "The fates might be stacked against me, but I'm going to stop him. Even if it's the last thing I do."

The pitying look on her face wavered, then melted into something far harder. Calculating. Appraising. "Are you?"

"I know what he'll do if I don't. I've seen it in visions. He'll destroy my city, my pack, my family."

She pursed her lips. "All cities. All families. And every pack that does not submit."

"Why?" Jaxson growled.

Rather than answer, the goddess walked to the pillars and stared out at the night sky. "We loved the same things, once. Each other. Nature. We both fought so hard to protect it. But he no longer believes you have any place in it. He'd rather start anew than try to fix the world."

I approached as close as I dared. "Please, tell us how to stop him. The legends say you tricked him and trapped him before. How do we do it again?"

When she spoke, her voice was very far away. "And what do your legends say I did?"

I motioned the loremaster over.

She shuffled up and licked her lips. "That to stop the Dark God's war on the two-legged people, you secretly gathered waters from the river of dreams and then called him to your side. You spent the night dancing and drinking and, uh..." The loremaster glanced nervously at me, then Jaxson, before continuing. "You danced as lovers do. Amidst the merry-making, you slipped the magic waters into his wine, and when he fell asleep in your arms, he did not wake. He has been trapped in dreams ever since."

Normally articulate and captivating, the loremaster was holding back, and with fair reason. The story was not one that in retrospect, I'd want told around a campfire.

Her version was so vivid, I'd seen it in my mind like a movie as she'd recounted it, images leaping from the fire and filling my senses. I'd seen the Moon let her dress slip, and how she moved ever so perfectly to arouse and seduce the Dark God.

Just the memory of it had me hot in the pants and thinking of Jaxson. I wasn't sure if the Moon had werewolf senses, but I tamped my wandering thoughts down *fast*.

But it didn't seem she was paying any attention to me and my problems. The Moon just gave an exasperated sigh and paced across the temple. "Does everyone believe that seduction is a woman's only power? I'm a huntress, for fates' sake."

The loremaster bowed low. "I'm sorry, great goddess. The legends were passed down many times, and I am sure some were elaborated in false ways."

The Moon scowled at us and worked her jaw in frustration. "No. It's pretty close to what happened—we'd been lovers before, and I knew it would work. It just pisses me off that people only remember the spicy bits. Yes, I seduced him and got him drunk. But he's a god, and I knew that the river of dreams wouldn't hold him forever. While he slept, I created a prison in the Dreamlands—a spell woven among three pylons of power. I sacrificed much of my magic to do it. He should not have been able to break free."

I crossed my arms. "So what can we do? I'm assuming he won't fall for potions in his wine again."

She laughed, though it was a little hollow. "He's a man, but not a total fool. Anyway, you're not his type." She traced her fingers through her long sliver hair, though her eyes flicked at Sam for just a second. "Maybe that one might have some luck, but I doubt it."

I blushed on my friend's behalf. Apparently, the Dark Wolf God had a thing for blondes.

Thank God I'm a natural redhead.

Shaking off the horrid thought of having to seduce the Dark God, I asked, "What can we do? How do I stop him?"

The goddess huffed with amusement. "You will not be able to overcome the Dark Wolf God, young twin-soul. He draws his magic and strength from the presence of wolves. If you get close, you'll just make him more powerful—and he's more than all five of us could handle." She turned and began to pace, twisting her hair as she spoke. "No, you can't confront him directly. You must enter the Dreamlands and restore my spells. I suspect they must be weakening, because the incantations were flawless."

She turned and wove an image of three large moonlike orbs. Columns of glowing light rose from each of them—the magical pylons that trapped the Dark God in the realm of dreams.

"How do we get there?" Jaxson asked.

"I will show you the way," the goddess said.

16

Savannah

My stomach lurched. I'd thought we found an ally to face down the Dark God, but we were on our own. "You won't come with us?"

A shimmer of sadness danced across her face, and the room suddenly felt as if it were drowning in a sense of deep longing.

"I cannot enter the Dreamlands anymore. To bind him there, I had to bind myself to this realm." Her mouth formed a distant and wistful smile. "I haven't dreamt in a very long time."

For a second, we were all silent, then Sam spoke. "I don't get it. Anyone else get it?"

The Moon's expression sharpened. "I'm like a counterweight —" She stopped abruptly and eyed us. "Actually, I don't like that analogy at all. I order you to forget it."

We nodded, and she waved her hand impatiently. "Think of the Dark God as a thief prowling in your bedroom. I slammed the door shut and locked it, with him on the inside, and me out in the hall. For me to return to the Dreamlands, I'd have to unlock the door between the realms, and that would let him come barreling through."

"Shit," Sam said.

She spoke for all of us.

I pulled my fingers through my hair. "So what can we do? How do we restore the pylons? Do we use our magic?"

The Moon looked shocked, and she put a hand to her chest. "*Your* magic? Don't be silly. That would be like holding the door shut with Scotch tape. It will take my magic, and it will take a lot."

For a second, shame overcame me, and I felt wretched and unworthy—as if the goddess had picked me out for humiliation.

But then I saw the flicker of sorrow in her eyes.

She wasn't being mean. She was speaking the truth, and she was preparing to give up more, perhaps, than I could possibly imagine.

I felt it in the air, and I could smell her emotions. Despair. Loss. Resignation.

When I'd first learned about my magic—which felt like years ago—my aunt warned me that when sorcerers and sorceresses enchanted something, they gave up a little of their soul. It's why they did it rarely. It's why my Fury, filled with spells woven by my father, meant so much more to me now, even than it had before.

It was his soul.

Was it the same for gods and goddesses? If so, how much had she given up to trap the Dark God? How long had it been since she could even dream?

She nodded as a grim determination shaped her features. "I will open the way for you and entrust you with my power. But you must go now, before the pylons weaken further."

The Moon explained the way we would take and what we had to do, and when she was certain we were clear on the instructions, she prepared to summon her power.

She held her hands up but paused. "I would stand back if you don't want one hell of a moonburn."

We quickly retreated to the edges of the columned entrance.

For a second, I heard her speak, and then a blinding light ripped through the space. The temple shook, and it felt like someone had hurled me out of a plane.

Power and magic rushed over me, and then, with a thunderous clap, it was gone.

It took a moment for my eyes to adjust. The Moon stood unsteadily in the center of the sanctuary. Her shoulders drooped, and every motion she made spoke of deep and complete exhaustion.

Three glowing stones spun in the air before her, each the size of a golf ball. She held out her hand, and they gently landed in her palm. Her eyes brightened as she touched them, and she gave a faint smile, but she didn't seem to have the strength to keep it there.

She approached. "These are my moonstones. Take them, and guard them jealously. They contain my power and must only be used to repair the pylons. I hope it is enough."

A faint worry built within me.

"If the Dark God discovers we have these, will he come for them?" I asked.

She gave a halfhearted laugh and held out the stones. "He wouldn't be so foolish. Just touching one would scar him in ways that even he couldn't heal."

Swallowing hard, I held out my hands.

Hesitantly, as if parting with a precious keepsake forever, she placed a glowing sphere in my palm.

I gasped as warmth and light poured through me, extinguishing the aches and fatigue in my muscles. The world turned bright, and the temple glowed with a vividness I'd never imagined possible. Everything was pure.

"You each should carry one," she said softly. "The power of all three together will be too much."

She handed two identical moonstones to Sam and Jaxson. "Be careful with these. I would not pass them over unless the need was dire."

"We will" I whispered as I slipped the stone into my pocket. "You can trust us."

She gave me a hard, appraising look. "I'm no fool. I'm a goddess, and that gives me the power to see glimpses of the bonds of fate. All three of you are tied up in this deeper than you know."

Her tone sent a shiver down my spine, and she gave a weak smile as she looked from me to Jaxson to Sam. "I just hope that you are strong enough to follow the path laid out for you."

We all nodded, but it was not without apprehension.

The Moon turned and waved her hand. A blast of energy swept through the room as a shimmering portal tore through the air. It pulsed and undulated, with silver magic burning at its edge.

"This is your path into the Dreamlands. The orbs will recognize my magic as soon as you arrive. Follow the telltale glow, which will serve as a beacon. If you get lost, the moonstones will guide you to my power."

We nodded.

The goddess reached into her pocket and retrieved an ornate silver crescent made of filigree wire. "When you have repaired the pylons, use this talisman to return."

Once we'd memorized the spell to activate the talisman, we gathered at the edge of the open portal. A wild, windswept landscape flickered beyond, and cold air rushed toward us.

I became keenly aware that I was only wearing socks on my feet. Of course, I could travel as a wolf, but how would I carry the moonstone? I glanced between my precious black boots and the goddess. "If you didn't like my offering, could I maybe take it back?"

She gave me a pained expression and waved her hand. "Please. Remove them from my temple and burn them. They profane this space."

I rushed over, slipped them on, and quickly laced them up, then rejoined the others.

While I did so, Jaxson took the loremaster's arm. "Stay here. Wait for us."

She glared at him. "Absolutely not. This will make too good of a story."

He shook his head. "You're staying, and that's an order. If we fail, someone needs to know what's happening. Warn them."

The loremaster gritted her teeth. "Fine. But don't think I don't know what you're doing. Leaving the dead weight behind."

Jaxson smiled softly. "This is the way it must be. Call Regina and let her know what's going on, and make a plan to move forward without us. Anyway, I'm sure the Moon has many stories that will befit the pack. This could be a good chance to get some juicy details."

He turned and headed over to join Sam and me at the portal.

The loremaster waved dismissively. "Fine, fine, fine. But you're coming back. Otherwise, we're all screwed anyway."

The Moon gestured to the shimmering portal and the wild landscape beyond. "Go quickly. Sweet dreams, and good luck."

I reached out and grasped Jaxson's hand, and we stepped through.

17

Savannah

A vast, windswept moorland stretched before us. Snow-capped mountains rose in the distance, fronted by forest-covered rolling foothills. While it was not night in the Dreamlands, sunlight filtered down through clouds and a pale sky.

The damp cold bit through my clothes, and I shivered. “This is nothing like the Dreamlands we visited last time.”

“Our legends claim that the Dreamlands are made up of hundreds of realms, each unique and inhabited by different creatures,” Jaxson said.

I rubbed my arms to warm them, and Jaxson’s jaw tensed. He pulled me close, which sparked another flurry of shivers for all sorts of other reasons.

I tried to focus on the task at hand.

The Moon had anchored her spell in the Dreamlands with three massive floating orbs infused with her magic. We had to find them and recharge them with the moonstones she’d given us. I was pretty sure the moonstones were more than just mundane receptacles for magic—they seemed to be pieces of her lifeforce, judging by the way she'd withered the moment she handed them over.

My gaze settled on a derelict castle perched on a rocky outcrop, our first destination. She hadn't given us any details about it, just that it was a ruined keep. "Maybe fate will throw us a bone, and this place will be populated with friendly furry creatures."

Fate had been a sour bitch so far, so I didn't get my hopes up.

"Unlikely," Sam said dryly. "What do you say, shall we go storm the scary fortress?"

"Let's go." I touched my pocket where I'd stashed the moonstone. A faint glow filtered through the fabric, and like I'd downed a shot of Red Bull, I felt my magic spike.

I could get used to having a battery of the goddess's power.

We started down the gentle slope as a light fog moved across the quiet landscape. Patches of bright pink flowers contrasted with the bleak, yet eerily beautiful, scenery. They looked like a type of strange heather, and their blossoms shrank when we moved through them.

My boots squished over patches of moist earth. Even though it had been bold to ask, I was deeply relieved that the goddess had let me take my Swiftleys.

Jaxson and Sam moved quietly on either side of me, their postures tense and alert. The moonstones in their pockets gave off a similar glow to mine, and together, we probably looked like strange beacons bobbing over the hills like will-o'-the-wisps. Hopefully, no watchers decided to take an interest. At least no one stopped us on our way up the slope to the fort.

Black and orange lichen covered its crumbling walls. The place seemed long abandoned, but a faint pulse of magic radiated from it, warm and soothing like the magic coming off the moonstones.

"It's in there," I whispered. "Do you feel it?"

Sam nodded as she climbed the outcrop of volcanic rock that spilled out of the gentle slope on which the castle was perched.

"Stay alert," Jaxson said as a raccoon-sized animal scurried into a gap in one of the fallen walls. "We have company."

The faintest scent of tar rose on the breeze, and my nerves hummed. Get in and get out. That's all we had to do. The quicker, the better.

I glanced up at the stone wall, which towered above us at least a hundred feet. Apart from several windows that pierced it, there was no gate or entrance. "Should we go around the other side, or—"

Sam gave me a wicked grin and leapt ten feet in the air. Her claws dug into the stone, and she scrambled up the wall like a goddammed spider monkey.

Jaxson looked back at me with a glint of amusement flashing in his eyes. "You good?"

"Perfectly fine," I snarled. He knew I hated scaling heights.

Slipping my claws out, I raised my chin and jumped onto the wall. My claws sank into the moss-stained limestone, and I heaved myself up, my muscles feeling exceptionally strong with the extra kick of moon magic.

Jaxson followed and somehow made it look even easier than Sam had.

Despite my moon-fueled burst of energy, I was breathing hard by the time we reached the top. I pulled myself up and slung one leg over the crumbling wall.

From there, I had an intimidating view of our surroundings. Just below the outcrop, about a hundred yards in the distance, a dense forest stretched out as far as my eyes could see. The wind carried scents of moss, earth, and the acrid odor of freshly laid asphalt on a hot day.

That last part was definitely unexpected, and I had no idea what it implied.

My breath hitched at the sight of the giant stone orb in the paved courtyard below. Hauling myself over the wall, I carefully descended. Sam was already on the ground, but Jaxson stayed just below me, I supposed to catch me if I fell.

I sighed in relief when my feet finally hit firm footing, and I quickly moved to inspect the white stone orb.

The thing measured at least twenty feet in diameter and levitated about four feet off the ground. The closer I got, the stronger the Moon's power grew, vibrating through me like a drumbeat just beyond the edge of hearing.

There was something both beautiful and ancient about the orb's simplicity. There were no magic runes, no ornamentation, no pretense at all. It was just her power made manifest, holding the Dark God at bay. The thing was completely smooth apart from a little notch at the top, a perfect match for a moonstone.

The problem was how to get it in. The orb was levitating just a few feet too high, and I couldn't reach the damn notch in the top. There was no graceful way to get up, and I didn't want to scratch the thing with my claws lest I damage it.

Or, more likely, it might damage me.

What would happen if I touched it? Just patting the moonstone in my pocket gave me a jolt of power. It could be like jamming your hands on the wires at a power transfer station.

Screw it. I gave the orb a fast tap. Cool as a cucumber.

Still not sure I wanted to scale it with my claws, I reached for the moonstone in my pocket, but a blur of movement from across the courtyard froze my hand in place.

"We've got company," Sam said, and Jaxson was at my side in an instant.

We scanned the courtyard. For a moment, the only sign of intruders was an intense acrid odor, and then two figures bearing curved swords slipped out from behind a collapsed portion of the castle's upper story.

"Holy shit," I whispered as my skin prickled. "What are those?"

One of the figures was double the height of the other, but they wore identical threadbare trousers and an oversized capelet with a hood. They appeared to be men, but their ashen, weathered skin and gray eyes indicated they weren't human.

"Savy," Jaxson said as he slowly stepped forward, "put your moonstone in the orb."

The instant I moved back toward the orb, the two figures bounded across the courtyard, and they were on us in a second.

Shit, they were fast.

Sam kicked the smaller figure as he lunged at her, and he ricocheted off the wall, but he recovered in a breath and crouched for another strike.

Jaxson ducked under a singing blade that almost took off his head. Panic surged through my veins, and my magic flared. Instinctively, my hand flew out, and a ribbon of shadow shot forward, wrapping around the sword that kissed Jaxson's chest.

What the hell?

That had never happened before. I tugged on the wisp of shadow, and the weapon flew out of the bastard's grip. Shock cut his grisly features, and he growled before jumping onto Jaxson.

Exhilaration coursed under my skin. Crushing the lion monster with my shadows had been awesome, but this...this was even better. Had the moonstone given me this new magic?

I flung the sword on the pavement behind me, then shot another shadow ribbon at Sam's attacker. It wound around his neck, and then, with a flick of my wrist, I flung him across the courtyard.

Holy crap!

He hit the stone wall adjacent to us, and his limp body

dropped to the ground like a sack of rocks. For a second, it looked like he was smoking, and then he burst with a piercing light that exploded across the courtyard.

I screamed as my eyes burned.

"Fuck!" Sam shouted. "What the hell was that?"

I blinked a couple times until the bright spots cleared from my vision. A pile of ash lay where there should have been a body.

That was definitely one way to go out with a bang.

Jaxson was locked in combat with the other figure, and I had no doubt he'd make short work of him.

"Watch out, they go nuclear when they die!" I shouted. "Don't get too close!"

Jaxson cursed and kicked the creature in the chest, sending it flying back.

I scrambled over to the orb. *Here we go.*

Crouching, I jumped with my arms wide and landed on its upper surface with less grace than a drunk girl in heels on the dancefloor. I cursed my throbbing ribs and inched my way up until I could reach the little notch at the top.

Before I got there, another blinding pulse of light consumed the space, and I pressed my face against the orb to shield my eyes.

"I hate those fucking things!" Sam swore.

After a moment, I opened my watery eyes.

"Are you okay up there?" Jaxson shouted.

"Fine! Just a sec." Once I was sure I wasn't going to slip off, I scrambled up the last few feet and deposited the moonstone in the opening.

The inaudible thrum of the orb intensified, and it emitted a warm glow, casting a column of light high above the castle—a pylon.

I slid off the orb, landing firmly on my feet. "One down, two to go."

Jaxson stalked toward me like a predator. His clothes were torn and tattered from the lion attack, and a glistening gash stretched across his chest where a sword had sliced him. Sweat and blood covered his brow, and *God*, was he beautiful like that.

Clink.

Something bounced on the pavement below the orb. The moonstone. I bent down and picked it up. The thing was warm to the touch, but all of its magic was gone.

"Are you hurt?" Jaxson asked Sam.

"Apart from my eyes, no." She glanced over at me. "Thanks, by the way. Your magic is getting wicked good."

"I'm beginning to use my shadows, but I'm not quite sure how this works. I think, in part, it might have been the magic of the moonstone. It gave me a little boost."

That wasn't entirely accurate, though. My magic *was* getting stronger, almost by the day. But using it was also sapping my energy more and more. Without the magic of the moonstone, my muscles felt like jelly.

Jaxson pressed the moonstone he was carrying into my palm. Its magic spilled into my body, filling it with a new reserve of power, and I felt strong again. Invincible.

"Thanks." I peered up at him, but I couldn't help my gaze from dropping to his fresh wound. It was already knitting, but his shirt was torn and bloodied. "Sorry I didn't get to you sooner."

"You had my back." He touched my cheek and gave me a look that sent fire through me and made my knees tremble. "I'm going to thank you later."

I cleared my throat, suddenly feeling overheated. "Let's get this show on the road."

Sam chuckled. "Now I know how to get you moving."

My cheeks flushed, but I couldn't help the smile that spread. "Shut it, Sam."

I pocketed the spent moonstone just in case the moon goddess wanted it back, then followed Sam as she vaulted up the wall. Damn, that girl had no fear of heights and was also a showoff, but I loved her, even if trying to keep up with her was probably going to get me killed.

At the top, I balanced on the broken remains of a tower and gazed out over the forested landscape.

"Are you seeing what I am?" Sam asked.

My heartbeat skyrocketed. Two areas in the forest, separated by at least a kilometer, glowed. They hadn't been there earlier, which suggested that they were tied to the orb we'd just recharged.

I smiled. "Bingo."

18

Savannah

Rich notes of amber and hickory filled my nose as we entered the dense woods. Dusky orange leaves littered the forest floor, and the thick boughs overhead blocked most of the sunlight from filtering in.

Countless tiny lights floated through the air—like lightning bugs, only smaller and more brilliant. I reached my hand up, and they swirled around my fingers. "What are those things?"

Sam plucked one from the air and inspected it. "No idea. Radioactive gnats?"

We quietly and cautiously moved through the trees, keeping a wary watch on our surroundings. Unlike the moor just outside, there was a cacophony of noises in the forest: the rustling of feathers, the scurrying of something in the underbrush, and the creaking of branches overhead.

I scanned the area as my imagination ran wild, knowing that many creatures dwelling in the Dreamlands were far worse than anything my imagination could conjure. Memories of the noctith demons and the grasping roots in the cave in Forks rose from the depths of my mind, making my skin crawl.

Ahead, something—a woman—moved between two trees. She was gone as quickly as she'd appeared. I blinked, unsure if my mind was playing tricks on me. "Did either of you just see that?"

Jaxson and Sam silently shook their heads, and their bodies tensed as they scanned the area. But there was no sign or scent of her.

Creepy magic?

We kept moving, and after a while, a subtle glow filtered through the forest. The orb had to be just up ahead. My pace quickened, but I kept my footfalls light. A circle of bright, almost fluorescent, mushrooms had grown below a large, twisted oak.

"A fairy circle," Jaxson said, his eyes still scanning the forest. "Don't step in it."

Fairies?

I frowned. There was still a huge world beyond Magic Side I was totally unaware of. Once we defeated the Dark Wolf God and weren't fighting tooth and claw for our lives, I couldn't wait to learn more about this world I was now a part of.

As I skirted the fairy circle, a flash of movement over Jaxson's shoulder drew my attention. I tensed, and then he followed my gaze, but there was nothing out there—or at least not anymore.

The trees thinned, and then another flash of movement. "There!"

Darting from tree to tree, I moved closer until I caught sight of a pond about the size of a soccer field. A stacked-stone retaining wall lined the edges, and what appeared to be a limestone tower or turret rose from the center of the water. The orb hovered above it like some strange planet or giant marble. Aside from a faint golden glow emanating from it, the orb was identical to the first.

Had the movements I'd seen just been reflections of the orb glistening on the water?

I chewed on my lip, searching for a boat or a bridge, or really anything that we could use to get over to the turret. "This is going to get interesting."

"Well, it seems like you can manipulate things with your shadow magic now. I suppose you could use your shadows to send it over," Sam said matter-of-factly.

I glanced at her. "You're a genius, Sam."

My magic was still so new, I hadn't even considered it. But if I could pull swords out of people's hands and restrain lions, I should be able to move things as well, right?

I had no effing clue how to do it, but why the hell not try?

"Just don't drop the damn thing in the water," Jaxson grunted.

And there was that. But none of us could fly, and I wasn't keen on finding out what lurked in the waters of the Dreamlands.

I scooped out the moonstone he'd given me at the castle and looked at it forlornly. Its magic vibrated in my hand and made me feel like I could do anything. If only I could have one of them for keeps.

I pulled my attention from the moonstone and concentrated on calling my magic instead. After a moment, it began flowing through me like a cool stream, and shadows coalesced below me.

I exhaled harshly, focusing my mind on creating those ribbons from earlier. But only more shadows formed at my feet. Why wasn't it working?

"Keep trying," Jaxson said. There was a hint of unease in his voice, and I sensed Sam moving behind me. "Focus and find a way to get that rock mounted on the orb."

The more I concentrated, the more the shadows boiled and moved, but they didn't form a ribbon. As I strained my mind, the hair on my neck began to rise. Something was here. Fear crept up my spine, and my shadows disappeared as I turned to see what was going on.

Jaxson and Sam had felt it, too. Both looked out over the pond at a woman standing in the shadow of the trees.

An ethereal vision. Vines and leaves wrapped around her, and white and yellow flowers stuck out of the long tresses falling over her shoulders. She was beautiful, but like so many things in the Dreamlands, I had the uneasy feeling that she was deadly. Like a bright red berry or a spiky caterpillar. The aura around her said, *Don't touch.*

"We've got this." Jaxson's voice was stern, his expression sharp. "Focus on the orb before more creatures or guardians show up."

Right. I was more than happy not to have to deal with the creepy forest lady.

Closing my eyes, I drew my magic around me again, focusing on the way it tickled when it spread under my skin. I pressed my eyes shut and took a steady breath. *Come on, Savy. Focus.*

The tingles gradually moved down my arm and to my free hand, and when I opened my eyes, a single black ribbon snaked out of my palm. Excitement and giddiness thrummed through me. Angling my hand down, the ribbon twisted and grew until it was several yards long and twirling in front of me as if waiting for my command.

In a weird way, it was cute.

Tenderness blossomed in my chest at this magic that I'd spawned. It was a part of me as much as I was a part of it.

I opened the fist holding the glowing moonstone, and just as I would speak to my wolf, I spoke to my ribbon. *Can you take this stone and place it on top of that orb in the lake?*

The ribbon paused, then jerked toward my hand. Two smoky tendrils grew from it and wrapped around the moonstone until it was completely veiled. Then the ribbon took it and began moving out over the water. When it seemed the ribbon would snag, it grew longer and continued moving.

My magic was like a whole other entity inside of me. Kind of like Wolfie, I mused.

The wonder that filled me was cut short as Sam shouted, "Savy, watch out!"

I instinctively jerked backward and landed on my ass, *hard*, as a green blur whizzed past me.

Damn forest lady.

I flipped over and pulled back to a crouch. Sam rushed to my side.

Where was Jaxson?

Where was the moonstone?

Panic surged within me, and I jumped to my feet. The shadow ribbon was still attached, but it was struggling to stay above the water. I pushed more magic into it, and it steadied. I sighed audibly, my nerves twitching like jumping beans. *Just a few more feet.*

As the ribbon carried the moonstone upward, a damp hand clutched my throat and yanked me to the ground.

It all happened so fast.

The wind burst from my lungs as my back slammed into the mud. I blinked my eyes open, and my vision focused on the face above me. Pale green skin, dark green eyes, and long, flowing hair with flowers strung in it.

The woman's lips curled in a growl, revealing a set of pointy teeth, and her grip on my throat tightened.

I didn't dare release my concentration to shock her with my magic. Everything I had was maintaining the ribbon, and I knew I couldn't do both at once.

So I did the next best thing: I ejected my claws and whacked her in the side of the face.

Loosening her grip slightly in shock, she reeled back and

slapped her free hand to the bloody claw marks I'd left. Her eyes flashed with anger.

That's right, I've got thorns.

A flash streaked through my vision and pulled the forest lady monster off me. Her hand reached for my throat, but then she was gone. I sat up, gasping, but quickly pivoted back to the lake, just in time to see my ribbon dissipate into vanishing wisps of shadow.

The moonstone plunked into the pond just below the turret. *No!*

Horror hit me like a freight train, and I screamed in frustration, though it came out more like a screech. My throat was dry and bruised after the forest bitch had strangled me.

Heart pounding, I spun around. Where was she?

Fuck—where were Jaxson and Sam?

I was alone, and the situation was bad, bad, *bad*, and I had to decide what to do quickly. I couldn't worry about the others; they were probably chasing the tree lady. We needed every moonstone we had, so getting that one back was on me.

Time for a swim, Wolfie.

19

Savannah

I glanced around the pool. Apart from the creaking of branches, it was quiet. I stashed my jacket and the talisman beneath a fallen log, then cursing, I took several deep breaths, then dove into the pond. After swimming in lakes most of my life, I knew to make my angle shallow.

The icy water squeezed my chest, which left me mildly hyperventilating when I came up for air. Keeping my head above water, I freestyled it to the stone turret in the center of the pond. Mosses and small ferns covered the base.

Who the hell put a tower in the middle of a pool?

When I reached the turret, I tried finding the bottom of the pond with my feet, but they hit nothing solid. Treading water, I took a few more deep breaths, then dove into the murky green water.

I was so fucking stupid. *This* was so fucking stupid.

The cold water pressed in around me, and I cleared my ears as I kicked downward. The only bright side about this situation was that I had my Swiftleys on. I swore I'd kiss the Moon's feet for giving them back.

By the time I'd swum a dozen feet down, my lungs were screaming. I swung my head around, peering through the dark water. A gentle glow shimmered off to my left.

Gotcha.

Then something brushed my thigh. Shit. Things were *definitely* lurking in the water.

Trepidation wrapped around my heart, and the rising panic only made the burn in my lungs stronger. I frantically kicked toward the glowing moonstone, glancing around me, half expecting to see some monster come out of the darkness.

Dizziness began to fog my mind, but I kept kicking until my ears were throbbing and the rocky bottom appeared. The moonstone shone like a beacon in the dark. I scooped it up in my fist, then pushed off the bottom, shooting to the surface like a torpedo.

As soon as my head broke the water, I launched into a coughing fit. Through my blurry vision, I saw Jaxson burst out of the forest, his shirt and arm bloody. His eyes locked on me, and relief flashed across his stricken face, and—

Something grabbed my ankle and towed me down. I barely sucked in a breath of air before I was pulled under. Kicking with my free leg as I was rapidly towed toward the muck, I connected with something solid and fleshy.

Oh, my God.

Panic and survival instinct flew into overdrive, and I began thrashing and flailing, hoping I'd strike something sensitive.

The grip on my ankle loosened, and I was free. Coiling up near the bottom of the pond, I looked around the dark, murky water. Shit, shit, shit. I didn't want to stay down here, but I also didn't want to risk swimming to the surface, where I'd be an easy target.

I called my magic, feeling it fill my aching chest. *Come on, you bastard, show yourself.*

As if answering my summon, a face appeared from the darkness. Red and blue splayed out around her head like a crown, and brilliant scales covered her arms. Though I couldn't make her out perfectly, she seemed to have the torso of a woman and a fin where her legs should be.

A nymph or mermaid? I wasn't certain of the difference—or that they'd even existed until that moment. All I knew was that the creature looked more than happy to drown me and drag me off to her lair.

As I tried not to lose my shit, the fish woman surged forward. All I saw were teeth before I blasted her with my magic. A shriek reverberated through the water, and I kicked to the surface. Gasping, I grabbed hold of the slick rocks at the base of the turret and pulled myself out of the water.

"Savannah!" Jaxson roared.

I slipped the moonstone into my pocket and climbed the turret as fast as I could in case the fish woman jumped out after me. There were enough handholds and gaps between the rocks that the ascent was easy with claws. The thing was only fifteen feet tall at most, and I was at the top in seconds.

I craned my head back and frowned at the orb hovering high overhead. Jumping up and clinging on for dear life didn't seem viable, so I was going to have to risk using my shadows again.

As if reading my thoughts, a black ribbon snaked from my palm and danced in front of me. Wonder squeezed my chest. My magic was blossoming, and I felt a deep...*affection* for it.

I'm getting jealous, Wolfie teased. *But seriously, what's going on? I faded out for a bit. Why are we wet? I thought the plan was to avoid the water...*

That didn't sound good, but one thing at a time.

I'll explain later, I said as I swallowed the rising lump in my throat and prayed that the shadows didn't drop the stone again.

A tendril broke free, and after winding around the stone, it plucked it from my palm. The ribbon snaked up around the orb, and I didn't dare break my concentration for a second—not to look down at the water or back at the shore. About twenty strangled heartbeats later, a soft clink echoed from the top of the orb, and in the space of a breath, the stone sphere began glowing brightly and a column of light rose above.

My shoulders relaxed, and I slumped onto the corner of the turret. Sam stood at the edge of the pond with her hands on her hips and a worried expression on her face, while Jaxson prowled the edge of the lake, looking murderous.

"I'm fine! I'll be right there," I shouted. "Let me get the spent moonstone back!"

Jaxson stopped pacing and watched me like a hawk. I sensed his agitation and protectiveness.

After a minute, there was another soft clink and a sound like a rolling marble. I glanced up to see the spent moonstone drop over the edge of the orb. Acting almost on instinct, I thrust out my hand, and a tendril of shadow jetted out.

It caught the moonstone in midair.

I'm getting good at this. Did you see that, Wolfie? I asked as I reeled in the stone and tucked it in my pocket.

No response.

Dread settled deeper in my gut. My wolf wasn't taking to being in the Dreamlands. Maybe an effect of the Moon's magic? Or the Dark God's...

Time to get the hell out of here.

Slinging my legs over the edge, I climbed back down the turret, praying to the gods that the fish woman had retreated to her lair, because there was only one way I was getting across the pond.

Before I could think twice about what a poor decision this was, *again*, I dove into the water and swam as fast as my anatomy and Swiftleys allowed. It only took a minute to get to the edge of the pool, where Jaxson and Sam were waiting.

I guess my shocking touch discouraged the mer-bitch from getting handsy again.

Jaxson reached down and, gripping the back of my shirt, plucked me out of the water like I weighed nothing. As soon as my feet hit the ground, he pulled me to his chest, his arms caging me in. The pulse of his heart thudded against mine, and I instinctively relaxed in his warm embrace.

He took my face in his hands and looked at me with an intensity that made my insides gooey. "You're frozen. Don't do that shit again."

I understood it as, *Don't almost get yourself drowned*. I couldn't agree more.

My throat was dry, and all I could do was nod. I placed my hand over his and was about to pull him to my mouth when he froze as stiff as iron in my arms.

Every sense I had immediately went on high alert.

Something was wrong.

The back of my neck tingled, and there was a new vibration in the air. I glanced toward the orb. The pylon of light rose from the top, just like the other. What I felt was from something else.

A low rumble moved through the forest behind us, and the scent of ash and burning trees flowed around me. A magical signature filled the air, one so powerful that I could barely breathe. It pressed in all around me as if I'd been buried in a cold and dark avalanche.

A man stepped from the forest on the far side of the pond—or rather, the forest backed away to reveal him.

At that distance, I shouldn't have been able to clearly see his eyes, but it was like he was standing right before me, and they were all that I could see. Glacier blue and as hard as ice, they practically shone with rage and contempt and power.

Arcane symbols covered his bare, muscled chest, and tattoos of snarling wolves covered each shoulder. His long, dark hair whipped in the gentle breeze.

It was the only thing gentle about him. He was beautiful and utterly terrifying.

His signature was so strong, it practically burned my skin, cold and brutal like frostbite. One look at his cruel expression told me that he'd never had any love for the creatures that were mere shadows of his two-legged form, and never would.

I knew him the instant I saw him.

The Dark Wolf God.

20

Jaxson

The Dark Wolf God—a creature of nightmare and legend. Now he was here, separated from us only by a small expanse of water.

An ocean wouldn't have been enough.

He wore the form of a man, but I knew that was a lie. There was no humanity there, only cruelty and malevolence and hate for all of us who walked on two legs.

Awe nearly overcame me. His signature was like the rumble of an earthquake, and stronger than that of any mortal I'd met. He was like the Moon, but everywhere she was bright and warm, he was cold and dark.

Every part of my soul wanted to charge forward, to wound and slash and kill or die trying to protect my mate. But I had no doubt that we couldn't stand before him.

"Time to go," I growled.

Sam exhaled. "I'm with you on that. Let's get the fuck out of here, Savy."

The god cocked his head like a predator and closed his eyes.

His mouth moved, and even though I couldn't hear what he whispered, I could read his lips. *Take her.*

Savannah rushed over to a fallen log and pulled her jacket out from beneath. "One sec. The talisman is in—"

Her voice cut off as one of the Fae creatures burst from the underbrush and grabbed her by the throat. My mate kicked and fought, but she was off balance, and the creature hauled her toward the forest. Then they were gone.

Everything turned red as rage filled my mind, and my wolf fought for release. All thoughts of the Dark God vanished, and without hesitation, I charged to where she'd been.

Their scent was gone. Had they teleported?

Fear clawed in my chest, and I looked around wildly, scanning the trees, but there was no sign. Suddenly, with a flash, they reappeared briefly at the base of a large oak thirty feet away. Savannah struggled and elbowed the Fae creature in the face, and then they disappeared again.

What the fuck was going on?

"Get Savy and open the portal," Sam growled from behind me. "I'll try to buy time."

I flipped around. *Triple fuck.*

Sam stood rigid, her moonstone gripped in her palm, staring down the Dark God as he approached.

"No, you're not! Get the fuck over here, Sam!" I bellowed, infusing my voice with command. She was beyond brave, but I wasn't going to lose either of them.

Savy materialized, this time alone. She staggered back, claws dripping with blood. "How do you like that, tree bitch?"

I charged to her side, my protectiveness in overdrive. "Open the portal!"

I turned to make sure Sam was with us, and my blood froze.

Like prey transfixed, she hadn't moved an inch. The Dark

Wolf God stalked toward her with a predatory curiosity that made my skin burn.

"Run! Now!" I roared, unleashing my presence.

That snapped her out of it.

She turned and bolted. But the Dark God chased, delight in his eyes. I charged to intercept, with Savy suddenly at my side.

She threw up her arms and raised a black wall of shadowy bands between them—but the Dark God simply ripped his way through and was on Sam in a matter of strides.

She stumbled, and my heart stopped.

As she landed in the dirt, Sam whipped around and hurled her moonstone. It slingshotted through the air, striking the god in the chest. A flash of light detonated, and a forcefield of blinding magic swept outward like an impact wave.

Stones, leaves, and branches tore free and whizzed through the air. I braced Savy and myself against the trunk of a nearby tree and turned my back to shield her from the blast.

My ears were still ringing after the light died away. Sam climbed to her knees, and shock and disbelief flashed across her face.

A shimmering sphere of light wrapped around the Dark God, caging him like a beast.

The Moon's magic, meant to power the binding spell, now bound him instead.

I had a sinking feeling that it wouldn't last long.

The Dark God's gaze locked on Sam, and there was no question that he intended to murder her. Rage radiated off him, and he roared. The ground shook, and the surface of the pond churned, but his prison held.

"Release me!" he growled. His voice was thunder and fury, yet cold and imperious like a mountain. "You do not know what you are doing. I would free you from your cages of concrete and steel and lies."

"Fuck that!" Sam yelled as she scrambled to her feet.

Several glowing cracks formed in the shimmering sphere as he threw his shoulder against it.

"Let's go!" Savy twisted free of my grasp and darted toward Sam with the crescent talisman in hand.

As I ran to join them, the Dark Wolf God turned his hateful glare on Savannah. "*You.*"

Savannah paused and bared her teeth. "Yeah. *Me.*"

His glacier-blue eyes flashed with bright light. "You are mine."

Savannah screamed.

Reeling backward, she doubled over and dropped the talisman in the dirt.

What had he done?

I was at her side in a second, and I shouted at Sam, "Get the talisman! We need to go, now!"

Savy looked up with a distant and volatile expression.

My blood curdled. Something wasn't right.

Savy's fangs released, and her body began to quake as she seemed to struggle against it. Violence and rage flashed in her eyes, and before I could react, she tore free of my hands. Her claws burst from her fingers, and she lunged for Sam. "You will pay!"

Sam screamed in surprise as Savy struck her, and she stumbled back, landing in the dirt. Four red gashes of torn flesh glistened from Sam's chest. Horror and pain cut her face, and she looked up at Savy in disbelief.

Fuck.

I dove for Savy as she dove for Sam, clamping my arms around her like iron bands. But her free arm swung wide, and she sank her claws straight into Sam's neck.

The color drained from Sam's face as blood streamed down

her front, and yet, she still struggled to free Savy's hand from her throat.

"Stop! That's Sam," I growled, as I tried to pull Savy free without hurting Sam. Savannah's skin was hot and trembling, and her signature had changed. She wasn't present any longer. The Dark God had taken over.

I poured my magic into her, letting my alpha signature envelope us. "Let her go, Savy. *Now.*"

A cry tore from her throat, and her body trembled. I sensed her magic fighting against that of the Dark God's. I kept my touch firm and gentle and pushed more of my magic into her. "Come back to us, Savy. Come back to me."

She contorted her spine and squeezed her eyes shut, then screamed as she released her grip. Sam stumbled back with a gasp, and then her legs buckled.

"Oh, my God..." Savy whispered, and sank to her knees. She blinked a few times, as if clearing a haze from her eyes. "What have I done, Jax?"

A roar of rage tore through us as the Dark God bellowed in his cage. There was a resounding crack, and streams of light began pouring from fractures in his golden prison.

We had seconds before he broke free.

Savannah frantically crawled to Sam's body. Blood flowed from her neck, pooling under her shoulder in the mud.

"Savy!" I seized the Moon's talisman and tossed it to her the moment she looked up. "We're in the Dreamlands. If she falls unconscious, she'll be transported to gods know where! Get us out of here!"

She caught it, and with tears streaming down her face, she shouted the words of the spell. The sky tore open as a shimmering silver portal formed.

The air shook as the golden sphere groaned and cracked

again. Rays of light streamed around us as the Dark God began to break through the wall of magic. *Fuck!*

Savy helped me carefully lift Sam's limp body from the mud, and we rushed through the portal as the golden sphere exploded behind us, followed by a deafening roar.

We hurled through the ether and stumbled out into the temple in Delos, covered with blood and mud.

The Moon leapt up from a recliner that hadn't been there before. "What happened?"

"Help us!" Savannah shouted. "She's dying!"

The loremaster hobbled over. "My dear Sam, no!"

"Put her down!" the Moon commanded.

I brought Sam over to the recliner. Her arm slumped over the edge, and a glistening trail of blood streaked down her fingertips, dripping onto the stones below. The blood flow from her neck had slowed, and she wasn't breathing.

The Moon knelt and traced her hands over Sam's body, then shook her head. "It's too late. She's too far gone."

21

Jaxson

The Moon's words rocked me to my core.

"Do something," I growled, as despair claimed me. "You're a goddess. You must be able to heal her."

Savy collapsed to her knees beside our friend, her face twisted in emotions that tore at my very soul. "Please. Save her."

I dropped down beside Savy and pulled her to me. "Please."

An agonized expression cut across the Moon's face, and she pressed her fingers to her temples. For a moment, she was silent, and I held my breath. At last, she spoke. "Okay, okay. I'm not supposed to meddle with death, but I sent you on this journey, and technically, by law, nobody is allowed to die on this island. I'll help her."

I could practically feel Sam's soul leaving this world. "Do it."

"I'll need your help. We need to call her back from death's domain. Place your hands on her, like this." The Moon pressed her palm over the gashes in Sam's chest.

Savy used the back of her wrist to wipe the tears from her eyes, then placed her hands lightly over the gouges on Sam's neck. Her pain and shame and horror filled the room, and I wanted so desperately just to hold her, but we had to save our friend first.

The loremaster and I placed our hands on Sam.

The Moon closed her eyes. “Now, in your minds, call her back to us, and I’ll do what I can.”

I howled in my mind as I would call to my wolves, and the Moon began to speak in a strange tongue. But my howl wouldn’t stay silent. It broke from my lungs, and my voice echoed off the roof of the sanctuary.

Savannah added her howl to mine, and the loremaster, too, until Delos became a temple to that single sound.

The Moon's magic flowed into Sam, and a soft glow emanated from her palms. Slowly, Sam’s breathing returned, and her heartbeat began again.

My howl caught in my throat.

Beneath my hands, the ragged flesh pulled closed, and Sam’s eyes fluttered open.

“Where am I?” she croaked as the Moon stood and stepped back. “I had the strangest dream...”

A sob tore from Savy’s throat, and she folded herself over her friend, pulling her into an awkward embrace. “Oh, my God, Sam. I’m so sorry.”

Sam peered up at me with a distressed expression. “Um, you can let me go now.”

I swallowed a laugh, and the tension in my body eased. Sam wasn’t touchy-feely, and I could sense her unease with all the attention.

Savy staggered to her feet, her eyes glistening. “Will you ever forgive me? I...it wasn’t me.”

Sam sat up and rubbed her blood-soaked chest. “I know.”

“He took control...my wolf, she went wild. I couldn’t hold her back! I saw my claws...”

Sam reached out and took Savannah's hand. "That wasn't you. It was the Dark Wolf God."

"The Dark God?" The Moon Goddess interjected, worry lacing her words. "You actually saw him? In what form?"

"Seven-foot-tall stunner of a man beast, with a penchant for murder. Does that ring a bell?" Sam asked, turning around.

Moon covered her mouth and looked away. "Then he's free of all his bonds."

Dread coiled in my gut. "What does that mean?"

"When I cast the spell on him ages ago, he was bound as a wolf, fully conscious but stuck in a dream," Moon said softly, her gaze distant as if she were recalling the memory. "If his form is corporeal, then that spell has broken, and he's grown powerful."

"The bastard was radiating magic." Savy said distantly.

I could sense the guilt and shame eating her up. I wanted to pull her close and take it all away, but from personal experience, I knew that was impossible. Savy would have to slay her own demons, and I'd be there to hold her up if she needed me.

Still, I moved to her side and took her hand, certain that she needed me now. It trembled in my palm, and I tightened my grip slightly.

The goddess's eyes flicked among the three of us. "The moonstones! Did you recharge all of the orbs? That will still lock him in the Dreamlands, even if he's able to roam free there."

"Just two," Savannah whispered.

"But you still have the third?"

Silence stretched out, and the Moon put her hands on her hips. "What happened?"

"I threw the third one at him so we could escape," Sam muttered.

The Moon's eyes went wide. "That will have hurt him gravely. He and his minions abhor the touch of my magic—that's why the orbs powering my spell are still standing. But unfortunately, while you may have caused him lasting agony, you've only slowed him."

Sam scowled. "Well, I hope it hurt a fucking lot."

The goddess sighed and pinched her brow, and began pacing back and forth.

I cleared my throat. "What can be done at this point?"

She paused and met my gaze, and her blue eyes flashed with concern and defeat. "You hope that the two moonstones are enough to keep him in his realm."

"And if not?" Savy asked.

"Then he will tear your city to the ground."

Fuck.

The Moon clasped her hands behind her back and began to pace again. "You may still stand a chance. Because you recharged two pylons, he'll be at a fraction of his strength. He may not even be able to fully enter your world. But whatever form his magic takes, it will be terrible enough."

My mind raced. "You say he'll attack our city. Are you certain? Will he use a portal, somewhere we can ambush him?"

"He won't need a portal. He'll tear a rift between your world and the Dreamlands. It could appear anywhere, but the choice will be deliberate. It will appear wherever he will be strongest—and he draws his power from the presence of wolves."

"Dockside," I whispered. "We have the largest concentration of werewolves in the Great Lakes."

"Is there still a way for us to stop him?" Savy asked.

For a moment, sadness crossed the Moon's face, and then she reached into her pocket and withdrew a moonstone, this one duller than the others. Cupping it in her palms, magic flared, cascading around the goddess like a solar burst.

It only lasted seconds, and when she opened her palm, the moonstone was glowing—but the Moon herself seemed far, far dimmer that when she'd first appeared to us, and her signature had weakened dramatically.

This was costing her much.

"You'll have to return to his realm in the Dreamlands and recharge the final orb. That is the only way to ensure that he stays there." She glided over to Savy, her movements graceful and fluid, and handed her the stone. "But it will be dangerous. He will guard it jealously now that he knows what we are up to, and I am certain he will wait for you there, in his full power."

"So we're screwed," Sam said, coughing slightly.

"Use it if the opportunity is right. Otherwise, it might buy you precious time if you use it on him like you did before. I'm sorry I cannot give you more."

"Thank you, Moon," Savy said. "We're in your debt."

The goddess sucked in a deep breath. "Perhaps. Or perhaps it is *I* who am in your debt. If the Dark God returns...he'll come after me after he wipes out you and the rest of humanity."

"Let's hope it doesn't come to that," the loremaster said, thumping her cane into the stone. Her eyes flicked to Savy before settling on me with a knowing look. "It's time we return and lick our wounds before the battle."

The Moon stepped back. "Farewell. You still have my talisman. Keep it. If you need to return to or from the Dark God's realm, it will bring you back to the spot you left."

We made our farewells and headed for the front of the temple, but at the last minute, Savannah took my hand and turned back.

The Moon raised her eyebrows. "Yes? Was there something else?"

Savannah swallowed. "This was my fault. I attacked her. The Dark God took possession of my wolf. I tried to stop him, but if it wasn't for Jaxson, I would have lost control..."

She was unable to finish the thought.

Sorrow and pity crossed the Moon's face. "It's not your fault, my child. He is the god of wolves. It is his power to control and command them."

Savannah shook her head. "I don't accept that. How do I stop it from happening again?"

The Moon studied her for a while before she finally reached out and touched Savy's shoulder. "This is no normal wound."

She adjusted her shoulder uncomfortably. "It was a gift from Victor Dragan, the sorcerer who brought back the Dark God. He cut me with a Soul Knife."

"He did more than cut you, Savannah. He severed a part of your wolf's soul. That missing shard is the Dark God's way in, like a gap in your armor. Through it, he can take possession of your wolf, and through her, he will take control of you."

The blood drained from her face. "What can I do?"

"You must find a way to heal the wound."

"You brought Sam back from the dead. Can you heal Savannah's wolf?" I asked.

The Moon shook her head. "If I could, I would. But this is a sinister magic over which I have no control. You will have to find another way to fight his power."

Savannah bowed her head. "Thank you."

We turned to leave, but the Moon spoke up. "You three faced the Dark Wolf God and survived. Not many in history can say that. You've made it this far. You will find a way."

Savannah nodded, and we walked off. Once we passed beyond the pillars, the temple faded, and when I turned around, only ruins remained.

Savy's face burned with anger, and she glared out over the island.

I gently brushed her hair behind her ear. "It will be okay."

She shook her head and met my eyes. "He used me to hurt

her, Jax. Never again. I don't care what I have to do—if I have to lock myself away, so be it. Never, *ever*, again."

Her words resonated with so much pain that they cut like a knife. The Dark God might have nearly killed Sam, but he'd tried to destroy my mate's soul.

Anger and despair threated to overwhelm me, but I pushed them down. That wasn't what she needed right now.

I wrapped my arms around her and didn't let go.

But she didn't soften in my embrace. She remained hard, a blade in a sheath, ready to strike. "I'm going to stop him, Jax. I'm going to find a way."

22

Savannah

I drew in a shaky breath, staring out the floor-to-ceiling windows of Jaxson's apartment. Dark clouds rolled in over the lake outside, while a deluge of emotions warred inside me: dread, shock, revulsion at myself for what I'd done.

I set the glowing moonstone and talisman on the counter. Despite the magic coursing off the moonstone, I still felt drained and...broken.

I squeezed my eyes shut, but the image of blood pooling beneath Sam as her lifeless form lay on the ancient stones of the temple rose in my mind. Red seeped into the weathered cracks of the temple floor.

The same red that had covered my hands.

He'd taken control of my wolf.

I'd fought as hard as I could to stop the shift, but he'd made me attack her all the same.

But the thing that twisted my stomach and planted fear in my gut was that a small part of me had actually savored his power as it coursed through my body. I'd felt invincible. Unstoppable. No longer afraid.

It had felt...amazing. And I wanted more.

What did that say about me?

Sam had brushed it off. Forgiven me. Told me it was all right a dozen times. But how could I move past knowing that I'd almost killed the closest thing I had to a best friend?

I *had* killed her. If not for the Moon, Sam would be dead.

Wolfie? Are you there? We really need to talk.

But there was no response. There hadn't been since the Dark God had taken control.

I was desperate to hear her voice and terrified that she blamed herself. He had come through her. One second, she'd been there, and the next, she was gone, and it was only him.

Now it seemed there was no one.

If you just need time, I understand.

Thunder cracked outside, and rain began pelting the glass. Dread coiled in my belly, and I felt myself sinking. Drowning under the weight of my shame, fear, and the duty I had to the pack. And beneath it all, a terror that something was truly wrong with my wolf.

What could I possibly do? How could Sam—or even Jaxson—look at me the same way? I was becoming a monster. A puppet. And I had to stop it, whatever the cost. I had to stop *him*.

Jaxson strode across the kitchen, snapping me out of my storming thoughts. He drew two lowball glasses from the cupboard, and reaching for a bottle of Maker's Mark, he set the glasses down hard and filled them an inch. He hadn't said a word since we'd returned, and he watched me now with an intensity that set me ablaze. His mood was dark, violent, and *hungry*.

Streaks of light illuminated the lake, followed by a deafening rumble. It was like the heavens were mirroring the anguish inside me.

Jaxson moved around the marble island, eating up the

distance between us. My pulse quickened. My God, he was a vision. The hard lines of his jaw were set, and his green eyes blazed. Dried sweat and blood painted his neck and thick forearms. A gorgeous, terrifying beast. Heat sparked low in my belly.

I wanted to melt into him. To let him take away some of my anguish, make me forget the demons that haunted my nightmares.

He took a step toward me, and his fingers brushed mine as he handed me a glass. Electricity surged up my arm, and I sucked in a shallow breath. How did this man bring me to my knees with a single touch? With a look.

He said nothing, but his eyes took me in, peeling the hardened layers I'd formed over the past decade to protect myself. Mistrust. Anger. Defiance. They were ways I'd learned to cope with the shit life had thrown at me. But somehow, in this moment, this man stripped them away, one by one, baring my soul. Naked. Exposed. Undone.

My chin trembled, and the impulse to flee rang through me. I hated feeling vulnerable and exposed, weak. But Jaxson held me in place with his gaze, and soon, the inexplicable urge to let go for just one moment beckoned. To get lost in this man and forget everything, just for tonight.

"You have to release that guilt, darling," he said, his voice rough but tender.

My throat tightened, and I fought the tears that threatened to spill. "It's not that easy..."

Knowing flashed through his eyes, and his jaw tensed. Anger and aggression pulsed off him, but they weren't directed at me.

"Let me take some of your burden." He stepped toward me and brushed his rough fingers over my cheek. I leaned into his touch, wanting to unload my pain and hurt.

"I don't know how," I whispered.

And that was the honest-to-God truth. I'd never opened

myself up to anyone before, and I wasn't sure I knew how to do it. Maybe I was too broken and fucked up. Hot tears flooded my eyes, and I looked away.

But Jaxson took my chin and tilted my face up to his. Though his features were harsh, his eyes were soft, his touch tender. "You need to lean on me. You need to let me stand by your side and help you fight your battles."

A tear broke free and spilled down my cheek. Jaxson rubbed it away with his thumb, and his gaze dropped to my lips. "You've been fighting on your own for too long. You did what you had to in order to survive, but you have to stop carrying everything on your shoulders. You've got the pack. You've got *me*."

The words lodged in my throat. My heart felt like it was splitting open, and I wanted so badly to let Jaxson in, but I was afraid.

He held my face like he was reading the pain carved into it. Like he could take it away. "Do you trust me?"

Yes. Despite all the uncertainty and warring emotions, I knew that beneath his hard, domineering exterior, Jaxson was kind. He fought for the ones he cared about. But would that be enough to keep him from wrecking my heart?

My chest rose and fell with short breaths. "I trust you, Jaxson."

At my words, he leaned down and kissed me gently. Desire burned through my veins, and my center ached with need. His lips were warm, and as his tongue parted mine, dipping into my mouth, a whimper escaped me. His fingers tangled in my hair, and he broke off the kiss, looking down at me with something almost like compassion. "What do you need, Savy?"

Forgiveness for what I'd done. Strength to face what was coming. Hope that there would be a way through all of this, that there would be a future.

My eyes slowly traced over the man in front of me. He was all of those things, and so much more.

"I need you," I said, the truth breathlessly spilling from my lips. "Everything that you are. Everything we can be, together."

His own breath stopped as if somehow, breathing would break the spell. And I understood in that moment how much he'd wanted that answer. Needed it himself.

I rose up on my toes and lightly kissed his lips. And when our mouths parted, I whispered, "I need my mate."

Heat flashed through his eyes, and as if the beast had been unleashed, he took my mouth in his, devouring me.

The kiss was possessive, an unspoken promise to cherish me, protect me, and ease my pain.

I let myself go, let it all go, the fear and guilt and danger hanging over our heads. I gave into the moment, forgetting everything but him.

His arm curled around my waist, and he lifted me. Still kissing him, I squeezed my legs around him while he carried me up the stairs.

He kicked the door to his bedroom open. It banged against the wall, but Jaxson kept moving past his bed into the bathroom. Flicking on the light, he set me on the countertop. I sucked in air, my breasts heaving and blood pumping. He traced my swollen lips with his thumb, desire and possessiveness written all over his face.

Fuck.

"I knew the moment we first met that I had to have you." Jaxson's rough voice skated over my heated skin, sending a volley of shivers in its wake. He slid his hands up my thighs, parting my legs. My pulse quickened, and I reached forward, gripping his bloodied shirt and pulling him toward me.

"I knew you were trouble," I said, peering up at him.

Dangerous, delicious trouble. I'd rebelled against him from the start, but in this moment, I was ready to submit to the beast.

His lips pulled into a knowing grin. "Trouble attracts trouble."

Kneeling between my legs, he removed one boot and then the next, all the while his eyes never left mine. Seeing him down there sent all sorts of dirty thoughts through my mind. My core throbbed, and I sucked in a shaky breath.

The lights flickered, casting Jaxson's features in shadow. His body was a map of hard angles, muscle, and power—a heady concoction that made my head swim and heat pool low in my belly. This man was devastation and sin. I wasn't sure which one I needed right now.

Maybe both.

Rising, he slowly moved his hands up my thighs to my waist, gently dragging my sweat-stained shirt over my head. Tossing it aside, he gazed down at me, his pupils dilating as they settled on my black lace bra. His fingers traced the outline of my breast and drifted down my skin until he found the top button to my jeans. For a second, his fingers paused.

My heart thundered in my ears, and I swore I could hear his, too, matching my own. I nodded assent, and he set the button free.

Every move he made filled me with the agony of anticipation. He was taking his time, cherishing every moment, but I needed him in me then and there. God knew how little time we had left together. Suddenly, I felt like I'd wasted every moment of my life that we'd been apart.

I sure as hell wasn't going to squander one more second. I leaned back on the gray marble counter, lifted my hips, and started shimmying my jeans and panties down over my ass. The cold surface stung my flushed butt cheeks, and I sucked in a sharp breath. "I need you *now*. I've needed you always."

23

Savannah

Jaxson's eyes dilated at my bare flesh, and he grasped my jeans and dragged them the rest of the way off.

"Fuck," he whispered, dropping my clothes, staring at my nakedness. "You're going to be the end of me, Savy."

Without taking his eyes off me, he reached over and turned on the water in the walk-in shower beside us.

Desire pulsed off him, and I couldn't ignore the bulge in his pants. Licking my lips, I cast him a vixen smile. "I hope not. There are so many things I want to do to you."

Gripping the bottom of his shirt, I tugged it up over his head and threw it to the ground.

"Show me," he growled, pulling me off the counter in a swift movement.

I fumbled with the button of his jeans and slid them off, my need burning when I took in his naked body. He must have seen the lust in my eyes, because when I looked up, he had a devilish grin on his face.

Then he pulled me to him, unclipping my bra and slipping off the straps as he trailed kisses down my neck. The bra dropped to the floor, and he palmed one of my breasts, taking the other in his mouth. I gasped when he grazed my nipple with his teeth, and then his hand moved down my stomach, dipping between my thighs.

"Savy..." he growled, feeling the slickness at my center. He gripped my ass cheeks, and with a single motion, he hiked me up to his hips.

He stepped into the shower, still holding me, and I gasped as gloriously hot water rushed over my back.

But all I could think of was his hard length pressed against my tummy, and I couldn't help but move against it. The emptiness ached inside me, begging to be filled.

"Please, Jax," I whispered.

"Please what?" He nipped my ear, sending flames down my neck.

"Take me."

Greed flashed through his eyes, and he obeyed. His mouth claimed mine, his touch hard and urgent. I met his kisses with equal measure, my nails digging into his back as I pulled him closer, needing to close the distance between us.

I gasped as he pressed my back to the cold tile, and then a moan slipped from my mouth when he reached around and his fingers slipped inside of me. My hips bucked against his hand as his thumb rubbed me just where I needed him to. "More," I rasped.

He lifted my hips and positioned his length at my center. I whimpered as he pushed into me, slowly, nudging himself deeper.

My God.

Pain and pleasure arced through me, and the world and all its problems faded away.

I had been running for so long, I'd lost all sense of direction. I'd been stumbling and hurtling through life, just trying to keep both feet moving. But finally, I'd found the thing I'd been running toward all along.

"I need you, Jax," I whispered. "Not for this moment, or tonight. But every moment that's going to come after."

He pressed his forehead against mine. "I'm yours. I always have been."

I knew then that we would only be complete together.

I began moving my hips against him. With a shudder, he growled low, then pulled out and slammed into me. I dragged my fingers down his back, tugging him to me, desperate to join our bodies.

How had the fates known exactly what I needed, and who I needed to pull me from the darkness? Whatever happened next outside the walls of Jaxson's penthouse didn't matter. He had restored my faith in one thing, at least: someone, somewhere was looking out for me, and there was a plan for us.

Bracing one arm against the tile, the other on my hip, Jaxson fell into a rough rhythm, our bodies slick and moving in tandem. He fucked me hard, and I met each thrust, needing more. I was more synchronized with him than I'd ever been. My fears and doubts melted away, and soon, nothing existed but the two of us, complete in each other. Every movement we made left me with no doubt that I was made for his arms, and that he was made for me.

How had I ever run from this?

I kissed him with everything I had, claiming him as my own.

I tried to hold on, preserving this moment for as long as I could, but pleasure swelled until I couldn't resist it any longer.

I split apart.

My back arched off the wet tile, my vision darkening as flames ripped through me. Jaxson grunted and thrust deeply, rocking into me as a roar tore from his throat and his muscles flexed.

He buried his face in my neck, our bodies heaving as we came back down together. "My gods," he said gruffly, a hint of astonishment in his voice.

My gods was right.

Every muscle in my body was weak and quaking, but just being next to him gave me the strength I needed.

He pressed gentle kisses along my jaw, and I felt his smile against my skin. "You're mine, Savy."

"And you are mine." I turned my head and found his lips, and we kissed, long and slow. No longer desperate, but savoring every sensation.

This man. He was everything.

~

Jaxson

There are moments in life that we know will change the course of things. A decision. An action. A twist of fate that alters everything and sets into motion a cascade of events, for better or worse.

The night I stepped into that shithole bar and laid eyes on Savannah. The day she decided to seek out her family and ended up in Magic Side. Those moments had changed everything.

Pressing a kiss to her lips, I set Savannah down on her feet. She was a vision. Water cascaded down her curves, and when she smiled up at me, my heart stilled. Her eyes were no longer stormy and blazing like the tempest outside, but calm and complete.

It was a feeling I shared—one that I'd never felt so strongly before.

Savannah took the loofah and lathered it with soap. Reaching up, she began to clean the lingering blood and grime that coated my skin. As she stepped behind me, she pressed a kiss to my shoulder, whispering, "Thank you," before she continued scrubbing my back.

"For what?" I asked.

"For being exactly what I needed."

I closed my eyes for a moment, recalling the fortune teller's tent where I'd had my first glimpse of Savannah through a crystal ball. The seer had drawn three cards for my fate. The second had been a woman subduing a lion by gripping it by its jaws. The card for *Strength*.

Turning, I took the loofah from Savy, soaped it up again, and began to wash her. The fates never chose the easy paths for mortals, but they were always the paths they needed to follow.

"You've always been exactly what I needed. I just was too blind to see it," I said.

Trepidation flickered in her beautiful eyes, and she swallowed hard and looked away. "I know you never wanted a mate, Jax. And if that's still the case, I understand."

She had no fucking idea, did she? Once, that had been the truth. After seeing what Stephanie's death had done to my brother-in-law, I swore to reject my fated mate, if I had one. But something had flicked on when I'd met Savannah, something that made me feel alive again. And the truth was, it terrified the shit out of me, feeling this way about someone.

I ran my fingers along her jaw. "No. I never wanted a mate until I met you. You changed everything."

She turned her face and kissed my palm, and when she looked back up at me, there was a hint of smile.

My heart swelled. Maybe we were crazy. Maybe we were doomed. But I didn't give a damn. Savannah was my mate, and I chose her.

We finished up, and I stepped out of the shower, grabbing two towels from the closet. Securing one around my waist, I wrapped the other around her bare body. Desire flared, and she must have sensed it, because she cast me a wicked grin as she took her towel off briefly and rubbed the drips from her wet hair.

Thunder raged outside, and rain drummed against the window in my bedroom.

Barely decent once more, Savannah took a step forward, tracing her fingers over my collarbone. "I hope you're not going to just tuck me into bed and then leave again."

Her citrus sunshine scent made my head spin. Intoxicating. Those lips, plump and inviting to be devoured.

I shook my head. The last time we'd fucked and showered, I'd put her in my bed and left. Propriety or not, I'd been an asshole. "There is no way I'm leaving you tonight," I said, my voice rough.

She turned and walked into my bedroom, then glancing over her shoulder, she let the towel slide, revealing nothing but bare skin. Lightning streaked, casting Savannah in a brilliant glow. My mouth went dry as my eyes devoured the sight. Her damp crimson hair fell down her sleek back as she climbed up and kneeled on my bed, her toned thighs and round ass on full display.

"Well, then, alpha. Come and claim me," she said, peering over her shoulder at me with a come-hither smile.

Fucking hell.

24

Savannah

Savannah. His voice moved through me like quicksilver. Crawling beneath my skin and clawing at my mind.

The Dark God.

You are mine, Savannah. Submit, and I will spare your friends and mate. Resist, and...

My claws reached out to rip into Sam's throat.

I gasped and jerked awake. Fear thrummed through me, and my chest rocked up and down with heavy breaths, but Jaxson's arm pulled me tightly against him. My heart was hammering, but Jaxson's steady breathing and the warmth of his skin against my back returned me to the present.

The air felt like ice and the faint traces of smoke lingered. I wanted to believe it was only a nightmare, but I knew better. Dreams were the Dark God's domain, and he'd just put an ultimatum on the table. Submit, or else.

Sam, Casey, and my aunt. I'd turned on them all. I was certain that it had been his influence from the start, and he was only growing stronger.

My pulse quickened as rage coursed through my blood. *I will never submit.*

Careful not to wake Jaxson, I gently lifted his arm off me as I slid to the edge of the bed. My heart ached at how soundly he was sleeping. I leaned forward and kissed his lips, but he didn't stir. More than anything, I wanted to crawl back into his arms and bury myself in his warm embrace, but dark thoughts had taken root, and there was no way I could shut off my mind.

The storm had passed, but the sky was still cast in shadow. It had to be late, almost morning. I crept into the bathroom, pulled a white bathrobe from the closet, and then slipped out of the room.

What was it about the middle of the night that made the darkest thoughts stir?

The witching hour.

Quite literally, because I was bewitched by the damn Dark Wolf God. I scoffed as I padded down the stairs into the kitchen. My body ached from the intense lovemaking Jaxson and I had done. Warmth pooled in my belly as I touched my lips, which were still swollen and slightly bruised.

But then the wound on my shoulder began to burn, and *he* was in my thoughts again, breaking through from the world of dreams. *Your wolf has submitted to me. It's time that you do.*

"Get out of my mind, you bastard," I hissed. Making my will like iron, I pushed as hard against him as I could.

Eventually, the pain in my shoulder subsided, and the sensation of his presence faded.

Wolfie? I asked, hope welling in my stomach for a moment—but there was no response.

Despair tore at me. The fucker had taken up residence in my soul, and somehow, he'd taken control of my wolf. But I knew she would never submit. As different as we were, in that, we were the same.

Wolfie had to be in there, fighting back. I knew it.

The Moon's words repeated again and again in my mind. *He severed a part of your wolf's soul. That missing shard is his way in, like a gap in your armor. Through it, he can take possession of your wolf, and through her, he will take control of you.*

Yet the goddess didn't have any idea how to fix it.

What the hell was I going to do? How could I be sure that I wouldn't attack Sam again? Or Jaxson? Or Casey? My gut twisted, and shame burned my eyes.

Thoughts thrashing through my mind, I paced the kitchen until pink and orange hues lit up the sky over the lake. If I couldn't stop the Dark God from taking control, it wouldn't just be my friends or Jaxson who'd be in danger—it would be the whole city.

Dread coiled like a constrictor around my heart, and I found that I could no longer escape the truth: no matter the cost, I had to shut the door. And there was only one way to do that.

But could I bring myself to do it?

Jaxson appeared in the doorway wearing nothing but a pair of sweats, powerful and gorgeous. My breath hitched, and my throat suddenly went dry.

He wasn't going to like my plan, but I couldn't do it behind his back. I wouldn't. What we'd shared last night had changed everything. We were mates, and I needed him at my side as much as I knew he needed me.

He must have sensed my unease because he frowned, and concern flooded his expression. "What is it, Savy?"

Chest aching, I bit my lip. "*He* spoke to me again in my dreams. Threatening all of you. We're out of options. I need to sever the Dark God's power over my wolf before it's too late."

"We'll find a way to heal your wolf," he said, his eyes dropping to the wound on my shoulder.

"There's no time. His control is getting stronger. He won't let me give up the Soul Knife, and I wouldn't have been able to push him out in the Dreamlands without your help. We have to do this now, and we have to be sure."

"What are you suggesting?"

I stared at him, my pulse pounding. Why couldn't I say it? It was despicable, and shame burned my throat.

Jaxson's eyes turned dark, his features lethal. "No."

He knew.

"It's the only way, Jax." My voice cracked as a sob lodged in my throat. "He'll take over again and try to stop us. I wouldn't be able to live with myself if I hurt you or Sam or Casey again."

"I'm not letting you *bind* your wolf." He strode across the kitchen, his voice cold and sharp as glass.

Thinking about binding Wolfie was one thing, but hearing Jaxson say the words sent bile up my throat. I squeezed my eyes shut. "It's the only way."

"Bullshit." Jaxson slammed a mug down as he started the coffeemaker.

I walked over to him. He was gripping the counter and looking down, and I placed my hand over his. "You have no idea how much she means to me. This is the last thing I want to do, but that fucker is in my thoughts. His hold over my wolf is getting stronger."

"Anything but that, Savy," he said solemnly.

His breath heated my cheek, and the weight of what I was about to do cut deep. Wolfie would be pissed and hurt, but what other choice did I have? She'd gone silent, and I couldn't communicate with her.

"It's the only way I can stay in control." I squeezed Jaxson's arm and slipped out of his hold. "Once we get the missing part of my soul back, I'll have Laurel remove the binding spell."

Jaxson's fury was palpable, electric and all-consuming, like it was sucking the air from the room. He looked over at me, a storm raging in his eyes. "I can understand Laurel doing this, but you? Can you really do that to your wolf after all she's been through?"

Another sob lodged in my throat, and I sucked in a sharp breath. I knew that Jaxson wasn't intentionally rubbing salt on the wound in my heart—he was just laying out the facts—but it hurt just the same.

"I must," I whispered. "She'll understand."

Jaxson raised his brows. "Will she? The betrayal will cut deeply."

I lifted my chin, but my body was trembling. "My wolf isn't there anymore. When I speak to her, the Dark God responds. When I tried to hand over the Soul Knife, he wouldn't let me. I have no choice."

"The Moon told us that we need to find a way to heal your wound from the Soul Knife—that's how he's controlling you."

"We're out of time. I nearly killed my best friend yesterday. Next time he tries to take control, I might do something worse. I've already attacked Casey and Aunt Laurel once. If he'd made me use the Soul Knife instead of my wolf form..."

Jaxson stiffened. The disappointment in his eyes hurt more than his anger.

I set my jaw, searching for confidence I didn't have. "We bind my wolf, and then we find a way to heal my soul. It's too risky if we do it the other way around. I won't let him take control again."

Jaxson turned and strode to the windows, and gazed out over the same city I'd been looking at moments before. What did he see down there? His pack? People worth saving? People worth doing terrible things to protect?

I didn't dare speak—I just let the reality of the situation do its work. We knew of no other way.

Somehow, I expected his shoulders to drop in defeat, or for

him to fly into a rage. But when he turned back to me, his expression was hard and determined. "I hate this, but I will always stand by you."

I swallowed, realizing that a part of me had wanted him to stop me, to rail against me. But neither of us had that luxury. What had to be done, had to be done.

Stepping close, I wrapped my arms around him. "Thank you."

25

Jaxson

A couple of hours later, we pulled up in front of a redbrick building as the sun was just beginning to lighten the sky. Savy said it served as Laurel's workshop, which was a piece of information I wouldn't soon forget.

"Are you really sure about this?" Sam asked from the back seat. She'd showed up this morning to check on Savy. After her initial shock had worn off at the proposed plan, she'd insisted on coming along. I assumed she was almost more worried about what I'd do when Laurel bound Savy's wolf. I still had no idea, myself.

As we'd driven over, Savannah had slipped into silence like a heavy fog, lost in thought. I could sense her emotions warring against each other—determination, fear, shame, sorrow—each trying to gain the upper hand. As if stirred from a dream, she nodded. "Yes. You two can wait outside, if you want."

"Not a chance," I growled as I climbed out of the truck.

"Same," Sam said.

Laurel stepped out of a red door behind a narrow set of stairs that fronted the building. Crossing her arms, she met my gaze.

Her hair was pulled back, and she wore a long, flowered dress. Despite the morning sun, dark shadows from behind cut across her form, betraying the hard and ruthless soul lurking beneath.

Savy stepped around the truck, and Sam and I fell in step beside her as the three of us walked across the parking lot.

I scented Laurel's irritation. She hadn't been expecting Sam and me to be there.

At the top of the steps, she pulled Savannah into her arms. "This is the right call."

My wolf surged in my chest, and I growled low. "For you or for her?"

"Jax," Savannah snapped at me.

I flexed my fists in irritation. I wasn't going to mince words. There was a chance, albeit small, that Savannah would change her mind, and I was going to make sure Laurel didn't convince her to do something she'd regret.

"Come inside." Laurel gestured for us to enter, but as soon as Savannah passed, Laurel stepped in front of me. "This is her choice, Jaxson."

My jaw tensed. "It wasn't before."

Guilt flashed in Laurel's eyes, and she lifted her chin. "It is now. As it should have been from the start."

She turned and followed Savannah inside. Sam shook her head as we showed ourselves in.

A dimly lit hall led to a library with antique furniture and oriental rugs. The dusty scent of the leatherbound books lining the shelves left the threat of a cough lingering in my throat. The packed shelves were a testament to the depth of Laurel's arcane knowledge. As much as I didn't trust her, I knew her capability all too well. If anyone could find another way, it would be her.

"Are you sure there's nothing else you can do to keep the Dark God from taking over Savannah?" I asked Laurel as she searched through a drawer in a large oak desk.

She frowned. "Unfortunately, I've found no other way. I've searched my spell books, but there's nothing powerful enough to block his magic. Maybe if he hadn't already managed to establish a presence over her...but he's a god, and his power is, frankly, incalculable."

A determined fury rippled through my veins. Whether he was a god or not, Savannah Caine was my mate, and I'd do anything and everything to protect her.

Savannah placed her hand on my arm. "It's okay. This is going to work."

I could tell she didn't fully believe it, but even so, her touch calmed the beast inside me.

Sam locked eyes with Laurel. "Is it reversible?"

"Yes," she answered, then met my gaze with an accusatory stare. "And with Jaxson's pull on her, I don't know how long the binding spell with last. Your mate bond is probably what broke the spell in the first place—and that could be a problem for us now."

Had it been our bond or the Dark Wolf God?

Something flashed across Savy's face, and I could tell she was wondering the same thing.

"Where's Casey?" Savannah asked, her hand tightening around my arm.

As if she'd summoned the devil, her cousin stalked into the study. His brows shot up as he looked between Sam and me and his mother. "Seriously? *They're* going to be here?"

"I was going to ask the same thing about you," Sam muttered.

Laurel didn't look up from the book she was flipping through. "They're here, and I don't think there's any point in arguing about it. But for now, Savannah and I need the room to prepare. So all of you, out. Including you, Casey."

"I'm not leaving," I growled.

Laurel snapped her head around. "I'm not going to bewitch her in your absence, *alpha*. She needs to learn the spell, and that will take concentration. You're a distraction."

"I need to learn a spell? I thought you were going to cast it," Savannah whispered.

"I did that once before when you were too young. But this must be your decision, all the way down. I'm not going to make it for you again."

Savannah traced her fingers over the pile of papers on Laurel's desk. "But what if I mess it up?"

I tensed, but Laurel laughed. "You won't. You are bright and capable, and I'm an excellent teacher. Casey and I will cast it with you, but you will need to take the lead."

Savannah's mouth opened, but Laurel swept away from her, opened the library door, and gestured with her hand. "The rest of you, out. Casey, make sure they don't touch anything too deadly."

26

Savannah

I gaped at the pages of symbols and incantations that Laurel had spread on the table. “I don’t think I can do this.”

“Nonsense,” Laurel said. “Don’t be intimidated. We’re sorcerers, not mages, so we cast with our souls, not with books and overly complex spellcraft. These are just notes to help you see how the spells work together. But you won’t have to memorize much—you have to *feel* it.”

“It *feels* like this is going to be complicated.”

She shook her head. “Sorcery is about intent and willpower. Even if you’re not perfect with the spell, as long as you know exactly what you want, you will achieve it.”

As long as I knew what I wanted...but did I really want to chain my wolf?

Aunt Laurel took my hand. “Savy, you’re headstrong and have more force of will than just about anyone I’ve ever met. It’s time you put that strength to use.” She slid a page across the table and tapped it with her fingers. “Now concentrate as if your life depends on it, because it very well might.”

An hour later, my brain felt like a lemon smashed in a press.

"I think you've got it," Laurel said.

I rubbed my temples. "God, I don't think I even remember my own name anymore. My head is swimming."

"Oh, I know it's a lot to download, but you need to understand how it works. How to bind and unbind. They're two sides of the same coin. Do you think you can do it?"

I squeezed my eyes shut. I could see each page of notes perfectly in my mind. I'd always had amazing recall, but this was putting it to the test.

Sweat slicked the palms of my hands.

This was going to be the most horrible thing I'd ever done—betraying my own wolf. But I had to. No matter how much the risk or how she might resent me, I was almost certain that she would hate me more if I did nothing, if I let the Dark God turn her into a weapon against my family and friends.

Even now, when I looked at my aunt, I could still see her lying in the hallway at home, covered in blood.

Had that been his influence, even back then? How long had he been pulling my strings, subtly manipulating my actions?

It had to end.

I rose. "I think I've got this. Let's do it now, while I've still got my nerve."

Laurel led me to the small office where Jax, Sam, and Casey were waiting. Jaxson's eyes instantly locked on mine, and I nodded. *It's time.*

His expression was hard and impatient, and unfortunately, it didn't seem like he'd cooled off much.

"We're ready," Laurel said in a hushed voice.

"Finally!" Casey belted. "I was getting so tired of these two yakking on about wolf stuff."

"I don't think you stopped talking for more than a minute the entire time," Sam moaned.

Jaxson stood and took my hand, and we all followed Laurel

into her "workshop" downstairs. Prickles skated along my skin as I gazed across the black stone floor that was elaborately etched with runes.

The last time I'd been inside was just under a month ago, for demon training. Man, how had my life gotten so complicated? I thought it had all been too much then, but now I was so in over my head that it felt like I was on a one-way trip to the bottom of Lake Michigan in concrete boots.

Laurel strode across the room and set her cloth satchel down, taking out a brown glass bottle and a burlap bag.

"What the hell is this place?" Sam asked, looking around the room. Between my nerves and Jaxson's simmering anger, the tension in the room was combustible.

"Laurel's workshop," I whispered.

Jaxson took it all in, resentment evident on his face. "You've been here before?"

I shrugged, ignoring his burning gaze. "Once. She summoned some demons to teach me how to use my magic."

"Wonderful," he said dryly.

Laurel started walking, flicking her bottle and spraying droplets of liquid on the floor.

Sam began to move around the edge of the room, and Casey was beside her in a second. "Don't touch anything."

"The only thing I'll be touching is your balls when my boot connects with them," Sam growled.

"Feisty." Casey smirked and turned on his heel.

My anxiety was already mounting, but Jaxson's unease and ire pulsed off him like a sun flare, making me even more nervous. I could tell that he was using every ounce of his restraint. He didn't want me to do this. Hell, *I* didn't want to do this. But some part of me, deep down, knew that it was necessary. I had to believe that somehow, Wolfie would understand... wherever she was.

"Casey, set up the braziers," Laurel said as she finished splashing holy water, or whatever the hell it was, around the room.

My cousin positioned four braziers within the outer circle of runes. He filled each one with honey-colored pieces of kindling, then tossed a handful of sticky crystal gravel on top. Then, with a wink at Sam, he launched four successive fireballs into the braziers. Flames roared to life, licking the ceiling.

Show-off.

Sam scoffed. Casey was definitely enjoying this.

Laurel, who was untying the burlap bag, shot him a sharp look over her shoulder.

"Dirt?" Jaxson arched his brows at Laurel. Holding the bag, she'd begun pouring a thin line of dry dirt in the shape of an oval.

"This is a circle of confinement. It will focus and direct the magic of the spell." She tossed the empty bag beside her belongings and retrieved several sprigs of dried leaves. Crushing them between her palms, she sprinkled them into the dirt oval.

"We wouldn't want to accidentally bind your wolves," Casey added, looking between Jax and Sam with a glimmer of amusement in his eyes.

A muscle in Jaxson's jaw twitched, and I placed a hand on his arm before he took a step toward my idiotic cousin. "He's just joking."

Still, doubt tugged at me. Images of the files Laurel had on each of the packs in North America flashed in my mind, and my gut twisted.

Laurel glanced in our direction, preoccupied. "You think I'm foolish enough to start a war? Anyway, I doubt I could bind your wolves without your permission. The only reason we were able to bind Savannah's was because she was a baby."

"She was helpless, you mean. Unable to object to your sorcery," Jaxson said sharply.

Laurel squared her shoulders but didn't take the bait. "You're here because I allowed you to be here, Laurent. Don't forget that."

"You think I'm afraid of you, LaSalle? Just give me a reason to rip out your throat."

Casey tensed, and flames flickered to life in his palms.

Damn it all to hell.

Sam's claws slipped free. I knew her well enough by now to recognize by the straightening of her shoulders that shit was about to get real in here.

"Enough!" I stepped forward, standing between the four of them. "You need to put aside your differences. What I'm about to do is messed up on so many levels. I *need* your support. All of you."

Laurel sighed and offered Jaxson her palm. "She's right. This is a dangerous spell. We need our minds focused. I'll put aside my differences if you will."

Jaxson looked at her for several long breaths, then finally shook her hand.

Casey took half a step toward Sam, but she turned. "Nuh-uh, fire boy."

"Let's get on with this, then." Laurel locked eyes with me and gestured toward the dirt oval in the center of the runes.

I tightened my hands in fists to keep them from trembling and stepped into place.

"What's with the creepy circles?" Sam asked.

"For your protection," Casey answered. "In case things get a little hairy."

The four of them positioned themselves inside the outer circle of runes. Laurel raised her palms, and two ribbons of light snaked out, moving across the symbols on the floor. They looked remarkably like the ribbons I'd fashioned with my shadows, only hers were made of light. As they touched the strange sigils, each illuminated until a ring of glowing runes surrounded us. The air crackled with magic, a sound curiously like Rice Krispies in milk, and my ears popped.

"This is a circle of protection," Laurel said. "As long as you're within it, nothing outside of the circle can harm you. *Don't leave.*"

Sam gave me a *what the fuck have you gotten us into* look.

Laurel pulled a sheet of weathered paper from her back pocket. She unfolded it and glanced at the cursive writing and symbols before placing it on the floor beside her.

My heart thudded. "Notes? Why'd you make me memorize it?"

"It's been decades since I've performed this spell. I know it well, but it never hurts to have the instructions. Are you ready?"

Absolutely not.

I tried reaching out to my wolf one last time. *Wolfie? Is this okay?*

No response.

I'm doing this to protect you, I said into the silence.

As if reading my mind, Laurel took my hands and smiled. "Long ago, your mother, father, and I cast this spell to protect you. Today, Casey and I are going to help you protect yourself. You can do this, Savannah."

I nodded. "Okay."

"Now lie down. You won't want to fall."

"Fall?"

She shrugged. "The binding might get a little rough."

Okay, what the hell was I getting myself into?

With a final wary glance at Jaxson, I took what might have been my last breath and leaned back onto the cold stone floor, resting my arms at my sides.

Laurel took her spot. "Clear you mind of everything but your intention, then summon your magic and begin the spell. We will help you shape it, but you'll have to form the bonds yourself."

Even though my nerves were failing me, I tried to calm my racing heart with long, deep breaths. Finally, when I began to feel a modicum of control, I called my magic.

Icy chills spread over my skin as shadows began spiraling around me. As the power built in my chest, I began to chant the words of the spell that my aunt had taught me. Hard words, to make my shadows like iron.

Then I wasn't the only one speaking. Laurel's whispers moved through the room like a breeze. The flames in the braziers flared, and the scent of nutmeg burned my nostrils. Her whispers turned into chanting, and light poured out of her hands as she held them in front of her.

Nausea rooted in my gut as the room outside of the circle of protection began spinning. Or was it the shadows that were creating the illusion of spinning? It felt like we were in the eye of a hurricane or tornado.

Although I knew how to cast the spell, I realized that I had absolutely no idea what to expect.

Not breaking my chant, I glanced at Jaxson and Sam—she was either in shock or awe, but Jaxson's gaze was fixed on me. I locked onto it, like a beacon in a storm. I knew how much this didn't sit right with him, but in the end, he'd left the choice up to me. And he was going to stand by it, no matter what. Something about that made my stomach flip.

A rising wind tore at my hair.

"Casey, join your power with ours!" Laurel shouted over the gust. "Savannah, you will need to open yourself up to our magic. Let us in."

Fire and light swirled around me, blending with my shadows. I called it all to me and into me. Like a smith at a forge, I was the iron, while they were the heat and hammer, molding and shaping the power I called forth. The shadowy ribbons of my magic suddenly grew hard.

I gasped, and my back arched off the stone as an unexpected wave of sorrow rose from the depths of my soul and flooded my chest. A choked sob escaped my throat as every muscle fiber clenched and my vision darkened. I couldn't see Jaxson, but I felt his presence reaching for me.

"She must do this alone! Do not risk breaking the circle." Laurel's voice echoed through my warring mind.

I fought against the rollercoaster of dread, sadness, and deep heartache that pulsed through me, tearing apart my insides like a cyclone. I gritted my teeth as my mind felt like it would break. What. The. Fuck. Was. Happening. To. Me?

My skin began to crawl, and a low rumbling rose around me. Could the others hear that?

The rumbling grew into a growl that shook the building to its core, and my heart seized as the wound in my shoulder began to burn.

The Dark Wolf God had arrived.

27

Savannah

I gnashed my teeth together as I felt *his* cold presence sinking into my body, more strongly than it had ever before. Had I somehow stepped out of the circle of protection? I gasped for air, but the weight of the shadows crushed against my chest.

Everything was a dark fog.

Panic gripped my heart, and I forgot the spell. I called every ounce of magic I could still summon and desperately pushed against the presence of the Dark God.

You cannot have me.

In the distance, I swore I heard Sam's and Jaxson's voices. I sensed their agitation. Anger.

"I don't know," my aunt said.

What didn't she know? But I couldn't open my eyes. It took every ounce of strength I had to fight the press of the Dark God's magic.

Let me in. The words echoed in my mind until I couldn't tell who they belonged to anymore—my aunt or the god.

Then the dam broke, and my magic crumbled all around me.

A force slammed into my torso, and I gasped as a dark, electric power spread through my body. I'd felt the same thing moments before I'd attacked Sam in the Dreamlands.

I raged against the Dark God's control, but my fangs and claws slipped out, and the beast inside of me surged toward the surface.

Darkness wrapped around my heart, and an overwhelming power settled within me—no words could quite describe it. All-consuming. Immense. Divine.

He was magnificent. I wanted to lose myself in his power, like an addict giving in to the rush of dopamine coursing through their system. I was spinning in it, a shooting star soaring through the cosmos, unaware of the world below...until my consciousness returned in a rush.

Fight!

A piercing scream deafened my ears, and I realized it was mine. I struggled, but my arms and legs were pinned. Agony rocked through me as my bones snapped and my sinews stretched, preparing for a shift. But into what?

This didn't feel right. In fact, everything about this felt...wrong.

Wolfie, where are you? I howled.

Submit, the dark voice commanded.

Rage bubbled up my throat, and I thrashed under my captor's grip, but it was iron.

Jaxson's voice broke through the mind-numbing pain that had seized my body. "Savy, come back to me."

How? I was trapped. The Dark God had sunk his claws into me, and though I was fighting the shift with everything I had, I knew in my heart that it was a losing battle.

How could you win against a god?

Because you're a badass bitch! Wolfie's voice broke through the recesses of my mind.

Elation and a burst of energy surged through me, and I reached for her. *You're back!*

I felt her strength rise as Jaxson's power poured into me through his hands.

I seized their strength. They must have been giving me everything, because even though my insides were torn and fractured, I was indestructible. Luminous. Filled with power like I'd never had before.

Get out! I roared.

Together, my wolf and I threw our strength against the Dark God. My wolf howled, and then something tore as we ejected him from our body.

His snarl of rage echoed through my mind, but that horrible weight was gone from my soul. Well, *almost* gone. My wound still burned as if he still had a claw in me, one I couldn't tear free. I collapsed back onto the hard floor, gasping. The stone burned, but I barely had the strength to move.

"Savannah!"

I forced my eyes open. Jaxson looked down at me, his features stricken with pain and fear. He wrapped his strong arms around me and cradled my head in his hands.

"She must stay in the circle!" my aunt yelled. "She must bind her wolf *now*!"

Bind my wolf? My mind wheeled like a top until I remembered where I was.

What are we doing here? Wolfie asked.

She was back. And oh, my God...

"She is mine!" The Dark Wolf God's voice shook the floor beneath me.

He's here! Right here!

With a gasp, I raised myself onto my elbows. Shadows and flaming embers spun through the air outside of the circle of protection, and inside the swirling vortex was the Dark Wolf God, like a prince of darkness in human form.

His beauty was staggering, a mix of shadow and flame and power. All-consuming. He stalked around the circle like a predator, testing its strength, looking for weaknesses.

Terror filled my body as his divine gaze locked on me.

Wolfie surged against my ribs. *Let me out. I'll tear his throat out.*

I struggled to hold her back.

The Dark God paused and cocked his head to the side and his face darkened with sinister fury. "Your wolf does not know that you are planning to bind her? I thought you, of all your kind, would be different."

Shame hit me like a slap to my face.

Bind me? He's lying, right? Wolfie whimpered. *What's going on?*

I rolled onto my hands and knees. *I have to, Wolfie. Just for a little while. He's using you against me. I promise I'll let you out once we find a way to defeat this fucker.*

Her pain and betrayal tore through my heart like a dagger. *You can't lock me away again! I don't understand!*

Tears streamed down my cheeks, wetting the etched runes in the stone below. *I have no other choice! I can't give him control. It's the only way to keep the pack safe.*

Don't do this, Savy! Wolfie pleaded.

Wolfie... I was sobbing now. The black stone slick beneath me. A crash ricocheted through the room, followed by a heart-wrenching roar.

"Uh, Ma..." Casey said. "Let's get this show on the road. That fucker is breaking through the magic barrier."

The Dark God howled again and banged against the protective circle. The air between him and us pulsed and shimmered as the spells weakened.

Laurel knelt beside me, shouting over the wind in the room.

"Savannah. Listen to me—you must finish the spell. I can't keep him at bay for long."

Panic and fear and regret tore through me.

"No! I don't want to do this!" I cried. "You said this was my choice."

She reached for me. "Trust—"

The Dark God's magic poured back into me. I lashed out with a clawed hand and snarled in a voice that wasn't my own, "I am his!"

Laurel jerked away just in time, and before I could fight off the possession, the transformation took me again. My spine cracked, and my mouth turned into snapping jaws.

Jaxson pinned me and held my wrists against the ground. Sadness cut his features, but his resolve was like iron. "Come back to me, Savannah."

His alpha presence slammed into that of the Dark God's, and I was crushed between them. Their magic fought and churned, until suddenly I was free. I stopped the shift.

Laurel reappeared beside Jaxson and looked down at me with anguish in her eyes. "I'm sorry, honey. We must act now. Finish the spell. Bind your wolf."

Sam dropped beside me. "It's going to be okay."

It wouldn't be okay until Wolfie and I were free of the Dark God's power.

My head rolled to the side. Casey stood at the boundary, arms raised, pouring flame and power into the circle of protection that held the Dark God at bay. Laurel was inches away, though I'd nearly just killed her. Sam, the friend I trusted more than anyone, was crouched beside me. She extended her claws and looked beyond the barrier as if somehow, she could fight the Dark God herself.

And Jaxson. My heart...

This really was the only way I could protect myself and the people I cared about.

Tears brimmed as I squeezed my eyes shut and began to chant the spell with all my strength and power. Seconds later, Laurel began chanting along with me.

Wolfie's howls sliced through my mind as I lay there on the hard floor, Jaxson holding my limbs like I was a sacrifice. And in a sick kind of way, I sort of was. Or at least, Wolfie was.

Please forgive me.

"You call yourselves wolves?" the Dark God roared. "How dare you do this? Without your wolves, there is nothing worth saving."

His magic raged against me, but with Jaxson's strength, I held him at bay.

My body shook with anger, but I wove our magic around me, forging bonds of fire and light and shadow. Iron bonds wrapped around the beautiful part of my soul that I had come to love—my twin, my wolf.

A weight clamped down on me, and my eyes sprang open. I gasped in pain and horror at the sudden hollowness inside.

The light from the glowing runes around us faded. The Dark God was gone, and so was my wolf.

In her place was a fury at Dragan, who had cut me. At the Dark God, who'd forced this on me. And at myself, for not being able to find another way.

I would free her. And I would have my vengeance, no matter the cost.

Though I wanted to scream until my lungs bled, it was all I could manage just to roll to my side and whisper, "I'll release you, Wolfie. I promise."

But there was no response.

28

Jaxson

One moment, the Dark Wolf God was beating his fists through Laurel's magic ring of protection, and the next, he was gone.

His absence left a vacuum that my shame, guilt, and anger readily filled. The flames that had been whipping around the room seconds ago were extinguished, and the shadows had dissipated, but not those that were still inside my heart.

Ashes drifted to the floor outside of the circle of runes, which had lost their glow.

"Holy shit," Casey said as he dropped to his knees, spent. Laurel looked gray and completely drained. How much power would it take to keep a god at bay?

Almost too much. I'd almost lost Savannah to him. I'd done what I had to, and I'd never forgive myself for it.

I brushed a strand of hair from her cheek. "Are you okay?"

Her eyes locked on mine. "She's gone. I will never be okay until my wolf is back."

I nodded and pulled her onto my lap, cradling her as she buried her face in my shoulder. Her tears dampened my shirt, and the aching hollowness in my chest spread through the rest of me like a sickness taking root.

My wolf had gone silent, but I felt his anxious pacing in my soul.

I'd seen the Dark God take control. I knew that it had to be done. But I wouldn't be able to forgive myself for not finding another way.

For a long time, no one spoke as Savannah's emotions poured out. But finally, she wiped her cheeks and reluctantly climbed to her feet. "I'm going to fucking destroy him," she swore. "I'm going to get my fucking wolf back."

Her eyes were hard and her fury burning, but that couldn't hide from me what was really in her heart: defeat, grief, and loss.

"We're here for you. We'll get you through this," Casey said, squeezing her shoulder. "And when this is over, I don't care if you go back to being a wolf or not."

Savannah smiled weakly and pulled her cousin into her arms. "I'm going back. Don't get used to this."

Sam still knelt at the side of the circle, brooding in her thoughts.

"What's wrong?" I asked.

As if I'd just pulled her from a dream or nightmare, she blinked the fog from her eyes. "The Dark God...what the fuck, Jax? That was..."

I'd never seen Sam this disjointed before, and she'd seen some shit.

"A close one." Laurel finished. "He wasn't supposed to be here."

"His chains are loosening," Sam whispered. "If we'd just recharged the last seal...then—"

My fists clenched as frustration seeped into my veins. "It doesn't matter. The past is the past. We need to lick our wounds and find a way to stop him."

"I agree," Laurel said. "I didn't realize how powerful he was. We must act quickly. *Together*. If he truly is returning to Magic Side, we'll need the help of the Order."

"He'll attack Dockside," Savy muttered. "He draws power from wolves. It'll be there, where he's strongest."

"We can speak to the archmages, come up with a plan," Laurel said. "We're not on good terms, but we can bury the hatchet to protect the city."

"So can the pack," I growled.

Casey whistled and cocked his head sideways. "Wait a second, is the alpha of Dockside agreeing to work with both the LaSalles and the Order? I never thought I'd see the day..."

I wasn't in the mood to deal with Savannah's idiotic cousin. I grabbed my jacket from the corner and gave him a passing glance. "Careful. You might not."

Savannah strode to the other side of the room and held out her hand.

My blood turned cold as the bronze Soul Knife materialized in her palm. She rammed it down into a crack in the stone, and walked back to her aunt. Holding out her hand, she said, "I need you to break the spell that connects me to the blade. I have to get rid of it."

Laurel took Savannah's wrist in hers and began to trace lines over her skin. Glowing spirals of symbols appeared on Savy's palms, and then, with a flash and the sound of swarming bees, they dissipated into curls of nutmeg-scented smoke.

Savannah threw her arms around her aunt. "Thank you."

"I wish you didn't have to carry so much," she whispered. "I wish that I could do more."

Eventually, Savy slipped out of her arms. "You've freed me from the Dark God and the Soul Knife. That's enough for one day."

Savannah turned to retrieve the blade, then hesitantly

looked toward me. "Can you take it until the archmages can put it in the Vault? I've carried it long enough."

I would carry anything for her. Whatever she needed.

As I wrenched the knife out of the crack, its sinister energy tingled along my arm.

Evil.

It was the blade that had wounded her, that had let the Dark God in.

Not wanting to touch it any longer than we had to, I slipped it through my belt. "The sooner we get rid of this, the better."

"Hold on." Laurel scooped up the spell she'd placed on the floor earlier, folded it, and handed it to Savannah. "Take this. For when you're ready to unbind your wolf. Between the two of you" —her eyes flashed to me—"you'll have no trouble at all."

Of that, I wasn't so sure.

29

Jaxson

The lowball glass rang against the marble countertop as I set it down. I poured a generous helping of whiskey and swallowed it, then measured out another. The amber liquid burned but did nothing to appease the demons clawing at my soul.

How the fuck did it come to this?

The events of the day flashed before me. Handing over the Soul Knife to the Order. Hours spent making plans with the archmages.

But like a storm cloud hanging over it all, I saw the pain and grief in Savannah's eyes as she bound her wolf. As I helped her do it.

Even when I shut my eyes, her face was there, tortured and heartbroken—an image burned into my mind forever.

I snarled, a recriminating whisper beneath my breath, "Fuck you, Laurent, you bastard."

Guilt and shame festered inside me like a disease. I downed the whiskey and slammed the glass onto the counter, sending a fine crack through the crystal.

I was her mate, for fuck's sake. This—*this*—was exactly the sort of thing I was supposed to protect her from, and yet, I'd failed.

Every fiber of my body had screamed at me to break off the spell. Instead, I stood by—hell, I'd pinned Savannah down—while Laurel chained her wolf. Once, I was ready to gut Laurel LaSalle for the same sorcery, but now, I was complicit in it.

Beyond unforgiveable.

Scrubbing a hand over my face, I poured another drink and stalked into the living room, where I sat down on the couch. The quiet sounds of Savannah moving upstairs filtered down, and a deep ache settled in my chest.

How could she even look at me after what we'd done?

My thoughts whirled as I searched every corner of my mind for some other path we could have taken, for a way to make it all go away. But the liquor slowly moved through my veins, and exhaustion settled over me. The fight was taking its toll.

Kicking off my shoes, I laid back against the couch and closed my eyes. I just needed a goddammed minute of quiet. A moment to breathe.

What would it have been like to live without a sword hanging over our heads? My thoughts drifted to the forests up north, where I'd gone to run my wolf as a youth. I would take Savannah there, to a quiet land with trees and waterfalls and plenty of game. I'd give anything just to be able to hunt there with her, to run without fear or monsters at our back. I could practically smell the woods around me and could feel my paws digging into the moss and moldering leaves as I sprinted through the trees.

And then, I was dreaming.

Branches and brush dragged against my sides as I ran. I could sense her running somewhere nearby.

But this wasn't the forest of my youth. I knew the strange vibration of the place—the Dreamlands. *His domain.*

A rush of scents and signatures pummeled my senses, but amidst it all, one thing stood out like a hundred blazing suns—the scent of forest fire, a searing cold that burned like dry ice, and the taste of charcoal and ash. The signature of the Dark Wolf God.

Pure hatred replaced the elation of the run. Would I never be free of him?

With my senses sharpened to a point, I wove cautiously through the forest of gnarled trees. The sonofabitch had brought me here for a reason, and I had no illusion that I was safe in his realm.

Finally, a faint glow pierced the dark woods ahead. Bloodlust urged me to charge forward, but I fought it back and slowed my pace.

I bent under a fallen trunk and stepped into a clearing. A set of stone stairs led to a platform within the ruins of an ancient building. A single arched doorway and several partially collapsed walls were all that was left. A portal?

Suddenly, I sensed the presence of others—wolves all around me, lurking at the edge of the pines.

Was Savannah here?

Before I could search for her, the air cracked with magic, and a low rumble vibrated the space. The air within the archway tore open in a rift of blue fire.

Then the Dark God stepped through, flames licking across his body.

An arc of power swept over the space, and I braced myself as it tore through the clearing, pummeling me with rocks and leaves. Branches snapped and creaked behind me as the magic dissipated into the trees.

Wolves whimpered in terror.

Baring my teeth, I gave a low growl and stepped forward to challenge him. *Get the fuck out of my dreams.*

"Dreams are my domain, Jaxson," the Dark God growled. "You will listen to what I have to say."

His voice shook the ground, and the vibrations thrummed in my chest.

"Your world is dying, and I know you sense it," the god said, clenching his hand. Suddenly, the forest was gone, replaced by a mirage of brick buildings and skyscrapers. Chicago.

"They call this civilization, but it is destruction. They poison everything they touch. They spread death and disease and misery," the Dark God growled.

My gaze was drawn to the trash lining the roads and littering the parks. A haze of exhaust hung about the tall buildings; the sounds of blaring horns emanated from the traffic-filled streets.

Out across Lake Michigan, clouds of soot rose from the steel mills that marred the Indiana Dunes where Savy loved to run, and rusty slurry poured into the water where I'd seen her swim.

"Do you not see that there is no limit to what they would destroy to gain the slightest comfort?"

In my mind, I saw the forest of my childhood overrun with bulldozers. It was replaced by visions of strip mines filled with toxic water. I shut my eyes, but the images of destruction and pollution came fast and furious, until revulsion knotted my stomach.

"You are all complicit," the Dark God snarled. "You drive their cars and wear their clothes, but you are not one of them. You are better, something more—wolfborn. There is still a part of you that is pure. That is wild and beautiful and worth saving. But you are trapped in a prison of concrete and steel."

The Dark God turned to the wolves beginning to cautiously approach. "I offer you freedom. Discard the shackles of your human life—the clothes, the phones, the masks you wear to hide your true form. Help me heal the land and cure the disease that infects it."

The breeze picked up, becoming violent and turbulent. Plumes of flames and smoke billowed into the air as Chicago's skyscrapers collapsed one after the other. People who'd escaped the buildings were incinerated by the violent windstorm of flame until there was nothing but desolation, and their ashes choked my lungs.

The Dark God's voice boomed over the chaos. "Your world can be reborn, and you, my chosen people, will rule over it."

Vines and trees sprang from the rubble, snaking over the concrete like writhing creatures, burying all traces of humanity. A pack of wolves raced through the trees that sprouted up, hunting fleeing deer.

For a second, every part of me wanted to chase after and to join the wild pack, but I braced my paws against the earth and bared my fangs in resistance.

I knew him for what he was.

With a guttural growl, I shifted into the form of a man and stood defiantly before him.

"You are not a god of wolves, but of death," I snarled. "And you would remake the world in an image of death."

The god turned on me, his eyes blazing. "Traitor! How dare you accuse me of anything!"

He descended the ancient steps, the scent of disgust and fury emanating off him as he addressed the gathered wolves. "You helped a coven of sorcerers bind the wolf of another werewolf! An alpha who would do that to one of his packmates no longer deserves the trust of his pack, but a man who could do that to his own mate—now *he* is a monster."

Rage consumed my thoughts, even as guilt tore at my soul. But before I could lunge, Savannah's voice cut through the clearing.

"*You* are the monster!"

I spun to see her emerge from the trees, naked and fully human.

"Look what the sorceress has done!" the Dark God shouted. "Just as humans destroy that which is wild, her coven took what was pure and good and tore it from her soul, leaving only corruption. If sorcerers could to this to their own blood, what makes you think they will hesitate to do it to all of you? They will tame you and imprison you."

"*You* did this!" Savannah shouted at him, and strode forward, the shadows and trees quaking with her fury. "*You* left me no choice."

"There is always a choice," the Dark God hissed. "You were my chosen, a twin-soul born to wake me from my slumber and be my avatar. You were *mine*."

"I am my own," Savannah snarled, and leapt from the trees. The shadows whipped around her like a building storm. I felt her power and rage shaking the stones beneath our feet. "And I won't let you take my city, my pack, or my wolf."

The Dark God laughed. "But I will."

His callous confidence sent rage pulsing through my veins. I knew I couldn't kill a god, but I sure as hell was going to try. With a roar, I sprang forward, claws out.

Something shattered, and I stumbled to the ground amidst broken glass.

Everything was wrong. Where was the Dark God? The forest?

Where was my mate?

30

Jaxson

My vision slowly shifted into focus. I was in my living room, standing unsteadily beside the couch. The whiskey glass lay on the floor, shattered. Early morning sunlight shone through the penthouse windows.

With my heart hammering, I rubbed my throat, which still burned.

Just a dream—but what did that mean anymore?

Footsteps thundered down the stairs, and Savannah emerged, wrapped in a sheet that trailed behind her.

"Jaxson, are you okay? I heard a crash."

I shook my head. "Just a nightmare. Sorry."

"I had one, too. You were there, and the Dark God. I saw visions of him destroying the city, and I spoke with him..."

My heart slowed to a crawl. Fuck. "I had the same dream."

The shocked silence hung between us. Savannah licked her lips. "Do you think the others—"

I kissed her to quiet her question, one I wasn't sure that I could face.

If our whole pack had had similar dreams, I could soon have chaos on my hands.

Our mouths moved together as we found the sweet solace and comfort that we'd shared two nights before. Once Savy finally relaxed in my arms, I led her into the kitchen to make coffee.

As I started the brew cycle, my phone rang, and I glanced down. Regina.

I swiped it off the counter. "Yes?"

Her worried voice cut across the line and straight into my gut. "I just got five phone calls, Jax. Everyone in the pack has had the same dream, and it's bad. I had it, too."

I fought to keep my breath steady and my mind in control. "It was the Dark God. This is his magic."

There was a pregnant pause before she spoke again. "The council has called a meeting, Jaxson. You need to be there in three hours. I tried to head them off, but you'll need to explain. People are freaking out, and there's only so much damage control that I can do."

What the fuck? How was this moving so fast?

"I didn't call a meeting," I snarled.

"Your father did."

For a second, I didn't know what to say. I just hung up as those three words sent my mind spiraling into rage and darkness.

"So everyone knows what I am now?" Savannah asked from behind me. Her voice was quiet but on the edge of despair. "That I chained my wolf? That I'm the twin-soul that's meant to take all their souls?"

"They know what we did," I said as I turned. Her expression broke my heart. "They may not understand the rest."

"Are they going to turn on me?"

Protectiveness surged through me, and I closed the distance with her, pulling her close. "No. Never."

Savannah peered up at me, and that feeling of being unable to breathe returned. Gods, she was so beautiful. And broken. And she didn't believe me.

Before I realized what I was doing, I reached up and traced my thumb over her cheek. So soft and warm. I'd exile anyone who tried to lay a finger on her. "Let them try to do anything. I haven't met a soul who could take you on."

She smiled at that, and my heart swelled.

I'd fallen into the deep end with this woman, and though I'd fucked up by not realizing what was going on sooner, I could still make things right.

She leaned into my touch, her gaze intense like she was trying to reach into my mind. "What do we do?" she whispered.

I released my hand and stepped back. She must have felt the loss of contact equally as strongly as I did because her brows pinched together. Sadness and confusion swirled around her, but I couldn't move past the festering guilt inside me. I needed to set things right.

"We meet with the council." I scooped up my phone, which was now exploding with calls and messages. "They're panicking because they don't know what's happening or what to do. We need to show them that we have a plan—that we have the Order and archmages on board."

"Do you trust the council? Regina was going to drag me in front of them for killing a wolf in self-defense. What do you think they'll do now that they know I'm the one who's supposed to steal their wolves?"

"The pack and the council don't know that. They know that you're tied up in the prophecy, but the exact words are only known by a few. I didn't know until I spoke with my father."

"And unfortunately, he'll be there. And they know I've chained my wolf as well..."

My father had warned me once that if I found a twin-soul, I should *kill them. No matter who it is, no matter the cost, do it without hesitation.*

I nearly rammed my fist through the wall. "You've made sacrifices for the pack, Savannah—sacrifices that no werewolf should ever have to make. We'll remind them of that."

"Jaxson—"

I lifted her chin to look her in the eyes. "Do you trust me?"

She searched my expression before finally admitting, "Yes."

"This is my pack, not my father's. They will follow me. All that matters is defeating the Dark God, and we all need each other to do that."

It will likely be a losing battle, my wolf said.

I knew it. But sometimes, life didn't give you a choice. When it set you on a path, there was only one direction to go: forward, even if it meant to your doom. Deep down, I'd known this the moment I'd met Savannah.

This woman would be my salvation and my ruin.

31

Savannah

Three hours later, I found myself standing in front of a portal that would whip us from Magic Side and drop me straight into the clutches of the werewolf council.

Last night, I hadn't thought that my life could get any more fucked up. At the time, I'd just been the awful bitch who'd bound her wolf. This morning, *everyone knew*. That, and also that I was the herald of the end times.

Was I just supposed to march in and beg for the council's mercy?

The other option, of course, was to run. Until I crossed the portal's threshold, there was still a way out.

The portal was in an old stone gazebo, not far from the Garden of the Wolves. The hidden doorway opened into the dark gray nothingness of the ether. No horrid gargoyles or monsters guarded the way.

It was what was on the other side that was the problem.

I nervously adjusted the backpack hanging over my shoulder. I could feel the Moon's magic radiating off the moonstone inside, and it helped me steel my nerve. "Where does this lead, exactly?"

"The gathering place," Sam said. "A private island in Lake Michigan. It's a spot where the leaders of all the Great Lakes packs can meet in secret."

Great. How convenient. No witnesses.

"How many pack leaders are we talking about?" I asked, my voice betraying a chagrining amount of trepidation. I'd assumed the council would be Magic Side wolves, faces that I knew, or at least that knew of me. Fatal assumption.

Jaxson adjusted his leather jacket and shrugged. "This was short notice, so probably a dozen. But they'll bring representatives of their packs, so maybe thirty or forty wolves."

That was a couple dozen more than I'd been expecting. "Is this wise? It sounds like it could go badly."

Jaxson studied my face as if he were deciding something, then finally spoke. "I'll be honest—maybe. Our pack lives in the city, and we're fairly open minded. Many of the alphas in our council are traditionalists, and they're all familiar with your family and hate them. Now that the Dark God is breaking free, they'll be looking for someone to blame. At this point, that's us."

More than any of his words, the tone of his voice was what raised the hair on the back of my neck. "And yet, we're going."

"Fuck the council," he snapped. "We're trying to save everybody's asses. We're not going to tuck our tails. We're going to show up and control the conversation so that men like my father don't."

I took a deep breath, looking for the same internal confidence. Unfortunately, the voice whose confidence I needed right now was gone, and there was only a sorrowful void in her place. My stomach tightened. While I'd lived without Wolfie for most of my life, there was no going back to that existence—not after knowing what it was like to have her as a part of me.

I needed her.

I closed my eyes as I mustered my courage. What would Wolfie say? Probably something like, *Screw those guys. We fought the Dark Wolf God himself. The council is nothing. Just nip them in the butt, and they'll go running.*

Stifling a glimmer of a smile, I jammed my hands in my pockets and nodded to the portal. "Okay, let's get this over with. Show me to the execution."

Jaxson reached out and lightly squeezed my shoulder. "Defeating the Dark God is all that matters at this point, not being a twin-soul, not binding your wolf. We need to make sure the council understands that. We have a plan to stop him—we just need to sell it. Don't show fear. I won't let anything happen to you."

I studied the lines of his face. Though I could feel his confidence, I sensed an unspoken *but*. I was going to be fine—*but* what about him? Although I'd gone against his wishes, he'd stood at my side. What did that mean for the alpha? Would the pack leaders turn on him for being complicit in a choice I'd made?

My heart accelerated, and when he turned to go through the portal, I held back.

Jaxson glanced at me, questioning.

"Are you going to be okay?" I asked. "Could this council of alphas hold *you* accountable?"

The corner of his mouth twitched up. "I'd like to see them try."

That wasn't a no.

"I'm worried about this, Jaxson."

"Don't be." And with that, my mate vanished into the portal.

Fuck.

I sighed in exasperation, and then, with my heart drumming,

I stepped through. My stomach spun as the portal sent me hurtling through the grayness of the ether.

After a disorienting moment, my feet hit solid ground, and I tumbled out of the portal into a dark evergreen forest. Tall pines loomed all around us, though I also caught the scents of beech, maple, and moss drifting through the woods. The soft wind rustled the needles and carried the sound of waves and the scent of lake water, not far off.

The calm before the storm.

Sam stumbled out after me and gave me a thumbs-up.

"Ready?" Jaxson asked.

I nodded, and he began leading us down a faint trail of crushed moss and brush. My nose flared at the scent of wolves, though it wasn't as strong as it should have been. One consequence of binding my wolf meant that my senses had diminished. Along with my ability to shift, I'd also lost my strength.

My gut twisted. Could I still heal?

My mind began a new kind of calculus, remembering how many times the Dark God's minions had nearly killed me. Our next showdown would require a completely different approach if I was going to live.

It wasn't likely either way, was it?

Probably sensing my distress, Sam sidled up and took my arm, though there was barely enough room to walk side by side. She gave me a strained but genuine smile. "Don't worry. Jax is technically head of the council, so even if they've gone behind his back, he'll know how to handle them. And if not, I'm here to crack some skulls."

Guilt and shame soured my mouth, and I squeezed her arm to me. "Thanks for being here, Sam. After what happened the other day, it means everything. You need to know that I'm really, *really* sorry. What I did—it's tearing me up."

She scoffed. "Are you still worried about that scratch? It was nothing. Remember, I grew up in a pack. Life was *rough*." She patted the arm looped through mine. "I broke this forearm alone three times. You've got nothing on seven-year-old werewolves."

"It was more than a scratch," I whispered as I tried to keep my emotions under control. I'd flat-out mauled my best friend in Magic Side. I'd never unsee what I'd done—her blood dripping from my hands.

Her eyes went gold, and even with my weakened senses, I could smell her abject hatred. "*You* didn't attack me. *He* did, using *you* like a weapon. Do you know how pissed off that makes me? He used *my girl* to hurt me. That's fucked up twice over. That bastard will get what's coming to him."

The memory of the Dark God's roars of outrage after Sam had pelted him with the moonstone brought a thin smile to my lips. "You saved our asses, and you sure pissed him off. I don't know which I appreciate more."

Her eyes twinkled. "Man, if I had more moon magic, I'd vaporize that asshole. Just holding those moonstones felt like I was glowing from the inside out. Is that what your magic feels like when you use it?"

A shiver ran through me. I'd acclimated to the feeling of my magic—hell, I was already taking it for granted—but there was no denying that my magic felt dark, like ice water running over my skin.

It felt like *his*.

It wasn't the first time I'd had the thought, and doubts nagged at me. Was the sorcerer part of me just as corrupted as the werewolf? Had it been so from the start?

Sam gently nudged my shoulder. "You okay? I sort of lost you, there."

I forced a smile. "I wish Casey could have seen what you did. His eyes would have popped out of his head with jealousy."

She laughed. "That, I would like to see."

Before long, the scent of wolves strengthened, and the trees above began to thin. I could feel their signatures and could practically taste their anticipation.

We ascended a small slope, heading toward what I assumed was the center of the island. As we climbed, I tightened my grip on the straps of my bag and kept my gaze locked on Jaxson's back. I let each footstep be a hammer, forging my resolve into a blade of steel. I'd been wronged. I'd been toyed with. I'd been pushed to the brink.

But I was *not* going to be pushed any longer.

Jaxson brushed away the last of the branches as we emerged into a clearing near the top of the hill.

Two jutting boulders formed a gateway into an open area beyond—a natural amphitheater of stones. I could see and smell dozens of wolves sitting in the space, and my mouth went dry. *Here we go.*

Four werewolves blocked our way forward—two were in their human forms, while the others were wolves. Their build betrayed their role: muscle.

A woman with long gray hair and dark eyes glared at us. I could feel the heat of her signature burning brightly. Definitely an alpha.

She inclined her head. "Jaxson."

He nodded in return. "Camila."

The tone of their voices was not kind.

Her eyes flicked to me, then back at him. "The council is waiting."

Jaxson tilted to look past her, and his fists tightened. "Everyone is already assembled? You met before we arrived?"

"We had to discuss procedures and options. This is a grave situation, Jaxson. I'm not going to lie, what you two have done..."

She looked at me but didn't give me the dignity of ending the sentence.

I wasn't going to give these wolves the satisfaction of watching me grovel while they treated me like a criminal. Stepping up close beside Jaxson, I said, "You're right. This *is* a grave matter. The Dark God is loose, and we're all screwed if we don't do something about it. So if you all haven't spent your time making a plan for how to defeat him, then you'd better put away your claws and hear what we have to say."

She gave me a warning smile and stepped aside, waving us through. "I think we are all *very* interested in what you have to say."

Every instinct I had told me to run, but I fought them down. I wouldn't show fear. I strode toward the entrance to the natural amphitheater with my chin held high.

Camila reached out and stopped Sam from proceeding. "You cannot enter."

She was taken aback. "What? Why? I'm with them. I've sat in on dozens of meetings in the past."

The gray-haired woman shook her head. "The Dark God changes everything. This gathering is for alphas and elders only. And the accused."

"Accused?" Jaxson growled. "I thought this was a council of wolves, not a kangaroo court."

Camila stiffened. "This is not a trial. Yet. But you will need to account for your actions, or we will take steps, despite your position on the council."

Sam snarled at the woman. "This is bullshit."

At that, the two black wolves rose off their haunches and moved toward her, teeth bared and menacing.

Sam drew her claws. "Don't even think about trying anything. I can take you both."

I instinctively raised my hands to draw my claws as well, but there were none there. *Shit.*

Camila smiled, though her voice was pregnant with warning. "A disruption would not reflect well on your friends, Sam. Considering how much hangs in the balance, I would put your claws away. Do you need to be escorted back through the portal to Magic Side, or will you wait by the lake for our decision?"

Jaxson growled, but I knew we had to deescalate before this got any worse. We had to persuade these wolves, not fight them. I reached out and gently touched my friend's shoulder.

"Go, Sam," I said softly, trying to muster a confident air.

"Fuck!" She snarled and withdrew her claws. "Are you sure? There are a lot of wolves here, but most of them are toothless by now."

I held back a smile as Camila tensed. "Thanks. We're good."

"Stay close," Jaxson said. "Call Regina. Let her know that there's bullshit about to go down, and to be ready."

Sam withdrew, frustration and anger tugging at the corners of her expression.

With a thankful nod, I headed toward the circle of wolves, but before we'd gone more than three paces, Sam jumped up on a large boulder and turned to face the wolves in the stone ring beyond. "Listen up, alphaholes!"

All faces turned to her, and my gut plunged. What was she doing?

"Since Savannah Caine discovered our world one month ago, she's been abducted, hunted, and nearly killed by rogue wolves operating in your lands! And when pack members turned traitor and tried to murder her family, she kept her mouth shut to protect our pack—even before she was one of us!"

Sam's eyes blazed gold, and her voice vibrated with anger. "She rescued me from blood drainers, and when a fucking sorcerer trapped two dozen of our wolves in the Dreamlands,

Savannah went back in for them even after she escaped. She nearly died getting them out."

"Get down," Camila hissed. "How can you defend someone who bound their wolf?"

Sam leapt to the ground in front of the gray-haired alpha. "She gave up her wolf to protect our people!"

She stepped around Camila, up to where the black wolves blocked her way. "How dare you people judge her for that? She's more wolf than any of you, and she's done more to oppose the Dark God than any of you have or will."

With that, she spun and stalked off toward the woods. "Fine. I said my piece. I'm fucking calling Regina."

I heard the heavy murmur of the council behind me, but I could think of nothing but the crumbling sensation in my chest. I'd never had a friend like Sam in my life. "Thank you," I whispered as she disappeared into the trees. Her words meant more to me than anything, and I could feel Jaxson radiating with pride.

"Is she going to be trouble?" Camila asked, her gaze locked on Sam.

Jaxson gave her a wicked grin. "Only if you are. Let's go."

With that, he shoved past her, and together, we stepped into the ring of wolves.

32

Savy

One glance at the expressions on the gathered werewolf council made it clear that this was going to get dark.

Some were in human form, and some were wolves. I was almost overwhelmed to be in proximity to so many powerful signatures, elders and alphas both. It was a sea of dangerous and unfamiliar faces. The loremaster was the only one I recognized from our pack.

All eyes locked onto us, but I kept my gaze fixed straight ahead, focused on one werewolf sitting directly across from us. His face was like Jaxson's but much older. He lacked the perfection of my mate's features but none of his ferocity.

Jaxson's father.

His expression stopped me in my tracks: abject hatred.

My stomach spun. For all his fury, Jaxson had never once turned his eyes on me in that way, and I thanked God he hadn't.

Screw this. I'm done being judged.

I raised my chin and stepped into the ring. My wolf might be bound, but I was still a *wolf*.

We've got this, I said to Wolfie, though I knew she wasn't there.

If, somehow, we lived through this and I could release her, would she ever speak to me again after what I'd done?

I closed my eyes and let the despair have its moment. When I opened my lids, I was all fire, while Jaxson was practically an inferno of rage beside me.

"You came," Jaxson's father said flatly, holding back the anger in his voice.

Before I took another breath, they were both in the center of the ring, face to face, staring each other down. While his father was built like a mountain, my mate still loomed over him and commanded the attention of every wolf in the clearing.

"What are you doing?" Jaxson bit out. "You're no longer alpha of our pack. You abandoned that role."

"The chairwoman asked me step in, if necessary. We both agreed that the council had to be called, so I did."

Jaxson bent his head low to his father's ear and spoke quietly, though we could all hear. "Why not come to me? I'm the head of this council."

"Because you should have come to us. Because there's no time. Because the current head of the council has abandoned his pack and his wits, bewitched by a LaSalle. Someone had to do something."

"Do something? We've been fighting every day to stop this. To save our pack," Jaxson snarled, his voice razor sharp with a fury I'd never heard before. "Where have you been? Fishing?"

His father's voice remained quiet and level. "I didn't realize that the alpha was harboring a twin-soul, or I would have been here in a second and dealt with her myself."

In an instant, Jaxson's shirt ripped along the seams as his body swelled. Fur rippled along his arms as his fangs and claws shot out and his eyes turned the color of the sun—but he stopped the shift right there, holding it in the space between man and wolf with a foot in each of the two worlds, master of both.

That trick required absolute control of your wolf, a thing not many could manage.

"She is my mate," he growled in a voice that was neither his nor his wolf's. "No one touches her."

His words dropped like a hammer, and shocked noises filtered through the council. Jaxson's father's expression hardened, and his pupils dilated. "So the rumors are true, then. It's worse than I feared."

Jaxson didn't respond, nor did his gaze leave his father's face.

If I'd had the strength of my wolf senses still, I might have been able to untangle the emotions raging in the space between them. It looked and sounded like the knife edge of violence, but it hid so much more.

Betrayal. Pain. Affection. Pride. Fury.

They were close, or they had been, once.

I swallowed, barely able to breathe from the tension in the air. Finally, his father submitted and stepped away. "Fine. Take your place at the head of this council—but make no mistake, you two are the ones on trial here."

Jaxson looked at the stone where his father had been sitting, a weathered rock wrapped in roots. He turned his back on the council and strode to my side, his eyes burning with gold. "If we are accused, then I will stand by my mate."

I licked my lips. He was transformed and more savage than I'd ever seen him. His power washed over me as he approached, and I had to fight down the raw desire that rose as he took his spot, standing by me while all the others stared.

After a stunned moment, Camila walked to the far end of the court and addressed the gathered wolves. "Now that that's settled, I will run this meeting. We've all shared a dream of the

Dark Wolf God. This woman here—a LaSalle by blood—is a twin-soul and the one who set him free. In accordance with the prophecy, that's enough for us to condemn her. But beyond this crime, they have bound her wolf with sorcery. This is beyond the pale of anything I ever imagined a werewolf could do or would do. I don't see how we can let this stand."

Jaxson tightened his fists. "Savannah is part of my pack. She is under my authority, not yours."

"By tradition, an alpha who sits on the council accepts the council's decision!" shouted a man I didn't recognize. "Are you above our law now?"

"Only if the law no longer stands for what is right."

The gray-haired alpha raised her eyebrows. "Is that a yes, Laurent?"

"The Dark God is loose," Jaxson growled. "We've done everything we can to stop him. You can waste time accusing us of crimes, but you've also seen what's at stake. The threat he poses. We are *all* in peril. Stopping him is the only thing that matters."

Jaxson's father gestured at me. "We are in peril because of *her*. She's the twin-soul who was prophesized to set him free. She's corrupted you and released the Dark God from his prison, can't you see that? She'll take our souls and make us weak before him. We must deal with her here and now to protect our packs and families!"

Jaxson snarled, but before he could lunge at his father, I seized him and pulled him toward me, trying to soothe his rage through our bond.

"I am a wolf. I must stand for myself here," I whispered to him. We both knew it was true.

Slowly, the bloodlust drained from his eyes, and he nodded.

I looked to his father, my eyes hard and accusing. "Yes, I'm a twin-soul. And yes, I released the Dark God. I was trying to stop him, but the game was rigged."

Furious conversation erupted around the circle, but I held up my hand, and the crowd soon grew silent. "Victor Dragan conducted a ritual to bring back the Dark God. It required the sacrifice of a twin-soul. Once the spell was complete, the die was cast."

I looked around the assembly, trying to meet the gaze of every wolf there, even as I came to confront the truth of what had happened myself. "At the time, I didn't realize that it didn't matter which one of us died, just that one of us did. Had Dragan killed me instead, the Dark God would have been released all the same, and you'd be up against Dragan as well."

"You say you're trying to defeat him, but the Dark God said that you are his chosen. What evidence do you have that you're not his puppet?" someone accused.

I unslung my backpack from my shoulder and set it on the ground. Pulling out the glowing moonstone, I raised it high for all to see. Even just holding the orb, I felt the goddess's power in me, calming my fear, giving me strength. "The Moon herself gave us her power to use against him. We fought the bastard in the Dreamlands, and when he returns, we will fight him here."

A stunned silence fell over the crowd

Suddenly, a white-haired man leapt to his feet. "This is preposterous! The *Moon*?"

The loremaster rose. "It is true. The moon mother came to us at Delos. Not in all my years did I imagine I would see that happen. She pledged to help us. To help Savannah. We are not alone."

Shocked whispers swelled around us, but Jaxson's father stood and scowled at the changing tide of emotion. "Whether this story is true or not, we cannot overlook the threat. The prophecy says this woman will steal our souls!"

I spun on him. "That will not happen. The Dark God sought

to control me through my wolf, but I bound her to stop it. That means he can no longer take control of me."

An enormous man rose at the corner of the ring. "You admit to this sinister magic? That you and Jaxson purged your wolf? I don't think this council has ever faced a more perverse act."

Roars and accusations erupted all around me as vibrations of outrage filled the space, and the tide of sentiment shifted.

"We will have order!" Camila shouted, and she glared until conversation faded away to silence. "This is a grave act for which there is *no* precedent. Tell us, what, exactly, have you done to your wolf?"

My voice quavered more than it should have, but I dug my nails into my skin and set my chin in defiance. I would not be judged. "My aunt and I used sorcery to bind my wolf. Once this is over, I will release her again."

"This is the LaSalles' dark magic," Jaxson's father spat. "You know what these monsters are capable of!"

Renewed murmuring broke out through the crowd, and someone growled, "We should have wiped out those sorcerers years ago."

Another shouted, "Fiend!"

Though they didn't move from their spots, the council of wolves seemed to press in all around me as they hurled accusations. I could smell their rage and fear and horror.

All because of me. What I had done.

Anger twisted through my veins. Maybe once, I would have cowered before them, but not now. My wolf had made me stronger than ever before, and that spirit hadn't gone away. I let the strength of my own presence lash out. "Listen up!"

Their words died in their mouths.

I thrust my finger in accusation at the gathered wolves. "When I was a child, my parents bound my wolf to protect me from the likes of *you*. I had to grow up without half my soul and my pack because of *you* and your hatred for my family. Now, I've had to bind my wolf again to protect all of *you* from the Dark God. Tell me how that's fucking fair."

No one answered, and tears of rage clung to the corners of my eyes. "I'm empty, and I miss her more than my own breath. But I would do it again because if not, the Dark God would be right here, right fucking *now*. And he would tear this world to pieces."

Stunned silence fell over the circle. As my words sank in, I knew I had left something unsaid.

"Sam spoke to you from beyond the ring," I continued. "In the Dreamlands, the Dark God took control of my wolf and turned me against her. I nearly killed her. That's why I bound my wolf. To keep him out forever, even if it meant giving up the best part of myself."

Several of the wolves sucked in sharp breaths at my confession, but I raised my hand to hold their tongues. "This is what you need to hear: the Dark God made me turn on my best friend with his power. *That* is why he sent the dream, to manipulate and divide us. To sow fear and turn us against each other. Don't let him distract you from the truth. He's back, and it means the end of the world as we know it if we don't stop him."

I gave Jaxson's father a pointed look, but he turned away.

For a while, no one spoke. No attestations for me, but also no insults hurled against me, either. All of them seemed to be considering my words, speaking now with their wolves in the silent speech of our people.

Finally, the gray-haired alpha stood. "I agree, this dream was sent to divide. And your packmate, whom you wounded, has spoken passionately on your behalf. That bears great weight among our people. Despite her antics, I could smell the truth of her words."

The tightness in my chest began to release, but Camila

hadn't yet finished speaking. "These remain shocking revelations, more than any we've ever faced. The council must deliberate on how to rule. I ask you both to leave while we reach our decision."

My stomach dropped, but I felt Jaxson's signature surge, and when he spoke, it was in a feral voice—a single word that sent a shudder of terror down my spine.

"No."

33

Jaxson

Rage shook my body as I glared at the weak-willed council of alphas.

Fools.

The anger was a mercy, because without it, my chest would have burst with pride. My mate was strong and fearless—and she was staring down two dozen alphas and getting the better of them. Any other wolf would have run.

But now was not the time for pride. It was the time to make the wolves fucking submit.

Camila crossed the distance between us in challenge. "The council will rule on this matter, Jaxson."

The old steel battleship was the alpha of the Superior pack, and she was as cold as the water in Duluth. She wasn't to be trifled with, which was why she was running the meeting.

I stepped up to meet her. "Go ahead and make your ruling, but we will end this discussion right here in the open. Not behind closed doors, where you can hide your shame and treachery."

"That's not what—"

I swept away from her and stalked before the council. "The Dark God is back. The fate of our packs, of the world, is teetering on the brink, and by seeking to punish us, you're wasting time. It doesn't matter what's happened to bring us here, but this is the truth: without the two of us, there's absolutely nothing standing between you and the Dark God."

"The LaSalle woman is prophesized to take our souls," my old friend Mac, the Michigan alpha, growled. "We can't overlook that danger."

I threw my hand out toward Savannah. "This *LaSalle woman* is the only reason we have the slightest chance. How blind has your hatred made you? She killed Victor Dragan before his cult could possess more wolves. She negotiated with the Moon and risked her life to go into the Dreamlands to try to rebind the Dark God. She fought him and lived! Which one of you can make that claim? Which of you could do the same?"

Werewolves shifted uncomfortably around the ring as they faced the truth.

I stepped up to Mac, but my words were for all. "The Dark God sent you a dream to turn you against us. Why? Because we're your only fucking hope, and you know it."

In the stunned silence that followed, I rode their surge of emotion—fear, confusion, desperation— like a wave. The time was right.

I raised my hand. "As head of this council, I call an open vote. I want to see hands right now—in the face of what's coming, who votes to risk having us killed?"

Savannah stiffened but said nothing.

I let a minute of silence tick by. Not one wolf raised a hand or paw. They weren't stupid, just desperate to have some sort of control in the face of the Dark God. But this wasn't the time to cling to control. It was time to let go of old ways and prophecies and face the threat that existed here and now.

And that wasn't Savy or me.

"Who votes we be exiled immediately?" I growled at the shame-faced assembly.

Still nothing. Not one. Camila looked away, as did my father.

I nodded. "Good. It seems you need us right now. And we need you. Help us protect Magic Side."

"So what's this plan of yours?" Mac grumbled as he sat back and crossed his arms.

I looked to Savannah and nodded.

She swallowed hard as the tension passed. "We believe the Dark God will return to Magic Side," she said. "We don't know where he'll strike, but we think he'll open a rift from the Dreamlands. The Order and the LaSalles are preparing containment and banishment spells. We need people to support and protect them—"

My father laughed. "Do you really expect us to work with the *LaSalles* after all they've done to our people? To our family?"

Bitterness worked into the set of my jaw. Of all of them, he should've had my back. *The traitor.*

Then again, he probably thought the same of me. My sister, his favorite, had died trying to wipe out the LaSalles' wolfsbane operation. He'd never forgiven them. I hadn't, either, until I met my mate. It would take him time to do the same, if he ever could.

I met his accusatory glare. "I haven't forgotten what happened to Stephanie, not for one second. But our hands aren't clean, either, and everything is on the line. I've spoken to Laurel. She's ready to bury the hatchet. I am, too."

He studied my face, then looked to Savannah. After a long moment, he shook his head. "I can't."

Then my father turned and left.

His quiet statement shook my heart. There was so much pain and sadness there, bound up so tightly. I wanted to go after him, but now was not the time. I wasn't sure there ever would be a time.

"No fucking way I work with the LaSalles, either," snapped another alpha. "Do you have any idea how much wolfsbane they push into our state?"

Murmurs of agreement boiled up all around, and suddenly, I was losing them.

"Please!" Savannah shouted. "Yes, you hate my family. And with good reason, I know. But we're all in danger. My cousin wove a spell for our pack to protect them from Dragan. They're willing to come to the table. Please, for the sake of all your packs, put aside your grudges until this is over and work with us."

She studied their faces. "Before we left the Moon, she gave us a warning: the Dark God draws his power from werewolves. Don't give him your power by fighting your allies, by quarrelling, by sitting here and doing nothing. Please, help us."

The council members looked around, none wanting to show weakness.

Finally, Camila stood and smoothed her cloak. "What you say is fair, but I think that very few will be willing to work with your family. They might work with the Order. And for those who can look beyond the past, what is it that you need?"

A deep wave of relief surged through me, and Savannah closed her eyes as a heavy weight seemed to slip from her shoulders. When she opened them again, she was almost smiling. "We need knowledge. Everything your loremasters might know that could help us figure out how to stop him. If there are any diviners among you, we need to know where he will open the rift."

Savannah looked to me, and I nodded. "If you don't want to come to face him in person, fine," I said. "But send backup.

Weapons. Anything. And prepare your homes, because if we fall, you'll be next."

We spent the next hour in intense negotiation. Several packs bowed out entirely, but some were willing to send help, or at least to consult their loremasters—which was what we needed, more than anything.

Mac was already texting instructions from Savannah to his pack. After she walked away, he turned to me. "I'm sorry, Jax. I didn't know what you two had done already. After the dream and your father's call, I just got caught up in things."

"I know. We all did."

As the sun moved on, Camila took me aside. "The Superior pack will do what it can to help Magic Side. But make no mistake, you've not acquitted yourself here, Laurent."

Gratitude died on my lips as she continued. "Necessary or not, what was done to Savannah's wolf is unconscionable, and the council cannot abide it. I spoke with the high elders while you were making plans. We're agreed—if you don't undo what you have done, you won't have a seat in this circle. We will not accept you as the alpha of your pack. Only your father. Frankly, I cannot imagine how your pack will follow you, knowing what they do now."

I was to be shunned and replaced by my father? And they thought Magic Side would take that lying down?

I tightened my forearms to keep my claws in check and bent my head to hers. "You can tell the elders that if I can't bring back her wolf once this is over, I'll happily go into exile. But don't you dare ever challenge me again in this way or try to use my father against me."

"He agrees with us, you know."

"I know," I said, my heart aching as I started to walk away.

"And Jaxson..."

I paused at the way her words hung.

"Savannah is fierce and speaks strongly. But we cannot be blind to the prophecy, not when it's been proven right once already. She's a threat. We're letting you both walk away now, but if for one second it looks like she'll turn toward the Dark God, she will need to be dealt with. For the good of all our packs."

I didn't turn around, and when I spoke, my voice was more animal than man. "Let me make this clear. If anyone lays a hand on her, you'll wish the Dark God had gotten to you before I did."

Unable to restrain myself any longer, I left the circle of wolves.

34

Savannah

Jaxson stalked out of the overgrown ring of stones. His posture told me I needed to get to him before he murdered someone, so I broke off my conversation with the Ontario loremaster and hustled through the pines toward the patch of blue sky.

He stood at the edge of the rocky shoreline, overlooking the lake. Rage still coiled around him, so I stepped up and gently placed my hand against his back. I could almost feel his heartbeat and pulsing blood.

I said nothing, just let our connection do its work. Silently, we watched the waves roll in and break on the stones, then tumble out again.

Once his breathing calmed, I traced my fingers lightly along his spine. "Are you okay?"

He grunted. "My wolf was eager to have a conversation with Camila. Are *you* okay? I know it was a shit show, but you impressed a lot of pack leaders today."

"Well, I was certain we were going to get eaten when I stepped into the ring, so mild cooperation is a win."

"Thanks to you. You stood your ground and stared them down. You showed them how the Dark God is manipulating us. You convinced some of them, when I couldn't, to work with your family. A month ago, I would have thought that impossible, yet here we are."

Thankful for the praise, but too embarrassed to accept it, I gave him a wink. "Well, it helps to have an evil eldritch power bearing down on us all."

"You'd make a good alpha."

Regret tugged at me, and I looked back out across the water. "Yeah, if only I had a wolf."

"You will. Once this is over."

"If she forgives me." *If I can forgive myself.*

"She will," he grunted. "If Big Mac can set aside his grudges and work with your family, then your wolf will forgive you."

I shook my head and took his hand. "She's not the same as your wolf, Jaxson. Yours is a part of you. I'm a twin-soul—two separate souls in one body. She's another person, and I just kicked her out of her body because I couldn't control her."

He took my hand and turned toward me. "You did what was necessary to stop the Dark God. The hard choice."

I studied his face. He was smiling for me, but beneath it all, there was so much anger and pain. I reached up and brushed a lock of his hair aside. "Are you really alright? I mean, your own father turned on you today. That can't be easy."

His expression hardened, and he looked out over my shoulder. "I'm sorry you two met this way. Deep down, he's a good man, if hard and stubborn. He was just doing what any alpha would—putting his pack first. Trying to protect them."

"It's not his pack, it's your pack."

Jaxson shook his head absently. "Once an alpha, always an alpha. That's why he moved away."

Frustration and outrage pulsed through me, but I kept it locked down. "He turned on his own son."

Jaxson gave me the stark look of a weathered soldier. "Being alpha means putting the pack first. Always. Before everything, even family. Because thousands of people depend on you for work, for opportunity, for protection. He was trying to do what he thought was right."

I couldn't help but think of my own parents, who sacrificed everything to protect me. Family ties, community, maybe even their lives in the end. Jaxson had none of that.

I suddenly felt very rich and heartbroken, and I squeezed his arm. "That's toxic. You know that, right?"

He shook his head. "It's what being alpha means. It's how my father lived. How my sister lived. It's why I resisted our mate bond at first. I knew that if it came down to my mate or the pack, I would never be able to choose anything over you. That I would no longer be able to do what was right or necessary."

Jaxson had said some of these things before, but I'd never understood how deep the roots of his scars were. How could he watch his own father turn on him and still forgive him? Did he really believe that the man was just doing his duty?

Despite his words, I could sense how much the betrayal had hurt him. The low throb of a remembered pain. Old scars, a constant knife cut, layered over itself again and again.

He'd said many times that his sister was meant to be alpha, that she'd been born for it. I'd thought that he meant he didn't measure up, but I wasn't sure. He'd had the job dropped on him. From what Sam said, his father had broken down and just faded away, and Jaxson had been left holding Magic Side together. Whatever he'd been before that had disappeared.

I brushed my fingers along the edge of his cheek. "Tell me about the time before you were alpha."

He gave me a wistful smile, and I suddenly knew that I

hadn't even scratched the surface of the man beside me. He shook his head at last. "It was another life. It doesn't matter now. I'd have given it up a hundred times over to spend this one with you."

Warmth flushed through me at the soft intensity of his words, his attention. I blushed and looked away, suddenly conscious of what a walking disaster I was. "I'm afraid you get to spend your last few days on earth with the widely hated herald of the end times. How lucky."

He turned my face back toward his and met my gaze with hard, loving eyes. "You are *not*. You're the woman on whom all our hope hangs. I feel it in my gut. Don't let that dream or the council or the prophecy make you doubt yourself. I believe in you more than I do any prophecy."

Before I could deflect, he bent his head and lightly dragged his lips along mine. My body melted, and I closed my eyes as I pressed my mouth against his.

It was so soft, so gentle, the opposite of the hungry passion we'd shared two nights before. Tender. Beautiful and probing. Lips that weren't desperate but searched and discovered. And with each kiss, I found someone who fit perfectly against me.

Slowly, Jaxson's kisses traveled from my mouth along my throat. I tilted my neck and slipped my arms around him. Pulling him close, I buried my chin against his shoulder. He slowed and broke off his kiss just to hold me.

The world was collapsing so quickly around us, and I didn't want to let go. I just wanted to hold on to him forever in that moment. To draw it out. To never have to face the future or the past.

But eventually, I opened my eyes to face the world that was.

A woman looked back at me from the woods. I tensed and dug my nails into Jaxson's shoulders, and then she was gone.

"What is it?" Jaxson whispered. His body was taut and ready, but he didn't look around.

"Someone was watching us. Maybe someone from the council?" I disentangled myself from his arms and headed up the slope to where she'd been standing.

No sign. I sniffed, but my wolf-less human senses were pretty terrible. Why did people even have noses?

Jaxson did the same. "I don't smell anything but our own scents."

My heart began pounding. Magic? Ghosts? Could it be one of the Dark God's agents, spying on us? I closed my eyes, searching for the presence I'd felt at Pere Cheney and the Dreamlands.

Nothing.

"I don't feel him here. It's something else," I said.

Jaxson nodded.

We moved from tree to tree, searching for any trace, but there was no sign of the watcher.

Then a subtle movement in the corner of my eye pulled my attention. I whipped my head about as a faded figure stepped around a tree. She looked at me, then moved out of sight behind the trunk of a nearby pine.

My heartbeat accelerated as my wound began to itch. That meant one thing: we had an ethereal visitor.

"What did you see?" Jaxson whispered.

"A ghost. A woman."

We moved cautiously, scanning the woods. After a minute, the ghost emerged ahead and motioned to me with her finger, then moved off into the woods and was gone.

"She wants me to follow her, I think. Alone."

Still searching in vain for the ghost he couldn't see, Jaxson said, "Not a chance. I'm coming with you."

I shook my head. "I have the feeling that she won't talk if

you're there—just like the first time I met the witch of Pere Cheney."

He gave me a frustrated glare. "It could be a trap. One of the Dark God's agents."

"I don't think so. I don't feel his presence. And so far, ghosts have only given us warnings."

"So far," he muttered.

I started moving off into the woods. "I'll shout if I need you."

"I'm not letting you out of my sight," he growled quietly.

The spirit led me deeper into the woods, slipping from tree to tree. She was there and then gone again, like the glow of a blinking lighthouse in the night.

Where was she going?

Jaxson followed behind, keeping me in sight. The land began to rise, and soon, I found myself on a ridge, looking down at the waves battering stones on the shore. There was something hypnotic about the way the water churned, and something familiar. For a second, I saw a dark shape lying at the lake's edge, rocking in the water, and then it was gone. A black wolf. A memory I would never forget.

Billy.

I sucked in my breath, and the vision faded. The spot was similar, but that was a different place and time.

"You killed my mate," a woman said from behind me.

I spun and instinctually called for my claws, but I had none —once again.

The ghost stood five paces from me. I recognized her instantly from pictures.

Stephanie. Jaxson's sister.

35

Savannah

Stephanie's hair was dark and long, pulled over her shoulders, framing a strong yet elegant face. Grief and anger tugged down the edge of her lips, and she clenched her jaw.

My chest rose and fell. Each breath felt like dying. I'd killed her mate, and now, her brother was mine. How fucked up was that?

She stepped forward, and I took a tentative step back, closer to the ridge.

Was she a vengeful spirit?

Billy had hunted me through the woods and dragged me down like a deer. He'd been on top of me, ready to kill me. I'd done what I'd needed to survive, but how could I explain that to her? If someone killed Jaxson, I would never forgive. I would hunt them down and murder them with my bare hands, claws or no.

She took another menacing step toward me.

"I'm sorry," I blurted. "I know it doesn't change anything, but I'm so sorry. Sorry for Jaxson, and sorry for you."

I desperately wanted to say that I hadn't meant to kill him, or that it was only self-defense. But I could hear the words in my mind, and I knew those would sound like weak and feeble justifications. I'd killed her mate. For her, there would never be anything that could justify it.

Sorry was the only thing I could say.

She glared back at me. "I want to hate you."

"I understand," I said, backing up once again. My foot scuffed at the edge of the cliff, and some dirt trickled over the edge, but I didn't dare look behind me. Not with the ghost approaching, not with the look of fury on her face.

I tried to calm my breathing.

She looked away, then, back to where Jaxson stood. He was far off, and I had no doubt that he was at the cusp of bolting to my aid, though he couldn't see or hear her.

How was I going to tell him about this?

Still watching her brother, the ghost sighed. "You make him happy."

I bit my lip, unsure how to proceed. "He makes me happy."

When she looked back, her expression was softer, but only by a hair. "You don't have to be afraid of me, Savannah. I'm not going to hurt you. If something ever happened to you, my brother would go insane. He'd lose himself just like Billy did. You are my brother's mate, and there's nothing that I can do about that."

I didn't say anything, or even move a muscle. How could I respond?

She brushed her translucent hair over her ear. "I know my husband attacked you. That he was trying to kill you. I can't imagine the terror of that moment, and I'm sorry for it. But I want you to know that's not how Billy was. He was a kind man once. He would have been a fierce father, if we'd ever made it that far."

She looked to be on the verge of tears, and a deep sadness

welled up in me. I guess she'd been only a little older than I was when she died.

So many broken plans, for all of them. Stephanie and Billy. Jaxson. Their father.

"Jaxson said Billy had been a good man," I replied. "Loyal. I'm truly sorry. It haunts me." A part of me wanted to bolt and to run as fast as I could—to get away from the ghost, to get away from the bloody memories that I'd shoved deep down.

The other part of me wanted to go to her.

She hardened her expression and wiped away the glistening in the corner of her eye. "He was a *monster* in the end. I know that. The grief broke him. Kahanov used the cracks to pry him open and corrupt him, just like the Dark God is trying to do to you."

"I know," I whispered. "I bound my wolf to stop him. He got so close to taking control..."

She studied me for a long moment, evaluating me with a stern expression. "You're fierce, but you're going to fail. That means you and my brother will die."

The words sank into me like an iron blade, and whatever hope I had left drained from my heart. I stepped toward the ghost. "Please, you're here to help, aren't you? There must be a way."

"You're not whole. You'll never be able to defeat the Dark God as you are." Her words filled me with despair, yet her face revealed no emotion.

I took a step forward. "The Moon told me that the Soul Knife severed a part of my wolf's soul. That's how the Dark God is taking control. How do I get it back and heal the wound?"

She pointed to my shoulder. "Your wolf's shard is here with us. You must come to the land of the dead. That's why I'm here."

The land of the dead? *Right now?*

The forest began to spin around me, and I had to steady

myself against the trunk of a slender sapling that was clinging to the cliff's edge. The poor thing was clutching at the world just as precariously as I was.

In the last month, I'd discovered invisible cities and been to the land of dreams. I'd spoken with werewolves, demons, and ghosts. But entering the land of the dead? *For fuck's sake.*

I studied her face, but her expression gave me no clue. She just waited patiently for me to recover my senses.

Was this seriously where my destiny was leading me?

I had to defeat the Dark Wolf God and bring my wolf back, so I had to go after that part of my soul. What other choice did I have?

I took a deep breath and straightened, letting go of the tree. "How do I get there?"

She smiled and motioned through the forest at a path that ran parallel to the shoreline. "Follow me, but not without my brother. You two are mates. If you enter without him, he'll go insane."

Fuck. Me going was one thing, but Jaxson?

I knew without a doubt he would follow. I licked my lips. Time for a pretty crucial question. "Is there a way back?"

She smiled. "Yes. Your strands of fate still tie you to the world of the living. That's why you can return, but I cannot—at least, not in any form more than this." She gestured to her ephemeral body.

I looked back at Jaxson, and then in the direction of the council. "We need to prepare Magic Side. We've made plans with the Order and sorcerers, and we need to see them through."

She shook her head. "You've put everything in motion. They can defend Magic Side. *You* must defeat the Dark God. And you cannot do that while you're broken."

That meant putting it all in the hands of Sam and Regina, of

Casey and my aunt. I trusted them, but how would the pack respond without their alpha? Would the council still cooperate? Would they be able to work with each other without me to make peace?

Wolfie would have said, *Tough shit. Time they grew up and learned to get along...now come get me out of the fucking Deadlands, already!*

Doubt swirled in my mind. Could I trust the ghost? Was she really Jaxson's sister, or an illusion sent by the Dark God? All my instincts screamed that she was telling the truth, but how could one tell with a ghost? Their expressions weren't exactly like a living person's. More distant. And they had no scent, no tells.

As if reading my warring thoughts, Stephanie cast me a knowing look. "This isn't a trick. Jaxson and I were close. He'll be able to ask me questions that only I can answer. I'm sorry, but it's the best proof I can offer."

Would that work? Or could the Dark God's magic replicate her memories, too? My head spun. At some point, I'd have to trust my gut, and my gut said, *Go with it. How else will you get your soul back?*

I looked back at Jaxson apprehensively, and she followed my gaze. "I know that there's no reason to trust me in this, but the Dark God has no power in our realm," she said. "He's trapped in the Dreamlands. But once he escapes, he'll be able to enter the land of the dead—that's why our kind have been helping you."

"How do we find the shard of my wolf?" I asked.

"I'll help guide you, but you'll have to find your way to her." Stephanie gestured to where Jaxson crouched, waiting to come to my aid at a moment's notice. "Get my brother and meet me in the Garden of the Wolves."

Desperation and indecision muddled my thoughts. I would tell Jaxson, and then we would decide what to do.

I turned and started to walk away, but her voice stopped me.

"A warning, Savannah. The journey won't be easy. You have enemies in the Deadlands, and your wolf may not wish to return. That part...that's up to you."

Then she vanished like a rainbow in the sun.

My gut knotted as I walked back to where Jaxson stood waiting beneath the trees. Concern etched his face. "I heard only your half of the conversation. Who were you speaking to?"

My mouth went dry, and my chest constricted so tightly, it became hard to breathe, but I forced myself to meet his eyes. "Your sister."

36

Jaxson

The world dropped away.

Stephanie.

My mind whirled, completely unable to process her words. “Are you sure?”

Savannah nodded and stepped close, laying her hand on my arm. Her touch calmed the heavy seas, and the pressure in my chest released as the world seemed to steady around her.

I took a deep breath and closed my eyes.

I’d never had time to mourn my sister, only to put out the fires after her death. To keep the pack and the LaSalles from tearing each other apart. When I’d finally had a moment to look up from the chaos, too much time had already passed.

Yet I’d never imagined her as a ghost. I’d never thought of her as anything but gone.

When I opened my eyes, shadows of concern draped across Savannah’s face.

“Are you sure it was her?” I whispered.

“I think so. We need to meet her again in the Garden of the Wolves. She said you could ask questions...”

My mind reeled with the possibilities. Our pack had always prohibited speaking with the dead, but the chance to talk to my sister...it was intoxicating. I studied Savannah in every detail. Could it be true that my sister had returned to help us? Or to warn us?

I swallowed. "What did she say?"

Her hand traced up my arm. "We spoke about Billy. And the Dark God."

"Is that why she came?"

Savannah looked away, out over the water. "She came to warn us that we won't be able to defeat him unless I'm whole. She said we must travel to the land of the dead to get that shard of my wolf's soul back."

I sucked in a sharp breath and gripped her arms. "Savannah, I'm sorry, but no. Crossing the veil between the worlds is perilous. Our legends say that those who enter the Deadlands don't return. We'll be able to release your wolf once we stop the Dark God. Then you won't be in danger of being controlled."

She bit her lip. "There's more. She said that without my wolf, we won't be able to overcome him. We need to find a way to do this—I don't think we have another choice."

Blood pounded in my temples as a million doubts tore at me. My sister wouldn't lead us astray, would she?

Never. My father might be willing to throw me to the wolves, but Stephanie—I could always trust Stephanie.

I made Savannah repeat their conversation over and over, looking for any clue she might have missed. Finally, Savannah stepped back and threw her hands down. "Enough. My gut says she's telling the truth. We need to try."

I studied her, truly studied her: the fire that flushed her cheeks, the set of her jaw, the strength of her stance. My mate was the key to it all—to the prophecy, to the Dark God, to me. And she needed to be whole.

That had to come first, or we would all fall.

The others could handle everything else. The pack, the council, the preparation. Right now, my mate needed one thing.

I nodded. "Okay."

Her expression transformed as the reality of the situation sank in: we were going into the Deadlands. She nodded, no longer quite as confident. "Okay, then. We do this. We need to go now. Stephanie said we didn't have much time."

We skirted the shoreline back to the portal, where we found the loremaster and Sam, who was perched on a large boulder.

Sam hopped down as soon as she saw us. "There you are! What took you so long? People have been filtering out for half an hour. The loremaster said you two survived the trial, so what happened to you?"

Savannah gave her a hug. "Thanks for being here and speaking up. For *everything*. This might sound crazy, but Stephanie appeared to me, and we need to go to the land of the dead."

"Are you nuts?" Sam snapped.

Savannah explained everything, and when she was done, all Sam could do was run her fingers through her golden-blonde hair. "Holy shit. This is crazy—you *know* this is crazy, right?"

The loremaster thinned her lips and narrowed her eyes. "It will be very dangerous, Jaxson. It's not wise."

Savannah looked from the loremaster to Sam to me, flickers of doubt and despair creeping into the shadows of her expression. But I was set.

I laid my hand on Sam's shoulder, its weight the end of the discussion. "If this ghost turns out to truly be my sister, then we must go. You and Regina will need to organize the pack to defend Magic Side. Regina and I had started drafting emergency plans for defense and for evacuation. She'll know where to begin."

Sam's protest died on her lips as she looked between us.

Savannah brushed her red hair out of her face. "You can do this, Sam. The Order and my family are working on barricades against the Dark God's magic. Coordinate with Casey. You've kicked his ass, and he'll respect that. Plus, he thinks you're hot, so he's *way* more likely to cooperate."

I texted Regina a heads-up as Savannah unslung her pack and handed it to Sam. "The moonstone is in here. You used it once before. If anything happens to us, it should be in Magic Side, where someone can use it."

"You can't be serious about this," Sam said, her voice overwhelmed and unbelieving.

I slipped my phone into my pocket and addressed our loremaster. "Put your head together with the other loremasters. There must be some clue in the histories, no matter how small. Something we can use. I started, but maybe you'll have better luck."

She grasped my arm. "We'll comb through the legends, but if you're going to risk entering the Deadlands, you need to understand that there are rules. You cannot drink or partake of the food there. Do not sleep, and do not stay more than a day. If you do, you'll begin to forget the land of the living and seek only to join the dead."

I studied the lines of worry that creased her face. "No food, no water, no sleep. One day. We can do that."

She shook her head absently as she let me go. "Time is not the same there. And in the legends, those who enter are always seduced to stay. Everything in the Deadlands is a trap designed to keep you there. No matter how well-meaning your sister is, all ghosts call to the living to join them forever."

I glanced at Sam, who was on the verge of a nervous breakdown. "Stop that. We're coming back, and we'll be stronger than ever. Be ready."

She nodded, and the four of us headed toward the old portal in the woods.

A moment later, we stepped one by one out of the ether. The Garden of the Wolves was just as we'd left it, with wildflowers blooming all along the paths.

Savannah looked around. "I don't see her."

"I know where she'll be," I said as I inclined my head toward the top of the mausoleum. "With our ancestors."

Sam gave Savy an awkward hug goodbye, but Savannah shook her head. "Don't worry. We'll be back soon. And I'll have my wolf. Just don't let my cousin burn down half of Magic Side trying to protect it."

I squeezed Sam's shoulder. She was one of the best. A loyal ally, a friend. Family. "You've got this. Now go whip everybody into shape."

"Gods, please come back," she pleaded.

"We will." Then Savannah and I turned and headed along the winding paths until we reached the old, weathered mausoleum.

"Any sign of Stephanie?" I whispered.

Savannah shook her head, and we circled the building. When we came around the front, we stopped short. My chest tightened, and my mouth went dry.

Stephanie stood beside the door, framed by the pillars and the deeply carved letters on the lintel above: *LAURENT*.

I could see her. Actually see her.

She hadn't aged a day, though she was translucent, and her face had a distant look that it hadn't worn in life. Every muscle in my body urged me to run her, but instead, I placed my hand out protectively in front of Savannah. "Who are you, spirit?"

A sad smile touched Stephanie's face, an expression I'd learned to resent as pity when I was younger, though it made my heart ache now. "You haven't changed at all, Jaxson. Stronger. Tougher. But still the same man."

I hardened my heart. "You need to prove who you are. What's the first thing I stole?"

"That I know of? A six-pack of Miller. You made me cover for you. We drank it together and threw the bottles into the lake because we were young and stupid." She brushed her ethereal hair guiltily away from her face. "I told Father, you know."

Shock overruled my suspicion. "*What*?"

I remembered every detail of that first heist—the jitters of deciding to do it, the thrill of escape, the glory of those cold beers, purchased with audacity alone. But I didn't recall getting ratted out.

"He caught me tipsy later," Stephanie admitted. "I gave you up. He was so pissed—*at me*—for snitching. He said that it was more important that you trust me than him."

"I had no idea."

She cocked her head in a condescending big sister way. "He didn't punish you because he didn't want to reveal that I told. He said we'd have to carry each other through life. But I think now that I look back on it, I just let you carry me. You still are."

She stepped close, as if she wanted to touch me, but stopped herself. "You need to stop carrying everything, Jaxson. The past, the future, the shadow of my death."

"I'll put it down when the pack is safe. When the Dark Wolf God is defeated and Savy is safe. What must we do to heal her wolf?"

My sister gave me an expression that I couldn't read. "You follow me."

She brushed her hand over the door of the mausoleum, and there was an audible click. Then the door slowly opened to reveal dark gray nothingness—the entrance to the Deadlands.

37

Savannah

I stared into the emptiness where the inside of the family crypt should be. Instead of a burial space, it was a swirling, milky gray void. Another portal.

"Is this always here?" I asked.

Jaxson's sister stepped to the threshold. "No. The Opener of Ways created it for you two alone. You may enter the Deadlands through it, and you may leave again."

My mind spun. "Who is the Opener of Ways? A god?"

She gave me a sly smile. "A god who governs the boundaries between life and death. Let's just say he doesn't wish to see the Dark God free. You don't need to know more than that."

Her tone had a sense of finality. *Mysteries we're not supposed to pry into.*

And to think I used to enjoy a good mystery.

With my heart straining in apprehension, I crossed my arms for some sense of security. "You promise that this is a round-trip ticket, right? I don't want to just walk into some deadly field of magic, get killed, and then—voila, we're stuck in the Deadlands because we're dead."

"You may leave the Deadlands again through this doorway. But once you do, it will close forever."

Well, that was a relief, frankly. The last thing I needed was a doorway for more ghosts to get into my life.

I turned to Jaxson, who had a determined expression etched on his face. "Are we really doing this?"

Though the set of his jaw and the hardness of his features persisted, his eyes softened. "Not if you don't wish to. We can find another way."

I glanced at Stephanie, who waited patiently but expectantly beside the portal. "I don't know that we have another way. I need my wolf, and I trust your sister."

He held out his hand. "Then we go together."

I uncrossed my arms and clasped his hand. A shiver ran along my spine, like stepping out of the snow and wind and into the warmth of a firelit cabin. Heat and a deep sense of belonging washed away my fear. "Let's do it."

Wordlessly, Stephanie slipped into the portal and disappeared. Hand in hand, we followed.

A wave of cold rushed over us, and my stomach dropped. Rather than the tumbling sensation of traveling by portal between places in our world, this felt like breaking through the surface of a frozen lake and plunging into the icy water below.

I shivered with relief as we emerged into a clearing enclosed by misty gray woods. Enormous pines stretched above us into the sky, and a low fog hung about the base of the trees.

I turned to look behind us. The mausoleum was there, though in this place, it was rundown and covered with moss. There were no other signs of the garden or of Magic Side.

I squeezed Jaxson's hand and let go, although I didn't want to, and inspected the portal. "This is our way back?"

Stephanie nodded. "Once you have the missing shard of

your wolf, you may return to the land of the living through here."

I surveyed the woods around us. Nothing was quite right. The place gave off a disconcertingly eerie feeling, and it almost seemed like the trees themselves were growing from the mist.

Jaxson sucked in a sharp beath, and I turned. Stephanie had her hand on his shoulder.

"I can feel you," he whispered.

"I exist in this world, not yours," she said.

With that, he embraced her in his strong arms. A lump formed in my throat, and I looked away to give them a moment of privacy. Yet I felt his emotions pulsing through me, as if our hearts were connected—and his was full to breaking.

"I miss you so much," he choked.

"I'm sorry, Jaxson."

And while they said nothing more for a long while, I was certain their own hearts were speaking in the silent language of wolves.

After several minutes, Stephanie finally pushed back and looked between us. "Your time here is short. You must find Savannah's shard and get out."

"How do we locate it?" I asked.

"I can feel it," Jaxson said. "It pulls on me in the same way I can feel you pulling on me."

A deep and twisting sense of betrayal strangled my throat. I couldn't feel anything.

Was it because I'd chained my wolf? Was I so completely cut off that I couldn't feel a fragment of my own soul, even while Jaxson could?

"Which direction?" I croaked out, unable to hide the hurt in my voice.

He gestured into the featureless woods. "That way."

"Your shard will be roaming with the ghost packs," said

Stephanie. "There are many, but in this place, they're mostly wolves from Magic Side and nearby. She's part of my pack."

Trying to put on a brave face, I adjusted my jacket and zipped it against the chill. "Okay, let's go get her, then."

"We must proceed cautiously," Stephanie said. "Wolves aren't the only creatures that roam these woods. Your life force will attract many things that lurk here."

Great. Lots of monsters in the underworld, and we were the only snack for miles around.

There were no landmarks to measure our progress, only endless pines rising from the mist. It flowed around us as we walked, hanging thick and low around our legs.

"Is the whole underworld like this?" I asked Stephanie.

"No. It's as diverse as the land of the living."

Fantastic. We wound up in the extremely creepy part.

After twenty minutes, a loose stone broke from the roots beneath my feet, and I stumbled.

Something didn't feel right about the stone—it was too angular. I bent over and fanned my hand to brush away the unnaturally thick mist.

Half a brick. I picked it up. It was yellow and crumbling, bearing a diamond-shaped maker's mark with the letters CHI above BRI.

A Chicago brick?

Were we walking through ruins of a building? I tried to fan away more of the haze, but that wasn't effective—it just curled back around.

"Was there something here once?" I asked Stephanie, who was patiently waiting for me to get my ass in gear and stop playing in the mist.

She looked back without emotion. "A building. Perhaps a home or workshop. When the building died, it chose to come here."

"Buildings die?"

"All things die, even places. Once, it was full of life, people, hopes and dreams and morning work routines. You two are the only things here that haven't died. The trees, the animals, even the mist—all are dead."

The mist?

I imagined the way that the fog in the woods around Belmont burned off as the sun rose. I'd never thought about it being a thing that died.

"You said that the building chose to come here?"

"There are many afterlives. We all choose one way or another."

That left me with a burning question: why had my soul chosen this place?

Eventually, the mist began to thin as we moved into rolling, forested hills. I wasn't sure how long we'd been traveling. Time was as formless as the fog around us. There was little sunlight punching through the gray sky, but it was impossible to tell if it was changing its position or if we were.

The loremaster's warnings echoed in my mind:

Time is not the same there.

Do not sleep, and do not stay more than a day.

You'll begin to forget the land of the living and seek only to join the dead.

If time wasn't the same, how would I know when a day had passed? And would time pass differently in Magic Side?

I was about to ask Stephanie when she held her finger to her mouth, then pointed ahead.

We froze, and I silently cursed the loss of my keen wolf senses. What the hell was it?

I watched the point she had indicated for a minute. There was nothing at first, and then something large moved between the trees—a dark shadow, like a massive cat. For a second, a pair of red eyes stared back at us, and then, with a blink, they disappeared in a swirl of mist.

I glanced at Jaxson and mouthed, *Is it gone?*

He nodded but put his finger to his lips, then whispered, "There's something else."

My muscles tightened, and I scanned the woods. I couldn't catch any scent, but I sensed a signature. Evil.

Familiar.

An impact drove the air from my lungs, and I hurtled backward. My shoulder slammed into a tree, and my jaw cracked shut with the force. I dropped to my knees in the thinning mist and sucked in a painful lungful of air as I looked up.

A massive, hairless man had Jaxson by the throat. The Crusher—the murderer Dragan had possessed at Bentham.

I'd cut out his soul atop the roof of the prison.

Jaxson rammed his foot into the brute's gut. The Crusher gasped and hurled my mate aside.

A wolf leapt forward and bit the Crusher's arm, but he swung her away.

Stephanie? I hadn't even seen her transform.

With no claws to rip the murderous bastard apart, I called my magic. My skin went cold, and energy crackled along my arms.

He spun on me. "You bitch! I could feel you ten miles away, the moment you entered the Deadlands. You cut out my fucking soul!"

With that, he charged.

I darted left and released a blast of dark energy.

He staggered but didn't stop. My pulse thudded in my ears, and my breath came in short and ragged gasps.

Jaxson was on him then, tearing at him with his claws.

The Crusher spun and rammed my mate into the ground

with a single blow, then kicked him in the ribs, sending him flying.

Faster than I'd ever seen someone move, the beast of a man was on me, with his hands pressing the area around my ears.

Pain exploded through my head, and my knees went limp.

"I told you I'd haunt you, that I wanted to feel the slick pieces of your skull slip between my fingers. I just never thought I'd have a chance like this."

I screamed—and then the pressure released, and I dropped to the ground.

Jaxson ripped into the Crusher's side with his bloodied claws, while Stephanie sank her teeth into his leg. But the glint of madness in the brute's eyes told me he didn't feel it at all.

With a gasp of pain, I staggered deliriously to my feet and unleashed my magic. This time, I shaped the shadows with my mind, forming them into black chains that wrapped around him. Like a black serpent, they looped around his arms and body and began to constrict. He bellowed, but I let the rage and anger take me, and I tightened the chains.

He'd caved in the skulls of at least three innocent women in Magic Side and two prison guards. He'd almost done the same thing to me on the roof of Bentham, and he'd wounded Jaxson so badly that it had taken all the magic I'd had left to bring him back.

My skull still throbbed from where his hands had been. He wouldn't be my personal poltergeist through this life and the next.

He would never hurt my mate again.

With my own shout of rage, I pulled the chains tight, and just like the stone lions, I crushed him.

The sound of it made my gut churn, but I didn't relent. When it was all over and there were no more haunting gasps, I released the spell of shadows.

His lifeless body dropped to the forest floor, and the red drained from my vision.

My thoughts immediately went to Jaxson. He was standing to the side, watching me with a dark expression, and he nodded.

I didn't know what that meant, but I ran to him. "You're hurt."

The shadows on his face vanished, and he gave me a weak smile. "A few broken ribs, but I'll heal quickly. I got off much better than last time—except for my ego. The question is, are *you* alright? You can't heal anymore."

Relief surged through me, and I pressed my cheek against his chest, listening to the beat of his heart. "Luckily, I've got a thick skull."

To our left, Stephanie shifted back to human form. "Who the hell was that?"

I didn't take my head off Jaxson's chest. "A blast from the past, looking for revenge. He nearly killed us both once, but I killed him."

Her expression didn't waver. "Death binds us all together. Those who you've killed in life, if they are here, will be drawn to you. And you to them."

Uh-oh.

A month ago, I'd been a waitress. Now...*now* there would be many in the Deadlands who would be looking for revenge, and I was certain that would be true for Jaxson as well.

I disentangled myself from Jaxson's arms. "We'd better get going."

"Yes," he said, his voice totally flat, but I detected the hidden concern.

I stopped at the Crusher's corpse but jumped back with a start.

He'd begun to change—as if he were decaying, but faster. His skin turned to mist and started to blow away like sand from the top of a dune. In a matter of seconds, he'd completely disappeared.

"He's gone," Jaxson muttered.

"What happens when you die here?" I asked.

Stephanie gave me a hard look. "The end. There is nowhere else to go."

I blinked in surprise. "Oh."

Nowhere else to go. So the Crusher was gone forever? From our world, and now the next? Not only had I killed him with the Soul Knife, but I'd eradicated him from the afterlife as well. A dark sense of satisfaction swelled within me. "Good."

I began to walk away, but Jaxson grabbed my arm. "We're being watched."

I snapped my head up. A gray wolf stood on the crest of a hill, tracking our movements. The moment our eyes met, it bolted.

For a second, the sight of a wolf brought hope welling up in my chest, but it died instantly. It wasn't her—my wolf—nor any wolf I recognized.

Stephanie frowned, and I asked, "Did you know that wolf?"

"No, but I'm certain it was a sentry. We're in *his* domain now," she whispered.

"Whose?"

She turned and gave me a blank, emotionless look. "The ghost wolf alpha. He rules over all the ghost packs."

"Ghost wolf alpha? Did he send you to us?"

She shook her head. "No. He doesn't know about this. I came to you on my own, with the help of the Opener of Ways. There was no time to seek the alpha's permission."

That didn't bode well.

We continued through the rolling hills, moving more cautiously than we had before, but it wasn't long before Stephanie stopped us. "He's here. I can feel him."

Focusing my senses, I strained to catch any scent. The limits of my human perception betrayed me again.

"I have his scent—a powerful alpha," Jaxson said. "And I can sense his anger. What should we do?"

Stephanie backed up. "I don't know if he'll help us, but whatever we do, we mustn't aggravate him. He's quick to anger."

Great.

I waited, listening. For a moment, there was nothing, and then a strong signature washed over me—the scent of falling leaves and the taste of dark molasses, the sound of crackling flames and the feeling of cold stone on my skin.

And the rumbling of anger.

I opened my mouth, but before I could speak, an enormous shadow crested the hill. A white wolf the size of a truck appeared among the trees. His power was overwhelming, like the presence of an alpha, but grounded in a way I'd never felt before. It vibrated all around us in the earth, the trees, and the sky.

For a second, he glared at us with vicious golden-yellow eyes. Then words echoed in my mind like a landslide: *Only I may take life and death in my lands. You have violated and profaned my domain. You will leave.*

With that, the great beast charged.

38

Savannah

The monstrous white wolf thundered down the hill, hackles raised and growling.

Jaxson's claws erupted, and he moved between us, ready to shift mid-leap.

I snapped my hands back and summoned my shadows. Their dark, cold magic wrapped around my arms and billowed like a cape behind me. Energy crackled over my hands and fingers, and I stood my ground.

We needed to make peace, but the ghost wolf alpha seemed intent on tearing us apart.

With two quick steps, the monster closed the distance. His head snapped toward Jaxson, who leapt back.

Deftly avoiding the creature's jaws, my mate ducked and rolled to my side, and I unleashed the reservoir of magic from my hand. "Stay back!"

The shadows leapt across the space between us and cascaded over the white wolf's body. I tried to fashion the magic into a barricade like I had with the stone lions, but the chains of energy dissipated into nothing.

Shit.

The beast whipped his head toward me, and I threw up a wall of shadows between us and turned to run, grabbing Jaxson's hand.

But the giant wolf slowed to a halt...and laughed. *Darkness does not affect me. I can see your souls shining like bonfires in the night, and yours is broken, shadow creature. You are draped with cursed magic and bring true death into the Deadlands. Leave my domain, or you will perish here.*

His thundering words froze me in place, and my gut tumbled in dread. He could see all that? *Fuck.*

Every nerve in my body urged me to flee, but I resisted Jaxson's pull and held my ground. We needed the ghost wolf alpha's help. My wolf was in his land, and he would know where she was. Somehow, we had to face him.

I dismissed the wall of shadows and the magic from my other hand, leaving myself unarmed and exposed.

Before I could formulate my thoughts, Stephanie spoke. "Great alpha, I lead one of your ghost packs. I brought these two to your lands to seek a missing part of her wolf's soul."

I know who you are, and I know what she seeks. Neither matters. Take them back to the land of the living, where they belong, the great beast snarled in our minds.

Shock rolled through me. He knew I was looking for my wolf's shard? What was this creature? A god?

I took a hesitant step toward the giant alpha wolf. "Please, help us find my wolf. Without her, I can't be whole."

The alpha mirrored my step, and he lowered his head to look me in the eyes. *She is part of my pack. I will not let her return to you. She is mine now.*

His answer rumbled through me as low as an earthquake, but anger overran my initial shock. Alpha or god, how dare he lay claim to a part of me?

Before I could rein in my emotions, my fear dropped away, and I growled, "She is *mine.*"

The giant wolf's voice shook my mind. *I see everything, the living and the dead. I see the spells wrapped around your body. Spells you put there to bind your wolf. You are a monster.*

My chest constricted beneath iron bands of guilt and anger and doubt.

He knew. My corrupt soul was naked before him. How could I justify what I'd done to an all-powerful creature like this?

My breath shortened, and my mind spun as I tried to think. He was an alpha, a pack leader like Jaxson. I could appeal to that.

I licked my dry lips. "My pack is in danger. The Dark Wolf God has returned to our world. He seized control of my wolf because she was broken. I did what I had to do to protect my pack."

The great white wolf turned away from me and headed toward the trees. As he walked, he spoke in my mind. *You are the one who is broken. Only a broken person could do such a thing.*

It was an arrow through my heart, but it was true.

"Yes, I'm broken," I shouted after him, "but I'm trying to put the pieces back together, and that begins with her!"

He looked over his shoulder. *I will not let you take what is mine to be your captive. Be gone.*

Desperation and rage clawed at me. "You won't let me visit her or talk to her? Then she's *your* captive, chained to you as much as my wolf is chained to me!"

The giant wolf whipped around, clearly agitated, as he began pacing back and forth—as if considering whether to take a bite out of me. *She is part of the ghost wolf pack now.*

"She has no choice to leave?"

He planted his paws and growled. *She is happy here. She will not wish to leave. What right do you have to ask her? You—a monster who has bound her wolf.*

Tears of rage crept into my eyes.

Jaxson placed his hand on my back. His soothing presence flowed over me as he inclined his head in deference. "Alpha. Many of my wolves now run with your pack, but this one does not belong here. She was taken before her time, and she is needed in our world. If she does not return to the land of the living, the Dark God will send many more to join your pack before their time."

The alpha approached Jaxson. *I do not come into your domain to steal your wolves. Stay away from mine.*

"She is my mate!" Jaxson growled, his eyes flashing gold, but it had no effect on the alpha.

Desperate for anything I could do or say, I dropped to my hands and knees to address him on all fours as a wolf would. "Please let me speak to her. If she doesn't wish to return, then so be it. But let me try. Let her choose her own path. In the end, we'll all join your pack one day. Wait, and we will return."

The great wolf stepped close, and Jaxson tensed. The enormous beast towered two feet over my mate. One bite, and I'd be bitten in half. I swallowed, but I held my ground as he sniffed me.

Finally, he grunted and spun away, pacing again. *You are fearless for such a fragile creature. Brave and foolish enough to stare me down. But will you be brave enough to face yourself? To face what you have done?*

"Yes. Please, let us enter your domain."

You carry human things. Things from the living world. I do not allow those in my realm.

I stood and shrugged off my jacket and backpack, then began to unlace my Swiftleys. "Only my wolf matters."

Jaxson followed suit, pulling off his jacket.

You may not enter in human form. Only as a wolf.

His words sank into my chest like a frozen blade. My hands slowed, a lump formed in my throat, and I looked up to meet his knowing eyes. "I can't. I need to convince my shard to return first. If I release my wolf now, the Dark God will take control of her."

The ghost wolf alpha planted his paws and released a savage growl that turned my blood to ice. *These are not his lands, and the Opener of Ways has not granted him entry. He has no more rights or power here than you do. To enter my lands, your wolf must be free.*

Suddenly, everything came down to this point: release my wolf or fail.

My breathing quickened, but the decision was easy. Dark God be damned, we had to take the chance. "I'll do it."

For a while, the massive alpha just glared, but at last, he said, *Release your wolf. If you reconcile and she chooses, then she may enter my lands. And if the shard of her soul chooses, it may return with you.*

"Thank you, Alpha."

He turned his white head and looked off into forest behind me. I followed his gaze. The mist boiled backward from the pines to reveal a clearing and the glint of water that I was certain hadn't been there before.

His voice resonated in my mind. *A mirror is prepared for you. You must see yourself as I see you.*

I sucked in my breath and looked to Jaxson. We began walking toward the woods, but the ghost wolf alpha's voice stopped us. *You guided her through her first shift, young alpha, but she must do this part alone.*

Jaxson's body tensed, and his expression turned dark, but I knew the ghost wolf alpha's words were true.

I placed a hand on my mate's arm. "Take this time with your sister. And don't worry, I'll return. *With* Wolfie."

He clasped my hand against his arm for a moment, then released it. "I know."

Jaxson stepped aside and watched me walk away. When I looked back, his face was ashen, as if every step cut his soul.

39

Savannah

Alone with my guilt, I descended through the trees down to a small lake. The eternal mist of the place hung low along the banks and crept in silken tendrils over the water.

Stepping to the water's edge, I looked down. The shimmering silver surface reflected the flat gray of the sky and the dark green of the pines. But my reflection was just a wisp of shadow, a dark, featureless silhouette in the water. I was empty, missing my other half, and this place had no illusions about it.

A lump formed in my throat. It was time to start putting myself back together. To repair everything I had broken and torn apart, everything I had hidden from and lied to myself about.

Closing my eyes, I recounted the spell Aunt Laurel had taught me—the spell to release my wolf. I'd memorized it and looked it over a dozen times since, but terror still took me.

Would I be able to do it without her help or Jaxson's? Would I be trapped without my wolf, unable to recover the shard of her soul and face down the Dark God?

Taking in and holding a deep breath, I pulled my shirt over my head.

Okay, Wolfie, it's time for me to undo all the damage that I've done. I hope that somehow, you can forgive me.

Going over and over my aunt's spell in my mind, I unbuttoned my jeans and pulled them off. One by one, I piled my human things on the grass until I was naked, the way I had been born. The way *we* had been born.

The two of us.

Forcing down the doubt and guilt churning inside, I stood up straight and summoned my magic. Slowly, ice water trickled around my skin, and the cold began creeping in. I inhaled slowly, filling my lungs with air and my body with magic until I was shivering and vibrating with power.

Opening my eyes, I began to weave the unbinding spell. As I spoke the words of the incantation, my power flowed out with my breath, the magic pulsing the air around me.

My skin began to burn, precisely and painfully, like a tattoo of fire. Flashes of light flickered, and then runes began to glow all over me—spells of binding. They wrapped around my body like chains of writing, but as I tried to tear them apart with my magic, I found that they were stronger than forged iron.

Anger consumed me. I'd had a hand in making this spell, and I should be able to break it.

I pulled down my magic from the ether until it was a burning ball of ice in my chest. I pressed out with all my strength until my legs were quaking and cold sweat dripped from my skin. My lungs hurt, and my arms shook, but I kept pressing outward. I felt the spell chains bite into my skin, yet they wouldn't break.

"Let me go!' I growled.

Savy! a plaintive voice cried.

Shock tumbled through my mind. Wolfie?

My heartbeat accelerated, and I pushed even harder against my restraints. "Wolfie, are you there?"

I can't get out.

I fought the spell, anger and desperation fueling my magic. The beads of sweat cut through the frost forming on my skin, and I trembled with exhaustion.

You're slipping away! Wolfie cried. *Don't leave me!*

Panic set in, and I snarled in desperation.

We've done this before, Wolfie said, her voice like a shout, but barely audible above a whisper or an echo down a long hall. *Remember.*

I closed my eyes and concentrated. I tried to envision the bonds of magic, but instead, I saw another place.

A memory of a bare concrete room. An IV stand to my right with a blood bag and a tube connected to my arm. A fluorescent light buzzing overhead.

My arms were tied down with leather straps. The rogue wolves had drained my blood and injected me with magic inhibitor. My magic was fading, but so were the bonds that I didn't know were even there.

A month ago.

I remembered the terror. I remembered arching my back and pulling against my bindings with all my strength. Of begging "please" in a whisper to anyone who could hear me.

And then, someone had responded. Someone I'd never known was there. A guardian angel. A part of my soul.

Wolfie.

In that moment, she'd roared with fury, two decades of anger unleashed. I was trying to fight my way free of the operating table, but she was fighting free of something far more powerful.

As I was about to give up, searing pain had raced through my arms, like my very flesh was being torn from my body. One strap had snapped, and my arm had torn free. I'd seen it for the first time in the fluorescent light: claws and fur rising from my skin. My true form.

As the memory faded to black, the pain lingered. Intensified. My eyes shot open. I was staring wide-eyed out over the lake, with my knees sinking into the soft mud beside the silver water.

We'd broken through before. We'd do so again.

Reaching out for my wolf, I growled deep and low, letting my icy magic turn to fire. All across my body, the golden bonds of spell writing began to burn away into whispers of black.

I gasped as the transformation took me. My back arched, and my chest cracked. Fur erupted along my skin—except this time, it was black and made of shadow.

My head whipped back, and I howled.

My cry was cut short as the wind slammed out of my lungs. My body hurled backward, and I tumbled head over heels until I rolled to a stop in the mud.

With a groan, I levered myself up onto my hands and knees. Human hands. My heart clenched. Had I failed?

"Wolfie?" I cried as I stood.

I'm here, she said—but her voice didn't come from within.

I snapped my head up.

A black tendril of smoke had coalesced around my arm and trailed to where a dark wolf stood across from me. A wolf of shadow.

My mouth went dry. This had happened before—once when I'd attacked Aunt Laurel, and again on the roof of Bentham.

I tried to moisten my lips. "Wolfie, is that you?"

Yes, she said, pacing back and forth in agitation.

Scrambling to my feet, I took a step toward her. But she retreated hesitantly, and my heart broke. How would she forgive me?

Guilt took me back to my knees, then dropped me to my palms as the tears flowed. "I'm so sorry, Wolfie. I'm sorry I bound you, that after one month of freedom, I bound you again. I know I betrayed your trust. I didn't want to do it. If I could have asked you, I would have. I know that doesn't matter." I hung my head, looking at the muddy streaks on my legs. My chest quaked with sobs. "Please forgive me."

For a moment, there was no response, and then a wet nose prodded gently at me. *No.*

My heart stopped cold with the answer I'd feared most. I looked up to see the shadowy wolf lying with her head on her paws, inches from me. *You don't need to be forgiven.*

My throat tightened. "But what I did—"

It protected our pack. Our mate. Our family.

The tears hung in the corners of my eyes as I tried to read her expression.

Did you think I would see it any differently? she asked.

"Yes. I bound you. I heard your cries," I whispered through clenched teeth, because had I spoken any louder, I would have broken into more sobs.

The Dark God took control of me. He turned me on Casey, he turned me on Sam. Fuck him. You saved me from that. Do you think that's freedom, living in fear of what you might do next?

The world began to spin as all the vindictive words spiraled around me and guilt tried to block my ears.

Wolfie rose and nuzzled me.

I watched them attack you for it and call you a monster. Screw them. We may be twin-souls, but we are one. Our thoughts may be different, but we share the same body, the same blood, the same life. I know why you made your choice. And I know that deep down, you'd make it again—I would trust you to.

With disbelief and heartache straining in my chest, I reached out to touch her. She was shadow, but I could feel her warmth, the soft silk of her black fur.

Finally, I found words. "You were there? You heard—everything? Even though you were bound?"

I've always been there. I watched you grow up while I was bound.

I watched you fight off the Dark God. I was there when you stood up to the council this morning and the ghost wolf just now. And I watched you cry over the choice you made.

Shock washed over me as she nuzzled my fingers and continued, *My heart broke because I couldn't reach you. That I couldn't be there to comfort you. You are my person and always have been.*

Then I cried. I held her, and I sobbed with everything I had. I didn't let go of *my wolf*.

Minutes or hours later—I couldn't tell the difference here—I'd drained all my tears, and my breathing began to return. Wolfie butted her head against me. *Okay, reunion time is over. We have a fucking city to save. So let's figure out how to get me back to normal.*

I sat upright. "Normal. This isn't your true form? I thought that maybe since we're twin-souls, you finally broke free."

Wolfie blinked at me. *Oh, hell, no. This isn't my true form. We are one. We share a body. This is your funky voodoo magic. While black silk is striking, I'm a beautiful red wolf, or have you forgotten?*

My jaw dropped.

I was doing it? How?

Staggering to my feet, I looked down at my mud-covered hands. That tendril of smoke still streamed from my wrist to her form.

"So, I have no idea how to do this, but if you're sure, I'm going to try to reel you back in."

Do I get to drive after that?

"Of course. I need a break. I've been on two legs for too long. Fair warning, though, I don't know what I'm doing."

She seemed to smile, then looked out over the water. *You'll figure it out. You're in charge of magic. I just chase rabbits and bite bad guys really hard.*

I reached my hand toward her. My wolf watched and waited. I strained, trying to draw the magic back in.

Wolfie looked at me expectantly.

"I'm trying," I muttered.

What was I going to do? I took a sharp breath as I pulled for my magic.

Nothing happened.

Wolfie sat, and I squeezed my eyes tight. Frustration blossomed under my skin. I'd done this sort of thing before, hadn't I? With the Soul Knife. When Aunt Laurel had taught me to summon it. She'd made me memorize every detail: how the blade looked, its weight, the signature of its magic, the way it fit in the palm of my hand.

Would this be the same?

Eyes still shut, I imagined Wolfie. Not how she looked when we were in wolf form, but how she felt when we were together. How she filled that void in my soul. The way her off-kilter humor lifted my spirits.

Reaching out with my hand, that was what I called to me. The spirit that made me whole.

There was nothing at first, and then I gasped as ice water rushed over my skin. My eyes flew open. The shadows around Wolfie spun, pouring into me like my magic had once poured into the Sphere of Devouring.

But she wasn't devoured. I was filled.

Her spirit flowed back into our body, and a divine lightness spread through my limbs.

And suddenly, all the shadows were gone, and I was standing there alone on the shore of the lake.

"Wolfie?" I asked, chest heaving from exertion.

Holy shit, it worked! she exclaimed from that comfortable spot at the back of my mind.

I blinked. "You're surprised? You sound really surprised."

Wolfie hesitated for a second. *Okay, confession: I thought I was probably stuck forever as some sort of weird shadow wolf, and I was going to be okay with it, because at least we would be together, but hell, this is so much better.*

"It is."

Great. Priorities. Rinse off, because you're covered head to toe in mud, and I don't want it in my fur. Then get your stuff, and let's shift. It's time to get the rest of my soul back.

40

Jaxson

Savannah's howl ripped through my chest, and every fiber in my body screamed for me to run to her, to comfort her, to heal her wounds. "Let me go!" I growled, but the ghost of my sister held me back, gently but firmly.

"She must free her wolf alone. You cannot do this for her," my sister whispered.

It was true, but how could I sit there while my mate was in pain?

With a snarl, I turned and walked in the other direction, trying to block out the soft, undecipherable sobs filtering through the woods. I rammed my fist into a tree just to feel my knuckles break. Just to have something—the pain—to concentrate on other than my mate's cries.

Too quickly, endorphins cut in, and the bones began to knit. I pulled my hand back to strike again, but Stephanie grasped my wrist.

"I know what it's like, Jaxson," she whispered in my ear.

Bitterness tore at me. She and Billy had been so happy. Back when she was alive, he'd been brave and fierce. Before the grief had torn him apart and filled the cracks with hate and bitterness before the drink took him.

I understood his pain better now, how different it had been even from my own. If anything happened to Savannah, I would burn the world down.

"You truly care for her," my sister said.

I pulled my hand from her grasp. "Of course I do. She's my mate. Her pain is my pain, and being apart is like suffocation."

She gave me a knowing smile that made my blood boil. "It's more than being fated mates. I see it—you can barely take your eyes off her, and you watch her every moment. Wait for every word. Even if you weren't fated, I don't think you would have escaped her spell."

I rubbed my throbbing fist. It was true. I was fucking bewitched, and I loved it.

Loved *her*.

Would I ever have the chance to truly love her or know her? We were in the Deadlands, and the way things were going, it was very likely we would be reunited here soon.

She'd gotten a raw deal, but if the fates were kind, I could show her a better life in Magic Side. One without fear and constant running. One where she could trust the pack and learn our traditions. One where I could learn every detail about her past and dreams and desires, and make them all come true.

What would life be like without this blade at our throats?

Bitterness stabbed my chest. "I wish you could have known her, Steph. She's fierce like you. Loyal. Dedicated. I don't think there's a thing in this world that could stand in her way."

The faintest of smiles graced my sister's face. "I can tell."

I shook my head. "You can't. There's no way. She can be so hard and strong, it's blinding, but there's so much more." I sighed and scrubbed a hand through my hair. "I wish I could explain the way she sees the world. The first time I picked up one of her sketches, it was stunning. The lines were charcoal black and bold and angry, but together, they made the softest shades. It was like she was only drawing shadows, but those shadows made the light leap off the page."

Pausing to look up at my sister, I let the heaviness in my heart harden the corners of my mouth. "If she drew me, I wonder what she would see. Would I recognize the man in the picture?"

Stephanie crossed her arms. "I imagine she sees you better than you see yourself."

I grunted. "I don't see her clearly at all, but I want to. I want to know her when she's not running, not frightened, not trying to fight the world. There have been a few moments we've stolen, but not enough. And now, I don't know that we'll have many more together."

"She's fierce, but she's relying on you to believe in that future, Jaxson. That there *is* a future."

"It's hard," I whispered, though I would never have admitted it to anyone else.

She rested her hand on my back. "Then do the hard thing. Believe it's possible."

I looked back at the ghost wolf alpha, waiting patiently at the far edge of the clearing, watching for movement in the trees down by the lake.

Suddenly aware of the silence, I followed his gaze. Something moved at the edge of the trees. Savannah?

My heart raced.

She emerged into the clearing, naked and human, her red hair dark and dripping with water.

She was human, not a wolf. A weight descended in my chest. Had she failed? The howl—I was certain she must have broken the spell. But had her wolf somehow rejected her?

With a furious gesture, Savy tossed a bundle of clothes at the base of a tall tree and strode up the hill.

"She *is* beautiful," my sister whispered.

"Yeah," I replied absently, my mouth dry with anticipation. Yet instead of coming toward me, Savy made a beeline toward the ghost wolf alpha. I recognized the expression on her face all too well—trouble.

Godsdammit.

When she was angry, she had no fear, not of gods or monsters or the dead.

I moved to intercept, but before I could, she shouted at the alpha. "You want to talk to my wolf? Here she is!"

One step, she was human, and the next, she was a gorgeous, red-tinged wolf—a shift so fluid and fast, it was like cracking a whip.

My breath caught, and I stumbled to a halt. She'd never transformed so effortlessly before. Always, it had been pain and contortion and a struggle.

My momentary hesitation was all Savannah needed to close the distance to the alpha. She wasn't much taller than his knee, barely a mouthful.

She rammed her paws into the dirt, as he had done before her, and snarled. *You will lead me to my shard. Now.*

For a second, the massive white wolf paused, and then he snapped his jaws at her. *You dare make demands of me?*

My mate deftly spun out of the way, faster than I'd ever seen her move—a blur, almost a shadow. She was behind him before the giant wolf could spin around.

Then she bit him.

Oh, fuck.

In a heartbeat, fur erupted from my arms and claws from my hands, and I was sprinting to get between them.

Savannah snarled and flashed through his legs, leaving a

streak of blood on white fur. *You made my human grovel. Beg. And yet, you didn't listen. You called her a monster.*

I tried to shield Savy. "Stop this!"

The alpha swung around, and his jaws nearly grazed her, but she was gone, almost like smoke.

Was she smoke?

She was not worthy of a wolf, the ghost wolf alpha roared.

Savannah flipped around to face him. *She's the* only *one worthy of me. Release the shard of my soul. We may be part of your pack one day, but she is mine for now.*

The alpha lunged at her, but she was already gone. He snarled. *I could make you part of my pack with one bite, little red wolf.*

Now to his left, Savy's eyes went bright blue, and magic crackled like lightning around her. *I think not. We begged before, and you rebuked us. Now we're demanding. Release my shard. Take me to her.*

I swung to the massive white wolf's flank. "We had a deal, Alpha. A city is at stake. Lead us into your lands."

My sister appeared at my side, in wolf form now as well. *Please, great alpha, honor our bargain!*

The white wolf looked at all three of us, then back at Savannah, and gave an amused huff. *How did your human ever chain a creature as fierce as you?*

Savannah's wolf eased her posture slightly, and the crackling magic around her faded to smoke. *In the end, I let her. It was the right thing to do.*

The ghost wolf studied Savannah for a long time, his aggression naked. But finally, he nodded and looked off into the trees. A path through the mist began to form. *I will take you to your shard, but be warned: I do not think she will agree to leave. She is with her mother.*

41

Savannah

My heart skipped a beat.

Our mother was here, and the shard of our soul was with her.

Every emotion I had rushed into my mind, from elation to regret. After all this time, would I have a chance to see her again? To speak to her? What would she think of me? Would she be miserable in this place? Would my shard refuse to leave her side?

The loremaster's warnings about the underworlds came rushing back: *Those who enter are always seduced to stay. Everything in the Deadlands is a trap designed to keep you there. No matter how well-meaning your sister is, all ghosts call to the living to join them forever.*

The world seemed to shift and flow beneath my paws, and I stumbled slightly, but Jaxson stepped instantly to my side. "Easy there, beautiful wolf."

He reached out tentatively, then ran his fingers through my fur. Tingles rushed along my spine, electric, like I'd never experienced before. Wolfie and I absolutely melted beneath his touch.

God, it's good to be back, Wolfie purred in my mind. *If only we were alone.*

We were most definitely *not* alone. The ghost wolf alpha's glare was like the sun searing the back of my neck.

Sudden shyness overcame me, and with a sorrowful pang of regret, I slipped away from Jaxson's touch and pawed the earth. *Let's run together.*

He gave me a knowing smile, then quickly removed the last of his clothes and placed them in a neat bundle beside a fallen log.

I glanced back toward the lake. I'd dumped my clothes dramatically at the base of a random tree. It wasn't much different than how I'd been living at Jaxson's penthouse.

I hope nobody steals my boots, I muttered to Wolfie.

Do you know how bad those things smell? One of those strange cats lurking in the forest is more likely to come along and try to bury them, Wolfie teased. *I can't believe you actually offered them to the Moon. You were lucky we didn't get kicked out of the temple right there.*

Yup. My sassy wolf was back, and my heart was full. Between her and Jaxson, I knew I could get through this.

I tried not to look at the sexy naked man striding back toward me and did my best to rein in my sudden upwelling of desire, as my scent would betray me in an instant. Jaxson shifted swiftly and landed on all fours beside me—a massive wolf, though definitely not the size of the white monster.

Jaxson cocked his head in challenge. *Can you still run? You're out of practice.*

I gave our fur a shake. *I've been a wolf for a month, and I'm just as fast as you are. You don't want to see how fast I'm going to be once I get some real practice in.*

He grinned, and I caught a scent of approval. Damn, it was good to have my wolf senses again.

As soon as Stephanie trotted up beside us, the ghost wolf alpha turned to face the path he'd created through the mist. *Follow.*

With no more warning, he began to run, and we chased after.

I let Wolfie drive—or, more accurately, I didn't challenge her for the job.

The trees flashed by as we settled into a steady pace. My muscles rejoiced at running. It had felt like a lifetime since we'd run free like this. Something had been wrong, even when Wolfie was unbound before.

As I let go, I slipped down deeper into my wolf. She was in control, but somehow, I was there in every movement with her.

Everything feels different, I thought to Wolfie as we raced along the pine needle–strewn trail.

Something's changed, she replied. *I feel it, too. Maybe not all the bonds were broken before—the ones your aunt and father created. Maybe when you cast your unbinding spell this time around, the old bonds shattered as well as the new.*

Was that true?

It had certainly taken all my strength to break her free, and I'd felt like we were fighting against so much more than my own spell. And something about our union was definitely different.

Maybe it was my perspective. In retrospect, something had felt restrained about our relationship. I'd always assumed that something was just wrong about Wolfie and me, and that somehow, over time, I'd become one with my wolf, like Jaxson and his were.

But that wasn't my fate—I understood that now. I shared a body with another soul. We would never be one, but we'd never be separate.

I didn't need to learn to control my wolf. I needed to learn when to let go and how to listen, how to lead and follow, how to become one in the dance, because we would always be two souls together.

We didn't have to be like everybody else. We could be something more.

Wolfie glanced at Jaxson running beside us, perfectly in sync. There was an unspoken question in her look that I thought I understood.

What about him?

The fates had paired us together, just as they'd paired Wolfie and me. Could Jaxson and I learn the dance as well?

I knew for certain now that I needed him just as much as I needed her. I'd railed against our mate bond at first, but I didn't want to fight anymore. I loved that bond, cherished it.

I knew that just as I had embraced my wolf, it was time to embrace what we were: fated mates.

What would happen if I truly gave into the emotions we shared? To let my fear of our bond go? To embrace it, to nourish it, to let myself sink deeper in love with him?

As we ran, wolves I didn't recognize filtered in from the trees around us. The alpha's sentries?

Something was strange about them. For a while, I couldn't figure out what it was, but as we emerged from the land of mist and gray skies I finally understood: light was shining through their bodies.

They weren't translucent like the ghosts I'd seen before, but they weren't quite solid. I glanced at Stephanie. She was the same.

Ghost wolves.

Their numbers grew as we ran. They gave us no heed, and the alpha didn't slow, so we just kept running.

I couldn't keep my eyes off Jaxson. The way he moved was so

powerful and graceful that it left me mesmerized. And I could feel his joy at running with Stephanie again. Elation. A connection lost, restored—if even for a moment.

Would I be able to run like this with my mother? What about my father? What had happened to him? Could they be together?

A glance from Stephanie drove the fears from my mind. While normally placid, her eyes were overflowing with joy. *Run*, she said. *Savor this moment.*

So I ran, treasuring the beauty and flow of it.

Soon, we joined with more wolves, maybe thirty or forty. One of the ghost packs. My chest tightened as if something was pulling on it.

The shard of my soul.

She's here, I can feel it, I said to my wolf.

Me, too. Wolfie broke away from Jaxson and Stephanie and began desperately searching among the runners. I had to weave and dodge, but it was much calmer than our race through Magic Side had been.

I'm not going to jump into any water, Wolfie said. *Hope you're not disappointed.*

Yeah, yeah, smartass. Lesson learned.

The wolves paid us no attention, just kept their eyes forward, lost in the rhythm of their pace.

At first, there were too many unfamiliar faces, but then I spotted her. I could feel the tug of our souls guiding me forward, but I knew her in an instant. She was a mirror, our twin—yet also far more translucent than the other wolves.

She's only a shard of our soul, Wolfie noted.

My shard looked over her shoulder, and then, with a start, she veered off into the crush of wolves. We pursued, but she was just as fast.

Finally, she broke off from the pack and dashed up a small tree-covered slope, where she stopped and looked back.

I followed but halted ten paces away. My shard was wary and started pacing back and forth with her hackles raised. *Who are you?*

Wolfie piped up in my head: *Okay, you have to explain this one.*

Trepidation wrapped around me. I hadn't really thought through what I was going to say. I tentatively took a step forward and bowed my head. *I'm you. The part that's still alive. I've come to bring you home.*

She backpedaled slightly, sniffing the air. *I can smell that you're not of this place, but how is that possible?*

I deferred my gaze slightly so as not to threaten her. *Kahanov cut us with the Soul Knife. You died, but we were left alive.*

My shard gaped at us. *I can smell...truth.* She began to look a little woozy. *I remember...oh, fuck my life. Or death. Or just...fuck it.*

Yup, if I'd had any doubts, that was definitely our soul.

The shard cautiously approached, sniffing the air. *Kahanov was the last thing I remember. I was fighting him in the Dreamlands. I thought I'd lost. That I'd failed.*

There was so much pain in her voice, my heart bent beneath the strain. What would it have been like to die believing that you'd failed? With my head lowered, I began moving to meet her. *We won. We killed the bastard.*

A familiar light twinkled in her eyes. *Hell, yes. He was a bastard.*

I paused, not wanting to spook her. *Actually, he was being possessed by a ghost—a sorcerer named Victor Dragan. We killed him, too, but that took a little longer.*

Mirroring me, she also paused and cocked her head to the side. *You've—er, we've been busy, it seems.*

I nodded. *There's a lot to catch you up on, and we're not out of the woods yet. That's why I need you to rejoin us, to come back to Magic Side.*

She looked up and over my shoulder. *I can't return. I belong here, with the pack. Mom is here. I'm no longer afraid. I can just live.*

With a lump in my throat and a sinking feeling, I followed her gaze. The whole ghost pack was waiting on the ridge, not far off.

Aw, crap. And I was on a clock.

I turned back to my shard, taking a firmer stance. *Magic Side is in danger. Casey and Aunt Laurel, Sam and the whole pack. They need us. The Dark Wolf God is coming. They're going to fight, but we're the only one who can stop him.*

My shard gave the slightest whimper of frustration. *I don't want to go back to fighting for my life every day, of always running, of always being afraid. I'm tired, and I just want to be at peace. My pack is here. Our family is here. Stay. We could all be together again.*

My heart twisted. I longed to see my parents, and I wanted nothing more than to be at peace without having to fight for every breath, but I shook my head. *Our pack is in Magic Side—Sam, Regina, Tony. As are Casey, Laurel, and Uncle Pete. Even Zara. There's a whole roller derby team depending on us.*

I turned to look back at Jaxson, and a flutter of warmth moved through me. *And our mate. We have a life ahead with him if we can just get through this next tricky bit.*

My shard's eyes went wide. *Our mate? But...*

Oh, right. She'd been cut out before he revealed that juicy bit of information. *You've got a lot of catching up to do. Trust me, it's worth it. Like, very spicy.*

Really? she asked, and I could smell her astonishment. And curiosity. Hell, I'd certainly been curious at one point myself. But there was more to Jaxson than the hot sex. And the amazing abs. And the low gravel of his voice, and the way he knew how to move his hands...

I cleared my throat. *He's thrown his life on the line again and again to protect me, and when my heart was breaking, he was there to hold and comfort me. Once, I couldn't stand him, but now, I can't stand the idea of being without him. I've never experienced life the way I have when I'm near him.*

She gave me a wry look. *Wow. The sex is that good, huh?*

Oh, right, she knew me. I met her eyes with a smile. *Out of this world. A dozen times better than anything I've had before. Trust me, you don't want to pass on that.*

My shard looked back to the alpha on the hill and the ghost pack. Was our mother somewhere out there? It didn't matter—I had to push her over the edge.

I stepped close. *I know this place is safe and that the pain and fear are over. But trust me, before we met Jaxson, we'd never truly lived—and we have a lot of living left to do.*

My shard paused for a long time before she spoke again. *Okay.*

Okay? Joy swelled in my chest. The nightmare of being broken would be over soon.

My shard shrugged. *Hell, I'm not going to miss out on all the fun with Jaxson if it's as good as you say it is. And seriously, I'm not going to leave our friends and family in danger. Would you?*

Of course not. We were the same.

She gave me a wolf grin. *And why pass up a great opportunity to get killed again by a god? I've already died once. It's only deeply traumatizing.*

I dipped my head. *Thank you.*

She turned to look me in the eyes. *But let me run with Mom one last time.*

My stomach twisted. I needed that as much as she did, if not more so. *Can you take me to her?*

With a decisive shake of her fur, my shard headed back toward the waiting pack, and I followed.

Jaxson approached cautiously with an expectant look, and I gave him a nod. *Success.*

My shard eyed him with an appreciative, if slightly apprehensive look.

As we neared the pack, the ghost wolf alpha stepped forward. *You have chosen to rejoin the land of the living.*

Yes, my shard replied.

He bowed his head. *I have given my word. You may go.*

A great weight slid off my shoulders. He'd been so cold, I was terrified he would still try to stop her.

It was really happening. I was going to be whole. Head spinning with elation, I advanced to stand beside my shard. *How do we...reunite ourselves?*

The alpha's reply sent low reverberations through my body. *Run together and become as one.*

My heart began hammering. *May we run with the pack?*

The ghost wolf alpha's eyes turned hard. *One day, but not today. You have made your choice, and now you must leave my lands. Your place is not with the dead, but with the living.*

My stomach knotted, and my shard whined in protest. As if in response to the sound, a silver wolf darted down the hill.

I knew her instantly from her scent, even though I'd never seen her like this: my mom.

42

Savannah

My mom slowed as she approached.

I was so overwhelmed, I could barely breathe.

She looked between us, a torrent of emotion surging in her eyes. *You're...alive.*

A lump formed in my throat, and unable to articulate everything I wanted to say in wolf speech and gesture, I simply nodded.

She took a swift step forward and rubbed against me. Even though the sun still slightly shimmered through her form, I could feel her, just as much as I'd been able to feel Stephanie's touch.

Joy flooded my body, and my heart began to sing. For a long time, we just nuzzled against each other, reunited after sixteen years apart.

I don't know how long we stayed like that. There was so much unspoken, but we didn't need to speak at all.

Finally, the ghost wolf alpha's voice boomed in my mind. *The sun sets. You must leave us now.*

My mother stood back. *You've come to take this one away from me.*

A sudden dread began to rise in my chest. How could I do this to them? To *myself*? But I had to, and I hung my head. *Yes.*

Don't leave, my mother pleaded. *Run with us.*

All the joy inside of me died. There was nothing I wanted more, but I couldn't.

We have to go.

My mother rubbed against me. *Come with me—your father will want to see you. I run with the pack, but I reside with him in the woods. I can take you there. The journey's long, but his heart will soar to see you.*

My heart wasn't soaring. It was screaming toward the earth.

My parents. After all these years, this was my chance to reunite with them—to tell them about my life in Belmont and Magic Side, about Jaxson, about everything I'd become. To spend time with them—time I'd squandered when I was young.

I looked up at the ghost wolf alpha. *Please, may I run with the pack? Just to see my father again.*

Stay or go, I do not care, the alpha rumbled. *The choice is yours. But it is permanent, and if you do not return to your world soon, that choice will be made for you.*

The loremaster had warned me that the ghosts would try to keep me here. To seduce me into joining them, not out of spite, I knew, but out of love.

But I couldn't stay, no matter how much I wanted it.

Tears welled in my eyes, and I buried my head in my mother's fur. *I need to return to Magic Side. Aunt Laurel and Uncle Pete, Casey, who you never knew, the pack—they're all depending on me. I have a life there. A love there.*

I nodded to Jaxson.

She inspected him with distraught eyes, then nuzzled me

again, each movement pulling on my soul. *I understand what you must do. Go—both of you—with my love.*

I'm sorry, I cried.

I'm not, she said. *I got to see you again for a moment, to know you're well and have found love, that you're doing great things in the world. One day, we will be reunited, my love. I'll tell your father. He'll be heartbroken with pride.*

I could barely stand for my grief. *Tell Dad I love him, that I think of him every time I sit in my car, that I'll learn every spell he inscribed so that one day, I'll understand what his magic was truly like. I love you both more than words can say. And one day, I promise, we'll run together again.*

The ghost wolf alpha growled from the ridgeline, and I could sense his growing anger. *The pack is waiting. You have what you came for—now leave my lands.*

~

Jaxson

I placed my head against Stephanie's. *I'll miss you. Thank you. This means everything.*

I'll watch over you, but you must watch over our pack. They need you. Go. She shoved me with her head, then trotted away.

A stabbing pain cut through my chest as she melted into the pack of ghostly wolves.

She was never one for long goodbyes.

I looked to Savannah and her shard. *Ready?*

With a last mournful look at the ghost pack, they nodded.

Then you heard the alpha—let's run, I said.

Reluctantly, we left the ghost pack behind and began the long journey back to the mausoleum, following the scent of our old trail.

I poured my strength into each stride and set a feverish pace. Savannah, never to be outdone, kept up, as did her shard.

We wouldn't be able to maintain the sprint for long, but the loremaster's warnings were burning in my mind. I wanted to get Savannah and myself away from the ghost pack before her shard had second thoughts.

The three of us bounded along through the trees and sparse underbrush of the wooded hills. I had no idea what time it was. The sun here kept doing tricky things.

Eventually, Savannah and her shard settled into a steady pace beside me—twin wolves, identical in every way, except one was just slightly translucent and allowed the light to glisten through. It was almost impossible to take my eyes off them, and I found myself slowing slightly just to keep them in the corners of my vision.

Before long, we entered the mist, but I didn't slow our pace. I could still smell our path, and we needed to leave this place as quickly as possible.

As the sky began to darken and the light became more diffuse, Savy's shard began to fade as well.

Focused on the grueling run, Savannah said nothing, so I kept my mouth shut.

Stride by stride, her shard disappeared, and Savannah began to take on a new glow—a life that had been missing from her since she'd been wounded. Without warning, she suddenly shifted into human form, swift and perfect as before. As I pulled to a stop, she stood and braced herself against a tree.

Then she began to cry.

I shifted in a split second, and she slumped into my arms. "It's okay, darling."

She dug her nails into my back and wept into my shoulder, her whole body shaking. My heart raced as I held her, and I tried to flood her with all the love and confidence and strength I had.

After a while, she sniffed and rubbed the back of her wrist under her nose. "God, Jaxson, look at me. I'm a mess. But I'm whole."

My spirit leapt. "It worked?"

"My God, it worked!" She grasped my arms. "Do you know what this means? I'm free. The Dark God can't control me anymore. *I'm free*!"

I looked down at her shoulder. "Your wound—it's starting to close."

Beaming, Savy threw herself into my arms, and I sucked in a sharp breath as she pressed her bare body against mine. Then, just as quickly, she was out of my embrace and pacing.

"I remember it all, Jax. All her memories of this land, they're mine. Running with my mom and the ghost pack, and even seeing my dad again—their love, their pride. My heart is overflowing." She closed her eyes as an expression of grace lightened the shadows of her face. "I thought the ghost wolf alpha had denied me a chance to be with them again, but all those memories my shard made in this land, they're a part of me now. All the questions I was dying to ask, she asked. I'll have it all because of her."

She turned away and wiped her eyes.

Unsure of what to say, I gently traced my fingers down her back, then wrapped my arms around her and lightly kissed the side of her neck.

She reached up and ran her fingers through my hair. "I don't know how to explain it. I'm glowing. I'm exploding from the inside out. I have my wolf and my shard, and I'm free of my bonds. Honestly, I don't think I've ever been whole before."

I smiled. "I'm looking forward to knowing the whole you, but I'm afraid it might be more than I can handle."

She pivoted so that I found her in my arms again, smiling up at me. "I know you can handle it."

And with that, she kissed me. Not a hungry kiss filled with passion and lust, but a soft and tender touch.

Desire, adoration, and devotion flooded my chest, and I pulled my mate to me, dragging my fingers through her hair. I wasn't used to these feelings, but they stirred something deep inside of me I couldn't quite describe. I'd burn the fucking world down for this woman. And whatever the fates had in store for us, I'd spend every last breath making sure she was happy and loved.

Though the urge to make good on my word right then beckoned, reality came rushing back. We had to get the fuck out of here before it was too late.

I broke off the kiss and dragged my thumb over her jaw. "While I want nothing more than to disappear with you for a while, we'd better get home."

Savannah closed her eyes and sighed forlornly. "I know. Just promise me something, Jax."

"Anything, darling."

She opened her eyes and gazed up at me with a look that slayed. She was so godsdamned beautiful. "Let's make it out of this alive."

My heart damn near shattered.

"I promise," I said, putting on a smile, though my chest was cracking as fear and protectiveness and doubt tried to cleave their way out. I shouldn't be making promises I couldn't keep.

"Let's go see what your crazy cousin and Sam have been up to," I said, trying to lighten the mood. And with a single motion, I shifted and bounded into the trees.

Savannah was right on my heels, and we were running.

Eventually, we found our way back to the lake, and

Savannah hurried to the tree where her clothes were still scattered like a mad racoon had rummaged through them.

She shifted back into human form, and I followed suit. "We can leave all that. We'll be slower on two feet."

"*You* will, but I have my speed boots, and I'm not leaving them behind. The Moon may not have wanted them, but they *are* my prized possession, thank you very much. We also can't leave our phones."

A fair point. With a grunt, I grabbed my clothes, making sure that my phone and wallet were still there—not like anyone here would steal them. Old habits.

Savannah pulled on her jeans, then slipped into her top. "Let me carry your things. You run as a wolf, and I'll keep up in my boots."

Once she was dressed, I passed her my bundle of clothes. "Okay, let's go."

With that, we were off and sprinting.

The tall pines rose from the dense ground mist that eddied around their bases. It was impossible to judge the time, but we must have run several miles when the clearing appeared ahead.

At the opposite end was the derelict mausoleum, covered in moss and leaves. Relief hit me when I saw the gray, churning emptiness inside—the portal was still up.

"Thank God," Savy gasped, her chest heaving from exhaustion as she laid my clothes on the grass.

I shifted back into human form and quickly dressed, then took her hand. "Let's go home."

43

Savannah

The ether closed in like the ocean depths, icy and oppressive. Every inch of my body screamed. Unlike traveling to the Deadlands, coming back was like passing through molasses. The distant whispers of the dead followed us, and I swore I could feel their freezing grip trying to pull us back into the Deadlands. My pulse quickened as my panic rose, but then the weight and the pain and the exhaustion released.

I gasped and stumbled across the limestone floor of the mausoleum, and Jaxson's arm swooped around my waist, steadying me.

"We made it." My throat felt like sandpaper, but my strength was slowly returning. The familiar marble catacombs rose around us, lining the walls, and a candle flickered on a pedestal in the center of the room.

Jaxson cupped my cheek, his fingers lingering on my jaw. "You did it."

His eyes flashed a honey gold, and my heart stuttered as a flurry of emotions flooded me. Overwhelming. All-consuming. I cared about him in ways I'd never experienced before, and it had nothing to do with the mate bond. This man was everything. I pressed my hand over his. "*We* did it."

An explosion rang out nearby, and the mausoleum shook.

"What the fuck was that?" Jaxson released me and crossed to the metal doors. They creaked as he opened them, and his body immediately tensed. I stepped up beside him and froze. The magical barrier around the garden must have been breached.

Smoke rose in the distance above Dockside, and an orange glow lit the darkening sky. Ash and burned metal stung my nose, and the echo of screams carried on the breeze.

He's here, Wolfie said.

No. We weren't ready. It wasn't time!

Jaxson already had his phone pressed to his ear. It rang once, and with my wolf senses back, I heard Sam's voice. "Jax! You're alive! Where are you?"

"The Garden of the Wolves. What's happening?" he answered.

An explosion echoed through his phone, and Sam cursed. "The Dark God's cracked open a rift in Dockside. Something's happening to the wolves. You've got to get out of there."

Terror iced my veins.

"Where are you?" Jaxson's voice was calm, but every muscle in his body was taut.

"The Indies. On my way to Laurel's—" Screams cut her off. "Fuck. All hell's broken loose. The demons and the Order have erected magical barriers to the north and west. Laurel and the sorcerers are putting one up on the south. You better get here fast."

Magical barriers? Would that be enough to contain the Dark God?

"Got it. But I thought we had more time," said Jaxson.

A brief burst of incredulous laughter rang through the phone. "You've been gone for three days. Hell, I'd almost given you two up for dead. Glad to be mistaken, but your timing could be better."

"Yeah, well, thanks for the welcome party," he said dryly. "We're on our way."

"Be careful, Jax. Some of the wolves have gone AWOL. They're attacking people—" she began, but the line disconnected.

"Fuck!" Jaxson pocketed his phone. "We'll cut through the park, and when we hit the streets, we'll make tracks. My truck is parked a few blocks from Eclipse."

"Will we be able to get through the barriers?"

"I fucking hope so."

We moved silently through the garden. My muscles felt like jelly, and my magic was still replenishing, but I felt whole again with Wolfie and the shard back.

It's good to be back, Wolfie said. *We'd better not die tonight.*

We didn't come this far to lose.

As we emerged from the woods around the mausoleum, I skidded to a stop and sucked in a breath. "Look at that..."

Jaxson followed my gaze up to the brilliant streaks of light that painted the sky. It was beautiful and eerie. Green and yellow lights flared to the north, while vivid reds flashed to the west like the northern lights on steroids.

"Those must be the magical barriers," Jaxson said.

The sky to the south was still dark, suggesting the sorcerers hadn't gotten theirs up yet. Were they waiting for us? I hoped that was the reason, and not that the barrier had already fallen.

We took off into the park, the familiar scents of oak and damp earth easing some of the fear that had taken root in my gut. What were we going to do?

Close the rift and lock the bastard away, Wolfie answered.

Easier said than done.

Tires screeched up ahead, followed by the crunching of

metal. We stepped out of the wooded park onto 63rd into an entirely different world.

Chaos.

I'm gone for a few days, and all hell breaks loose, Wolfie remarked.

A man darted by, his shirt torn and a look of utter terror on his face. Acrid smoke burned my throat. A light post bowed over the street, its bulb flickering. The SUV that had struck it was half on the sidewalk, steam rising from its dented hood.

Shrieks pierced the air, and a faint, dark mist drifted down the street. Flickers of golden light flared inside it like a million twinkling stars in a midnight sky. *That* wasn't natural.

Jaxson towed me across the road as I took in the madness. He'd said something, but I barely registered the words, too transfixed by the strange mist that moved like an ethereal creature.

On our left, a figure careened out of the mist. Hair sprouted from his arms and neck, and when he turned, his yellow eyes locked onto me. His face was that of a wolf.

Dread chilled my skin. Half wolf and half human, he was stuck in a shift.

"Jaxson, look," I whispered.

As I did, the man's body jerked, and a blood-curdling scream tore from his throat. Then he bolted toward us like a rabid animal.

Jaxson shoved me to the side as the man leapt at us. Searing pain shot through my upper arm as the man's claws dragged through flesh. I staggered but regained my footing as Jaxson threw him into the side of a brick building. His body slumped to the sidewalk, unconscious.

Jax turned back to me, worry cutting his face as he glanced at the wound on my arm. Blood dripped down my fingers, and the thing burned, but I already felt my skin beginning to heal. "It's fine. Just a scratch. Come on!"

I took off down the sidewalk, keeping an eye on the strange mist expanding around us. Jaxson's truck was parked up ahead, shrouded by the sparkling haze.

Shit.

We stopped a few feet from the truck. The magic pulsing off the mist smelled of ash and flame, but it was so frigid that it raised goosebumps on my skin: the Dark God's signature.

"I don't think we should touch the mist," I said.

"We don't have a choice, darling," Jaxson whispered, as if reticent to alert the weird fog to our presence.

He was right—we needed to get to the truck, and fast. The mist had crept in around us, blocking off all exits, almost as if it were pursuing us.

Hunting.

Jaxson palmed his keys and unlocked the truck. "Ready?"

What options did we have? Any way we moved, we'd have to face the haze. I nodded, and we darted toward the truck. Tingles cascaded over my skin the instant the mist enveloped me, but otherwise, I felt nothing. I reached for the passenger door, and—

Wolfie howled in my mind, and pain rocked my body. I doubled over, my claws slipping out as I felt a shift coming on, but it wasn't me who was in control.

The Dark God's presence infiltrated me like the floodwaters of a broken levy. I clutched my head and saw Jaxson across the hood, struggling. He was affected by it, too.

Stop fighting me, Savannah. The Dark God's voice pierced my mind.

This douchebag clearly doesn't know you at all, Wolfie growled.

I would have laughed, but the agony that tore through my

body was too strong. Anger simmered under my skin, and I latched onto it as I drew my magic inward.

Get out!

I thought of Sam and what I'd done to her. Of my aunt and uncle and cousin, all depending on me. I didn't survive this fucking long to give in to *him*.

With a burst of energy, I forced the bastard out. The aching pain ceased, and I had control over my body again.

Jaxson leaned against the hood of the truck, his head tilted down and the corded muscles in his forearms popping. He was fighting the Dark God's magic, too.

Shadows poured out of my fingers, and with a flick of my wrists, they launched forward, driving the mist away from Jaxson. He growled and straightened, his gaze locking on me. "Let's get the fuck out of here."

With a quick nod, I flung the door open and slid into the passenger seat. Jaxson was beside me in seconds, and the truck rumbled to life. He hit the gas, and we lurched forward. Jaxson swerved around another wrecked car in the street, and I looked out the side window, which peaked above the low-lying haze.

Things were fucked. The mist had completely enveloped Dockside, by the looks of it. It pressed in around the truck, the sparks within it flaring and flickering, as if it were alive and agitated.

I shivered and steeled my nerve.

This was going to be one hell of a fight.

We've been fighting our whole life, Wolfie said. *Let's finish this.*

44

Jaxson

The tires of my truck screeched as I pulled onto Razorback Avenue. My skin still crawled from the Dark God's magic, and a deep dread churned my soul. When he'd forced the shift, I'd heard him loud and clear, as if he'd been standing right beside me. His words repeated on loop in my head: *I will take her from you. Tonight, your soul will be ripped in two.*

I glanced at Savy. She clutched the door handle, her brows pinched together, looking as beautiful as ever, even as we perched on the edge of a knife. I sensed her fear, and my chest ached. Fury rippled through me. I wasn't accustomed to feeling helpless. I couldn't lose her. I *wouldn't.*

The further south we drove, the more wolves and half-shifted people appeared from the flickering fog. It was like hell had been ripped open and was spilling into Magic Side.

I caught sight of Eclipse as we roared through Dockside. Smoke billowed into the sky, and I tightened my fists on the steering wheel.

A gray wolf strutted across the road up ahead, and I slowed down as smoke clouded the air. I didn't need to crash right now.

The Dark God's magic was pressing in around us, and I had a sick feeling that it was only a matter of time before he infiltrated our minds and bodies again.

Savannah pointed out the window. "Holy shit, Jaxson, that woman!"

I followed her gaze to the sidewalk where a young woman, Fae by the look of her tipped ears, was in the early throes of a shift. On her neck was a dripping wound. My blood curdled. She wasn't a werewolf—what was happening?

"It looks like she was bitten," Savannah said, then looked at me. "Could it be lycanthropy?"

"Impossible."

Lycanthropy was a rare disease transmitted from werewolf to non-wolf that brought on wolfish aspects, but it had been nearly wiped out in our world.

I slowed the truck as we rolled by the woman. Claws tore from her fingers, and she screamed as the bones and sinews of her body rearranged themselves.

"Oh, my God," Savannah gasped. "Can we help her?"

She rose, half woman, half wolf. Just like the other poor bastard we'd seen.

I hit the gas. "Lycanthropy or not, this is the Dark God's work. There's nothing we can do for her now."

I wasn't certain that was the truth, but we had no time to stop.

Guilt tore at me as I watched the woman in the rearview mirror as we sped away. I was at least partially responsible for this shit, but I wouldn't risk Savannah's safety by stopping and helping those poor souls. My mate was everything to me now, and perhaps our only chance at stopping the fucking Dark Wolf God.

"It's the mist," Savannah said quietly. "He's working through it...taking over peoples' wolves and making them go crazy."

Godsdamnit. If she was right and the Dark God was using the mist to infect people, how long did we have until he turned the whole island? Before newly transformed and apparently crazed wolves started infiltrating Chicago?

A loud thud hit the back of my truck. I looked in the mirror to find another half-shifted man clawing at the window, scraping up my new paint job. *Motherfucker.*

"Hold on," I growled.

I hit the brakes, and the tires skidded and screeched across the asphalt. The man slammed into the window of the bed and flew over the roof, rolling on the sidewalk. I ground my teeth. He'd broken an arm and was pretty busted up, but he'd live.

Savannah turned to me, shocked.

"What?"

She shook her head and looked out the front. "Nothing, just a moment of déjà vu from the night I met you."

A sick turn of fate.

Dodging cars, debris, and rampant wolves made the rest of our trip to the Indies painfully slow. Up ahead, a piercing wall of light illuminated the sky. The sorcerers must have erected their magical barrier.

We'd better be able to fucking get through.

Savannah had her phone to her ear and was tapping her fingers anxiously on the window.

"Savy?" Her cousin's voice sounded on the line.

"Casey! We're almost to the border with the Indies. Can we drive through the barrier that just went up?"

"Savy, damn it! Yeah, it only keeps the Dark God's scourge out, but anything else has free crossing. But we have physical barricades, too—piled-up dumpsters and shit. Cross at the intersection of 73rd and Ironwood. Get your ass over here. We're being bombarded by crazy-ass wolves."

"Be careful," Savy warned. "And don't get bitten. We'll be there in five minutes."

"Fuck! Where've you been for the last three days? I was afraid you were dead!"

"Only sort of. I'm back now and ready to kick some ass. Keep the drawbridge down."

She hung up and dragged a hand through her hair. "I still can't believe we were gone for three whole days."

I tightened my grip. "The loremaster told us time was different in the Deadlands. We've lost any chance to prep."

Savy shook her head. "Doesn't matter. We trusted Sam and Regina, and it sounds like they did their job. We're alive and moving, so that's good, but we need a plan. We've got to find a way to close that rift."

I grunted with dark amusement. "A plan to close the rift? Right now, I'm just trying to keep us alive and get us out of Dockside. Let's hope the Order—or hell, your aunt—has a plan to shut it."

Swerving onto Ironwood Ave, I immediately slowed. The translucent magical barrier along the border to the Indies was nearly blinding. It rose into the heavens, emitting a brilliant white glow.

But the strange, flickering mist crept around the buildings, drawing nearer.

The closer we got to the magical barrier, the more blinding it became. I could barely keep my eyes open as we roared through the wall of light.

As soon as we were through, I slammed on the brakes.

The truck fishtailed and screeched to a stop just in front of a makeshift barricade of overturned dumpsters and a shipping container.

I parked on the shoulder and climbed out, and Savannah scrambled after me.

Casey's head peeked over the barrier. "Get your asses over here, now!"

Claws scraped on asphalt behind us, and I spun.

Three rabid-looking wolves lunged toward us, but before I could extend my claws, magic ripped through the air.

Wind and electricity whipped around us, and a fireball grazed my head. It blasted into the lead wolf just as he leapt for Savy and drove him howling into the ground.

I grabbed Savannah's hand and pulled her with me to the barricade. We jumped over, and the barrage overwhelmed the attacking wolves. They retreated, leaving one unconscious. Or dead.

Savannah flew into the arms of her cousin. "Casey!"

"Holy crap, you made it," he said, squeezing her. "Thank the gods. Mom's about to have a stroke."

Sam stormed over and pulled Savy from his arms to hug her, too, then turned toward Casey, her face a mask of rage. "How many times do I have to tell you to knock that shit off? Get your people under control! No fireballs. No lethal magic. Those are *our people*! They're just not in their right mind!"

Casey threw his hands in the air. "What do you expect me to do? Those furry bastards are vicious and were going to take a bite out of my cousin. I don't care who they were."

Sam locked him with a steely gaze, and he took a step back. "No fireballs," she snarled.

The sorcerers and wolves guarding the perimeter watched them with held breath.

Casey let out a big sigh. "Fine. But we can't take any more losses—I've already got two of my boys bit and infected. We're doing this my way." He twirled his finger in the air, signaling to one his cronies, who was parked beside a series of black crates. "Wolfsbane it is."

Had he lost his damn mind?

Two of the crates were full of black cannisters of wolfsbane, while a third was stacked with gas masks. Casey grabbed three masks, tossed one to Sam, then strolled over to Savy and me and handed us each one.

"Casey, you're kidding right? You know that wolfsbane hurts us," Savy said. "Half the people here are werewolves."

"No shit. But unless you have a better idea, *this* is how we keep *them* out."

Sam looked at me expectantly. They all did—werewolves and sorcerers alike.

Casey's people were bruised and battered, and even our wolves—who could heal—had tattered clothes and seemed exhausted. By the looks of it, they'd been holding this position for a long time, and shit wasn't going to ease up.

"Do it," I growled. "But don't kill anyone."

"You got it, boss." Casey spun and waved his buddies over.

Sam touched my arm. "Things are bad here, Jax. There's a mist that turns our people crazy—or, more accurately, puts them under *his* control. And anyone bitten becomes...a hybrid. Half human, half wolf, and completely mad."

I nodded. "We've seen the transformation happen, but we didn't know how it worked, exactly."

Sam looked at Savy. "Whatever you do, don't go into the mist. He tries to take control. It's...*horrible*. We can't be anywhere near it."

Laurel LaSalle's shout cut through our conversation. "*Savy*!"

She came running up the street and pulled Savy into her arms for a lingering hug. Finally, she released her. "You're okay?"

Savannah smiled. "Let's not leap to conclusions, but I'm complete. What can we do to help?"

Laurel's eyes darkened. "As far as we can tell, the Dark Wolf God has opened a rift in Dockside. His magic—that shimmering mist—is pouring through. We must close it before he collects enough power to cross through himself."

"How do we do that?"

"Follow me," she said.

She led us to a makeshift workbench, where her husband, Pete, was hunched over. The top was inscribed with a circle of spells, and in the center sat a silver object that looked like an astrolabe. He glanced up and smiled, but his eyes were weary. "It's done, I think."

Laurel peered down at it. Worry and doubt swirled around her, but she steeled her nerves and squeezed her husband's hand before looking to me and Savy. "We'll find the rift, and I'll use this talisman to sew it shut. This is the needle, and my magic will be the thread."

For a moment, Savannah admired the talisman on the workbench, then looked up at her aunt with an expression of deep sorrow. "This is amazing, but I don't think sealing the rift will be enough."

"What do you mean?"

"We need to go back through to bind the Dark God in his realm before you seal the rift. Otherwise, sooner or later, he'll make a new one," Savy said. Though she spoke with confidence, I saw the despair and fear in her eyes.

We'd gotten lucky last time, escaping with our lives. Returning to the Dark God's realm to finish what we'd failed was likely a one-way ticket.

"Bind him? How could you possibly do that?" Laurel asked.

"Long ago, the Moon bound him there, but her spells were failing," Savy said. "We've started the process of repairing them, but we have one left. If we succeed, the spells will recharge, and the Dark God will be stuck in his realm for good."

Understanding shadowed Laurel's face. "You're going into his realm, to face him?"

"If we don't, all this will happen again." She lightly touched the astrolabe in Laurel's hand. "Once we lock him away, will that thing be powerful enough to close the rift?"

Laurel looked off to the shining barrier, a tear shimmering in the corner of her eye. "It sure as hell better be."

45

Savannah

As soon as he was done with us, Uncle Pete dashed off to tend to the wounded, and dread writhed in my gut like a sea of snakes.

The longer we spent on our side of the barrier, the worse things seemed. I could see the cracks—overtaxed spells, exhausted wolves, and hurt and barely standing sorcerers. Whatever had happened while we were away had taken its toll, and it was only going to get worse.

The shimmering barrier above us flickered as trails of mist leaked through.

"Is the barrier okay?" I asked my aunt.

Her face took on a dark expression. "It's failing already. Too many of the sorcerers maintaining the barrier have gone down, and the rest are tiring."

Casey rejoined us. "I don't think we can take another charge like that last one. It was twenty or thirty wolves all at once, and they're regrouping." He tossed Sam a riot gun. "One shot. Wolfsbane suppression cartridge. You're going to want to have it. I just wish we had more."

She started to open her mouth, then snapped it shut.

"Regrouping?" Jaxson asked.

"They come in waves. They're totally feral for a bit right after they shift, but then they seem to fall under his control—it's like he's playing with pieces on a chessboard."

And if I hadn't gotten Wolfie back, I would have been his queen.

Casey grimaced. "You guys should take a look at what we're up against."

He led us through the blindingly bright barrier and out of the other side, where we crouched down behind a car.

The sparkling mist had risen, though it stopped ten feet short of the wall of light. Further into Magic Side, the dark fog rose above the tops of buildings, massing like a storm cloud in the air—a cloud in the shape of a wolf's head. All around us, the Dark God's power vibrated through the city, shaking the very asphalt beneath our feet.

"I don't think your barriers are just weakening," Jaxson whispered. "His power is growing. Can't you feel it?"

I nodded.

"Maybe," Casey said as he passed over a pair of goggles. "These are infrared. Check it out."

I pulled them on and popped my head over the top of the vehicle.

There were dozens upon dozens of hybrid werewolves out there, lurking in the glistening fog, maybe even a hundred. All waiting for a final, brutal assault. My gut twisted. "Holy shit." I sank back down and passed the goggles to Jax. "I think we've got a problem."

How were we ever going to fucking close the rift? There was a sea of feral werewolves and dark magic between us and it—wherever it even was.

On the other side of the barrier, our team wasn't looking so hot. The sorcerers and werewolves who weren't hurt were exhausted. On this side, the Dark God's strength was only growing.

We were going to fail.

My head slumped back against the undercarriage of the car, and I fought through my memories for any solution, or even just a shard of hope. I pressed my fingers against my forehead. What had the Moon said?

She'd warned us about this: *He draws his power from the presence of wolves.*

Well, he was in Werewolf Central in Dockside, and his mist was making more of his hybrids by the second. It was only a matter of time before it would break through the spells and flood over the city, turning everyone it touched into a monster under his control.

How great would the Dark God's power be then? Every person that he turned made him that much stronger.

The horror and despair of the moment crashed down on me like a wave, sending my heart tumbling into the churring darkness. And slowly, the horrible truth sank in—fighting the prophecy was futile. Despite everything I'd tried, there was no way to beat it. The words kept repeating over and over in my mind, like a bully taunting me on the playground: *In seven days, he will walk the earth once more, spreading madness among the living.*

Well, seven days had passed, and the entire city was going mad. But even as I sank further into despair, one phrase burned brighter than all the rest: *The twin-soul will steal the wolves from every werewolf who resists them and will leave your people weak before the Dark God.*

I still had a part to play. And it was, somehow, to betray everything I held dear.

Bitterness clouded my vision. But then, like the moment you see the other side of an optical illusion, when the goblet becomes two faces, everything changed.

My pulse began to beat faster and faster as the words of my damnation slowly transformed into a terrible glimmer of hope.

It was time to fulfill my fate.

Mind spinning, I staggered to my feet. "We need to talk to Laurel. Right now."

I didn't bother waiting for a reply, but rushed back through the barrier, with Casey and Jax on my heels. I found Laurel down the block, working through logistics with Sam and Regina.

I skidded to a stop, and she looked up in surprise. "Savy, what's wrong?"

Sam, Jax, Casey, Regina, and Laurel. Their eyes were all on me. Chest heaving, I looked from one to the next. "Our position is hopeless. There are too many. They're going to break through."

From the expressions on their faces, they knew it was true.

"We have one chance, but it's going to take an enormous amount of power," I continued. "We'll need all the sorcerers, and even then, I don't know if that'll be enough."

"What are you talking about?" Laurel asked.

The horror of the words sitting on my tongue was almost too much to bear. I met Jaxson's eyes. "We need to bind their wolves—all of them. A massive spell, to encompass all of Dockside."

Their faces froze in shock.

Casey whistled. "Holy shit, Savy."

"You can't be serious," Jaxson said, his voice practically failing him.

"I am." I took his hand in mine and begged him to listen with my eyes. "The Moon warned us that the Dark God draws his power from wolves. He's possessed half of Dockside. If we bind them, we free them from his control."

"This is madness!" Regina said.

I didn't look away from my mate, the only one whose approval mattered. "The prophecy said I would take the wolves of our people and make them weak before him. Well, in doing so, we take away his army *and* his power. Maybe without them, he won't have the strength to come through the rift."

Jaxson's churning emotions were an open book: shock, horror, and despair. "Savy, this—"

"I know exactly what I'm asking, Jaxson, and how horrible of a choice this is. *I've lived through it.*" My eyes welled up as the truth sank in. "I think fate has been preparing me for this moment my whole life. I know how to cast the spell, and I know how to reverse it. I know what it's like to have my wolf taken, and I know that it can be undone."

Comprehension dawned, and shadows of deep sadness fell across his face. He entwined his fingers with mine but couldn't find the words to speak.

"I have to become the monster of the prophecy to save our pack, to save us all. This is the path the fates ordained for me. I can feel it. Trust me."

His jaw hardened while his fingers tightened. "I trust you to the ends of the earth, in this world and in the next."

"You're alpha. It's your pack. But I believe it's the only way we can hope to weaken him, and the only way to stop the barriers from being overrun."

"You're certain you'll be able to reverse the spell?" Jaxson asked, his voice so flat, I knew he was repressing all emotion.

"I can. I've done it before. But you need to understand, if you have any doubt—those people out there have already lost their wolves to *him*. He's the one in control, not them. We're taking their wolves to give them back."

Finally, Jaxson nodded. "We must do it. I'll explain it to the wolves here in a way they'll understand."

Sam wiped her eyes and silently agreed.

Regina looked at me, and I held my breath. Finally, she nodded. "No way I let some fucking god take control of me or my wolf."

I let out a long and shaking sigh.

My aunt crossed her arms and knotted her fingers in her shirt. "To cast a spell that large, we'll need everyone here. I don't think we'll have the strength to keep maintaining the barrier after that."

I shook my head. "We have to risk the barrier—it's failing as it is. Even I can see that."

Dark expressions shaded everyone's faces except for my cousin's, which sported a giant grin. "Okay, this is a batshit crazy plan, and there are major consequences if we fail—so I love it. However, there's a big problem. This barrier keeps all magic out, not just his. If we leave the barrier up—which I *highly fucking* recommend—then we've got to go into the mist on the other side to cast the spell."

Shit.

What we needed was a windstorm. Unfortunately, Neve wasn't answering her calls, and I was pretty certain that the Order had their hands full with their barrier.

"Are any of your people really good with wind magic?" I asked.

Casey scratched his chin. "Yeah, I know a couple of folks who are windbags. What, we just fan the mist away and hope we don't get overrun with wolves?"

"Yes."

He looked to the others. "This sounds like a fucking fantastic way to die. I'm in."

One by one, they all agreed.

Aunt Laurel touched my arm softly, compassion in her eyes. "I'm sorry that we have to do this. That you must carry this."

I clenched my hand around Jaxson's. "Don't be. This is my fate. It always has been."

46

Savannah

Once the decision was made, we flew into motion. Aunt Laurel gathered her strongest sorcerers, Casey organized a team of bodyguards, and Jaxson spoke with the pack members manning the barrier, explaining what we were planning to do. I knew it had to be one of the hardest conversations of his life. At least they would be safe from the binding spell behind the wall of shimmering light.

What about me? Wolfie asked. *I mean, I'll take one for the team, but...*

You'll be fine. I'm casting the spell outward, not inward this time. And just like Casey doesn't usually fireball himself, you'll be okay.

I gotta say, that's a relief, my wolf replied.

Ten minutes later, Casey pounded on the side of his RAV4. "Okay, people, suicide mission time, let's rally. Savy's got the plan, so listen up!"

Heart pounding, I faced the gathered crowd. My mouth went dry, and my throat was tight, but I forced out the words. "We're about to attempt something very dangerous. If there was any other way, we'd take it. But to save werewolves on the other side of the wall from the Dark God's power, we'll need to bind their wolves."

Murmurs flowed through the crowd, though most knew what to expect by then—the rumors had gotten around quickly.

I pointed to the vehicles parked by the barricade. "We're going through the wall, and as soon as we're out there, they'll be on us. Be prepared. Circle up the vehicles and make a wall, and expect heavy resistance." I looked from one person to the next, seeing hard and grim faces. "Let's go take back our city."

Casey beat on his car door again. "You heard her! Everybody load up. Glorious deaths for the sorcerers, while the wolves get to watch us die. Win-win!"

Half-stifled smiles erupted around the circle as werewolves and sorcerers sheepishly met eyes. We all knew that at this moment, all we had was each other.

My cousin had a knack for saying the wrong thing, but in just the right way. Also, for saying the wrong thing in the wrong way, but right now, he was winning them over with bravado.

I felt a flicker of pride.

As sorcerers began to load into the vehicles, Casey waved his arm. "Remember, wolfsbane and non-lethal spells only! No blasting anyone with magic. They may look like monsters, but these are our friends. They're just having a...*ruff* day."

He winked at me and whispered, "Get it? *Ruff* day?"

I glared at him and shook my head. "Jokes like that are going to get you killed."

He shrugged. "Yeah, probably, but boy, have I *lived*."

I felt that puns like those were more like inner death.

Jaxson stalked over, his body rock hard with tension and his expression as dark as I'd seen it. "I should go with you. I can resist the spell."

I shook my head. "If we're going to go back into the Dark God's realm, you'll need your wolf. We can't risk it getting bound, and we won't have time to make a circle of protection." Seeing his face fall, I took his hand and entwined my fingers with his. "But I expect you to be there at my side the second after it goes off."

He placed his head against mine. "I will be."

Heart pounding, I wanted to hold on forever, but I knew it was time to face my fate.

I loaded up in Casey's SUV. "Let's do this."

Grinning, my cousin blared the horn.

A sorceress waved her hands, and the shipping container that was serving as a makeshift roadblock levitated. Casey hit the gas, and his RAV4 roared through the shining wall of light, followed by a convoy of three more vehicles.

I shut my eyes against the light, but I still saw stars when I opened them again on the other side.

We skidded to a halt a hundred feet beyond the barrier. The other vehicles pulled up alongside to make a makeshift wall—not that it would slow the wolves much. One of Casey's old girlfriends bailed out of the rear of the vehicle behind us and unleashed a massive gust of wind. The sparkling mists billowed back, away from our vehicles. That was our cue.

We all jumped out into a magic windstorm. As soon as our feet hit the ground, the crazy-eyed hybrids charged, jaws wide and claws out.

Riot guns echoed beside us as our bodyguards fired wolfsbane cannisters into the converging pack.

I blocked out the cries of pain as I ran to Laurel's side, where the other sorcerers and sorceresses had gathered. There were eight of us in all—most beaten, bloody, and exhausted.

A crash of metal and glass thundered behind us, followed by howls of agony, but I didn't look back. I had to trust that Casey's people could hold the line.

Laurel extended her hands. "Everyone, link up, with Savy in

the middle. We don't have a circle to work with, so we'll have to be her circle. Give her your strength and power. Help her control and shape the spell."

They joined hands around me. I looked at their hard and fearful faces. Some I knew, some were neighbors, and some I'd never met before, but we were all risking our lives here together.

My stomach knotted with thankfulness and remorse, fear and hope.

Laurel began to chant a spell I didn't recognize, and the others followed suit. Soon, their clasped hands started to glow, and magic began to swirl around the circle between us.

Don't forget to leave me out of the spell, Wolfie half-teased. *Twice bound is enough.*

I've got you, I told her, then steeled my nerve and closed my eyes. *Showtime.*

The magic whirling around the circle poured through me, and I felt my body burn with power. Not a single power, like the Moon's had been, but many—the signatures of seven others. Individual tastes, scents, and sounds merged into a maddening cacophony that threatened to overwhelm my senses.

Focus, Wolfie said. *You're a wolf—you can manage sensory overload.*

With a deep breath, I pulled in more of their magic until it felt like my body would dissolve into pure light.

I had this.

I knew the spell. I hadn't merely cast it—I'd *lived* it for decades. Once my aunt had taught me the words, I realized that they'd been wrapped around me my whole life.

Those words had *been* my life.

I began to speak them, enchanting them with the precision of my father's runes and of Laurel's spellcraft. The magic reverberated through my body and into the ground we stood upon.

Suddenly, a scream broke my concentration—a voice I knew well. *Casey*.

I whipped my head around, and horror flowed through me. One of the savage hybrids had my cousin pinned down, his arm in its jaws. Blood poured from his mouth.

The words seized in my throat.

A bodyguard threw up her hands. Light flashed, and a bolt of electricity shot forth. The werewolf and Casey flew apart, but hybrids attacked them both before he could recover.

"Complete the spell, Savannah!" my aunt shouted. "They're getting overrun! It's their only chance!"

I tore my eyes from my cousin and hardened my heart. I had to stop this. I hurled my head back and threw my voice toward the heavens.

But when I spoke the words, they didn't come out in human speech, but as a mournful howl.

Thunder cracked, and energy ripped through me. All the air vanished from the center of the circle, and for a second, my voice had no sound.

Then an explosion of power rocketed outward.

I felt my life pour into this moment. The chains that had bound me would now bind others. The spell that had protected me from the Dark God's control would now protect them.

The bright shockwave rolled through Dockside, ripping through the Dark God's magic and burning away the mist.

I staggered forward, drained and dizzy, and dropped to my knees.

Or I would have, except strong hands grasped me and pulled me up. Jaxson held me against him as tears filmed my vision. "You did it, Savy."

My body and magic were drained, and my soul felt ready to collapse into dust. But his touch meant that none of it mattered.

I wanted him to hold me forever, but I pushed back and took his hand. "Casey's hurt."

We rushed to my cousin's side. There was blood everywhere, and he had huge gouges on his chest and arms. His eyes rolled toward me. "I don't feel so good, cuz..."

"I told you to be careful!" Laurel sobbed.

Uncle Pete dropped down beside his son and pulled out a bright green flask with a shaking hand. "Hold on, Case, this is going to sting."

Casey's eyes went wide, and his pupils dilated in terror. "No! Not that, I choose dea—aaaaggghhh!" he screamed as Uncle Pete poured a smoking silver brew over his wounds. The flesh boiled and bubbled and slowly knit back together, and a reeking cloud of vapor billowed into the air, the thick scent of burning skin and hair.

I almost lost my cookies.

"Shit! It's so bad!" Casey moaned as he rolled over. "Why can I taste it? It's a fucking topical salve."

My kneeling aunt buried her face against Casey's arm, but after a moment, Uncle Pete pulled her back. "Give him a little space. He'll heal."

Casey looked up at me with a wild expression. "They fucking bit me! That's how it spreads. I was in the spell, right? I'm not going get it, right? I don't wanna be a werewolf!"

Pete looked to Laurel, and her face darkened. "We don't know how the magic works, but your father's potion seems to be doing the trick."

My uncle waved to one of the other bodyguards. "We need to get him inside and under observation."

We helped Casey to his feet, and then his old girlfriend—the one who had caused the windstorm—got under his shoulder and led him back to the car.

"I'm a war hero now, you know..." he muttered hopefully.

Clearly, he was going to be okay.

People rushed in all directions around us, helping the wounded as well as the hybrids, who'd all returned to human form and were wandering about in horror and confusion.

Jaxson gripped my hand as distressed cries rose around us. I could feel his heart break, and he wanted to go to his people. But we had work to do.

Tearing her face away from her wounded son, Laurel looked to me. "You did well. I think you saved a lot of people."

She looked as exhausted as I felt, and I shook my head. "I bought us time is all. His magic is going to keep pouring out of the Dreamlands unless we can restore the Moon's spells and seal the rift."

She nodded, tired lines showing on her face, and turned to her husband. "Pete, do you have the talisman?"

He pulled two potions out of his satchel. "Yes, but you're in no shape to keep fighting. Drink these."

We each took one, and a subtle dread of what it might be weighed on my shoulders. I was about to go face down the Dark God himself, and yet, that potion—drinking it was a truly terrifying prospect.

I popped the top, clinked potions with Laurel, and kicked it back.

I regretted everything I'd ever put in my mouth the moment I tasted it. The sticky black substance made my stomach churn, and I was certain it would have been better to have been born without a tongue.

"This is particularly bad, Pete," my aunt choked.

"What *was* that?" I whimpered.

He grinned wide. "Homemade restorative—think Red Bull for magic. I make them extra bad so that I'm not tempted to drink them myself and stay up late."

Even as he spoke, I felt new energy begin to flow through my veins.

He handed the talisman to Laurel. "Be careful, my love."

She kissed him. "Take care of our son. Make sure he doesn't turn into a wolf."

"I'll do what I can."

Laurel sent the sorcerers and sorceresses who had helped us back to the barricade. "Get some restoratives from Pete and prepare to move the wall. We need to seal off the area immediately around the rift. Lock him down."

They rushed away, and she turned to Jaxson and me. "Should we get this over with?"

"We'll take my truck," Jaxson said.

We headed back across the flickering barrier, and Sam bolted over. "You guys aren't going without me."

I grinned. "Wouldn't dream of it."

As Regina and Pete took control of the chaos, we loaded into Jaxson's truck, and then, with a set of bodyguards in the SUV behind us, we roared into Dockside.

The place was in shambles. Buildings had been looted and were burning. Lost and confused people wandered aimlessly.

Jaxson's anguish was so strong that I was sure even Laurel could read its signature.

He pointed toward the skyline in the northeast. "There's a glow on the horizon, over in the direction of Eclipse. That bastard better not have opened a fucking rift in the middle of my restaurant."

Luckily, it wasn't there.

As we rumbled across the Diagonal, Jaxson hit the brakes, then began to back up.

In the middle of the street, two blocks up, a black hole burned in the sky, from which the sparkling fog poured out. Light shone from its edges, but there was nothing in the center.

"Found it." He flipped us around, and we drove forward cautiously. The closer we got, the greater the destruction: overturned and burning cars, broken windows, and everywhere, scared and confused people.

Laurel called the Order to report what we'd done and the location of the rift.

We pulled to a stop half a block away and got out.

The rift floated about a foot off the ground. As if riding the mist, the energy of the Dark God infused everything around us. My spell had cleared the air...but not for long.

"Are you sure you have to go through?" Laurel asked me as the team of bodyguards formed a perimeter around us and the rift.

I nodded. "We need to recharge the last of the orbs, or he'll break through again."

She took my hand. "Please be careful. I can't lose you. Not again."

Sorrow sank into my gut, and I gave her a hug to hide my grief. "I can't lose you, either. Or Casey, or Uncle Pete. I swear I'll be back."

If she were a wolf, she'd have known that I didn't believe my own words. But Laurel just squeezed me tighter. "I'm not closing the rift until you come out, you hear?"

"Do it at the first sign of trouble. I have a talisman from the Moon. We can use it to escape, if need be, but I'm not sure where it'll send us. If the Dark God shows his face, shut it instantly."

I turned away quickly so she couldn't see my tears and stepped up in front of the rift. It radiated with his signature, vibrating through us into the ground—a slow hum, a song of death and destruction.

I took Jaxson's and Sam's hands and gave each a smile. "Here we go. Let's end this."

47

Jaxson

The ether whipped around us, as we stepped from Magic Side into the Dreamlands and certain peril. Would it be the last time any of us saw Dockside?

No matter how much that thought tore at me, I was with my mate. That was what mattered. And if there was no time left for us in this life, perhaps we could find happiness in the next, like Billy and my sister.

I looked around as I prowled forward, still holding Savy's hand. A light mist drifted through the trees, and my skin felt damp and sticky. Auburn leaves littered the ground, and large, twisted oaks stood guard like silent sentries. By its scent, I could tell it was the same forest we'd visited earlier.

Two pillars of light rose toward the heavens in the distance —the two pylons we'd recharged before.

Only one left. Something told me that it wasn't going to be as easy.

The place was eerily quiet, and the pounding of my heart sounded like an anvil.

I looked over my shoulder. The rift was still open behind us. I hoped that Laurel would do the right thing and close the opening if it came down to it, but I prayed to the gods that she wouldn't have to. Savy and I had gone through hell and back, and I wanted her to myself for one moment when we weren't fighting for our lives.

My mate clutched the moonstone Sam had given her, and I could sense the euphoria she felt holding it.

Savy pointed toward the woods where I could just make out a faint glow shimmering through the leaves. "The moonstone is pulling me that way. The orb has to be over there."

I sniffed the air, noting at least a dozen scents. "We need to go quiet and fast. There's no way that the Dark God has left the orb unguarded."

One by one, we rushed through the trees, moving quickly but keeping our footfalls quiet.

Suddenly, a black blur rushed through the trees on our left, and we skidded to a halt.

"We've got company," Sam hissed, as she reached for the riot gun Casey had given her.

I could smell them. The scent of musk and tobacco. Three powerful signatures, but none of them matched the Dark God's magic.

"We know you're there," I growled. "Come out and play."

Three massive black wolves erupted from the dense undergrowth. One was enormous, with silver-tinged fur. A thing of nightmares.

They were on us in seconds.

The giant silver-tinged wolf charged Savannah, and I threw myself between them. We collided and went tumbling. I rammed my claws into his chest, even as he clamped his jaw down on my forearm.

I drove my fist into his face over and over until the wolf's grip slipped and he crashed into the ground, rolling once before he was on his feet again.

My arm ached where the bastard had managed to sink his fangs into me. Sam grunted as she rammed her foot into another.

Savannah blasted one of the wolves with her magic, but even as she did so, a fourth emerged on our flank.

Fuck.

I repositioned so that Savy and the other wolves were in my line of sight, then glanced behind us. I could see the orb and stone tower. We were so close, and the way was clear.

"Get to the orb now!" I shouted at Savy. "Sam and I will keep the wolves at bay!"

"I'm not leaving you!" she snarled, unleashing a blast of magic.

"They're going to cut us off, and I'm betting the Dark God will be here soon. We need to chain him before he arrives, or everything will be lost. Run!"

Savy opened her mouth to protest, but I poured my presence into her and roared, "Go!" With a hiss of frustration, she threw up a cloud of darkness to cover her escape and raced toward the tower.

Good luck, my love.

A black wolf chased after. I charged, tackling it, and holding it down. Its claws raked my side, but I gripped its neck and twisted until it snapped. The body went limp beneath me even as another attacked.

From behind, the massive wolf howled, deep and low, calling in reinforcements. *Fucking hell.*

We were already cornered. Sam had fought off one of the wolves but was backed up against a tree by another. I couldn't keep track of how many there were—they kept ducking in and out of the brush.

The smaller wolf limped around her, while the silver-tinged leader stalked forward. His ears flicked back, and he growled low. Sam was a fighter, but the massive wolf wasn't a normal shifter, that much was clear. She didn't stand a chance against them both.

The limping wolf lunged. I met him midair, bodychecking the beast with my shoulder. He skidded through the decaying leaves with a grunt.

I looked around, adrenaline pumping. The large wolf had Sam pinned. She growled and managed to kick him off, but bright red scratches streaked her arms and face. She jumped to her feet and crouched as he charged again, jaws wide.

No.

At the last second, Sam sprang into the air. The wolf swiped her leg as it barreled beneath her, and she grabbed hold of an overhanging branch. Swinging one leg over it, she pulled herself up.

I squared off against the massive beast, but Sam's eyes went wide. "Jax, behind you!"

An arm swung around my neck and pulled me back against a tree in a choke hold. I grunted and dug my claws into the pale green flesh, recognizing the signature of the Fae creature. I'd killed one of them last time.

She hissed and sank her teeth into my shoulder. Stinging pain cascaded across my chest, but I was more concerned with the massive wolf who was now stalking toward me.

The tree fairy had me pinned, and she was remarkably strong.

Sam dropped to the ground and started yelling at the large wolf, but a smaller one was at her throat in seconds. They were fucking everywhere.

The large wolf paused and cocked his head to the right, listening. I couldn't make out anything other than the hissing of the fairy behind me and my thudding heart. Suddenly, he tensed and bounded into the trees, heading in Savannah's direction.

Double fuck.

Rage burned through me, and I swung forward, snapping the fairy's arm. A shrill screech deafened my ears, but the fairy's hold around my neck released.

I shot forward and grabbed the hind legs of the limping wolf as it bore down on Sam. I swung the beast into the tree, then jumped on him and ended him with a swift snap of his neck.

"Holy shit," Sam huffed as she propped herself up against the twisted trunk and cradled her arm.

Before I could respond, there was the sound of crashing trees and a blood curdling cry of pain.

My mate!

48

Savannah

I sprinted through the forest, no longer taking time to move with caution. Grunts and snarls and the sounds of battle raged behind me. Fear for Jax and Sam tore at me, but I gritted my teeth and kept going even as my instinct urged me to turn back.

Everything depended on me getting the moonstone to the final orb. Failure wasn't an option.

I darted through the widely spaced oaks, the leaf litter soft under my boots. Though it was easy going, I had virtually no cover.

The glow up ahead grew stronger as I neared. It couldn't have been more than a quarter mile from Jax and Sam.

I jumped over a fallen trunk and slowed as the orb came into view. Like the one in the middle of the pond, this one was floating above a stone turret, but in a small clearing. Lichen covered the stones, and bluebonnets colored the grass around it.

"Thank God," I whispered, counting my blessings. I really didn't want a repeat of *Lady in the Water*.

My breathing sped up, but I steadied it as I crept forward, moving cautiously. At first, nothing seemed out of the ordinary, but then the hair on my arms rose, and a chill worked down my dampened back. The forest was dead quiet, the light mist blanketing any sound, but someone, or *something*, was out there.

Stalking me.

What do you think, Wolfie? Shadows pooled around my fingertips.

In the trees. Forty feet to our right.

I felt it then. A signature, or rather, the lack of one. It was like whatever was moving toward us was blocking its magic, and in its place was a hole. A big one.

A shudder worked through me. *Fuck this.*

I touched the moonstone tucked in my bra for good luck. The Moon's magic seeped into me, and I delighted in the surge of euphoria and energy, as if my batteries had instantly been filled.

Go time. I sprinted toward the tower with its floating orb.

Before I could cross the distance, a shape shot out of the other side of the clearing in between me and the tower. I jerked to a stop, my heels digging into the grass as I spun.

It was a man. He was masking his signature, but the way my instincts were blaring told me he was freaking powerful...whatever he was.

He cocked his head as his piercing light eyes took me in. *Dangerous* was written all over this guy. He stood over six feet tall, his face chiseled, and his body lean and taut. He didn't look over thirty years old, but I sensed he was far older.

Bad news, Wolfie growled.

No shit.

Delight flashed in his gorgeous eyes, and his lips pulled up in a devilish smile. "I wouldn't do that if I were you. I'm looking for a new toy, and I happen to bite."

Who the hell was this guy?

A howl cut through the forest, drawing the man's attention.

A signal, but not from Jaxson or Sam. One of Dark God's wolves was calling for backup.

We were running out of time.

I summoned my magic, and icy shadows streamed down my arm. I collected them in my free hand and hurled them at the man. Like a net, they fell over him, shrouding him in darkness.

Then I took off, my boots tearing up the damp grass. I made it to the stone turret in seconds and leapt onto the side. It was a good two to three feet taller than the one that was submerged in the pond, but my claws dug into the stone, and I pulled myself up to the top of the tower in three heaves.

A whoosh of wind blew below, and a hand gripped my ankle, pulling my foot out. I slipped, hitting my left knee hard. Pain cascaded down my leg, and I screamed as claws tore into my ankle. My kneecap throbbed, and I dug my claws into the stone, anchoring myself as I peered down.

The man from the clearing was staring up at me with an amused and lethal expression. *Fucker.*

I twisted sharply and kicked him in the face with my free leg. He snarled, but his grip on my ankle released.

I released a burst of magic. A shadow billowed from my hand like a lance and rammed into his chest. He collapsed into the undergrowth with a bellow of pain.

The world seemed to turn upside down.

The forest beside me erupted as if a comet had struck, and an unearthly growl sent a cascade of shivers through me.

My head whipped up in time to see the Dark God step from the wreckage of trees. His dark hair whipped in the wind, and the tattoos on his bare chest burned with lethal light.

His signature of smoke and searing heat pulsed outward like a solar flare. Gritting my teeth, I fought against the urge to cower. Fighting it went against everything that felt right, and Wolfie whimpered.

"I warned you, Savannah," the Dark God growled.

In that moment, I knew that our time had just run out.

For a second my mind froze in terror. Then I desperately grabbed for the stone tucked in my bra. Before I could pluck it out, the Dark God threw his hand up. An enormous tree ripped from the ground and slammed into the turret.

Branches tore into my skin, and the impact sent me hurtling off the top of the tower. The breath was blasted from my lungs as I crashed into the hard earth of the meadow.

I groaned. *Why wasn't this pillar the one inside the pond?*

Chest aching, I picked myself up off the ground and desperately scrambled for the moonstone where it had tumbled from my grasp.

Sam and Jaxson charged into the clearing around the orb, and I shouted, "Watch out!"

A wave of magic tore through the forest, ripping trees from the ground. It crashed over them like a tsunami of dirt and branches.

Jaxson and Sam pulled themselves from the wreckage as the dust settled.

The Dark God approached, his movements precise and calculated like a predator's, exuding limitless power and confidence. "I gave you a chance, alpha, to save your world! And yet you let this sorceress bind the wolves of your pack? You are far more corrupted by human thought than I ever suspected."

His presence washed over us, and Sam dropped to her knees, a scowl cutting her face, while Jaxson staggered back, and I fought the urge to submit.

"Fuck you," Sam said, glaring at the Dark God. She was still on her knees, but she betrayed no sign of fear. She was pissed.

"I remember you." The Dark God's jaw tensed, his eyes blazing with fury as she unslung the riot gun and aimed it at his head. "How could I forget. A little wolf with a bite. But if a moonstone did not stop me, what do you think you will do?"

I couldn't help the shudder that worked down my spine, but Sam was unaffected—amused, even. She smiled as she peered through the scope, then said, "It will fucking hurt. Go to hell."

A crack erupted from the gun, and a second later, an explosion knocked the Dark God several feet back. A fog of wolfsbane enveloped him, and he bellowed with savage fury.

The smoke burned my throat, and I couldn't help coughing even as the Dark God emerged from the smoke. Glass was embedded in his chest and arms, and his face was filled with, rage, vitriol, and a lust for revenge.

"You will pay for that, little wolf!" He was on her in a second —faster than I'd seen any creature move. She screamed in agony as he ripped into her shoulder with his claws and kicked her to the ground.

"What does pain matter to me?" he snarled.

Jaxson raced forward, and I gritted my teeth and summoned every last ounce of magic I had. Shadows raced across the forest floor, gathering at my feet, as I felt the familiar cool energy course through my veins with every pump of my heart.

My fear of him was gone. I was enraged. At Kahanov, at Dragan, at the Dark Wolf God and his buddies.

For everything that had happened to Jaxson, Sam, and me.

Rage fueled my magic, and ribbons of darkness whipped out from my hands, wrapping around the Wolf God like black chains. My soul strained as I pulled them tight.

The Dark God snarled and struggled against them. "You'll find I'm not so easy to bind as your wolf!"

"She just has to hold you steady!" Jaxson growled. He seized a long, shattered branch and charged forward with it like a lance. The Dark God roared in pain as it sank into his chest, and his eyes turned bright blue. Jaxson released the branch and tore into him like a savage animal with his claws. Blood poured across the Dark God's skin.

Then, with a thunderclap, my shadow chains shattered. I staggered back, and the release of power snapped my hands back like rubber bands.

The Dark God unleashed a blast of power that sent Jaxson and Sam flying backward. He snapped off the branch that Jaxson had lodged into his chest, and then broke it in two. After inspecting both pieces he lunged forward and rammed one of the pointed branches through Jaxson's right shoulder, pinning my mate to the ground.

He broke the second piece, and in a blur of motion, slammed it through Jaxson's other shoulder. My mate growled and blood pooled at the corner of his mouth. His pain was my agony, and I was blinded by white-hot rage.

Nothing else mattered—the pylons, Magic Side, my own life. I was going to rip that fucker's heart out.

I pulled out the moonstone and bolted toward them with a ferocious snarl, ready to blast the asshole to kingdom come. But I skidded to a stop as the Dark God placed the last remaining piece against Jaxson's throat.

"One shove, and I can end him," the Dark God growled. "So, it's your fate to choose. Try to chain me, and your mate dies. Drop the moonstone, and he lives."

49

Savannah

Blue flames flickered over the Dark God's skin, and he pressed the stake against my mate's exposed throat.

"Finish the spell—" Jaxson croaked.

No.

I couldn't live without him.

Jaxson had become my world. It wasn't just the mate bond, but with every single moment we'd shared in the short time we'd been together. I knew for certain that Jaxson was mine, and I was his. I was head over heels in love with him, and there was no way I could give him up.

"Drop the stone!" the Dark God roared, as he swung his arm back for a killing blow.

The stone quivered in my hand, and pain ripped through my chest as if my ribcage had been torn open and my heart pulled out. A guttural scream tore from my throat as my body jerked back and a blindingly fast blur leapt out of me—my shadow wolf.

I'll protect our mate, shouted the fearless little voice I'd come to know so well. *You save our pack.*

In two strides, my shadow wolf rammed into the Dark God, snapping at his throat. He stumbled back and released Jaxson. She tore into the Dark God with all the anger and fury I'd ever felt.

My twin soul was a little wolf no longer, but a snarling monster born of legend. Black shadows poured off her like flames, and her claws were savage and cruel.

Go! Wolfie shouted in my mind.

Time slowed as the Dark God's minions burst from the trees, charging toward me as Jaxson, Sam, and my wolf fought off the Dark God.

I had one chance to save them all.

Heart pounding, I spun and charged toward the orb with wolves on my heels. I leapt and landed on the side of the tower. Pain jolted through my knee, and my angle was off. The air expelled from my lungs in a gasp, and I immediately began to slip off.

No, no, no.

My claws sank into the soft stone, and I dragged myself up. I had to get to the top. My pulse was off the charts, and panic filled my chest. I just had to get the moonstone in place. If we weren't going to make it out of here, at least we'd trap the Dark God in his realm forever.

It took every ounce of strength I had to leap onto the orb and pull myself up and over the curved surface. Howls echoed through the forest, and I heard Sam's cry of pain.

Holding on with one hand, I pulled the moonstone out of my bra and swung my arm up, slotting the enchanted stone into the oval nook at the top of the orb.

It clicked in.

For an eternal moment, there was nothing.

And then, there was light. The orb pulsed with unimaginable power, and a blinding column of light burst into the sky.

A shockwave of magic raced through the forest, knocking the wolves at the base of the turret over. Lightning bolts crackled from the orb, drifting across the meadow. Searching, hunting for the wolf they were meant to bind.

The Dark God.

Jaxson, Sam and my wolf had him cornered, but even though they fought together as a pack, they were overmatched. The Dark God was too fast, too powerful, and charged with magic.

And now he was desperate. He roared and lashed out with his claws sending Jaxson flying back, then unleashed a spell into my wolf.

I felt her pain as she howled, and I nearly fell off the orb.

I had to get to them. But around the base of the tower, the Dark God's servants were staggering to their feet. *Shit*!

A desperate plan formed, and I called what little magic I had left. Like icewater flowing through a pipe, two ribbons of smoke snaked out of my palms, and my idea sprang to life.

I blanketed the clearing in shadows to confuse the wolves and cast a ribbon toward the top of the tallest tree, where it coiled around a branch several times. I tugged on it to make sure it was secure, and then, taking a breath, I stepped off the orb.

Hold on to your tits, ladies.

My ribbon caught me, and I swooped over the clearing like Tarzan on a vine. Pain burned in my arm where the shadows were rooted, as if they were bound to muscle and bone. But I lost altitude fast, and my ribbon gave way just as I made it into the forest.

The impact was hard, and sent me tumbling, but I quickly scrambled to my feet, claws out, but drained.

Whatever I had left to give, I would.

The Dark God turned on me, eyes burning with fury. "What have you done?"

In answer, a lightning bolt burst from the orb and blasted into the Dark God's chest, as if called by the very sound of his voice. He gasped and staggered back, but the lightning did not disappear. It formed into chains of electric light that snaked around his ankles and wrists.

His eyes went wide with horror. "No! I will not be bound again!"

My heart skipped a beat. It was working!

The chains of light pulled the Dark God back toward the orbs, and though he raged against them, they held like iron. His corded body strained against the golden bonds. Sweat glistened on his skin, and his strange tattoos blazed.

He was striking and terrifying, but I knew now that the Moon's magic was stronger. That *we* had been stronger.

"It's over asshole," I said, my voice sharp and cold. "Enjoy eternity in the company of yourself and furry friends."

"Seize them!" the Dark God howled as a lightning storm filled the sky above us. Then with a crack, he was gone, pulled back through the trees by the Moon's spell, leaving a trail of broken branches like the wake of a tornado.

Holy shit.

He was gone. It was over. Hope flickered in my chest, and—

My shadow wolf darted past me, colliding midair with a brown wolf charging from behind.

Sam screamed, and I whipped around. A giant wolf was trying to drag her into the woods.

My palms tingled, and sucking in a breath, I channeled my magic into my rage. Casting my hands forward, I released a blast of magic at him. The ball of shadows struck the wolf head-on, and his body flew twenty feet back into a large oak. He didn't rise.

"Badass," Sam grunted as she climbed to her feet. Her left

arm hung limp, and her shoulder was tattered where the Dark God had scarred her.

Wolfie growled behind me. Two wolves lurked at the edge of the trees. But then, with a snarl they turned and fled.

Yeah, I thought so, Wolfie muttered after the fleeing beasts.

I dropped to my knees beside Jaxson. Blood was everywhere, and a broken branch still protruded from his shoulder. The Dark God had barely left him breathing.

The ground quaked, and I felt a deep tremor of magic surge through the earth.

"The rift is collapsing," Jaxson choked, agony on his face. "Get Sam, Savy. Promise me you'll go through the rift."

"No. We're getting out of here together. Hold still while I take these out." My voice was steady and calm, the exact opposite of the emotions that were tearing through me.

He was bad off. I needed to heal him, but I was so drained.

You're running on fifty percent power, Wolfie said. *Let me help.*

My fearsome shadow wolf limped over. She was battered and wounded, but there was no hiding the triumph in her eyes.

Still, seeing her hurt pained my heart. *Uh, Wolfie... you were absolutely incredible, but you don't look so hot right now. Are you okay?*

She gave me a toothy grin. *Nothing that being back together won't be able solve.*

With that, my shadow wolf leapt back into my chest, expelling the air from my lungs. I gasped in pain as her sensations merged with my own.

Oh, I hurt a lot, by the way, she said.

But despite the pain, strength flowed through me—*her* strength, filling me with power and life.

Our strength, she said.

I gripped the stake in Jaxson's right shoulder and pulled it free. He growled, but his gaze never left mine. "Savy—"

I ripped the left one out before he could finish, and he growled with pain.

Then I kissed him. Our mouths entwined, and I poured my magic into him as he groaned in agony and desire. Life and power and love, burning though us—healing me even as it healed him. It was pure ecstasy.

But suddenly, the ground shook again.

"Guys?" Sam said, her voice pitched an octave too high. "As hot as it is to watch you make out, I think something's happening to the rift. It's time to go."

I looked up. A plume of magic spiraled into the sky to the west where we'd come from.

Shit. Would the rift completely collapse without the Dark God's power? Or was Aunt Laurel losing control? What would happen to everyone on the other side?

I pulled Jaxson to his feet, and the three of us charged back the way we'd come.

As we burst from the cover of the woods, I took one glance behind my shoulder, and my stomach churned.

The pillars of magic rose high above us. But behind them, a dark cloud grew—a cloud in the shape of a black wolf. Lightning cracked through the air as the dark shape pushed against the bonds of the spell, but it held.

A roar of anger shook the land as we neared the rift, which flickered and rippled with unstable magic.

Time to get the hell out of here and lock that bastard away for good.

Grabbing Sam's hand with my right, and Jaxson with my left, we barreled through the silver-black tear in the sky.

50

Savannah

Smoke and ash burned my throat, and every inch of me screamed in agony. The return through the rift had been twice as bad as the journey there.

I exhaled in relief as my feet landed on asphalt, but dread rocked me the moment I looked around.

Aunt Laurel stood across the street, her arms outstretched. Lightning bolts of magic cracked and flashed between her hands, and the skin on her palms was scorched and blackened. Sweat beaded all over her with the strain, and the pain and determination in her eyes undid me.

I ran toward her, but Jaxson's arms locked around my waist. "I need to help her, Jax!"

"No."

I fought against his hold, but deep down, I knew he was right. I had no idea what spell she was working, or what it would do if I got too close and interfered.

An orange aura blazed around her, and the energy snapping the air above was electric and searing. My heart cracked. I could see the agony etched in her strained expression.

"It's done! He's locked away! You can close the rift!" I shouted.

Her attention was distant, but a subtle flicker of acknowledgment flashed across her face, and she shut her eyes.

The fiery aura around her swelled, and the wind picked up, carrying leaves and trash in eddies. Tendrils of purple-blue light snaked out of her upright palms as if from a plasma ball. The heat coming off them scorched my face and arms, like I was standing too close to a fire.

Three successive streaks of lightning exploded out of Laurel's hands, piercing the night sky. The resounding thunderclaps erupted around us, and deafening pain struck my eardrums. Clutching my throbbing ears, I forced myself to stay upright as I watched my aunt.

Would she survive this?

Her hands were raw, and the tendons in her neck strained as she dropped her head back, angling her face to the heavens. The wind picked up, and Jaxson shielded me from the debris whipping around. A heart-shattering scream tore from Laurel's throat as a blindingly bright white ball of light burst from her chest like a shooting star. It flew into the rift and detonated in a blast of searing energy. The aftershock threw us backward, and the pavement scraped my exposed skin as I landed and skidded to a halt.

Shock and adrenaline dulled the pain. The wind died down, and an eerie quiet settled over the streets. I rolled onto my side, glancing over at Sam and Jaxson, who'd also been knocked over by the blast.

Jaxson was on his feet in seconds and pulled me up. I spun out of his arms, panic choking me. "Laurel!"

My aunt was on all fours, her head hanging and her body spent. I sprinted down the street and dropped beside her.

She whimpered at my touch but lifted her head to meet my

gaze. Her features were sunken and hollow, and I almost didn't recognize her. "We did it," she whispered.

Tears filled my eyes as I helped her to her knees. I gently took her hands and turned them to see the damage, and my stomach heaved at the sight of the ruined flesh. "What can I do? You're hurt," I choked.

She forced a small smile. "I've seen worse."

Really? Because she looked like she was at death's door.

"Laurel!" My uncle came dashing down the street. He sank to his knees beside her and kissed her forehead. "My love."

Moving away to give them a moment of privacy, I took in the damage around us. Scorch marks seared the pavement where the rift had been. Smoke and fire billowed from the buildings around us, and brick and glass covered the streets.

Dockside was in ruins, but the nightmare was finally over. Magic Side was safe, and we'd locked the Dark Wolf God away for good.

And we absolutely kicked his ass, Wolfie said.

That, too.

Relief settled over me, and I let out a deep sigh.

I was free. And she was free.

But I had one thing left to do.

I glanced at Jaxson. "I need to find a way to free the pack—to break the spell I cast."

Trepidation tightened my throat. It had taken seven other sorceresses and everything I had to cast the binding spell. And now my aunt, the strongest of them all, was too weak to even walk.

As if reading my mind, the strong arms of my mate wrapped around me from behind. "Don't worry. I'll help you put things right."

Although I just wanted to collapse into him, I twisted around in his embrace and met his gaze. "I'm so tired, Jax. I don't think I'm strong enough."

He reached up and cupped my cheek, brushing my cheekbone tenderly with his thumb. "You're the strongest person I've ever known. I have no doubt you can do this."

I sank against his palm, savoring his warmth and the strength of his touch. "Magic is different, Jax. I could barely free my own wolf. How will I free them all?"

He shook his head. "This is your spell. You can break it."

I pressed my head against his hand, then stepped back. "I'll try."

Striding to the center of the street, I opened my mouth to speak the words of the unbinding spell Laurel had taught me, but I paused. Breaking the spell had been so hard, like cutting through roots or chains. I'd nearly passed out from the struggle. There was no way I could do that for every wolf I had bound. But maybe I didn't have to cut through the binds I'd created. Maybe there was a way to take them back.

Aunt Laurel had told me that with every enchantment, a sorceress left a little of their soul behind. Well, I'd scattered my soul across the city, bound to every wolf in Dockside. But they were *my* bonds—and they were mine to withdraw.

Closing my eyes, I reached out with my mind, feeling for the traces of magic I'd left. For a moment, there was only the darkness behind my eyelids...and then I saw them in the thousands, twinkling like stars in the sky, a thousand tiny shards of my soul.

I reached out as I would with my shadow wolf and called them to me. *Come home.*

I felt Jaxson step up behind me, his warmth and presence flowing through me, giving me strength.

Stretching as far as I could reach with my magic, I pulled. *You are mine. Come home.*

My body shook with the strain, and Jaxson's hands braced against me.

Then I felt the magic chains I'd woven begin to slip. At first, it was just one or two, but it soon became a torrent. The spells unraveled and spiraled into me, a thousand tendrils of magic that flowed over my skin like ice water.

My eyes flew open, and I gasped. The world around me seemed to glow, taking on a richness I'd never seen before.

The wolves were free, and I was whole once again.

51

Jaxson

Savannah collapsed into my arms, and for a long time, I just held her: my mate, my love, the woman who had saved my pack.

I combed my fingers through her hair as she quaked from exhaustion. How much time had passed I couldn't say, but finally she stirred.

"It's okay... I'm okay," she stepped back to prove her point, but was unsteady on her feet, and I held onto her arm. "Do you think it worked?"

I smiled. "Listen."

She paused.

Wolf howls echoed in the distance in every direction—a sound we all knew by instinct: the cry one makes when a lost pup had been found. Our pack members, no longer possessed or bound, and been reunited with their wolves. They were crying out with joy and calling to each other.

A broad grin stretched across Savannah's face. Fatigue ringed her eyes, but they shimmered with delight and triumph.

My heart leapt at the sight. She was radiant. Beautiful. Everything I had never known I needed.

Like a whirlpool, sudden need pulled my lips to hers, and we were kissing. Bruised, battered, and exhausted, but alive and churning with emotion.

Her mouth moved across mine, searching, needing, desiring. Every motion was a song of relief. I lost myself in her taste and tongue and the completeness I felt when I was with her.

I could barely contain the lightness in my heart. When Savannah was in my arms, it was like a part of me that I hadn't known I was missing had been found. Somehow, this woman made me whole, in a way I'd never thought was possible.

Finally, needing breathe, I broke away. Chest heaving, Savy leaned into my embrace as I dipped my head to her ear. "It's over. We're free. You did it."

"We did it," she muttered.

With a growl of admiration, I shook my head. "No. This, this was you. It was your idea to bind the wolves to weaken the Dark God, and your power that set them free. No one else would have been able, or even dared, to do that. You saved our pack. Our city."

Savannah reddened and I could smell the scent of her embarrassment at the praise. She turned her head to gaze out over the ruins of Dockside.

"The city doesn't look like it's been saved," she said. "If we hadn't lost so much time..."

Rebuilding would take time. The hallmarks of devastation stretched for blocks—broken glass, crumbled walls, burning buildings.

I gently pulled her chin back to me. "I know it looks bad, but this is a fraction of what could have been. You saw the visions. If we hadn't stopped the Dark God, this city would be ash and rubble, with half of its inhabitants dead and the other half homeless and running for their lives."

She took a deep breath and straightened her shoulders. "I know. I just wish we could have done more."

"We did everything we could. Now, we pick up the pieces of Dockside. There is plenty we can do to heal the wound he left us."

Savannah tensed. "Sam. She was hurt."

"She's okay. She looks a little worse for wear, but she's already off helping the others."

A familiar truck pulled up, and Regina bailed out. She ran over and—uncharacteristically—gave me a hug, "Thank fates, you survived."

"I'm hard to kill."

She pushed back. "Not for lack of trying—you look like you've been through hell."

Regina gave Savy a hug as well. "Thank you for everything, Savannah."

Savy nodded and I crossed my arms. "Give me a rundown of the damage. I'm guessing it's bad since you're here in person."

"I had to see you. And yes, it's bad. A good portion of Dockside is burning. Firefighters are working to contain the flames. But we have a bigger problem on our hands. The people who were bit by the possessed wolves have some sort of lycanthropy, and it's not gone away. Some are managing to control it, but others are going feral."

Regina's words ran through me like ice water, and Savannah sucked in a sharp breath. "You mean, they're still turning into werewolves? We chained the Dark God and closed off the portal—"

"Doesn't seem to have stopped it. Some keep partially shifting, others are fighting severe fevers."

Savannah stiffened and went pale. "Casey?"

Regina's expression darkened. "We had him moved to the hospital. He partially shifted about twenty minutes ago, and now he's passed out and sweating a fever. Mira—one of our nurses—is looking after him now, along with a few others. She's a werewolf so maybe she can understand what he's going through—but I'm not sure there is anything we can do for him or the others."

Savy dug her fingers into my arm. "Fuck. He's got to be going out of his mind. This is definitely his worst nightmare."

Regina's eyes narrowed, and she crossed her arms. "He has been—difficult. Apparently, he keeps moaning *'I don't want to eat people. Do people taste okay?'* Let's just say it hasn't won him any sympathy from the hospital staff. Mira deserves a sainthood."

"There must be something we can do," I growled.

Savannah bit her lip. "Alia was going to try to make a Lycanthropy cure for my condition. Maybe she knows what to do."

That was one potion, for one disease. Mass disease was an entirely different story. "Any idea how many are infected?"

Regina shook her head. "No firm count but brace yourself for the worst—I'm certain it's going to be in the hundreds, not dozens."

I pulled out my cell, and although the screen was shattered, it still worked. "Fuck. Okay, I'll call Alia now."

Savannah looked over to where her aunt was sitting on the curb, her head drooped between her knees. "I need to go tell Laurel and Uncle Pete about Casey. I don't want them getting a call from the hospital. It should come from me."

"Do it." I dialed Alia.

The potion maker picked up in half a ring. "Jaxson? What the hell is going on in Dockside? Local news has been blacked out, and I can't get a straight answer. My demons tell me all the werewolves have gone rabid and are running all over town."

"Your demons are idiots," I growled. "But I do have a werewolf problem. Can you make a lycanthropy cure? For hundreds of people?"

"Shit. It's true—"

"Whatever you heard is certainly *not* true. I'll explain everything when there's time. Right now, I need you brewing potions. Whatever it costs."

She released an exasperated hiss. "It's not that easy Jaxson—brewing is going to take time. It's got to be in small batches, and I'm going to need to reduce a shit ton of wolfsbane."

I glanced over at Savannah and Laurel. "I can get you all the wolfsbane you could imagine. The LaSalles will be very motivated to expedite the process."

"Okay, I can have the first batch done in three days if you get me the ingredients tonight. But it will only be fifty or sixty doses."

"Are you willing to teach Pete LaSalle? I'll make it worth your while. This is an emergency. Name your price."

There was a pause. "I'll teach him. But giving up a recipe to that family, that's going to be expensive."

"Send me an invoice and a list of what you need. Get going now, and I'll let you know how many infections we're talking about but think in the hundreds." I hung up and pocketed my phone.

Regina raised her eyebrows.

"Don't look so worried. The hard part's over. We'll get through this."

She nodded. "I know."

I grasped her arm. "Thank you. For stepping up while Savy and I were gone. For protecting our pack. I know I put a lot on your shoulders."

"I can take it," she grumbled. "But dealing with the LaSalles was like herding cats. Big, bad tempered, sabretooth cats."

"That doesn't surprise me. Did the council give you any help?"

She shook her head. "Not much. Camila and Mac sent

people. Not many of the others—but it was for the best. Their wolves got possessed, just like ours. With a bigger response, the city might have been overrun before you got back."

"That doesn't matter. They're fucking cowards," I snarled, balling my fists. "We put out a call for help, and they turned their back."

Rage clouding my vision, I called Camila.

"Jaxson?" She answered, a tremor of fear in her voice. "What's happened? I'm getting conflicting reports."

"It's over. Savy got her wolf back and defeated the Dark God. We sealed the rift that he'd opened and chained him in the Dreamlands for good. But it was fucking close. And if we had fallen, if Savannah hadn't stepped up, the Great Lakes would have been overrun with thousands of blood-thirsty wolves. Not one of you would have stood a chance."

"Fates," was all she could muster.

I tried to keep my voice steady, but I wanted to rage. "Regina tells me your people were here and helping. Thank you. I won't forget that. But I won't forget that you are the one who put Savannah and me on trial."

"I'm sorry for that, Jaxson. But if what you say is true, then I think the council should no longer have any problem with either you or your mate."

My fingers tightened around the phone. "Oh, they have a problem. The fucking Dockside alpha is pissed. I think they've all forgotten who I am and what part of their livelihood I control. Call a meeting for three days from now. There will be a reckoning."

She hesitated a second. "Understood."

"Tell them that if they want to start making amends, to send workmen and supplies. I've got Dockside to rebuild." With that I hung up and took in the scene around me.

Savannah.

She was like a brilliant flame in the dark of night, calling to me. Brave. Beautiful. Triumphant.

She sat with her aunt, holding her hand. Giving strength to one more person, after she'd given everything she had to the city.

I didn't deserve a woman like her. But somehow, the fates had given me a chance to earn her love. A chance I wasn't going to fuck up.

I started toward them, but halted at a familiar scent, and scanned the surroundings.

A werewolf stood in the shadows of an alleyway, watching me. A muscular form, but tired. I knew the silhouette anywhere.

My father.

Not what I needed right now. I strode into the darkness. "What are you doing here?"

"I came to help," he growled.

"Why? Because you thought we couldn't handle it. Or because you realized you'd fucked up."

"Because I was wrong, Jaxson, and I'm trying to make amends. I shouldn't have brought you up before the council, but I was afraid that you and that woman were bewitched by the Dark God."

"That woman is my mate. She's a LaSalle, but you will speak with respect."

He looked away in submission. "Trust me, Jaxson, for what you two accomplished, I have all the respect in the world. For both of you. Regina told me you had to enter the Deadlands to stop this."

A chill filled me, but I nodded.

He sucked in an unsteady breath, and the scent of distress was strong.

After a long pause, he spoke. "You were gone three days, and I swear to the fates, there wasn't a minute I didn't regret every word we've exchanged in the last five years. Your mother and I weren't sure you were coming back, and it felt like my soul was breaking. I've spent so many years dwelling on losing Stephanie that… I can't lose you, too."

"Well, I'm still here," I grunted.

"I'll fix things between us, Jaxson. I'm going to try. I'm sorry for everything. For leaving you on your own, for dropping the pack on you, for being distant. Inaccessible." He put a hand on my shoulder, and I tensed. "I'm here. In the time I've got left, I need to focus on the son I have, not the daughter I lost."

Anger pulled at me, and I didn't try to hide it. Why had it taken nearly dying for him to see this?

I looked away, until I got control of my emotions. Finally, I was calm enough that I could meet his eyes.

"I saw Stephanie," I muttered.

My father stiffened and shock dilated his eyes as the implications struck home. He was speechless, and I didn't break the silence between us.

At last, he forced out a hoarse whisper. "You saw her in the Deadlands?"

"She led us there," I said, measuring every reaction.

"Is she…" He swallowed hard and licked his lips. Pain shown in his eyes as he searched for the right words. "At peace?"

I crossed my arms. "She is with Billy. They run together with the ghost wolves. I think she's found a peace that she didn't have when she was alive. We spoke a long time."

My father turned away, every muscle in his body coiled with tension and anguish. After a long moment his shoulders drooped. "I'm glad. That's all I want for her."

I started to walk away, but his hand stopped me. "Jaxson."

He met my eyes. "I know this isn't the right time, but I hope that someday you can forgive me. For abandoning you. For losing myself. For being such a shit father when you needed me to be there. I'm going to do everything I can to earn back your trust."

I shook my head. "There is someone whose trust you need to earn first."

He followed my gaze to Savannah, who was helping move a wounded man to the truck.

"She's my mate. My other half. When you've made peace with her—if that is even possible after what you said—then you and I can talk."

My father nodded. "I understand. Whatever I must do, I will."

Taking a deep breath, I nodded. "Good. Now I need you on the West Side at the hospital. They're triaging people infected with the Dark God's lycanthropy. They'll need an alpha to help guide the new wolves, and I can't be everywhere at once. The rest, we'll talk about later."

"Of course." He turned to leave but paused. "You did good, you know. I would have failed this test. The pack is lucky that they had you."

"They were lucky to have had Savannah," I growled as I walked away from my father and the pain of our past, and back toward my mate. Toward my future. Toward my strength.

My fate.

52

Savannah

One week later...

My eyes fluttered open.

Rosy hues painted the lightening sky outside of the floor-to-ceiling windows of Jaxson's bedroom. A few stars clung to the darkness, their brilliance slowly fading as golden fingers of sunlight reached toward the heavens over Lake Michigan.

My head rose and fell on Jaxson's chest, and the steady beat of his heart matched mine. I smiled as I peeked up at him, memorizing the curve of his lips and the way his lashes quivered when he was dreaming. Warmth and happiness filled me.

But I also had to pee.

Careful not to wake him, I gently lifted his arm off me and slid out of bed. Jaxson stirred but fell back into a deep sleep.

He's dead to the world, Wolfie said with a hint of amusement. *You really wore him out.*

I'd certainly done my part.

But that wasn't all of it. We'd been working twelve plus hours a day to put Dockside back together. I'd learned to install drywall and spray paint walls and run caulking. It felt like everyone in the city was pitching in.

I didn't usually see Jaxson from sunrise to sunset. He had his hands full with logistics and the council and tending to the infected werewolves, who needed help controlling their wolves while they awaited Aila's antidote. Some, however, had decided to join the pack, which is good, because we needed every hand we could get.

Then there was bartending every night. Eclipse was donating all proceeds to the rebuild, and the place had never been so packed.

I shut the bathroom door and sat down, groaning as aches spread from my ass to my spine.

If being on my feet wasn't enough, Jaxson had kept me on my back and knees all night. Even dead tired, we hadn't been able to keep our hands off each other. Heat spread across my cheeks as I recounted all the places in the penthouse that we'd made love. The shower, the couch, pressed against his living room window...

Don't forget the kitchen counter, Wolfie added.

The cold stone had been a delight for my overheated skin, but it was also hard. Five stars for the sex, but two for location.

After tending to business and brushing my teeth, I slipped into the bedroom and scooped up Jaxson's flannel shirt and my phone. I guess I really *had* worn him out last night because he didn't move an inch.

At least, we were finally going to get a break and get out of town. With the rebuild in full swing and most of our loose ends tied up, we were headed to Colorado for a week on a new adventure: tracking down my family—the werewolf side.

Mom's side.

According to her letter, my grandfather lived in a small town called Silverton in the Rockies. Besides our trip to Forks several weeks ago, I'd never been out West, and I was looking forward to driving cross-country and seeing the sights.

Wolfie was practically buzzing with excitement.

Starving, I beelined for the kitchen, and as if on cue, my stomach rumbled. I started the tea kettle and fetched the coffee from the freezer as I made a mental list of the things we needed to do before we headed to Colorado.

I dumped several heaping scoops of coffee into a French press and filled it with steaming water.

My phone vibrated. *You up?*

Casey? At this hour? Consider me shocked.

I responded, *The real question is, why are you up?*

Seconds later, he called me, and I smirked as I tapped the screen. "Late night, huh?"

"You don't know the half of it. Mom says you and lover boy are heading out of town? You need to stop by here before you go driving into the sunset."

I opened my mouth to respond, but a shiver of heat worked down my spine, and Jaxson's sexy woodsy scent wrapped around me.

"Lover boy, huh?" he whispered in my ear as he slipped his hands under the flannel shirt I was wearing. His fingers traced over my hips before settling over my tummy.

I pressed my back into him and looked up. "Hi," I mouthed.

"Good morning." He leaned down and kissed me, his touch slow and sensual. Liquid heat pooled between my legs, and goosebumps pebbled my skin. Jaxson smiled against my mouth. "You look good in my clothes."

"Uh, you still there, Savy?" Casey asked, reeling me back to reality. "Because I still am, and I can hear Jaxson talking sexy in the background. I mean, I can go if you're busy, but if things are gonna get interesting, I'll stay on the line."

Before I knew what was happening, Jaxson snagged my phone and turned the speaker on.

"Where are we supposed to meet you?" Jax asked, as he quickly kissed my lips then began working down my neck.

"The workshop. I'm there now. How about meeting me at eight?"

Jaxson froze and we exchanged shocked glances. By workshop, Casey meant the factory where my family made wolfsbane. I'd only been there once.

"You're kidding," Jaxson said flatly.

"I'm not, and you don't have to worry. It's totally above board. Regina and Sam are going to meet me here too, and they already gave me the third degree about it."

What the hell was going on in Magic Side? Had the world fallen off its axis? I gave Jaxson a confused look and shrugged.

"Fine. But no bullshit," Jaxson growled.

"Of course not. I'll see you then." The line went dead.

"What the hell do you think he's up to?" Jaxson asked as his hands moved down my thighs, leaving a trail of heat.

"No idea." I grinned up at him, delighting in the hardness of his body against mine. "What do you think you're up to?"

"No idea." Jaxson leaned down and traced his lips over my neck. "But we've got fifty minutes. Just enough time for breakfast and a shower."

Molten heat throbbed low and deep, and I whispered, "Breakfast? What do you want?"

He met my gaze, and a sinfully sexy smile ghosted his lips as he gripped my bare ass and lifted me up on the delightfully cold counter. "I have a couple things in mind."

My stomach was still grumbling with hunger—real hunger—an hour later when we pulled into the parking lot in front of my cousin's factory. I couldn't believe Casey was letting werewolves, let alone the alpha, anywhere near the place.

The security guards hadn't been able to believe it either, and it had taken three separate calls to get through the front gate.

We parked beside Regina's truck and hopped out. Jaxson immediately began speaking with her and Sam in hushed tones, but I made a beeline for my cousin, who I hadn't seen all week except for a couple of visits while he was still in the hospital.

He stopped pacing and hung up his phone the moment he saw me and gave me a big hug. I squeezed him back. "I feel like I haven't seen you in ages, and—" I paused and sniffed, then my eyes shot wide. "Oh my God... you're still a wolf?"

A sheepish expression flooded his face. "Well, sometimes I'm a wolf. I'm pretty good at shifting now."

The world spun. Had I just walked into the twilight zone?

"But... but you were going to take the antidote!" I stammered.

Casey gave me a deeply serious look. "There's a lot of people who need that medicine, Savannah. Not just me. I'm trying to be strong."

I shook my head. "Who are you and what have you done with my cousin?"

He stuck his hands in his pockets and rocked back on his heels in a self-satisfied way. "Hey, I'm just trying to turn over a new leaf. To be a better man. Or wolf man. Say *no* to prejudice and hate and fleas."

The shock of his words practically took my knees out from under me. Could getting bit and living through a shift have actually transformed my cousin into a noble and altruistic person?

I scrutinized him with all my senses.

Not a chance.

Then the pieces clicked into place. I suppressed a knowing grin that tugged at my lips, and gave him a hard, interrogating look instead. "There's a girl, isn't there."

"Absolutely not," he said, lyingly. "And if there was, it wouldn't affect my thinking."

I rolled my eyes. "Okay. Who is she, Casey?"

"You've got me all wrong Savannah, I'm a changed man!"

I crossed my arms. "You have to be seeing a werewolf. Nothing else would keep you this way. Cough up the details."

He gritted his teeth. "Okay, fine. Her name is Mira. She's part of the pack."

My eyes shot wide. "Oh my God! That was your nurse at the hospital! We got complaints from her for days!"

He shrugged. "I guess I just grew on her?"

My mind scrambled to assimilate information. Hell, he'd grown on me, but we were kin. I couldn't believe that it would happen with others. At last, I shook my head in disbelief. "I'm guessing she gave in just to shut you up. You *are* incorrigible."

"I couldn't help it. She is so hot, and always bending over me to take my vitals. My *vitals*. It just sounds hot. And she smells so good. I've got crazy senses now, and when she's aroused, it's like—"

I threw up my hands. "Nope! We're not going there."

"Hey, you should be proud of me. I'm building bridges. It's about making love, not war. Like, making a lot of love. Over and over. Werewolf stamina is amazing. How are you Jaxson not just having sex all the time?"

My cheeks burned.

"Oh," he said looking over at Jax. "Okay, that makes a lot of sense. I'm guessing that's why you're late?"

Jaxson glared from where he stood with my friends and growled low. "That particular conversation is done. Forever. Now, what the hell are we here for?"

"Alright, alright," Casey said. "Follow me."

53

Jaxson

There was no way to stop my heart from pounding as we followed fucking Casey LaSalle toward the large red brick building. I couldn't believe they were letting me within a mile of the place, or that Regina had even agreed to set foot on LaSalle land.

Although the security appeared shit, I knew better. The last factory the LaSalles ran, the one my sister had tried to shut down, was rigged with enough enchantments to blow a crater in Magic Side. And it had. The LaSalles spent a month rebuilding after the blast.

It had taken me years, and I still wasn't over it.

Casey opened a white metal side door and held it open. I paused on the threshold and glanced from him to Savy.

She nodded.

I stepped inside. Not for myself, but for the pack. For the hope for new beginnings.

Sucking in a sharp breath, I spun as my eyes adjusted. The place was far more complex than I'd ever imagined, a space the size of a football field with concrete floors and dozens of steel vats, copper stills, and tables.

"Where is everybody?" Savy asked from behind me.

I'd been so distracted by the impressive array of equipment that I hadn't even considered why we were the only ones here.

Casey stepped up. "We're planning on shutting down and refitting to take advantage of other opportunities. I pitched the idea to Reggie after a run to gauge if you'd be interested."

Reggie?

My heart skipped a beat as the words sank in.

We'd been trying to shut down the LaSalles' wolfsbane production for decades. After all this time, were they really ready to give in?

There had to be a catch.

I narrowed my eyes and looked from Casey to Regina. "And what sort of opportunities were you thinking about?"

"Trade deals. And free access to our docks," Regina answered.

"We agree to stop producing wolfsbane, and you cut us in on your operations," Casey said. "It's a win-win. And if you need better enchantments and wards—because trust me, that cut-rate work you had done by Mages Guild rejects doesn't cut the mustard—we'll be glad to offer assistance on a case-by-case basis, for a fee."

The floor moved beneath me. I could smell the truth in his words.

He was serious.

It would change the future of our pack—of packs all across North America. The LaSalles had a monopoly on the wolfsbane market. Cutting off that supply would mean fewer weapons on the market and fewer senseless attacks on werewolves.

I'd be a fool not to agree, but I knew it wasn't that simple. Money can change minds, and we'd need to lock them in so that in a year or two, as black market wolfsbane prices soared, they wouldn't be tempted to dip their toes back in the pond.

I crossed my arms. "How about we contract with you to run the enchantments on *all* our shipments? If you can handle them, they're yours."

Casey turned pale. "Seriously? Hell, yes, we can handle them."

He had no idea how big of a favor he'd be doing us by taking over the enchantments. Weak aftermarket mages' spells were just the tip of the iceberg. We had supply lines we had to keep hidden and protected, and our last group of enchanters—a coven of witches—had gone out of touch.

Of course, I wasn't about to let him know that.

I glanced at Regina to make sure she was onboard. Her scent betrayed no emotion—which was good since Casey LaSalle was still a fucking werewolf—but I could almost hear her crunching numbers in her head. Approval flashed in her eyes.

"It's done, then," I said. "The rest is up to Regina and our partners. If they're amenable to it, you can access our docks and negotiate trade deals."

"Holy shit!" Casey dragged his hands through his tousled hair. "Deal, Laurent."

Casey spent the next thirty minutes giving us a rundown of the place and explaining what he planned to do with the leftover equipment and supplies. In short, his father was going to help him transition to a smaller operation of producing over-the-counter potions, which Casey hoped they'd be able to sell across the Great Lakes region.

His words faded into mumbles as I wrestled with the implication. Regina found my side as Casey continued the tour.

"You okay with this?" she asked. "I wasn't trying to go behind your back—he was hesitant to approach you directly after everything... with Stephanie."

I nodded. "Shutting down this operation is what she wanted.

And if she can make peace with what happened to her in the afterlife, then I can do the same in this one. You did well."

"What about the council? Will they object to us working with the LaSalles?"

"After what Savy and Laurel LaSalle did last week?" I scoffed. "They'll swallow whatever issues they have. Plus, I'm squeezing the other alphas so tight for not showing up that they can't tell their nuts from their eyeballs. Don't let up the pressure while I'm gone."

"I won't, and I've got nails," she chuckled. "When do you get back?"

"A week. You're alpha until I return."

Regina shook her head. "I'm not. But I'll remind everyone who is, and that should keep butts moving."

"I'm serious. I rely on you for a reason."

She gave me a wry smile. "Smart man."

Savannah joined us. "Laurel just texted me, and I'd like to stop by to see her before we leave."

I slung my arm around her waist and breathed in her citrus sunshine scent, which mingled with the coconut shampoo she loved so much. "Then we'd better go. I don't need to be around here any longer."

"I might drive over with Casey, if that's okay."

"Just wear your damn seatbelt," I growled, glaring at her cousin.

He raised his hands in front of him and frowned. "I happen to have an excellent driving record."

Doubtful.

We stepped outside and said our goodbyes. My mate climbed into her cousin's car, laughing and feigning shock at his jokes, and I shook my head.

"Things are really changing around here," Sam muttered.

"It's her," I whispered. "She's changed everything. I'm not

sure how to react to anything anymore."

In the short amount of time she'd been in Magic Side, Savannah had managed to accomplish something that most thought unimaginable—a truce between the LaSalles and Laurents. Defying a prophecy. Defeating the Dark God.

Sam laughed. "True."

I turned to my truck but frowned as I got a look at her left arm. "You're not healing like you should."

She looked down at her shoulder. "That thing? It's fine but will probably leave a scar."

"You're a werewolf. You shouldn't scar."

"Yeah, well the Wolf God gave it to me. Fates knows what sort of crap he had under his nails. Probably poison. But it's already better than it was yesterday."

I opened my mouth to protest, but she thrust her hands down into her pockets and stepped close. "Listen, I'm going to head out of town for a while, so I might not be here when you get back. I need to head up north next week and sort out some family business."

I eyed her, searching for more, but she'd locked her emotions down. "Everything all right?"

"Yeah, just family bullshit. I'll be back in a month or two. Will that be a problem?"

"No. You deserve some time off. Call if you need anything." I didn't know much about Sam's background other than it had had some rough patches.

"I'll be fine. You two enjoy yourselves." Winking, she clapped me on the back and headed to Regina's truck, which was already running.

Regina gave me a two-finger salute as the two pulled out of the lot behind Casey's RAV4.

As I left the lot, I gave the redbrick building one final look.

Stephanie would be proud.

54

Savannah

By the time we arrived at my aunt and uncle's house, I was laughing so hard I was crying.

"Am I right, though?" Casey glanced over at me as he turned off the car. "Werewolf sex is off the charts."

I shook my head and rubbed my sore abdomen. "So what, it's so good that after years of hating werewolves, you're just going to be one now?"

"I'm deciding. Pros: amazing sex and superhuman strength. Also, bigger dating pool. Cons: I shed on the furniture. So far, the pros have it. I've never felt so alive in my life! Mira, Sam, and Regina have been taking me for runs every night. I never knew growing fur and running on four legs would be so great."

"*Regina*? Are you sure? Like the woman from the warehouse, Regina?"

The world had definitely fallen off its axis. There was no way Sam, let alone Regina, would be taking time out of their busy lives to teach my cousin how to be a wolf. They *despised* him, didn't they? Hell, his face was on a wanted poster in Eclipse.

But Casey didn't sound like he was shitting me. "Yeah.

Reggie and I are buds now. I mean, she was a cold bitch at first, but I think I'm growing on her."

I choked. "Reggie?"

Regina the ice queen? Regina, who'd missed no opportunity to give me shit about my family?

A whole lot had happened in the past week.

A whole lot had happened in the past month.

I spilled out of the car, clutching my still aching stomach. Casey was acclimating to being a wolf way faster than I think anyone thought possible. Not only was he thrilled with his heightened senses, but he wanted to learn everything there was about werewolf history and the origins of the Magic Side pack.

Frankly, it was astounding. But that was my cousin, batshit crazy and completely unpredictable. I loved him all the same and wouldn't change anything about him.

A big part of me was desperate to have him stay a wolf, though I barely wanted to admit it.

I bet he smells real bad, Wolfie said.

Probably.

I bounded up the steps and fell into Laurel's embrace. "It's good to see you."

She released me and wiped a few stray tears from her eyes. Her hands were bound with gauze, but she didn't appear to be in pain. "Savannah, you look absolutely refreshed and—"

"Just fucked?" Casey stepped up beside me with a shit-eating grin plastered on his face.

Laurel's eyebrows shot up, but then she smiled and nodded. "Yes."

"Oh, my God." I walked past them into the house. The warm, buttery vanilla aroma of freshly baked cookies bombarded me. I followed it into the kitchen, noticing several cardboard boxes stacked on the kitchen island beside a tray of cooling cookies.

"Help yourself," Laurel said, following me in. "I packed up a container for the road, along with a few other snacks."

"Thanks," I said as Casey strolled into the kitchen and helped himself to two cookies.

"I mean it—for everything. Without you, we'd be screwed, and Magic Side would be in ruins."

Laurel shook her head, clearly not comfortable with the praise. "You and Jaxson are the real heroes. I'm proud of you, Savy, and I know your parents would be, too."

My chest constricted as I thought of them. I missed them so damn much, it hurt. But I knew they'd be proud, and that felt good, even if they weren't here to see it.

A truck rumbled up outside, and Laurel glanced at the window. Jaxson.

"You two had better hit the road so you can make some headway before it gets dark." Laurel walked over to the three boxes on the counter. "Casey, will you help me carry these outside?"

"Sure, what are they?"

Laurel's eyes flicked to mine, and I sensed her guilt and shame. "Oh, just something that I've been meaning to get rid of for quite some time."

Casey heaved two of the boxes into his arms and disappeared down the hall. I lifted the corner of the last box and peered inside.

The dossiers on the North American packs.

I looked up at Laurel and blinked. "Why?"

She took my hands and squeezed them gently. "Because you opened my eyes and showed me that not everything is black and white. Because it's time to carve a new path forward. We need to be focused on the future, not on the grudges of our past."

I swallowed the lump in my throat, afraid that if I spoke, I was going unleash a flurry of tears. "Thank you," I whispered.

Casey reappeared and frowned at the two of us before taking the last box outside. We followed him to the porch, where I found Jaxson waiting at the bottom of the stairs with his hands in his pockets. Butterflies filled my stomach. God, when was that going to stop?

Hopefully, never.

Jaxson dipped his head in greeting to Laurel, and she did the same.

"A little house cleaning?" he asked, looking at the three boxes on the sidewalk beside him.

"Sort of." Laurel took a hesitant step forward. "These are for you, Jaxson."

He lifted the lid off one, and his expression darkened as he flipped through the files. For the first time in a week, I saw some of the old anger and frustration creep back into his posture. "What's the meaning of this?"

"My father collected data on all the North American packs. You know the hate he harbored for wolves, and…" She paused. "I kept these files and added to them over the years because I was afraid, and I needed insurance."

His fists tightened around one of the files. "So why are you giving this shit to me?"

"Because I want to start fresh. A clean slate, and that means letting go of the past. Savy binds our families together. Let's build a new future that we can be proud of. And for everything in the past—your sister, my father, all the anger and distrust—I'm sorry, Jaxson. I really am."

My stomach churned as the silence stretched. So many terrible things had passed between our families—would he really be able to forgive her?

For a while, it felt like no one breathed, but then Jaxson finally spoke, his voice strained. "Thank you." He shoved the lid back down on the box. "The Laurents aren't blameless, either. I must also apologize for my actions, but also for those of the pack and my father. It's high time we set things right."

Relief tugged on my aunt's features, and she let out a deep breath.

I looked between her and Jaxson. "We're good?"

Laurel nodded. "All good."

Jaxson met my gaze. Affection and devotion flashed in his eyes. "I'm tired of holding grudges. Besides, I can't be at war with my in-laws."

"I agree," Laurel chuckled.

Wait—what did he just say? Wolfie asked.

In-laws? Was he subtly asking Laurel's permission to...propose?

My heartbeat shifted into fourth gear. I wasn't ready for marriage—yet. There was still a whole lot of being *not married* with him that I was looking forward to. Besides, we were fated mates, for God's sake, so why would we need to get married? Also, I didn't need a man to ask anyone permission for my hand. That was between him and me, so if he was going to damn well ask someone, it had damn well better be me.

Jaxson gave me a devilish grin, acutely aware of my agitation. *Bastard.*

At the same time, I couldn't deny the warmth that spread through my chest.

"Casey," Jaxson said, gesturing to the boxes, "could you load these into my truck?"

"Glad to get rid of them. Having them around makes me feel like a spook."

Laurel handed me the bag of goodies she'd prepared for us as she walked me to Jaxson's truck. "Best of luck with finding your mother's family. Just don't forget that you've got family right here who are eager for you to come back."

"I'm just grateful that the fates, no matter how fucked up they are, brought me here in the first place."

"Me, too."

Jaxson opened the passenger door for me. "Ready?"

I gave Laurel and Casey hugs and promised to keep in touch, then climbed in.

As we rumbled through Dockside, I admired the work we'd done. There was hardly any trace of the hellstorm the Dark God had unleashed. The pack had really pulled together.

Sam met us as we pulled up out back of Eclipse.

Jaxson began unloading the boxes of files, and she peeked inside. "Wow, I didn't think there would be this much when you texted. You sure you want me to destroy all of these? Information like this could be worth a pretty penny."

"Burn them," Jaxson growled.

Sam sighed. "All right."

While they shifted the files into Eclipse, I loaded our bags into the back of my Fury. It had taken a rather heated debate to convince Jaxson to take my car—not to mention a heated make-up session—but it was the only way I wanted to see the world.

Thank God, we're finally hitting the open road, Wolfie said.

I traced my fingers over the chipped paint on the side of the door and across the hood. My father's enchantments flickered like pulses of energy under my fingertips, and a mix of sorrow and delight and pride filled me.

The back door to Eclipse closed, and I looked up.

"Are you sure you don't want to take my truck?" Jaxson asked as he strolled over.

"Absolutely. This baby was meant for the highway."

He lifted an eyebrow at me. "You sure about that? Because I'm not confident it'll make it out of Chicago."

We climbed in, and I turned the key in the ignition. The engine rumbled to life, and I smiled, feeling perfectly content.

"My father enchanted this car. It could make it to Colorado with only one wheel and no engine."

As I pulled out of the side alley, Sam slipped outside and waved. "I don't care how much fun you're having, don't forget to come home! We need you here!"

I waved back as a deep, warm glow rose in me. I had so many things I never knew I needed: dear friends who understood me, a loving family, and a place to call home.

Don't forget me, Wolfie chirped.

Never. *We've got everything we never knew we needed.*

"You know, it's funny," Jaxson said as he looked out his window.

"What is?"

He wore the most contented smile I'd ever seen him have. "How everything comes full circle in the end. A month ago, you ditched Belmont and came to Magic Side just to get away from me. And here we are together, heading back out of town in your Fury."

I smiled as I turned down the Diagonal and headed west. It was noon, and the sun was overhead. Not quite "driving into the sunset," as Casey had suggested, but it was good enough for me.

Excitement thrummed within every inch of my body, and my fingers twitched.

"The fates are funny, aren't they?" I said, and leaned over to quickly kiss him. "I wonder what they'll have in store for our next adventure?"

Thanks so much for accompanying Savy and Jaxson on all their wild adventures! If you've got an extra minute, please leave us a review on Amazon (mybook.to/Shadow-Kissed), Goodreads, and/or Bookbub. Reviews make a huge impact. They help us become better writers and keep us going when the writing gets tough.

While the fates have brought Savy and Jaxson's romance to a happy conclusion, in many ways, it's also a new beginning. Their friend Samantha is heading up north on a mysterious trip. Whatever her intentions are, you can be certain that her journey is going to take a dangerous (and steamy) turn!

Initially, we thought we might tell another heroine's story first (can you guess who?), but by the time we got to the end of Dark Lies, we knew it had to be Sam. Her tale was practically demanding to be told. And anyway, it's never wise to keep a *jealous god* waiting for long.

Sam's first book, *Wolf God,* will be here in October, but you can preorder it on Amazon (mybook.to/Wolf-God).

In the meantime, if you want a hint of how Sam's story might unfold, you can read a free alternate point of view scene of her showdown with the Dark Wolf God. All you have to do is sign up for our newsletter here: https://dl.bookfunnel.com/iem2e1rx02 (We never spam and you can unsubscribe at any time).

Finally, if you're interested in the history and archaeology that inspired this book, or want a first look at Wolf God, keep reading!

AUTHOR'S NOTE

Thank you so much for reading *Shadow Kissed*! It's hard to believe how much Savy and Jaxson's story evolved from the initial tale that we imagined while driving through the back-roads of Wisconsin.

As always, we love to weave real places and history into our stories (like Pere Cheney, which we discussed at the end of *Dark Lies*). In this case, Savy and Jax had to travel to the island of Delos in the Cyclades to meet the Moon. We were looking for ways to bring them back to the Mediterranean world, and this was the perfect opportunity. By some accounts, Delos was the birthplace of Artemis, the Greek goddess of the hunt and lunar light (she was one of three overlapping moon goddess, along with Selene and Hekate).

The site of Delos is now a UNESCO world heritage site. It was one of the most sacred religious centers and pilgrimage sites in the Hellenistic world. With several good harbors, Delos also became a thriving commercial port that served as a primary hub for trade in the Aegean, reaching a population of around 25,000 by the first century BCE, despite the barren landscape.

Savy and Jaxson arrive at Delos at a portal located in the

Minoan Fountain, near the Sanctuary of Apollo. Built in the 6th century BCE, the structure was originally a three-sided building that enclosed a sacred spring. Nine steps led down to a square well, hewn in the rock where the spring bubbled up and continues to flow until today. In the 2nd century BCE, the fountain house was refurbished with frescos showing nymphs and a river god, and it was dedicated to the cult of the Minoan nymphs with an inscription.

The stone lions that the Dark Wolf God sends to attack Savy and her friends were inspired by the giant marble lions that line the Sacred Way. They were the guardians of the Sanctuary of Apollo and its temples, as well as the sacred lake. While there were originally nine to nineteen, only four remain (certainly Savy and Jax will find a way to repair the ones that attacked them!)

The temple to Artemis (the Atremisium) is a tiny building, only about ten meters (thirty feet) across. We felt this was grossly unfair, considering the multiple large temples dedicated to the goddess's twin-brother (not to mention the entire sanctuary grounds). Fronted by six columns, the temple of Artemis originally held beautiful statues of the goddess as well as lions, and an ornate honeycomb decoration along the walls.

While Delos remains an active archaeological site, you can still visit it if you wish, by hopping a ferry from Mykonos (or if you know Myrto, she might be willing to let you use the portal).

While this is the last book in their series, Savy and Jax will certainly appear in future Magic Side adventures – just like Neve and Damian from *Wicked Wish* (mybook.to/Wicked-Wish).

Did you know there's a free prologue to the Wolf Bound series? In it, Jaxson investigates the murder of a witch and visits the seer at the full moon-fair, days before he meets Savannah for the first time. The fortune teller gives him his first glimpse of Savy, and foreshadows much of what would happen in the series. If you want to check it out, you can download it by signing up for our newsletter here: https://dl.bookfunnel.com/wgkpoqcjqa (don't worry, you can unsubscribe at any time, and if you're already a subscriber, you can download it from our members only area).

That's all for now, but *Wolf God*, Sam's first story, will be here in October (mybook.to/Wolf-God). You can expect a little more fantasy and romance, but it'll be packed with just as much action, dramatic plot twists, and colorful characters.

In the meantime, come check us out in our Facebook Reader group (Veronica Douglas' Magic Side Insiders) if you'd like to chat more about the books, interact with fellow readers, and get the scoop on what's up next. You can join here: https://www.facebook.com/groups/veronicadouglas

Thanks again for reading and stay in touch!

-Veronica Douglas

WOLF GOD

SAVAGE GODS: WOLF GOD BOOK 1

VERONICA DOUGLAS

WOLF GOD

SAVAGE GODS: WOLF GOD, BOOK 1

I defied a savage god, and now he wants revenge...

When the Dark Wolf God threatened my pack, I stood my ground and helped trap him in his kingdom. But you don't defy a god and go unpunished. Someone had to pay the price, and that someone was me.

Now, I'm his prisoner, and he wants to make me suffer. He won't hurt me—he just wants to break my will. But I'm tough as nails, and I can take anything he dishes out. I have to bide my time but the rising heat between us is more torture than I can stand. Why can his eyes hold me when chains cannot? I despise him and all that he stands for—he shouldn't take my breath away.

My plan to fight back crumbles when he puts the lives of my friends on the line. I have no choice but to cooperate and do his bidding. For now.

This one job buys their safety. All I've got to lose is my life, right?

Sam's first story will be here in October! (mybook.to/Wolf-God)

DRAGON'S GIFT: THE STORM BOOK 1

VERONICA DOUGLAS
LINSEY HALL

WICKED WISH

DRAGON'S GIFT: THE STORM, BOOK 1 PREVIEW

If you're ready for more Magic Side adventures and want to read a complete series right now, try: Wicked Wish (co-authored with Linsey Hall).

I'm at the mercy of a fallen angel.

I work for the Order of Magica, the supernatural version of the FBI. Sounds fun, right? Except I spend my days chained to my desk, writing reports, and wishing that I was out solving crimes. *Well, be careful what you wish for.*

When my best friend is abducted, my life in Chicago turns upside down.

I'll do anything to get her back—even work with Damian Malek, a wanted criminal, notorious crime lord, and dangerous fallen angel. He's hot, lethal, and he's the only one who can help me master my dangerous powers. I don't want anyone to know about my magic, but I have no choice if I want to save my friend.

Here's the catch: if the Order finds out that I'm working with Damian, I'll get canned. Maybe even be hunted for what I am. But if I don't give him what he wants, he'll reveal my secret to the world.

Wicked Wish features a rebel heroine, a dark angel hero, and slow burn romance. Prepare yourself for edge-of-your-seat adventure amongst ancient ruins and fantastical worlds.

If you enjoyed the archaeology, history, and daring in Linsey Hall's original Dragon's Gift books, this adventure is for you!

Begin the adventure now: mybook.to/Wicked-Wish

ACKNOWLEDGMENTS

VERONICA DOUGLAS

Thank you to all our readers and friends—you've been so supportive throughout this long and winding journey!

Thank you to Jena O'Connor and Ash Fitzsimmons for your patience and amazing editing skills! You two are incredible.

Thank you to the amazing readers on our advanced review team, with extra special thanks to our beta readers Penny, Susie, Amanda, and Margaret—your eyes are so sharp!

Many thanks to Lauren Gardner for all of your hard work. You are absolutely a lifesaver! And thanks to Caethes, for all your efforts to keep us rolling. We'd be lost without you both.

And finally, a huge shoutout to Orina Kafe for designing yet another mind-blowing cover! You truly are the best!

ABOUT VERONICA DOUGLAS

Veronica Douglas is a duo of professional archaeologists that love writing and digging together. After spending an inordinate amount of time doing painstaking research for academia, they suddenly discovered a passion for letting their imaginations go wild! A cocktail of magic, romance, and ancient mystery (shaken, not stirred), their books are inspired, in part, by their life in Chicago and their archaeological adventures from around the globe.

Published by Magic Side Press, LLC

www.veronicadouglas.com

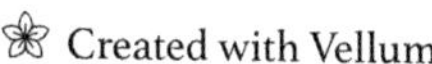

Printed in Great Britain
by Amazon

83748653R00215